Avalon Nightmares

Alexa Whitewolf

Avalon Nightmares
by Alexa Whitewolf

Copyright ©2018 Alexa Whitewolf
ISBN 978-1-9994499-8-8

Cover design by **Y. Nikolova at Ammonia Book Covers**

Second Edition

*A person often meets his destiny on
the road he took to avoid it.
- Jean de La Fontaine –*

ACKNOWLEDGEMENTS

Behind This trilogy was a bit of a surprise for me at every turn. I don't regret any which way the plot has taken me, nor my characters' fancy, but I might have rearranged the original release order if given a chance :) Of course, as it so happens with Merlin and his horde, that was not the case.

Book I, *Avalon Dreams*, was originally meant to be a standalone–also the reason why it's so long. By the time I realized it would turn into a series (a trilogy, at that!), I was already set on releasing Vivienne and Sébastien's story as a wrap.

Book II, *Avalon Wishes*, went back to the past and where it all started. Here, I–just as much as you, my readers!–was dragged into a time before Camelot, when dragons still lay hidden in hills. I took my time developing Merlin's story, and even Alistair got a bit more of a background than originally intended. Not to mention Morgana and Arthur, whose separate stories were a pleasure to get lost in.

Which brings us to Book III, *Avalon Nightmares*, where both plots converge into one storyline, back in modern day.

Get ready for a thrilling ride into the last installment of this series. To make this a bit less confusing, I included a sneak peak in the last pages of *Avalon Dreams*, as a refresher.

I have to give huge thanks to my family, most especially my

husband who ensured I had a never-ending stream of caffeine for those all-nighters I pulled to get this release ready! And to my furry babies, Zeus and Achilles, for indulging their mommy in the busy editing period and accepting shorter playtimes.

Thanks to the team behind this series, my editor and also my cover artist at **Ammonia Book Covers** whose vision for the covers really brings this to life! And as always, a huge hug to the fans of this series!

Happy readings :)

Previously in *Avalon Dreams*...

With the acolytes all gone, Sébastien looked to the river, as there was a keen tug in his mind. "Something's wrong. We have to get Vivienne, now."

Hold on to me, Alistair instructed, then entered into the lake.

The guardian followed him in, wrapped an arm around the dog's massive neck, and they sank in the water. An invisible energy propelled them forward, much quicker than if they had actually swam.

They arrived at the small patch of earth and could glimpse Vivienne in the distance. She was on her knees, bent over, with a semi-translucent barrier surrounding her.

The companions got out of the water and Sébastien immediately inched towards his beloved, while Alistair kept an eye on Carleigh. The necromancer was standing with a satisfied smirk, simply observing his half-sister.

Try as he may, the demon dog could not understand the

behavior. He could sense something had happened. Darkness's footprints were all over the unseen world his senses could capture, but he could grasp nothing concrete from its trail.

As he approached Vivienne, Sébastien observed the protective shield around her, and the energy crackling on its surface – like little zaps of electricity.

"Vivienne!" he yelled above the noise of the vibration.

The enchantress did not respond, keeping her head bent and hands joined as if in prayer.

"Vivienne!" Sébastien yelled again, desperation tinging his tone.

He moved Excalibur and struck the shield with it, only to be shoved back by an invisible force. The brightness and sparks glinting off the metal attracted Vivienne's attention, and she peered up at her lover.

Sébastien willed himself not to react, but the young woman's blank look shook him to the core. It was no longer the warm emerald shining with joy, rather cold and empty, as if she no longer experienced anything. There was no focus within, no shine of recognition – only a bleak, glazed stare and blank countenance.

The knight noticed Alistair out of the corner of his eye, but dared not blink away from Vivienne for fear of losing her completely. "Love, it's me, Sébastien."

Her lips moved and, with a sinking presentiment, he realized she was casting an enchantment, and remained unattainable to him.

Sébastien turned to Carleigh, pointing Excalibur at him. "What did you *do*!?"

"I did nothing," he chortled. "I simply reminded her of past mistakes."

She is putting up a defensive shield, Sébastien, Alistair rumbled. He sounded unsure, and the knot in the guardian's stomach got heavier. *Something odd took place here, but I cannot get a good read on it. Keep Carleigh occupied while I get closer.*

No problem, Sébastien promised.

He advanced to the necromancer with Excalibur humming in his hand. "You and me, it's time we end this unfinished business."

"You can always try!"

Carleigh used dark magic, while Sébastien relied on Excalibur to block attacks. Promptly realizing he was at a disadvantage, the sorcerer pulled his own weapon out of the cloak, and they went metal to metal. When the swords clashed, sparks shot out.

His blade is the opposite of yours, Alistair warned. *Darkness in its raw state. Do not let it cut you, as death will not be merciful.*

Got it, Sébastien assured him. *But what's wrong with Vivienne?*

I cannot figure out what he did to her, but she has externalized her spirit. All she has left are emotions.

How is that possible when I sense none coming from her?

Alistair hesitated, then informed him, *I can feel Carleigh's particular brand of magic within Vivienne, almost as if somehow it infected her. There is a bite on her ankle that I isolated as the origin, probably one of Carleigh's tricks. The problem is, in Vivienne's case, the darkness has no ambitions to feast on, so instead it is crushing her hope. Despair and remorse are taking over and she is poisoning herself, with nothing to pull her out of it. We must stop this before it is too late.*

Blocking the necromancer's blow, Sébastien growled, *Will killing him fix it?*

No.

Alistair, don't lie to me!

It is the truth! If your murder Carleigh, Vivienne will still be lost. You have to somehow reach her heart and remind her she has something to fight for.

Sébastien got distracted with Alistair's words – wondering how to get to his beloved. He blocked the blow a second too late and Carleigh's blade grazed his shoulder. A whoosh of something struck him and he gasped, Excalibur growing heavy in his hand.

"There, that wasn't so complicated," Carleigh smirked triumphantly. "Now, to finish off my lovely sister." He stepped to Vivienne. "Your champion is dying. Do you want more remorse?"

In a flash of desperation and fury, Sébastien used his remaining strength to creep on the sorcerer and bash him in the head with Excalibur. Carleigh dropped to the ground, unconscious.

"Keep an eye on him," he grumbled to Alistair, then stumbled to Vivienne's bubble.

* * *

The shadows in Vivienne's heart overwhelmed and grew until there was nothing but the worst of sentiments left. The curse was oppressing, crushing her, taking away her ability to breathe, yet not killing her – not yet. It was as though it yearned for her to give up, to taste the bitterness of defeat, before she would be put out of her misery.

Love, Carleigh, the world no longer existed, buried far away in an unattainable abyss where nothing could get to the memories. There was no salvation to cling to, no fire to light a way out.

Vivienne observed everything via a haze, unaware of the battle happening on the outside. Until *he* was in her head.

Love, I need you!

Sébastien's mental cry for help got to her. In the most obscure corner of her heart, something flickered, and Vivienne blinked at the surrounding reality. She noticed the knight outside her shield, bleeding, tendrils of obscurity flowing out of him.

In front of her eyes, Sébastien slumped to his knees, breathing heavily. She crawled to him, blocked in by her own barrier.

"Carleigh cut me with a poisoned sword," Sébastien said, his gaze trying to lock onto Vivienne's. "I need your help."

The enchantress bit her lip, wanting nothing more than to come to his aid. When she tried to search deep within, there was no tangible magic, only a wave of negativity.

"I don't have it," Vivienne confessed shamefully, attempting to bring down the shield – to no avail. "I can't even get out of here, Sébastien." Tears streamed down her cheeks as she noticed, helpless, the life edging out of him.

You must drop the barrier, Alistair informed her.

Vivienne looked in his direction, but gave a small shake of the head – freezing once her gaze landed on Carleigh's unconscious body next to the dog. In that moment, she knew that to save Sébastien, it was time to reach into the unknown, whatever the cost.

The enchantress closed her eyes, searching deep within, for what was left – a pool of obscure emotions and tainted magic. She attained and gathered some of it, keeping the image of Carleigh's unconscious body in view.

A life for a life! Within moments, Vivienne directed the darkness towards the sorcerer, and let the force loose.

Stop it! Stop her! Alistair cried in both their heads.

I can't, Vivienne admitted frankly, pleading with her eyes for understanding. *I will not stop and lose Sébastien. If I can't escape this makeshift prison, he has to live.*

Having heard the words, the champion lifted his heavy eyelids. Though woozy from the loss of blood and darkness eating at him, the knight vaguely recalled Vivienne's shields could only be entered by someone pure.

What's the chance that this whole fight with Carleigh didn't take away the last shard of light I had left? he thought, dismayed at failing yet again.

Despite the doubt, Sébastien knew there was no choice now. To be Vivienne's salvation, he had to stop her from making the biggest mistake of her existence.

Please, he implored the fates, *let me get to her.*

Sébastien urged himself to stand up, then passed the barrier, almost crawled through the transparency. There was a ripple as if he was walking under a waterfall, and he fell to his knees in front of Vivienne, mere inches between them.

"It's not necessary, love," he whispered. "Leave the shadows, and come back to me. I'm here, Vivienne. Accept your light magic back in."

Sébastien grasped her cold hand in his, and the pull was immediate. Their soul mate bond re-emerged to the surface, strengthened by the physical connection. Images of the past and present ran in the young enchantress' head, this time not distorted by her own agony.

Vivienne inhaled deeply and willed herself to let go of the darkness. Resistant at first, the tendrils finally released Carleigh.

Instead of calling them back to her, the young woman shunned them. She closed her eyes and breathed in deeply, begging pure spirit to come back to her and cleanse the darkness out.

The protective shield – reinforced by light magic – transformed into liquid, falling like rain showers to the ground, and trickled in tiny diamonds back to Vivienne. It covered the young woman's body in its entirety. In a blinding blaze, it was absorbed into her skin, reintegrating her body – the final missing puzzle piece.

The enchantress could now access her center again, filled with spirit. A burst of warmth went through her, warming her cold extremities and giving her the breath of air she desperately craved.

Vivienne opened her eyes, shifting her focus to heal Sébastien. He was lying down on the ground now, smiling weakly. It only took a scan with her otherworldly senses to realize the evil within him could not be cleansed away.

"It's alright," Sébastien whispered, reading the horror in his beloved's eyes. The fresh tears streaming down her cheeks were more vocal than any verbal warning. He squeezed her hand in his, proud to have kept her safe.

"No," Vivienne cried, "I've seen this before. *No!*"

With a resolute shake of the head, the enchantress placed

both hands above his wound, the incantation forming subconsciously. It glowed brighter than any others, due to Vivienne's intensity and the love backing it. Though the wound could not be mended, there was a way to extract the occult from within it – at a cost.

Vivienne, no! Alistair pleaded, reading the intention behind the magic, and inched towards her.

The young woman flicked a wrist to the dog, creating a barrier he could not penetrate. Alistair pawed at it, attempting to cut through with his claws and teeth, all the while continuously

begging her to stop.

The shield did not budge, reinforced as it was by the Vivienne's intense emotions. Without a care for her own life, she attracted the shadows to her instead, her magic extracting them out of Sébastien. At first hesitant, the tendrils of darkness crawled over the enchantress eagerly, being absorbed in the skin, feeding off her life energy.

The whole thing took only a few moments. The guardian blinked, conscious of his strength returned. Uneasiness stirred deep within him and he looked to the side, where Vivienne was lying down, close to unconsciousness. Alistair howled in anger, still blocked by the barrier.

Sébastien stood up and crawled nearer, cradling her in his arms. His lips hovered a few inches from Vivienne's, but she could barely move. He clutched her hand, hoping it would be enough to keep her with him.

"What have you done?" he whispered, chest constricting painfully, as though he was being torn in two.

"You saved me once," Vivienne stated, inhaling deeply as

her life force seeped out. "Now I can do the same for you. You can have a life with a good woman."

Tears came to Sébastien's eyes, and he willed the words past the lump in his throat. "It's always been you, my love, no one else. In all these lives we spent together. Please don't let go... Don't leave me again." He choked on the words. "I've tried to do everything different this time. *Please* stay with me."

Vivienne heard the words and tried to squeeze his hand, but her muscles would not listen. She slipped into a blackout, no longer in control of anything.

* * *

"No!" Sébastien yelled, gathering Vivienne's inert body to his chest. "Not again!" He sobbed against her cheek, hot tears streaming down his face.

Merlin! Alistair roared. *If you care so much about her, come and do something!*

There was no response for a few moments. Then, a rumbling vibrated in the lake next to them. Alistair headed over, lending his own magic out. Though the demon dog did not have the powers Vivienne now did to part the curtains of time, he could add his force to Merlin's, and help him push through –

consequences be damned.

With a huge nudge from his side, to contribute for the dog's lack of power, Merlin emerged and ran to Vivienne, having followed the fight from his time. With a wave of his staff, the barrier she had created disappeared, and both he and Alistair could pass through.

The mage moved his staff over the young woman, and it glowed fiercely. "She has absorbed all the evil, and it is potent.

I can heal it, but some will remain in her." Merlin scanned Sébastien for his approval and consent.

Why is she unable to heal this herself!? Alistair growled loud enough for anyone within the vicinity to hear.

"Even Merlin knows mages have limits."

The three males whirled around to see Carleigh standing, smirking, not unconscious in the least. A malevolent orb was conjured in his hand, and he was bouncing it up and down as he would a tennis ball.

At their shocked expressions, he flat out snickered manically, while they could only stare at him – and each other – in dismay.

When neither male joined in, Carleigh's laugh slowed to a chuckle, then a snort as he continued, "I knew my dear sister would not be able to heal herself, after having spent so much energy fighting me. And I knew you would come, old fool." The last words were spoken directly to Merlin, his evil glare fixated on the wizard.

Merlin stared back unflinchingly, still kneeling next to Vivienne's motionless body. He glanced at his pupil's body, then to his staff on the ground, and finally back to the necromancer.

"And what is it you wish to accomplish?" his deep voice thundered. "All this misery, this hate, to get what, exactly?"

"VENGEANCE!" Carleigh roared, his restraint slipping. With a deep breath, he pressed his lips tightly together and continued, "You ruined my life, hiding my real identity. And you cast me away. I expect what is due to me."

Merlin stood up slowly, leaning on the staff as though in pain. "And I suppose none of this has anything to do with the evil forces you struck a deal with?"

"And if it does?" Carleigh was still playing with the sphere, though his eyes flicked briefly to Sébastien and Alistair,

who had moved next to Vivienne.

"How can you imagine I will let you destroy this world, letting darkness feed on it?" Merlin questioned.

"I don't care what you intend to do, *master*. I will get what is due to me. Starting with her." He pointed an index to Vivienne, chortling in amusement as the three males closed ranks, effectively blocking her from his sight.

Sébastien advanced in front of Merlin, Excalibur drawn, his body a shield. Alistair faced Vivienne and blew a barrier over her, before joining the wizard's other side.

"Look at you, the three stooges," Carleigh cackled, before throwing the orb towards Sébastien.

The knight lifted Excalibur to cut through it, but at the last minute it did a wide ark and instead hit from behind, blowing him in the air. He landed a few feet further, rolling onto the ground, and got up almost immediately, gritting his teeth. With a meaningful look to the demon dog, Sébastien charged again.

Alistair, reading his intent, went to strike on the other side. They both arrived by the necromancer at the same time. Sébastien swung Excalibur, slashing him. At the same time, the dog barked thunderously and a large circle exiting his jaws, hitting the sorcerer full force.

There was an explosion as both Excalibur and Alistair's attack hit Carleigh, and the two protectors were blown backwards by the force emanating from it.

Merlin was about to step forward, but glanced over his shoulder as he heard a moan behind. Vivienne's hand was tightly clenched, and the sounds coming from her were of agony and affliction, like a hurt animal that was drawing its last breath.

The wizard glanced back at the thick cloud of smoke now emerging from where Carleigh had been. Sébastien and Alistair were getting up, approaching it cautiously from both sides.

Merlin passed the staff in a circle over Vivienne's form. The crystal blazed with a blue glow first, then red, alerting him to danger. He raised it closer to his left eye and surveyed the enchantress using the crystal.

"No…" Coughs from behind unfocused the mage from the disturbing picture he was seeing.

The smoke was so potent both protectors had to back away from the sorcerer. Alistair whined, making an effort to shake the

ash out of his eyes, whilst Sébastien furiously wiped away at his face with both hands. He felt a burning sensation as though he had entered a room filled with chemicals. When he finally managed to clear his vision, his jaw dropped to the ground.

What the hell!? Alistair echoed the sentiment.

Carleigh stood smugly where they had left him, not harmed in the least – not even a speck of dust. "You didn't really figure I had been standing next to your precious princess all this time without doing anything, did you?"

Sébastien glanced at Alistair, then Merlin. Throughout the entire fight, the wizard had stood there, observing, eyes glowing softly while in a trance.

Now, he shook his head, and there was fear in his gaze. "You couldn't have!"

"Become immortal, you mean?" Carleigh smirked wider.

"And if I did? What will you do now, old man?"

Sébastien, unfazed, circled around the necromancer and arrived by Alistair's side.

It matters not what his powers are, he stated for good measure to the dog. *All we have to do is capture and imprison him. Then we can figure out a way to neutralize him.*

Alistair gave a tight nod, not once taking his opaque glare off from the sorcerer. *It will not be easy.*

When has it ever been? Sébastien retorted, and gripped Excalibur tighter.

With his newfound immortality, Carleigh's ego had also increased, no longer careful of multiple attacks, as though he could withstand anything.

"No..." Merlin murmured, glancing from Carleigh to Vivienne, his shoulders sagging in defeat.

Snap out of it! Alistair threw at him, but the wizard's frame seemed more fragile compared to Carleigh's potent corruption. The shadows around the necromancer were larger, obscuring his feet to the point they resembled tentacles.

Carleigh brought both palms together, as though in prayer. For a few moments, his lips budged in an incantation neither of the defenders could capture, then he slowly disengaged his palms. A ball formed betwixt them, growing with each movement he made, until it was the size of an extremely large volleyball.

The orb was the same color as the previous ones – pitch black – but electricity crackled from it, like it was filled with lightning. From the mass of darkness at his feet, a snake slithered up Carleigh's leg, then over his forearm. Gluing itself to the ball, it was absorbed.

Merlin, be careful! Alistair roared a warning, but it was too late.

The mage used the staff to defend himself, the crystal shining brightly for a moment as a barrier was cast. When Carleigh launched the sphere, it hit the shield, and normally should have been shattered. Instead, it bounced a few feet away, hovered in the air, and went back to attack.

Carleigh cackled, eyes shining in delight as he watched the show. Merlin with both hands gripping onto the staff, maintaining a shield, and the orb incessantly striking. With each hit, the barrier wavered, and the ball gained in mass, expanding as it stole the magic and grew.

Sébastien gripped Excalibur and was about to head towards Merlin to help him. Alistair advanced in front of him with a meaningful stance.

Merlin can take care of himself. If we do not manage to injure Carleigh, or render him unconscious, this world will be lost.

Sébastien glanced at Vivienne, then her mentor, before nodding tightly to Alistair. *What do you propose?*

Alistair glared towards Carleigh, still lost in his own arrogance. Then he looked to Merlin, who was now on his knees, holding onto the staff as though his life depended on it. Strain showed on the mage's expression as he came close to breaking.

We can only attack him repeatedly, hoping we can distract him long enough for Merlin to attempt a counterattack. You got that, old man?

Merlin gave a tight nod in response across the distance.

Sébastien gripped Excalibur and without further ado, ran

towards Carleigh. Alistair matched his pace, jaws open and ready to attack.

The dog lunged first at Carleigh, only to be driven away by a wave of the necromancer's hand. He landed heavily on the ground, whining in pain. Still, he got back up and lunged again. At the same time, Sébastien swung Excalibur to attack the sorcerer's shield.

The singing sword hit the screen, cut past it, and there was a whoosh of air as the barrier collapsed. At the same time, Alistair aimed for Carleigh's throat – he never got to it. The tentacles at the necromancer's feet struck out, wrapping around his paws, and yanked the dog down to their mercy.

Seeing his predicament, Sébastien swung again high at Carleigh's head, with the certitude it would be blocked. He then dropped to a knee, cutting instead through the creatures at his feet. When Excalibur hit the darkness, the metal shone brightly, as though it was bathed in moonlight. The creatures hissed and edged away, releasing Alistair.

"You two are annoying me," Carleigh muttered, moving his gaze away from Merlin.

He raised both palms, one facing each defender, and released two bolts of malevolent energy. Before they could block it, the spell hit them full force and they flew back, landing to the ground – unconscious.

Carleigh laughed maniacally, then approached Merlin. "What say you, o great mage of the past? Ready to give up and accept your fate?"

Merlin's blue eyes met his, and the defiance remained as he declared, "Never. I will not let you win. I should have arranged for you to be suffocated in your crib, and saved us from all this."

"You *would* say that, wouldn't you?" Carleigh scowled at him. With a head signal from him, the orb of darkness increased the frequency of its attacks, constantly hitting onto the shield.

Merlin grunted, white-knuckled as he gripped onto the staff.

"Know this before you die, consumed by my darkness. I will let it take over this world, feasting onto each living thing. And when and if your king Arthur is reborn, I will ensure he is corrupted, as I did with your precious Vivienne."

"No!" Merlin glanced again at his pupil, lying unconscious, and it was the split move that cost him. There was a crack, and the staff broke in two. The wizard slumped to his knees, palms on the ground, panting heavily.

The sphere hovered in mid-air, waiting for its master's command – there was nothing defending Merlin now. With a nod, the orb hit the wizard full frontal, blowing him in the air until he landed roughly a few meters away, unmoving.

"Finally. My revenge is complete."

Carleigh placed his back to both Merlin and Vivienne, and elevated both palms to the sky. All that was left was to open a portal, and let the darkness swarm in. As he brought his hands together, a voice stopped him.

"Didn't your father teach you to never turn your back on your enemies?"

The necromancer froze, and the sneer died off his lips as he whirled around. Vivienne stood facing him, head bowed, shoulders straight, hair obscuring her visage. Carleigh's eyes narrowed. Something was different about her, something…

"Oh, that's right," the enchantress continued with an evil

snigger, her voice cold and devoid of emotion. "You never had one."

When she raised her chin, Carleigh's jaw dropped in shock. Vivienne's eyes were midnight black, her skin the color of cray. There was nothing human left in her features, as though they were now made of marble – all unnatural pallor and sharpened edges.

"You bitch!" Carleigh yelled, throwing a ring of energy at her.

The young woman raised her palm and caught the orb instead of deflecting it, to the necromancer's increasing shock.

"You're thinking, let's see…" Vivienne murmured softly, caressing the sphere as one would a puppy, "…that there's no way I should be able to hold anything dark. That it should burn me, affect me…" She laughed, meeting his gaze. "Surprise!"

The orb ascended in her hand, twirling at its mistress' command.

"You're bluffing," Carleigh muttered. "You cannot handle darkness, this is some trick you're pulling. When I took your light –"

"Yes, yes, you became immortal." Vivienne rolled her eyes, as though it was a story she had heard many times before. "And you left me in agony. They," she waved a hand carelessly towards Sébastien and Alistair's unmoving forms, "tried to get the good back into me. And it worked. Except you cut my poor, poor lover with your evil weapon, and guess who had to come to the rescue?"

"You couldn't have, unless –"

"Unless I let the darkness in me. Which I did. Ta-da!" Vivienne spread her arms, the sphere still bouncing in her palm, and twirled around in a circle.

When she faced Carleigh again, there was black lightning in her eyes, and her hair was flying wildly, animated by an unseen energy.

"Then join me."

She tilted her head, assessing the sorcerer as one would a bug. "Join you?" Vivienne repeated, forming the words as though foreign.

"Yes! Don't you see, sister? This is what we're intended to do, rule the world together. Join me...and we can both reap the benefits!"

Vivienne threw her head back and sniggered. "There can only be one master of darkness, brother. Or, in this case, *mistress*."

With that, she threw the orb back at him – but Carleigh had been prepared, a shield drawn up. He conjured another sphere, this one similar to the one used on Merlin, and threw it back to Vivienne.

The enchantress waited until the last moment, when the sphere almost hit her, before lifting a palm and stopping it in midair.

"You forget," she murmured so softly Carleigh could barely hear, "the darkness you put in your sword, which I absorbed from Sébastien, was potent, not diluted, like yours. Immortal or not, you are nothing compared to me. I am your queen, and once and for all, you *will* recognize it." Eyes flashing, Vivienne added, "Time to see some of my own wonders, *brother*."

With that, the young woman raised her other hand, a fire sphere in it. Carleigh could not believe his eyes – the element was still responding to her call!

He stared in shock as Vivienne added the sphere to the orb he had thrown her way, and rerouted it. The darkness flew his way and came to a stop outside the barrier, hovering for a beat, immobile in the air.

Then, it attacked – except once it hit the shield, it multiplied. With each strike, the orb duplicated, until there were hundreds such orbs hitting at once.

With a cry of defeat, Carleigh fell to his knees, and the spheres all fell upon him at the same time. Vivienne watched in satisfaction as he was brought to within an inch of defeat. She strode closer, to better hear his pleas for mercy.

"Why would you do this? To protect them?" Carleigh whispered instead.

"I care nothing for either of them. You ensured that, silly brother," Vivienne admonished softly.

Carleigh dropped to his back, weak from the attack, and gave into the blackout. Though he was immortal, what Vivienne had used with the fire and curse had sapped his strength. It was the perfect time to feed him to the same forces he served.

The enchantress raised her palm, ready to finish the necromancer.

"Vivienne."

She tilted her head to the side, to Merlin. He had crawled over, only a few feet away. Still on his knees, he lifted a hand pleadingly to her. "Please... You cannot give in to the obscurity. You are the best of us."

Vivienne smirked his way, her black eyes uncaring, "Which is why it's only fit I become your Queen of Darkness."

"This is not you," Merlin whispered, shaking his head.

"Please… I beg of you, think of Sébastien. Your lover, you did so much to help him. Will you shun him, too?"

There was a flicker in the enchantress' eyes and she turned away from the wizard, scanning the grounds for Sébastien's unmoving form. The moment of hesitation was enough, as Merlin's palm shone with a light, which he aimed at the back of her head. Vivienne dropped down, unconscious as the sleeping spell took over.

Merlin crawled next to her body and waved a hand in the direction of the other two defenders, bringing them back to consciousness. When Sébastien and Alistair came to a few moments later, he was still next to the young woman's inert body.

"Vivienne!" Sébastien cried, and staggered to her side, kneeling by Merlin. "Will she be alright?"

Alistair sniffed the air, noticing Carleigh's battered body, Merlin's demeanor, and Vivienne's unconsciousness – yet she been moved from her previous spot. He observed her unnatural pallor, and growled low.

What the hell happened here?

Merlin cased their surroundings, then declared, "Carleigh is defeated."

And you did this?

"Yes." The wizard locked gazes with the dog, daring him to defy.

Alistair concentrated his attention to Vivienne. *There is more potent darkness in her than before.*

"I can heal her, as I mentioned before. But there will be a shard of it left."

The mage had addressed the last words to Sébastien, a

query in his blue eyes, to which the knight pleaded, "Bring her back."

Merlin put one hand over Vivienne above her chest, and with the other levitated Carleigh's body nearer, placing the other hand on him. He closed his eyes and began withdrawing the obscurity from Vivienne.

The tendrils of evil were slow to exit, unwilling to let go of the power lying dormant within her. As soon as they poked their head in the middle of her body, the wizard unflinchingly yanked them out like weeds, and threw them into Carleigh's body to be reabsorbed.

She is still not breathing! Alistair panicked when Merlin finished the procedure.

Sébastien grazed her lips with his own, tears falling on her cheeks. "Come back to me, my love."

Vivienne's eyes fluttered open at the words, inhaling deep. Her irises were dark, but as she blinked, they cleared to a normal emerald green color.

Sébastien gathered her to him, crying in relief, and she wrapped both arms around him tightly. There was an odd sensation in her stomach, as though there was something she should be aware of, but had forgotten. In her lover's strong embrace, it went away, and Vivienne breathed in the fresh air.

When Merlin went to stand up, the enchantress clasped his withered hand. "Thank you," she murmured, her eyes shining with tears.

The mentor bowed his head and pressed a kiss to her forehead, warm once more. "You are most welcome, my dear."

"Merlin, I..." Vivienne gulped past the knot in her stomach, and continued, "I forgive you. For the past. I realize now you had tried to shelter me. My stubbornness to see you as the

enemy could have cost me my life. I cannot, and will not, err that far in judgement again." She surveyed Sébastien, then Alistair. "I need all of you by my side if I'm to fight evil here and defend this world. My sentiments, though important to me, should not come first in the fight for good. And Merlin... I hope you forgive me, too."

"There is nothing to forgive, Vivienne," he declared, the corners of his eyes creasing as he smiled. He was proud beyond words that she had managed to get past the hurt and perception of betrayal she had carried within for so long.

Merlin beamed at the couple, then inclined his head to Alistair, who was by his side. Undeterred, the dog warned, *You must bring Carleigh back with you and imprison him in such a cage he can never get out of, until we can figure out how to remove his immortality.*

The old mage acquiesced and levitated Carleigh's body back into the waters. As he was about to disappear, Alistair's voice stopped him again. *Something happened here, which you are hiding. I will find out eventually, old friend.*

Merlin squinted back at him, then at Vivienne in Sébastien's arms, but said nothing. He had faith in his pupil. With one last glance to the couple, the mage evaporated with the sorcerer's still unconscious body by means of the portal.

The transparent mirror wavered once he was gone and, with a nudge of Alistair's power, contracted until it was smaller, then finally disappeared. The water was once more limpid and blue, a true reflection of the sky.

Alistair turned to Sébastien and Vivienne, who were now

embracing passionately under the morning sun. He woofed in happiness, and they turned to him, smiling.

I dare say we all deserve a long vacation after this, the demon dog rumbled, and they laughed out loud.

Sébastien peered down at the gorgeous woman in his arms, eyes locked with hers, and whispered, "Anywhere you want, we can go. We have this life and the next to enjoy together."

"We did it, Sébastien," Vivienne grinned, tears of joy streaming down her cheeks. "We rewrote our fate, changed its conclusion. We can truly enjoy our happy ending now."

"As you wish, my lady." The knight bent his mouth to hers, this time in a longer embrace. When he drew away, his

heated gaze was the promise of passion to come, and the enchantress' body warmed in response.

As the sun rose behind them, Alistair narrowed his eyes. For a moment, a fraction of a second, he had noticed Vivienne's aura flare dark.

He opened his jaws to mention something, but found he could not. As he tried again, a familiar voice snickered in his head, *You will reveal nothing. You are bound to me from now on, demon lord.*

The dog whined low, but the two lovebirds were too caught in their moment to notice his distress.

CHAPTER 1

Sébastien was dreaming, lost in the fogginess of a beautiful forest, when it all erupted in flames. Smoke filled his nostrils, choking him and blurring his vision. In the distance, he saw Vivienne but could not reach her, his feet rooted to the ground as she ran further and further away.

Each breath brought more smoke, cutting off his air with every passing second. His lungs ached, desperate to escape the asphyxiation. Breathing was impossible, but it was the coughing fit that jolted Sébastien out of his sleep.

He jumped awake–and realized it had not been a dream.

"Vivienne!" Dazed and fighting unconsciousness, lungs afire, he shifted to his beloved. He could hardly see past her folded up form on the bed, so he relied on his other senses, catching the heat of her body.

He crawled across the mattress, which felt unsteady under his knees. The room spun and Sébastien realized he was close to passing out, having inhaled too much soot.

Despite the imminent threat, nothing could have stopped him from getting Vivienne out. He ignored the torture each breath brought, and after precious seconds his hand touched her.

Sébastien grabbed hold of Vivienne's shoulder, only to find her skin burning to the touch. A slight sheen of sweat coated it, yet she did not stir when he struggled to shake her awake.

"Alistair!" He looked around in a frenzy, but the dog–their protector–was gone.

At a loss, he kicked the covers and picked Vivienne up in his arms, carrying them both off the bed. "Wake up, love!" He half-shouted against her forehead, but still she did not move.

Vivienne moaned against his chest, hands clenched in fists, eyelids squeezed shut. She seemed to be in a hell of her own making–or someone else's. Unease settled in the pit of his stomach, and the knight moved. The quivering flames rose as though provoked, larger and more unstable than ever.

He halted in his steps towards the exit, frowning. On pure instinct alone, he inched closer to the door and the fire crackled in response. When Sébastien stepped back, curling his upper body around Vivienne to protect her, it dropped to mere flickers.

Sébastien glanced at the room, tightening his grip on Vivienne. Though flames still licked everywhere, the pollution was gone and he could breathe. Once he stopped listening to the pounding of his heart and the blood rushing to his temples, he realized there was no sound of wood being burnt, nor any dark marring on the white walls.

Magic.

It was clear even to his untrained eyes that this was no natural occurrence. Grounding himself to fight the flight instinct, Sébastien settled on the floor, as far away from the blaze as possible. He placed Vivienne astraddle him, ensuring it was his back that was the closest to the flames—should they flare up once more.

After one last suspicious glance to their surroundings, Sébastien focused on Vivienne. He cupped her face, his eyes drifting over her flushed cheeks and long, dark lashes. *Please let this work...* He hovered just out of reach, then pressed his lips to hers.

Sébastien had hoped a kiss would wake Vivienne up, nothing more. Yet the moment they touched, she came alive. She rose to meet his mouth, opening hers for his assault, all the while melting against him as though they were one. She was almost feverish, each stroke of her tongue demanding more.

Before Sébastien could pull away and calm his libido, Vivienne's hands ran through his hair, her hips pressing down into his. He groaned, unable to resist the invitation. The hand on her cheek moved through her long, black hair to grip it and angle her head. Moving her to his leisure, he turned the kiss seductive, no longer a battle for dominance but more a pleading for consummation.

Vivienne moaned at the change, causing his eager fingers to grab onto her hip for support. Each breath, each pant that escaped her was a catalyst to his own desires. In one fluid motion, Sébastien rolled them over into the soft carpet, pressing into Vivienne as he lost control, the flame of desire sneaking up on him...

Flames!

Sébastien lifted his head, gaze darting around. How he had forgotten their surroundings, and the danger they had been in, was beyond him. Despite his distraction, the walls were their usual pale blue, not a mark on them. He blinked in disbelief, unable to understand the contrast. A soft hand on his cheek brought his attention downwards.

Vivienne was awake and smiling, though her green eyes sparkled with something else. In the moonlight filtering from the window, he was blind to her expression.

His body, however, was not.

As if sensing his thoughts, Vivienne arched her back, pushing more into him. It was an open invitation, one as old as time itself, and Sébastien was powerless to resist.

Ah, what the hell...

Sébastien lowered his mouth to Vivienne's, pausing just above her lips. A deep groan built in his throat, almost a reprimand for his own impulsivity. Despite the storm raging in his body, he tried to slow down.

"Vivienne, I..."

She raised one leg up then, the silky nightgown falling to her hip. Sébastien gritted his teeth when her slim limb wrapped around his lower back, then tugged him closer.

"No talking," Vivienne ordered, then lifted her head and touched her mouth to his.

The blaze stroked anew, and Sébastien gave in before he recognized what hit him, surrendering to something far greater than himself. He ran his hands up Vivienne's sides, then his mouth followed the same path, until he found her ready center.

Her breathing hitched with every passing moment, and she dug her heels in the mattress, one hand clutching her sheet while the other tugged on his hair. Sébastien gave in to her pull and rose up once more, hovering above her. His eyes glittered with passion,

forearms tense with the force it took to restrain himself.

Vivienne lifted her other leg, running it up and down his thigh, biting on her lower lip. The last shred of his control snapped, and Sébastien crushed his mouth to hers while desperately tugging her underwear out of the way.

In one smooth stroke, he buried himself inside her, groaning in her neck. Vivienne's gasp of pleasure was his reward, as she tightened around him to the point he thought he saw stars.

"More," she panted in his ear. "Please."

Sébastien heard her plea, felt her body's insistence, and his own echoed the need. He thrust deeper, then pulled away, repeating the movement over and over. One hand caressed her cheek until her eyes opened and watched him, unwavering, then she could no longer hold back.

When Vivienne's back arched off the bed, her long groan of ecstasy in his ears, Sébastien finally gave in to his desire and let go.

Hours later, once she was asleep with no haunting nightmares, peace eluded Sébastien. He got out of bed, pacing by the window and trying to make sense of what had taken place, his mind too awake to allow rest.

Months earlier, the enchantress had suffered a traumatic event. On top of finding out reality was not what it seemed, she had fought her half-brother, the necromancer Carleigh. With the fate of the world hanging in the balance, they had dueled until it had almost broken Vivienne. It had been a bittersweet victory, ending with Merlin taking custody of Carleigh to imprison him.

In spite of a triumph that should have left them all feeling fulfilled and at peace, the truth was they were each recovering in their own way. Alistair, ashamed at not having been able to protect his mistress, had withdrawn and kept his counsel the last few weeks. Sébastien was still struggling to come to terms with almost losing his soul mate, then being allowed to remain by her side. And Vivienne herself seemed disoriented, unable to forget her experience or to move on.

Sébastien could not fault her. Before facing Carleigh, Vivienne had lived a peaceful life. Meeting him had yanked her from her version of existence and catapulted her into one she knew nothing about. Magic, sorcerers, dark and light... It was a world where she existed as the reincarnation of a mighty enchantress

from king Arthur's time–none other than the Lady of the Lake.

Though lately Vivienne seemed to have accepted her original duties as a champion of Light, nightmares plagued her. Due to their history as much as their soul mate bond, Sébastien could guess where they were coming from. Still, for a vision to create such havoc...

His gaze lingered on the unblemished surfaces. Though being without magic had never bothered him, in that instant he wished to at least understand what had inspired the outburst. Only one could answer his questions, and he was not around.

Movement outside drew his attention and he stilled, stare narrowed on the backyard. The fight with Carleigh was a matter of the past, but unease lingered at the edge of his consciousness. Their newfound happiness felt fragile–too much so. At any turn, something could arise and snatch it away. Convinced of it, Sébastien knew it was his duty as Vivienne's previous knight and current lover to protect her.

He moved closer to the curtains, peeking below. Shadows shifted and Sébastien tensed, then his sight adjusted and focused on a shape he recognized only too well. Alistair was pacing back and forth, his massive Caucasian Shepherd form agitated.

Large enough to reach past his hip, with a body more the size of a small pony, the demon dog was one of Vivienne's other guardians. He was also their ally and had helped in the last fight. Cursed into the underworld by gods he called siblings, he struggled to find a spot to belong.

On some level, Sébastien believed another path waited for Alistair, designed for him alone. But only time would reveal whether he was right or wrong, and he needed the company, especially as both him and Vivienne still had much to learn.

Their partner's behavior was enough to trouble him. At the present moment, Alistair was shaking his head as though arguing with himself. With each passing second, his tail swished back and forth fast, his muscles hunched with tension.

He'll wear out the ground if he keeps at it like that. Sébastien frowned in confusion as he recalled Alistair's absence from the evening's events. *What the hell is going on?*

* * *

I am done doing your bidding! Alistair could no more stop his growl than he could stop taking his next breath. With each passing moment his patience thinned, and he was half-tempted to throttle the spirit in his mind. *If only...*

You forget that you are bound to me, demon dog, the woman snickered. *Your opinion does not matter to me. Besides, what I seek is simple.*

He would have laughed at the outright lie, were it not for the rising tide of his fury. *You wish me to spy on my mistress!*

Since defeating Carleigh weeks earlier, someone had become linked to him. They could sense his moods, look into his dreams and order him around as well they pleased. Whoever it was had only grown stronger with time—and him more bound.

The first few times, blocking the presence had been possible. Yet with each passing day, it became further embedded in his subconscious, like a leech unwilling to let go.

For the moment, it wanted information. On him, on Vivienne, on Sébastien. He tried to keep away, even avoided his mistress in a lame attempt to protect her. Alistair knew he needed a better solution, but the road to freedom eluded him.

For many sleepless nights he had speculated as to the identity of his jailer. The only plausible theory was that it was an ancient deity out for revenge. But who and why, was a mystery. Besides, with the less than stellar powers he had left... Well. To put it mildly, there was no recourse when she had spelled him into obedience, unable to speak of it.

Be thankful I am not asking for more, the voice threatened. *Yet. Now be a good pup and go back inside!*

Alistair wanted to retort, but the minute the idea came to him, a spark of electricity shot through his body. He flattened down to the ground, biting a groan of pain.

Message received.

He waited a beat to ensure she had disappeared, then did as he was told and re-entered the house. Aggravation bent him out of shape and sleep would be elusive once more. For someone who had once directed a pantheon of gods, he was not accustomed to being defenseless.

Lost in their romance, Vivienne and Sébastien did not notice something was amiss, not that he could fault them. The two of them, more than any other, deserved happiness. *I will settle this myself—one way or another.*

"What's going on?"

Startled, Alistair turned from the entrance to see Sébastien walk down the stairs. Words stuck in his throat, a spell too powerful to break. He could only shake his mane in reply.

What are you doing up at this hour, knight?

A flicker of irritation passed Sébastien's expression, and for a second the shame of lying to him overcame Alistair. His ears flattened on his head and he looked away, unable to hold his gaze.

Without a word, Sébastien stepped past him into the living room. He headed straight to the crystal pitcher and poured himself a drink.

Night cap? Alistair tried to joke, but it fell flat.

Sébastien narrowed his eyes at him, then downed the glass in one shot. He paused, choosing his words, then spoke low. "Whatever secrets you keep, I will not pry them out of you. Not because I don't care, but because I owe you respect. After all you have done to help us, you deserve your privacy."

He crouched low, leveling with Alistair. Though the dog avoided his look again, Sébastien's gentle tug on his ear forced him to meet it. "I wish you'd trust me enough to share, buddy. But if nothing else, at least know that I'm here, whenever you *are* ready."

They stared at each other for two heartbeats, then Sébastien got to his feet and refilled his glass. "As for this," he lifted the amber liquid, "let's just say it's been earned."

Alistair joined him in front of the fireplace, ears perked in interest. *What do you mean?*

The guardian gazed in his liquor for a moment, eyebrows drawn together. There was no relaxation in his posture, rather a tension Alistair could sense even across the distance. When his revelation dropped, it was almost in a whisper.

"Vivienne burned down our room."

She did what!?

"Only she didn't."

The knight's confused onyx eyes met Alistair's, and for a second the dog was struck speechless. Then he shook himself out of the stupor and crawled closer, placing his head on his knee. *Explain. From the beginning.*

In between sips, Sébastien went through the nights' events, retelling what had happened. Alistair glanced to where his mistress now slept, unable to perceive a threat. Was it a coincidence that the presence had chosen that precise moment to steer him away?

Something is wrong. A piece of the puzzle eluded him, and one question kept coming up, though without an answer. *Who the hell did I piss off to this extent?*

"Alistair?" The dog focused back on the knight, acknowledging his pensive gaze. The dark onyx eyes narrowed in suspicion at his silence, but Alistair only sniffed worry on his scent.

I cannot make sense of this.

"That makes two of us," Sébastien muttered and downed

the remaining of his drink.

The recent stress might have triggered it.

"Stress?" Sébastien scowled, his fingers tightening on the glass. "How about the damn darkness Carleigh put in her!?"

Alistair sighed, then shook his head in response. *You are right. We let Merlin leave without getting all the answers we could from him. There has to be a better explanation to this, something more than...* He stopped, eyes riveted on the stairs once more. *Vivienne is stronger than this.*

Sébastien only stared into the fire, eyebrows drawn together in concentration. One hand still held the glass white-knuckled, while the other rubbed the back of his neck.

What is it?

At first, he refused to answer. But as if the weight was too heavy to carry alone, the confession escaped him in an anguished tone. "Something isn't the same, Alistair. I feel her as close as I feel my heart. There is chaos now where before there was none and I'm afraid..." The fire once more drew his focus as he finished in a whisper, "I'm afraid of losing her to what almost claimed me."

Let us not be hasty, knight. You said it yourself, Vivienne has odd dreams... Perhaps it's only a severe case of trauma, of shock waiting to pass.

"Maybe. I thought we were past that stage. First the lost memories, now these blasted nightmares... I only want her happiness."

Alistair nudged his free hand, causing Sébastien to concentrate on him. *What makes you think she is miserable? I know Vivienne and I have seen joy radiate from her these last weeks. Yes, these things leave scars, but they will heal too, with time.*

Sébastien sighed, then nodded. "I hope you're right. Even so, I'd appreciate your help next time this happens."

Alistair's ears flattened onto his head. He watched as Sébastien disposed of the empty glass on a coffee table, then returned upstairs. Guilt tore at him, but he reasoned that his reassurance had not been an outright lie. Vivienne *was* scarred. But if his suspicions were correct, the cause for the enchantress' turmoil would not be disappearing anytime soon.

And Merlin knew as much.

An idea formed in his mind. If he could contact his old friend and get his help in the matter, they could find a solution. Alistair settled down, grunting at the precarious situation they were all stuck in.

Lulled by the crackling of the fireplace and the silence in his head, he fell asleep. Yet even then, blank dreams eluded him and instead he dreamt of red hair and blue eyes, and smooth skin under his hands...

* * *

Where they existed, there was nothing. It could have been a castle, a ruin, or simply a space in time. At the end of each day– and there had been many–it remained an empty place, fixed but forever out of reach.

Despite the disconnection, the two beings living there had each other and it had been enough.

At the moment, deep within a forest they called home, a woman knelt by a stream. She passed a slim, pale hand through the transparent liquid, enjoying its coolness and detesting it equally. It reminded her too much of what she had witnessed.

As though picking up on her thoughts, wisps of silver escaped her fingertips and mixed with the flood. The steady stream bubbled, then formed a mirror for her perusal. In it, she saw an older man with blue eyes and a long, white beard. He was pacing in a cave, his wiry body bent over a cane.

He appeared to be in his late seventies, but the woman's gaze latched onto him with an obsessive frenzy. She knew the man even better than she knew herself. And despite his fragile appearance, she was convinced a spell hid his true image for easy camouflage. Underneath it was the body of the Halfling she had

fallen in love with, once upon a time.

The mage who had bedded her, betrayed her and stolen her kingdom to give it to Arthur.

Merlin.

Morgana glanced away, splashing the water with her palm. She blamed the wizard for what had happened and had eagerly watched Carleigh almost destroy what the wizard held dear... until they had captured him. The necromancer was arrogant, but not even Morgana had expected Vivienne's tryst with the dark side.

Again latching onto her thoughts, the water swirled and showed her a new image—of the sleeping enchantress.

After witnessing her power, Morgana spent many sleepless nights. She associated Vivienne with Merlin, and him with her pain. When they had all faced off, eons earlier, the Lady of the Lake had caused Mordred's death. Had she not protected Arthur, her boy would have lived—and she would have kept her talents. Despite their history, Morgana had to admit Vivienne would prove useful if she was on their side.

Though her son was had magic, it was impossible for him to part dimensions by himself. Such a feat was taxing even if done at an auspicious time, yet they had no choice if they ever wanted to escape.

That day was Hallows Eve–Halloween night in the modern world. The gates between worlds were thinner, and if Morgana had possessed her full Fae capacity, they could have broken the curtain of time and entered Vivienne's world. After all, if Merlin had been capable of such a feat, she should be too.

But the sorceress did not possess all her might, having given up her immortality to save Mordred's life. Whatever abilities remained were not adequate. They needed more allies, more power... And now that she had the potential to turn the Lady of the Lake to their side, she planned to use it. Nothing would hurt Merlin more than losing his protégée to the ultimate evil–forever. And with that accomplished, Morgana would take the revenge for all she had lost.

Movement drew her attention, and she stood to welcome her son. Mordred had not aged despite the eons gone by. Lean, with cropped dark hair and Merlin's sharp blue eyes, he was the image of his parents combined. Morgana could have been his sister rather than his mother, equally lithe and young in features.

Only the feral look in her expression revealed an older wisdom.

"Is it time, then?" He arched an eyebrow, almost afraid to hope.

For ages now, stuck in this loop of time, he had waited, forgotten. They had observed the world go round, until Vivienne reincarnated. Despite being in different dimensions, he still felt the connection between them, a tangible link that refused to vanish.

He became conscious of Morgana's sharp gaze on him. Lost in thoughts of Vivienne, he had not heard her reply.

"Mother?"

"It is time to pay your father a visit."

Spinning on her heels, Morgana then trotted to the end of the forest. Mordred followed her in silence, noticing how she kept her back straight, as though getting ready for a fight. In mere moments, they reached the mountain hidden from view, and the thick crystal gate that marked its entrance.

With each step taken towards it, Morgana's hands clenched in tight fists, and the doorway itself seemed to shine fiercer. Creator and creation faced off for the first time since Morgana had unleashed her power to shut the door, eons ago.

Mordred recalled how his mother had spent the remnants of her powers to secure their new home. The portal they had used lay beyond the crystal. It made it impossible for enemies to pursue them, sealed as it was by Morgana shortly after their arrival.

The only problem was that, as with most Fae magical barriers, this specific one had evolved and ended up becoming stronger than its mistress had ever intended.

Hard like ice, yet shining of a million rainbows, the barrier had withstood the test of time and pulled energy from the mountain, the earth, and most breathing things in their environment. To jump through and reach Merlin, they would have to break it.

Morgana lifted her palms, facing it. Her body was tense as a bow, filled by a foreign power, yet somehow she seemed fragile. Perhaps it was the pallor of her skin, the circles under her eyes, or the lost shine of her hair. Whatever the true reason, in that moment, Mordred was more aware than ever of what she had given up for him.

"Mother..." He touched her arm and Morgana turned to him. Her eyes shone of an unnatural light, lips pursed in concentration.

"We are doing this," she stated, narrowing her gaze.

"But what if –" Mordred hesitated, unsure how to voice his fear of losing her. Though Morgana had always doted on him, she had kept her distance emotionally. Growing up, it had not made it easy to connect, rather the opposite.

What am I...? Off balance at the startling thought, Mordred stumbled backwards.

The sudden introspective look at his own feelings left him with a bitter taste in his mouth. *What am I, deprived of love?* His mental tirade did nothing to calm him down, and his heart beat faster in agitation. For someone used to not showing sympathy, to only loving chaos, the prospects were alien and unwelcome.

Morgana touched his shoulder then, drawing his attention. "What is it?"

"I –" A pause, then he mumbled, "Are you strong enough? Without your immortality... I can go at it alone, mother."

"No." Her tone left no room to doubt, and neither did her expression. "Merlin is mine." And on that hiss, Morgana faced the gate, lifting her palms anew.

The air became saturated with sizzling energy and the crystal flashed warningly, as though sensing what was coming.

Fae magic had always been potent in Morgana's clutches. Fuelled as it was by the madness inside her, it altered the sorceress into a bomb ready to explode. Her eyes shone fiercer, sharpening to lightning with each passing moment.

The wind picked up next, surrounding her and blowing leaves and debris in the air. Morgana paid them no mind, not even when her own long, wavy dark hair tangled around her. The temperature dropped a few degrees, enough to chill her to the bone in the silky robe and cape she had on–more nightgown material than actual garment.

Yet Morgana did not register the change, lost in the high of the energy filling her. She stepped forward, placing both hands to the crystal, shuddering with it at the vibration. When she glanced backwards at her son, Mordred had front-row seats to the ruthlessness in her face.

"Now."

Mordred gulped, then joined his mother's side and added his own fists to the surface. He closed his eyes, gritting his jaw,

and let the fire inside consume him. The pulse grew louder, and the ground echoed with a faint wail.

Unable to resist it, Mordred blinked and lifted his gaze to the tip of the gate. Once standing proud, the crystal now trembled at the dual assault. With a final groan, a crack split it. For a moment, everything remained still–unerringly so. In the following beat, the wall collapsed, taking them with it.

* * *

Vivienne jumped awake in bed, panting. Fleeting images of a dark-haired man, shining sapphire eyes and wild, untamed magic hit her.

The flashes were quick to follow, assailing her with images of the unknown. Vivienne grabbed hold of her head in a desperate attempt to stop them.

"Love?"

Everything stopped at the sound of her lover's voice, and Vivienne could breathe again. She glanced at Sébastien, whose half-lidded eyes did not waver from her.

"I'm fine, only a nightmare." The lie slipped past her lips smoothly, but she could not hide her agitation. Wringing her hands, she took controlled breaths, struggling against something.

Sébastien reached for her, and once upon a time she would have collapsed in his arms gratefully. Instead, his touch had her recoil. "I said I was *fine*!"

Now wide awake, Sébastien took in her defensive stance, tight features and the vibe he could sense as surely as his own heart beating. "Vivienne, what's wrong?"

Was it my imagination, or did her eyes darken?

As though sensing his sudden distress, she shook her head. For a moment, his face blurred, replaced with a cerulean stare. Then it came back into view, and Vivienne could only shudder. *What's happening to me?*

Attuned to his beloved, Sébastien captured her distress and it left him wondering at its origins. Inch by inch, he moved closer to Vivienne. She had curled up in a corner of the bed, knees drawn up to her chest in a reflexive stance of defense. Hand extended in invitation, he kept silent and fought to maintain a calm expression.

Her eyes lowered to his open palm, and her erratic breathing quieted down. Eventually, she capitulated and crumbled in his embrace. "I'm so sorry." Tears fell, unbidden, and she was

helpless to stop them.

"Shh..."

Sébastien focused on holding her tightly rather than the raging inferno of questions he ached to get answers to. This is not the time. Confused, he dozed off with Vivienne held in the cocoon of his arms. His last thought before surrendering to the blissful oblivion was, *Now I have two things to bring up to her in the morning.*

CHAPTER 2

Far away from the lovers' dimension, yet close in spirit, stood a kingdom governed by the old pantheons—and one particular Fae with her own portion of paradise.

She swam in a clear blue lake, her hair the color of blood streaking the water and reflecting the sun's rays. The daily exercise kept her body toned, not that she needed it. Curves the envy of Aphrodite herself peeked, with skin like the most expensive marble.

Catriona...

The forest on the edge of the pool called her name, sensing her aggravation. From her mother, she had inherited a deep respect for nature. Coupled with her father's immense powers, the Fae was a true force to be reckoned with.

Catriona, let us help.

Ceasing to advance, Catriona shook her head in brusque

movements, then exhaled heavily and opened eyes the color of the bluest sky. Despite the perfect temperature, the dip had done nothing to cool her heated skin. And she knew just who was to blame.

The previous night, for the first time in decades, she had dreamt of the wolf god, Atrox. Their brief fling had been epic, and her flesh craved him still. Especially after the dream she had last experienced–one that had left her panting and soaked in sweat, her body craving an exertion only he could provide.

The redheaded Fae slipped out of the translucent pool, stalking to a spot on the ground where she plopped down.

On her back, Catriona stared at the sky and watched the multi-colored clouds spin round and round. She lifted her index, playing with the wind without really thinking it through. In her aggravation, it took her a few seconds to realize she was creating a tornado—but once she did, she released her hold on the element with a frustrated grunt.

Uneasiness had settled within her, similar to centuries earlier. It had been that same instinct that had pushed her to contact Atrox and gain his help with Merlin, her half-brother.

Catriona smiled wistfully at the thought of the wolf god. Though their time together had been short, and ended in the same manner, the memories of his touch still made her skin tingle in appreciation.

In fact...

Her eyes snapped open, narrowing at the sky above. It had been centuries since she had last seen Atrox—dreams notwithstanding. She had assumed he had taken to paradise after Vivienne's death, and had not sought him out.

And neither did he, her treacherous mind whispered.

Scowling, Catriona stood. In the surface of the lake, she could see her reflection, barely draped in a piece of cloth that concealed her bust, left her midriff exposed and continued to cover her lower body down to mid-thigh. Despite her rather skimpy clothing, the sun outside should have kept her warm. Still, Catriona shivered.

"After all, who would it hurt if I have one peek?" She reasoned aloud. "Atrox would never learn of it. And if he has forgotten me, then so be it."

Tossing her head back, she walked over to the tree in the middle of the meadow. Over ten feet high, it had a trunk the side of five normal seedlings. Sinuous roots dwelled deep into the earth, reaching down to reach the water hiding within its depths.

A massive crown of willowy branches dropped to the ground, and she touched them in passing. Inside it, Catriona had hidden something eons earlier.

Time to retrieve it. She placed a palm on the tree's bark, sensing its vibration all the way to her toes.

Please return what you have guarded for so long... She pleaded mentally, unwilling to disturb the ancient entity.

Though to the outside it looked like a regular willow tree, it was in fact the center of her universe in this realm so far isolated from reality. The tree was both portal and shield, an entrance and exit. It let her see into the beyond, and kept things for her, serving

as her constant protector.

As you wish...

After a moment, the branches rustled, and the pulse centered in the trunk. The dark wood blurred, and within it was a small hole. Catriona delicately put her hand through it and withdrew the other half of the fairy medallion she had gifted Atrox.

Cradling the precious treasure to her chest, she bowed her head to the tree and stepped back. A branch moved closer to her arm, caressing her from cheek to wrist. *Be careful, child. Fate is fickle with your kind...*

Catriona gulped, not so much at the warning as the fact the entity had spoken. It was rare to hear its voice, and the deep rumble in her mind was enough to give her pause. She glanced at her fist, hesitating.

The Fae was no stranger to fate. After all, it was her desire to help Merlin that had gotten her entangled with the wolf god. But the need to see Atrox again grew with each passing second.

"I have to know," she whispered, blue eyes glittering. "Please understand."

Only silence answered her, and the branch that had shifted was now inert. Feeling as though she had disappointed her benefactor, Catriona moved further away until she was back by the shore.

Only then did she open her palm, taking a moment to admire the delicately designed fairy on a simple silver chain. When her fingers touched it, she sighed in relief, before pulling it out into the sun.

Her eyes glowed an icy blue as the spell activated, then she closed her fist over it. She had expected to sense Atrox, or at the very least see him frolicking in paradise.

Instead, all she sensed a black hole of nothingness. Brow furrowed in concentration, Catriona tried again, with the same result.

"This is impossible," she huffed. "If he is in the realm of

the gods, I should have...."

Eyes glassy, she stared in the distance for a long time, gnawing on her bottom lip. Something did not feel right, and she vowed to find out what it was.

With a negligent move of her hand, Catriona dressed in a deep purple sheath and clasped the pendant around her neck. The miniature fairy rested in the hollow of her cleavage, cold against her bare skin.

Through her back, translucent wings delicately peeked. All Faes had them for ease of transport, and they could retract and expand at their owner's whim. In that moment, they fluttered in agitation as they caught onto their mistress' emotions. Unwilling to wait any longer, Catriona took off.

Once she reached the barrier of her territory, the Fae twirled her index and called the elements and nature itself. The tornado she had toyed with earlier was the first to answer, nipping at her heels like an obedient puppy.

With one last glance at the tree below, Catriona gave in to the currents and dropped within the tunnel, letting it carry her forth.

Bring me to the entrance...Get me into the gods' paradise.

It did not take long to pass through time and space, and the tornado allowed her to exit gently, floating almost to the ground. She had managed it again—arrived in forbidden territory, at the same darkened gate which held the secrets of the pantheon.

This was one place cut off from her, on account of an ancient rule instilled in both their kind—gods and Faes—after the Last Wars. However, with Fae magic being unruly, all rules tended to be flexible.

Catriona was about to put her powers to the test again when an ominous voice froze her to the spot.

"What business do you have here?"

Catriona whirled around, finding herself face to face with–

"Aequus?" Her disappointed tone only caused him to frown.

"Do I know you?"

Bulkier than his brother Atrox but with the same black hair and sculpted features, the god was striking. Dressed in a dark green toga held by a panther brooch, he was three times her size.

Her body's desires, long unfilled, could not help but notice his good attributes. But unlike Atrox's malicious eyes and playful spirit, all she caught in the god's emerald gaze was a cool calculation.

It was enough to moderate her senses, and Catriona regrouped easily, even more so at his next words.

"I demand an answer."

She tossed her hair back at his imperious, if slightly irritated, tone. "I am Catriona, daughter of Merlyddus and heiress of Faes. Where is your brother?"

Rather than respond, Aequus stared at her long and hard. His gaze traveled up and down her body, a flicker of recognition passing through it.

A smirk tugged at his lips, yet when he spoke, his tone was confused as though not quite believing what he was seeing. "I remember you now."

"I am not surprised," Catriona batted her eyelashes. "I am, after all, difficult to forget."

Aequus frowned for a moment, then his expression cleared and he laughed. After a brief hilarity, he sneered and stepped closer still.

"Yet my brother had no trouble casting you aside, did he?"

Stunned at his nastiness, Catriona took an extra second to process what she should have already guessed: he *knew*. Whatever had happened to Atrox, his sibling was involved.

Fury filled her, rising like a tidal wave ready for destruction. Her father had always warned against her inherited temper, but Catriona never listened. Ruled by impulses more so than rationale, once an emotion took control of her she had to see it through to the end, regardless of who she hurt.

Before she could pause for a breath—or Aequus could defend himself—Catriona lunged at the god. Propelled forth by her wings, she cut through the air and near-tackled him. Caught by surprise and not having expected her strength, Aequus stumbled backwards.

Hands out like claws, Catriona went after him and scratched his face, snarling in fury. Despite his bulkier frame, Aequus could not maintain a distance. He back-pedaled again, swearing under his breath.

The Fae doubled her attacks, moving under his lazy strikes with the agility of a cat—and all the grace of a feral panther. Aequus tried to grab Catriona's hands behind her, but one of her wings cut him.

She spun in place, a true tornado fuelled by rage. Her eyes shone cold ice, her palms gathering momentum, ready to launch a magical attack. A laugh echoed, distracting them both.

Catriona paused in her steps, tilting her head, a low snarl escaping her. "Who goes there?"

"At ease, Fae." The words were spoken softly, and Ardea stepped out of the shadows. A little shorter than Aequus but with bi-colored eyes—one green, the other black—she had inky hair and a beige toga.

Catriona settled not because of the goddess' words, but due to her mere presence. There was an aura of wisdom around Ardea, a calming spirit so in contrast with her siblings.

As though to prove said knowledge, Ardea cast an amused glanced at her brother. "You really should pick your fights wisely, Aequus. Have you not learned from humans how dangerous scorned women are?"

The panther god only scowled, wiping at his face and muttering under his breath.

Ardea ignored him and instead inched closer to the Fae. "You seek Atrox."

Seeing no reason to lie, especially with the scratches still visible on the other deity's cheek, Catriona inclined her head. "Yes."

"He is not here," Ardea admitted, eyes shining with unspoken emotion. "Not on this dimension, I fear. Come with me."

The goddess moved away, expecting the Fae to follow. Catriona stood rooted for a moment to the same spot, glaring at Aequus. Sensing the tension, Ardea touched his hand in passing and the god stepped back into the shadows.

Not liking the loss of control, Catriona grudgingly followed Ardea. They passed through corridors of fog and ice, then under a luminous barrier. The Fae shivered at the liquid coating her skin, then shook it off like a cat unwilling to tolerate water.

Ardea's low chuckle brought her out of her musings, and she realized they had come to a stop. Still on her guard, Catriona inspected their new surroundings. Everything was white, except for a transparent pond in a corner.

"What is this place?" she asked, unable to keep her eyes from taking it all in. There was an odd vibration of primitive and modern that rattled her nerves and set her on edge.

"'Tis but the Reincarnation Pool, Fae. Do you not perceive its energy?"

Catriona refused to answer, clenching her jaw instead. "Why bring me here?"

"For the truth. Atrox never cared for much while he was a god. When we banished him and he found Vivienne, we were all bewildered at the strength of their bond." She pursed her lips, grimacing. "Be that as it may, he only really loved her. After her death, he chose reincarnation so that he could be reborn again."

Catriona frowned, trying not to take the statement personally.

"See for yourself, I do not lie." Without waiting for Catriona's approval, Ardea grabbed her hand and stuck it in the water. As though zinged with electricity, the Fae's head fell back and she saw through their eyes...

In the gods' palace, Alistair walked around in a daze. When Vivienne had died, he had felt a part of him being yanked out, never to be filled again.

He did not notice, lost as he was in memories of his former mistress, that the ground underneath he walked on became more vivid, and the surroundings changed.

"Atrox."

Only her voice pulled him out of dark thoughts. Alistair glanced up at Catriona, mere feet away from him. The look she gave him, the regret in the cerulean gaze, hit him full force. There was a lump in his throat, then the proud former god fell to his knees and allowed the tears to fall.

"I failed," he stated hoarsely.

Catriona rushed over, hugging him to her. "You did not!" she whispered, knowing it would do no good. The wolf god let his sorrow out, recognizing only the Fae could understand how much he had tried to change the course of events, and how little impact he truly had.

Eventually, he pulled away, wiping at his face to remove all trace of weakness. Catriona kissed him with the barest touch and Alistair absorbed the healing she transferred wash over, welcoming it.

When he opened his eyes, she had disappeared and he was back in the gods' paradise. In the distance, he could sense Ardea's presence and followed it with wooden steps.

The goddess was standing next to a small pond, peering within. When Alistair was near enough, she lifted a hand and the water twirled. He glanced down, doing a double take at Vivienne's sleeping face.

"What is this?" he growled.

"I know it has hurt you to lose her, brother, but Vivienne will be reborn. If you so wish, you can join her in the next life."

Alistair tried to gauge whether it was a trick or not, but not sensing anything, he nodded. "I wish to return in her service."

It was at that moment Ardea yanked her hand out. Catriona blinked, focusing on the goddess' watchful gaze. Despite what she had witnessed, the uneasy feeling in her stomach did not pass.

"Thank you... for showing me," she murmured. The reality

of seeing Atrox make the choice left her shaken, and she guessed Ardea intended it so.

The Fae gritted her teeth at the goddess' next words. "Do not take it personally. Whatever good was ever in my brother, it was gone the moment he turned against his family."

"Thank you, for your honesty." Catriona spun away before Ardea could see her tears and took off.

Aequus appeared next to this sister, eyes glued to the flying redhead. "Atrox sure knew how to pick them."

Ardea only chuckled. She felt they had not seen the last of their brother just yet.

* * *

Back in her realm, Catriona wiped at her cheeks until they were red from her ministrations. "Why am I even crying?" She muttered, before plopping down on the ground, curling onto herself.

She knew why, deep down. Atrox's callousness, his complete dismissal of their fling–or whatever it had been– hurt. Though it only counted as a dalliance, Catriona could not deny her heart's desire. She missed her wolf.

"I must have done something terrible to be cursed such."

Catriona jumped to her feet with a gasp and spun on her heels, not trusting her ears. Sure enough, an apparition confronted her–of her father, the great Fae king Merlyddus. Leaves, dust and air tangled to form his shape, leaving her agape. After all, it was not every day one received a visit from the lord of all Faes.

After she became of age, Merlyddus had allowed her to create a separate realm for herself. Then, the recluse Fae retired away from the world, to a place only the enlightened elders like him lived in. He had not visited, aside from the occasional dream or word of caution.

Now faced with his image, Catriona bowed her head in deference, but remained aright. A queen in her sanctuary, she no longer answered to Merlyddus for every little thing. The exception to that was the one rule she had never broken.

Her blue eyes met a mirror in a wrinkled face with long white hair. He was past millennia old now, but still moved like a middle-aged man, instead of the elder he was.

The mutual observation was interrupted when his words registered. "Cursed?" Catriona repeated, her fine eyebrows drawing into a frown.

Merlyddus crossed his arms, and she could have sworn he grunted. "Yes, cursed with two children who have their choice of mates in the entire universe, yet end up picking ill-fated relationships."

Damn.

Merlyddus had long ago warned Catriona about falling in love, especially as a pure Fae. Because emotions led their kind, affection was akin to tying a noose around their own necks. Faes fell for one person and losing them could break them, due to their ability to love only once.

Nothing stopped them from finding solace in others of their own kind, but their heart was fickle and closed off to any other mate. It was a double-sided coin, both blessing and curse, if one found the right person.

Catriona shook with laughter at his statement, even as the breeze picked up around her in agitation. "Father, I do *not* love him!"

Merlyddus' image shattered, then the leaves fell back together. "Do you not, my dear?"

His wry tone so reminded her of Merlin that Catriona could only gape.

"Be warned, my beautiful daughter. The path to the wolf is afire with danger. Change your mind–and your heart's desire– while you still can."

As quickly as he turned up, Merlyddus disappeared,

leaving behind only an eerie silence. Catriona shivered in the gust,

no longer smiling. With her father's apparition, one certainty had taken ground in her mind: Atrox was in trouble.

* * *

Catriona waited until the middle of the night before once more attempting to breach the gods' paradise. When the door remained stubbornly locked, she called instead onto the element of spirit. As she was a being of magic, her every step in various realms left a track.

Surrounded by nothingness, Catriona followed her own footprints through the various corridors, ensuring to mask her presence otherwise. It was only once she was in the same room, with the vibrant pond, that she dropped all pretenses and dipped her hand back in the basin.

Her thoughts centered on Atrox, his kiss, his embrace... And the rest appeared on its own.

"I know it has hurt you to lose her, brother," Ardea was saying, *"but Vivienne will be reborn. If you so wish, you can join her in the next life."*

Alistair tried to gauge whether it was a trick or not, but not sensing anything, he nodded. "I wish to return in her service."

"And so you shall." With a wave of the hand, Alistair became a glowing orb which Ardea dropped into the pond.

Aequus appeared around the corner after he was gone. "You forgot to tell him one thing."

"He will figure it out," Ardea laughed, then stepped away. "Besides, being a canine may suit him better than we think."

Catriona yanked her hand from the basin, having now seen everything. She wasted no time in returning home and setting the forest alight with her magic.

Show me the path to the wolf god, a way to set this right.

The woodland shimmered, then the willow tree rose up, its branches no longer scraping the ground. *Do you realize what you ask?*

Catriona hesitated for a brief moment, and then nodded. *Yes.*

Movement followed amongst the woods, an echo of voices whispering, demanding, enthralling. In the forest's heavy depths, a plan formed and shortly after a path was revealed. It only took the Fae moments to tap into the events of time and witness what had

taken place.

The foreboding feeling in her chest grew heavier until she got to the end and witnessed Atrox's full dilemma.

That witch!

* * *

Merlin was restless, unable to find peace in his cave in the mountains. He reasoned a quick check of the prisoner would reassure him and ease the sense of some imminent menace.

He stepped out for a walk in the night, not bothering with his staff. Only the mossy green of the trees was visible, until they split apart to reveal the restored ruins of a castle.

Merlin had pondered long and hard where to ensnare Carleigh. Unwilling to put his own home to the use, he had created a bubble in time–practically a mirror dimension of that particular location. Accessible only to those who wielded power of the same caliber, the prison existed parallel to the modern world.

In terms of location, the wizard had chosen a tower house which had opened to the public. Ancient and in ruins, it was a historical site meant for tourists. Yet it was old enough that it confused Carleigh to the point he believed he had been imprisoned in the past, and sought no escape.

Not that he would have been able to achieve freedom anyway, as Merlin had covered his tracks. Stuck between past and present, forever bound to the rock, the necromancer was meant to spend immortality alone.

At least until Merlin removed it from him. The mage had spent the last months dwelling into researching the occult, attempting to restore balance and undo what Carleigh had done. And throughout, he prayed for Vivienne's health, disturbed by the darkness he had pulled out of her—and that which he could not.

Lately, dreams of his former lover, Morgana, had shaken him up further. Despite all the time that passed, he could not forget the raven-haired beauty, to the point he sometimes felt her eyes on him.

Merlin blamed it on the fact that their relationship had evolved from one extreme to the other. Yet no matter how many lies he told himself, the wizard knew it was his guilt and love that kept him returning to thoughts of the sorceress.

As he ascended the steps, Merlin shook his head to clear it. The cloak he wore over his simple tunic and shirt came to the knees, half-covering the regular cane he leaned on. Each step felt heavier, and he absently wondered why he had chosen this particular castle, of all.

A sharp turn came and he took it, head still bowed in dark ruminations. Out of the corner of his eye, he caught sight of a shadow.

Surprised, Merlin glanced up–and froze in his tracks.

"Morgana?"

Impossible!

At first he thought she was a hallucination, induced by the little sleep he had. But then she moved, and the moon enhanced the coldness of her eyes.

Merlin was a second too late in preparing his defense. Like a whip, her magic hit him full-front and he slammed back into the rocky build of the wall, at the way at bottom of the stairs.

"Morgana..."

His illusion fell, and he was at her feet her not as the bearded man, but with jet black hair and features that were only a tad sharper than when they had first met.

On the verge of losing consciousness from the hit to his head, Merlin glanced up at his former love. This was not their first duel, but a bone-weary fatigue washed over him. *How many more will have to suffer? I am sorry for failing you, Vivienne.*

Morgana knelt before him, smiling icily under her hood. She grabbed his chin with thin fingers, though her grip was firm. "Yes, darling, fall and surrender. It is my turn now."

His eyes closed and a void of nothingness welcomed him.

* * *

Glad to have avoided detection by the gods, Catriona hastened and returned to her realm. She landed next to the willow tree, brow furrowed in concentration. Despite what she had seen, something nagged at the back of her mind and caused her stomach to feel perturbed.

When the skies darkened above, she snapped out of it. A flutter started deep in the woods, and their rustling echoed across. Catriona stepped closer, then froze.

In front of her petrified gaze, everything was changing. The trees that were usually vibrant and conscious now dropped their branches, colorless leaves falling to the ground. Even the willow tree, so alive mere hours previously, seemed burdened.

Catriona bit her lip, then touched the tree bark–only to

stumble back at the intense apprehension vibrating through it. Chills raked up her spine.

"You are right to fear."

Somehow, her father's apparition did not startle her. She faced him, her breath quickening yet unwilling to accept what had caused the transformation. "What is happening?"

When he stayed quiet, her eyes flashed lightning.

"Have you not had enough conflict for the day?" Merlyddus countered.

Catriona frowned, not catching his meaning at first. Then she did, and tried not to read into it. "You kept watch over me?"

"Someone has to. You and your brother do not make it easy. It is never a good idea to displease the gods, Catriona.

Your lover should have expected as much."

The Fae narrowed her eyes at his chastising tone. "I am not a youngling anymore, father. I can do as I please." When his features did not soften, she changed the topic. "What is all this?"

His gaze darkened as it fell on the forest, but he did not shy away from the truth. "The balance is breaking."

"Why?"

Another silence.

"Is it Morgana?"

"Not only her. Your brother, you, Carleigh, even Vivienne and her protector. All your actions have fused into chaos, unfortunately tipping the peace one way. And with the Lady of the Light now dimmed, it is only a matter of time."

Catriona stepped closer, tilting her head to the side. "Do you not mean the Lady of the Lake?"

"She is that too, yes. But Vivienne's energy balanced Carleigh's darkness, just as your brother's existence offset Morgana's isolation. With them gone, the clock is ticking."

His tone was absolute, and that alone contributed more to her panic than what she could observe with her own eyes. "Why is this affecting my realm?"

"I warned you," Merlyddus said, no longer condescending. "By choosing to save your wolf, you have altered your own fate, once more. Now it is tied with his, and the outcome of this final battle."

Catriona was silent for a moment, pacing. When she faced her father again, it was with a determined expression. "I can fix this. Let me go to Merlin."

A deep sigh, then a murmured, "Did you not hear me,

child? He is gone."

"Surely you don't mean..." Catriona balked, unable to finish her thought out loud.

Merlyddus shook his head, then waved his hand until the leaves that had formed his shape instead showed her Merlin. Within moments, Catriona had witnessed everything –his capture, Morgana and Mordred splitting the dimensions once more, and Carleigh revealed to be in hiding.

"*No*! I must help him!"

Before she could do anything, the image disappeared, replaced by her father's expression once more.

"It is not wise."

"Father, please. Lift the restriction. Let me enter their realm."

Her pleas fell on deaf ears, as he only shook his head. "No."

"If not for me, do it for Merlin! Morgana is his weakness, we both know it. Atrox can be useful."

"Your wolf is but a mongrel in this fight, powerless."

Her eyes blazed. "He is not! And I will not sit by and do nothing, especially now that I am as involved as all of them!"

They glared at each other for a beat, icy sapphires battling to establish their opinion, until Merlyddus relented and sighed. "Always doing as you please, my darling daughter... Very well. You cannot go where they are, as I refuse to allow darkness to taint you. But as for the rest, the choice is yours."

Catriona inclined her head in gratitude, ecstatic at the small victory and at the fact her father would not stand in her way—much.

"How can I fix this?" she pressed.

"You would need a miracle. There is not enough light here

to offset the evil within."

Merlyddus disappeared once more and Catriona dropped to the ground, holding onto the tree with one hand. She had to help Merlin—and Atrox. *And perhaps one does not have to exclude the other.*

Straightening her back, she rose and headed to her home within the forest. She needed refreshments and a recharging ritual for the realm. If she planned to join the fight, she required a fortress worthy of the name.

CHAPTER 3

Merlin opened his eyes, dazed like he was coming out of a dream. The cold hit him first, then the numbness in his joints. He blinked, to find himself leaning against a hard surface, immobile. A quick scan of their surroundings revealed a familiar picture. He was in Carleigh's old room, where he had been imprisoned for the last months.

"Ah, the mighty Merlin is finally awake."

The voice could not be mistaken. Merlin hoped he was hallucinating, but his eyes fell on the necromancer, now freed from chains and standing only a small distance away in a corner. Out of reflex and pure rage he tried to move, but found his hands and feet were bound–and not with rope. The sorcerer's next words distracted him from further investigating his plight.

"Fancy little prison, is it not? You can thank Morgana for the idea."

Merlin glanced to where his ex-lover was staring out a

small window. He knew what she saw underneath: the mossy green woodland, the old huts and barges, all for the view of visitors. This particular jewel amid an otherwise emerald isle had become something of an experience to the past, a way to understand Ireland for what it had been.

Craggaunowen was as close to an open-concept museum as one could get. Merlin had chosen its sixteenth century castle as the prison to dump Carleigh in. He had even created a parallel dimension that mirrored the real world tourists walked in. Regular humans never guessed who hid in the tower, nor could they hear the necromancer's angry cries.

But the museum was more than just a castle and woods. It was acres upon acres of archaeological items displayed for sightseers to enjoy. Surrounded by mossy forests and long trail walks, one could view anything from a boat that had once crossed the Atlantic, to huts where the ancient people of the land used to live, decorated with furs and pottery. In this place, it was easy to get lost–as Merlin had discovered.

Now, his senses focused on his ex-lover. He knew, by the tension he sensed radiating from her, that Morgana was envisioning what her life had been. Once, long ago, they had both lived and laughed together. Only ashes of despair were left between them, tangible and bitter.

The mage cast his attention to what was holding him hostage. Crystal encased his entire lower body, imprisoning his hands up to the wrists. Only his naked torso and head were free. When he jerked against the bindings, sharp pain ratcheted up his arms, and a groan escaped him.

"It is useless, father."

Merlin noticed Mordred for the first time. His son had been

in the room all along, yet it had taken a moment to recognize him. Though he had the same jet black hair and blue eyes, there was a distant gleam in them that was almost alien. His mouth settled in a sneer at Merlin's distress.

"How is this possible?"

His voice shook, and he gulped repeatedly to steady it. The mage distinctly recalled the last time he had seen Mordred, blood of his blood, fighting ruthlessly against Arthur. Their battle had caused both their deaths.

He should not be here. This is not right.

Now that his senses were more conscious, he caught the blur in the atmosphere around Mordred, almost like a halo of malevolence. Whatever was done to revive him had not left things unscathed in the world.

Even as Merlin wanted to hate him, the young man had too much of him to disregard. To distract himself, he continued inspecting the room.

A quick glance confirmed they had brought him to the tower itself, ensuring magic chained him there. *My spell must cover us, despite my imprisonment. Somehow, he found* solace in the idea his powers had not been taken away, merely blocked.

His eyes returned to Mordred. *In another life, things would have turned out differently.* The thought struck him by surprise,

but he pushed it aside. It would do him no good to be sentimental, especially when faced with their unfeeling gazes.

Unless...

"Morgana."

She did not turn right away, but her back straightened and Merlin knew she heard him. Undeterred, he tried again, ignoring Carleigh's snicker.

"Please, look at me."

Merlin's chest squeezed painfully, oddly hollow when she remained immobile. The air itself in the circular room seemed to have stilled, in expectation of what she would do. The mage reasoned it was only their powers together that caused the phenomenon, unwilling to admit the truth.

Eventually, Morgana faced him. Over the years, her features had grown gaunt, giving her expression a fiercer beauty than Merlin had first seen. This was definitely not the woman he had mentored, but a hardened enchantress.

Sorceress, his mind corrected, to no avail.

The heart wants what it wants. Atrox's words of warning from long ago rang in his ears, but he shook them off.

Unable to tear their gazes off each other, the two ex-lovers stared, taking each other in. Despite Morgana's beauty, there was an untouchable air about her, a shadow in the depths of her gray eyes. A faint crackling of the air testified to the power she held. And yet something was missing.

Ever perceptive, Merlin continued his assessment. Morgana was wearing a long, blood red gown. It wrapped around her curves, hinting at what hid beneath, and his baser self-triggered images of a past too far gone to be recovered again.

Her skin upon his, her moans and his sighs–all too real, they echoed in his mind. Merlin had to tear his gaze from hers, unable to hold onto the darkened silver orbs and not want to touch her. *After all this time... and still nothing has changed.*

At a loss, he took a deep breath calmed his erratic heart. "How did you get here?"

Morgana smiled, taunting him with a slight upturn of the

corner of her lips. "Wouldn't you like to know?"

Merlin gritted his jaw, well aware of the web of lies he found himself caught in. Over the years, he had hidden her existence from Vivienne and even Alistair. Many times, he had come close to revealing the full extent of their past, but had reasoned it would do more harm than good.

Aside from wanting to protect them, the mage still had a hard time admitting how far his mistake had cost them all their happiness. Nothing he did could undo it, but perhaps the loss of memory for all concerned had been a blessing. In either case, it was definitely something he had taken advantage of, paying no heed to the warning cues destiny kept hurling towards him.

Now, that same secret had come back to bite him. Merlin glanced at Mordred, whispering in a corner with Carleigh. From the way the necromancer nodded in assent, he guessed nothing good would come of it.

There would be no escape, he knew that. His fate had been pre-written eons ago, and his Fae heritage had only pushed him further into it. It was time to pay for all his tinkering.

But not before he found out what the three planned and warned Vivienne. *I will not cause her pain again.* With that resolution firmly in mind, Merlin tried again. "How?"

"You made it too easy." It was Mordred who answered instead of his mother, stepping away from Carleigh. "You thought the magic you researched wouldn't leave a trace? The more you delved into the occult, the more you left footprints. There were so many... All we had to do was follow them."

Have I truly been so foolish?

"But Carleigh–"

"You may have hid me on a different dimension," the

sorcerer interrupted, "but you forgot your ex-lover was just as powerful as you." He glanced to Morgana, a faint sneer on his lips. "Perhaps not quite as immortal. At least, not anymore."

Morgana paled at the words, shooting daggers towards the necromancer. Merlin did not miss the moment, his sharp gaze zoning in their tense stances.

Momentarily forgotten, Merlin had time to recall his earlier assessment that something was missing in the sorceress. *Carleigh hints at a deeper loss,* he realized. But would Morgana really have surrendered that much to save their son?

And if yes, how had she survived at all?

Interesting.... Merlin noted her reaction and filed it away for future reference–if ever the opportunity arose to use it.

"Regardless," Mordred interjected and strode to his father,

"you have grown old and reckless with time. It was *much* too easy."

Merlin threw him an incensed look, all the while pondering how he would have liked to prove him wrong. Unable to do so, he focused on Morgana. There was no way he could relate to Mordred, even to plead for his life. But *they* had a history, no matter how much both had tried to forget it.

And judging by the fire in her eyes, Morgana would not let it go.

Which is exactly what I need.

The sorceress met his pensive gaze and smiled. She stepped closer until they were a hair's breath away. Silver orbs danced with mischief, and a long, elegant hand rose to caress his cheek.

Merlin could not have stopped from nuzzling into that touch if the entire world depended on it. For years, he had craved her, wanting so much to undo the harm caused. *One chance… I only need a second chance…*

As though hearing his thoughts, Morgana put her mouth to his ear, deliciously close but not quite there. Her sweet citrus perfume enveloped him and Merlin closed his eyes, lost to memories of the past. At least, until she spoke.

"You made it easy for me," Morgana whispered, "to come and take away all that you hold dear."

… Or perhaps not.

* * *

Catriona watched with dread as her brother courted death. Since her father had disappeared, she had spent the last hours on and off keeping an eye on Merlin.

She was far from comfortable sitting cross-legged on the ground near the willow tree. The bark was rough against her wings and back, and her thighs were cramping.

Catriona ignored the little discomforts, hands dug deep into the earth and touching the roots. Her eyes glowed incandescent as the air in front of her shimmered, showing Merlin's dilemma.

It was true Faes could only be killed by one of their own kind, or a god–thankfully, that meant Carleigh could not harm Merlin permanently. But Morgana was on the verge of insanity, driven mad by the loss of her child and a needless thirst for vengeance. Catriona could see it, even if her own brother could not, blinded as he was by his feelings for the Halfling.

"I need to help."

The words sounded odd in the night, which had previously been quiet. Small fireflies circled above her head, but the Fae paid them no mind. She was stuck, unable to do much– at least until Atrox went back to sleep. Then, she would try to contact him.

Earlier, after seeing all she had to in the gods' paradise, she had tracked down the wolf god. Connecting with him, however, proved more difficult. Despite her best attempts, something blocked his mind from hers, and it was not only the distance between realms.

Thus, the Fae had waited until his consciousness was no longer awake before attempting again.

As though hearing her through time and space, the image she saw changed from Merlin's shocked expression to a large Caucasian Shepherd pacing restlessly.

Catriona had been surprised at first to find Atrox in such a form. But underneath the docile exterior, she recognized snippets of the man she had known. It was in the way he paced like a lion in a cage and snarled at the empty air as though fighting an invisible enemy.

The vision had no sound, despite her best efforts. Catriona noticed he was in an enclosure of some kind, perhaps a house. A fire flickered behind him, oddly off balance. Her stare lingered on the flames, then fixated on the dog.

Whether tiring out or simply bored, Atrox dropped to the floor, placing his head on his paws and sighing heavily. Catriona could read in him indignation and anxiety–something was amiss, but what?

Aside from being stuck in a dog's body.

Catriona frowned, then dug her hand in the ground, clenching the earth between her fingers to center herself. It all depended on her ability to link to him, and communicate her warnings. *Everything relies on tonight.*

"Hear me, Atrox…"

Catriona kept her eyes focused on his shape until it was as clear as though he sat next to her. Still, her plea provoked no reaction.

"Atrox, listen to my voice... I need your help."

He moved then–but only to exhale heavier, then shift to the side. *Bloody mess this all is.*

Catriona jumped, startled at the rough timbre of his words, so familiar in her mind. She could now hear him, sense each breath he took.

She could also feel the heat from the fire—and it was that which held her attention again. It was due to that split second of focus that she caught it. A rumble on the ground, then the flames crackled once more. Only this time, they hissed as if alive.

Eyes widened in shock, Catriona witnessed two snakes of ashes escape the pit and slither across the floor towards Atrox. He was almost asleep, his breathing deepening, unaware of the peril he was in.

Catriona reacted on pure instinct, lashing out with the full force of her psyche.

"Atrox, watch out!"

* * *

Atrox, watch out!

The warning was so clear, Alistair jumped up–and away. Snakes of fire passed the spot he had last been on, then continued toward the curtains. In front of his startled gaze, they slithered about and disappeared into the wall.

Without the voice, he would have burned. *But who was it?*

Alistair stood frozen for a few more beats, staring in shock. He had been so tired, his mind preoccupied by more thoughts of Vivienne and his own dilemma, that he had not paid attention.

Who the hell saved me?

There had been a twinge of familiarity, not unlike the voice of his jailer. Despite his best efforts to identify it, he could not place it.

Sounds of crashing upstairs brought him out of his ruminations, and he ran towards them. He could hear Sébastien moving about, struggling to wake Vivienne up.

By the time Alistair entered the room, she was breathing in deep and the fire had eased away, leaving behind only a lingering taste of magic and chaos. The demon dog sniffed around, not liking the particular twinge of darkness he could sense.

In the eons he had spent as lord of the underworld, he had grown well acquainted with the inner goings of the occult. What he captured now was more potent than even then, almost reminiscent of…

The thought eluded him, and he shook his head in frustration. Instead of fixating on his own shortcomings, Alistair turned his midnight gaze to his mistress.

Vivienne had curled up on the bed, knees drawn up to her chest and rocking softly back and forth. Her arms were wrapped around herself as though in protection, but there was nothing in Sébastien's stance that warned of danger.

On the contrary, the knight was kneeling by the bedside, reaching for her hand with an expression of pain on his face. They both had dark shadows under their eyes, a testimony of the many sleepless nights they had spent lately.

It was not the first incident–nor did he think it would be the last. Something was definitely going on with Vivienne, affecting her more than it ever had Sébastien. Alistair could well recall a time when the guardian had dreaded tainting Vivienne, and his less than stellar experience as the Mafia's enforcer had only contributed to darkness taking a hold in his heart.

But lately, he seemed fine. Though still prone to occasional bouts of morose behavior, he was much more stable than Vivienne. Alistair coughed to get his attention, and after a moment, Sébastien turned to him.

The two males shared a look full of meaning, then Sébastien focused back on Vivienne.

"Love, we really need to talk."

She continued to sway, not quite hearing him. Then she lifted green eyes brimming with tears, her hand grasping his over the bed sheets.

"I'm sorry," Vivienne whispered, then promptly broke into sobs.

Alistair was struck at the transformation in her. Whereas before she had been level-headed, now Vivienne seemed ruled solely by emotions. Nothing they did helped, only worsened matters. And with each night she slept less, and more and more incidents arose, like the one that had just taken place.

We need to sort this out, Alistair warned Sébastien. *Try to find out what's causing it, what things she's having nightmares of.*

Sébastien gave a curt nod, but his gaze never wavered from his beloved as he squeezed her hand in gentle reassurance.

"What were you dreaming?"

Almost at once, Vivienne's demeanor changed. She let go of him, turning her face into the crook of her elbow. She wiped tears away with the back of her hand, before sighing. "I don't remember."

It was the same answer as before, delivered in a flat voice, and Alistair was tired of hearing it. Vivienne had become withdrawn and moody and keeping whatever was eating her inside would not help.

Before he could intervene, Sébastien spoke.

"Stop lying to me." Though his tone was neutral, there was a firmness that had not been there before. "If you don't wish to tell me, admit it. But don't lie, Vivienne. We swore honesty to each other."

"*You're* one to talk!" Vivienne retorted, scowling towards him now in a familiar display of temper.

Sébastien gritted his jaw but did not back down, only inched closer to her. "This isn't you. Yell at me all you want, but I know what I see. What the *hell* is going on, Vivienne?"

They stared at each other and the tension in the air rose a few notches. Realizing the two lovers were close to a quarrel, Alistair interceded before it got out of control.

Highness, we only wish to help.

"I don't need help!" Vivienne burst, standing from the bed. Her eyes had darkened, her face pale in the wake of another sleepless night.

Alistair's hackles rose at the sight, and even Sébastien was struck dumb. Then, just as suddenly as the sinister aura had flared around her, it disappeared. The obscure gaze was once more clear green, though Vivienne was left shivering.

She glanced between them in confusion, brow furrowed and bottom lip trembling. "What's happening to me?"

Alistair took pity on her state and marched closer to nuzzle his head on her bare knee. *The corruption Merlin withdrew from you.... He warned us it would not be all gone.*

"Remember how it influenced me, love." Sébastien got up and grasped her hand in his once more. "You cannot let it affect you. The more you give in, the more it controls you."

"I try, but it's hard." Vivienne pulled in a shaky breath, then released it and met Sébastien's gaze full on. "The dreams…

They're always the same. There's a man, reaching out to me. He says things that get to me, then I forget and wake up."

Sébastien glanced down to Alistair, and the dog shook his head infinitesimally. *I know not what to make of it either.*

"Why not tell me?" Sébastien asked Vivienne.

"Because I feel guilty, dreaming of another. And… I was afraid."

There was a lengthy pause, then Sébastien tugged on her wrist and pulled her in his arms, wrapping Vivienne in his embrace. "There is nothing that will tear us apart now that we are together. I vow it."

When Vivienne allowed the brief contact, Alistair thought it best to step out. The two lovers needed a moment, and he had to ponder what Vivienne had revealed. *Who the hell is seeking to get through to her?*

He barely reached the fireplace to sit down again when *she* appeared in his mind.

What happened this time?

Alistair groaned in despair, ducking his head and dropping to the floor.

* * *

Catriona stepped out of the water, having cleansed her body and spirit. With a flick of her hand, a warm breeze surrounded her and soon dried the dripping liquid from her skin.

Despite having undergone a ritual that normally calmed her, she found it did not help. All her hopes centered on Atrox and her recent success. She had reached him, warned him!

Quick on the heels of that thought was the realization their link had not been broken by chance—but by someone else. Anger pushed through the last of her calm demeanor, but she fought the urge to use her connection to the realm and start a fight.

No, what the Fae planned to do could be achieved by her strength alone. *No one messes with what is mine.*

The fact that Atrox was technically not hers–anymore–did not stop her. Catriona sat down on the ground, tucking her legs underneath her and closing her eyes. Her spirit traveled, searching, questing for that which opposed her.

Though her contact might have been brief with Atrox, it had been enough. She only had to linger around his essence to detect the unfamiliar something—some*one*—else.

When the energy hit her, Catriona's startled eyes opened. *Morgana.*

Burning of a cold fire, she settled deeper unto her haunches, determined more than ever. This was the connection between her brother and Atrox, just as she had expected and feared.

Morgana is the key–to everything.

* * *

Merlin knew it was a gamble, but it was one he had to take. He inhaled Morgana's fragrance once more, then spoke what was on his mind.

"After all these years, your hate has not lessened?"

Morgana pulled back abruptly, eyes flashing and hands clenched. "You took everything from me! Do you honestly think that betrayal has ebbed with time?"

No... But I had hoped.

Before Merlin could find a suitable answer, Morgana laughed coldly. "No, it has not. But I should not be surprised. After all, you have no idea what I went through. All these years, you had it easy, darling. So let me show you what real pain is."

Snakes of fire escaped her hands and she thrust them towards Merlin. They slithered up the crystal base, not melting it but rather solidifying it. When they touched his skin, their regular temperature surprised him, yet he remained wary of what would follow.

At first, he felt numb–then the blaze spread. Each serpent wrapped around one of his sides, circling him from bicep to rib and across his abdomen. Once they had each inch covered, little fangs dug into him, sending the fiery torment under the skin as well as over.

Try as he might, Merlin could not keep silent. He howled in agony, his gut churning as though his intestines were being scorched. It went on for long moments and when it stopped, he was left panting.

"You do not know pain," Morgana finished softly. "But you will. I will take away everything you hold dear."

"Vivienne." The name escaped him in a daze.

Morgana blinked, surprised, then laughed. "She is already lost, darling. The darkness you removed lingered–at least enough of it did. Soon, she will be ours."

Merlin searched her gaze, seeing the hate, knowing it was his fault, yet not understanding. "Why?"

The silver eyes that had once looked upon him with love glittered, but no response came. Instead, Morgana turned away, dismissing him as easily as she had condemned him.

It was Carleigh who stepped closer, bringing the evil surrounding him within a few inches of Merlin. "You thought imprisoning me would exclude me from the game."

He had kept his distance, enjoying the show, but now craved retribution. Tendrils of evil escaped him, crawling up Merlin's torso and leeching on, replacing the serpents. They bit into his skin and blood flowed, trickling down his chest. His vision blurred, and he found it hard to focus on anything.

Mordred's eyes danced at the spectacle. "Will they really ensure he is harmless?"

"Oh yes. Your father is as good as useless. These pets of mine will keep him in perpetual delusion–until we have no more need of him."

Carleigh snapped his fingers to get Merlin's attention, waiting until the wizard's pain-filled gaze settled on him. "You wished to know what I want now with my half-sister. She is no longer Light's champion, but her energy alone would be a great sacrifice, at least for starters. There is more than immortality I seek." He bent over and whispered in his ear. "I desire what you have: the freedom and power of a god or Fae. And I shall obtain it."

Merlin's eyes flashed with panic. What he had read...in the research on the occult... His thoughts muddled together, but one remained clear. *Vivienne! Danger!*

"Rest easy, darling. I will finish what I started," Morgana grinned from afar. "But first things first."

They left him alone, and Merlin fought back despair, struggling against his bindings. With each suck on his skin, his vision darkened, until only one question remained. *What have I caused?*

A dimension away, Catriona's heart constricted in pain for her half-brother.

CHAPTER 4

Leaving Merlin to the torment of his minions, Carleigh led the way out of the circular prison and down some dusty stairs. Morgana and Mordred followed him, their long cloaks brushing past the stone and wood with each step.

They continued in silence until the narrow staircase opened onto an older room, with an opening to a balcony. Barely half a foot of cement surrounded the outside tower, enough for the sentries of the past to have a look if they were being assailed.

Carleigh stepped into the tight space, breathing the fresh air with rapture. His cool eyes settled on the forest below, and the horizon further away. Sunrise had come and gone, but it was still early morning and a fog remained on the grounds. Free once more, he could appreciate the beauty of the landscape rather than hate the confining castle.

Mordred followed him on the rampart without hesitation, but Morgana lingered in the opening. A torn curtain fell miserably, and she pushed it out of the way.

The necromancer was silent, then turned his body halfway in the narrow space to better face both his opponents.

"I see no reason to dawdle. I know it is you who helped me in the past. What is it you wish now?"

"Merlin."

"Immortality."

Carleigh stared between them, then grinned widely.

"Merlin is mine to do with as I please once this is all over," Morgana explained.

"And I want immortality for my mother again," Mordred continued.

Morgana glanced at him in surprise, but her son did not react, face blank and staring at Carleigh. Something warmed in her chest at his concern. She had known the consequences of her act, perhaps more so than Mordred, and did not expect to shy away from them.

"Mordred…" She touched his arm, searching his gaze. "I made my choice peacefully."

Carleigh's features hardened, a faint sneer on his lips. "Be that as it is, you die a little more each time you use your powers."

A swift intake of breath was the only reaction from Mordred, as though he was stunned at the confirmation of something he had already known. Morgana had grown weaker with every dip into her Fae magic. Soon, it would burn her out. It was the ultimate price to pay for having saved his life.

Unconcerned with their private moment, Carleigh pressed forward. "What use is a Halfling to me, especially one as damaged as you?"

Morgana stepped onto the rampart then, pushed past her son and lifted a glowing palm. Carleigh sensed it when the surrounding air shifted, almost pushing him off the balcony and into the nothingness below.

Despite the irony, the necromancer recognized Morgana was still powerful, enough so to fight him if need be.

"Very well," Carleigh conceded, and the pressure around his head eased off. "I want to be a god, free from Darkness. Though I fully enjoy my extensive powers, I dislike being subservient to another entity. Full-fledged Faes and gods are not. Thus, it is my next ambition."

Mordred's eyes danced in approval. "You have guts, sorcerer. But before we go any further, I require your assurance that if we succeed, you will give us what we asked."

Carleigh's brow furrowed as he assessed both Mordred and Morgana. *A team player, I am not. But they may prove useful yet.*

"I agree to your terms and commit to fulfilling your requests once you help me achieve my goal."

Mordred glanced to Morgana, silently asking her thoughts on it. The silver eyes watched him, unwavering in their attention. Carleigh sensed the hairs at the back of his neck stand at their connection, something he was unaccustomed to.

After a beat, she inclined her head ever so softly.

"Agreed."

Mordred grinned, turning to Carleigh and holding his hand out. He gripped him by the forearm, squeezing in brotherly approval. "We have an arrangement."

Once he let go, Carleigh leaned on the railing. Below them, he could hear humans. The grounds had opened for visitations, but their existence between dimensions protected them all from their eyes.

He debated how much to share with the two, then admitted, "A few months ago, I tainted my dear half-sister. By sacrificing her blood to evil, I gained immortality. I had thought that would be the end, but it turns out Darkness wants more. It craves Vivienne's soul, because of her affinity for the elements and her weight in the overall balance."

Morgana drew closer, almost despite herself. "But that's impossible. She is a champion of Light, even corrupted as she is now. The only way Darkness could ever have Vivienne's soul would be if she denies her allegiance to Light and you take her life in a place of power, on a full moon."

If the sorceress' words surprised him, Carleigh did not show it. Instead, he inclined his head in appreciation. "Precisely. The problem, besides my capture in this realm, is that I need to find such a location."

Only the sounds of humans and the wind echoed around them for a few moments. It was Mordred who broke the silence, glancing at his mother. "There is one such place that has gained rumors over time…. Do you remember the circles of stone we used to travel?" At her encouraging nod, he breathed its name. "Stonehenge."

Carleigh blinked in surprise. "Yes, I know the place. The land is ancient, and there are always mortals around, easy prey for sacrifice. But first, we have to slip away from here. Can you two create a portal?"

"No," Mordred's tone was steely. "My mother will be too weak. I could, but I need someone on the other side to balance out the spell."

Carleigh's face darkened at the answer. "Then we may be

stuck here for much longer."

"Not necessarily," Morgana intervened with a loaded look to her son. "Tell him."

Mordred gritted his jaw, blue eyes shining fiercely. Carleigh had the uncanny sensation he was hiding something and wanted to keep on withholding it. At his mother's insistent gaze, he sighed and admitted, "I can work on Vivienne."

"How?"

"Since their birth, they have been linked," Morgana explained. "You may be her blood, but Mordred is her fated nemesis. Over the last few months, the precious Lady of the Lake has had dream after dream of my son, and they communicate. Give him more time, and he can twist her reality enough to bring her to our side."

"Then do it." Mordred scowled at the necromancer's order, but did not disagree.

"That takes care of the location, Vivienne, and our escape," Carleigh summarized. "Merlin is handled, so it is only a matter of time. How much, exactly?"

Rather than answer, Mordred countered with a question of his own. "Are you sure those leeches will hold my father?"

"Yes," Carleigh rolled his eyes. "There is nothing Merlin can do to evade their clutches, believe me. Now how long do you need for Vivienne?"

Mordred thought back to his last contact with the enchantress, then shrugged. "A few more weeks. It is slow work, especially with her protectors around. Her spirit fights against the change, but not for much longer."

Carleigh smirked in satisfaction. Soon, he could have what he always missed–and kill Vivienne in the process.

* * *

After days of being cooped up inside the house, the enchantress relented and agreed to Alistair's suggestion for a walk. They ambled aimlessly on the streets in Avignon, Vivienne holding his leash.

Despite the sunny late afternoon, it was not long before Alistair caught his mistress' change of mood. Her gait slowed, and she frowned at the ground as though it had offended her.

Noticing this, Alistair nuzzled her hand. *What is it?*

Vivienne met his eyes, but only temporarily before glancing away. "Nothing, I'm fine," she muttered. The demon dog sighed, shaking his head at her stubbornness.

Highness, after all this time by your side, I should think I know when something bothers you. Talk to me. When Vivienne still remained silent, he purposefully stepped in her way, causing her to pause before tripping over him. *Please.*

Vivienne glanced around, noticing a few others out for a stroll. Rather than respond aloud, she linked telepathically. *I'm tired, is all. Sick of these nightmares, of not feeling like myself.*

Alistair stepped to the side and they resumed their walk as he tried to find a way to broach the subject. In the end, he settled for bluntness. *I sense guilt in you, majesty, and so much sorrow. You cannot let this get to you. How can I help?*

I don't know, I... Vivienne trailed off, then restarted. *It is my fight to settle, but how to do it eludes me. It was almost easy when Sébastien was fighting these demons to advise him to be good and not give in. Yet now that I find myself in the same situation, I feel... lost.*

Alistair glanced up at her, noticing how Vivienne's aura

had darkened. *Highness, your light is what helped him out of his mess. What you carry with you cannot be thrown away, but you can learn to deal with it.*

Vivienne scowled at that, looking none too pleased. "As if I don't know that already."

An elderly couple that passed them threw her an odd look, having heard her words. She avoided their confused glances and ducked into the next alley. *All I need is for people to think I'm crazy now.*

You are dealing with many things at the moment, highness. Try not to be so hard on yourself.

"Right..." Vivienne shook her head, as though trying to shake off a bad memory.

A few more minutes passed, then they turned into another alley. Vivienne kept going, but Alistair spied shapes trailing them.

We have company.

Vivienne peered over her shoulder, noticing the three men after them, all built like fighters.

Let us go back into a public place, Alistair suggested.

The presence chose that moment to appear in his mind, its tone unequivocal. *No. Let Vivienne unleash her powers on them.*

Never! Alistair growled.

Vivienne looked down in surprise, slowing down. A whistle from behind had her look again–they were nearing.

Without warning, she whirled around and faced them.

Highness, this is not a good idea. Alistair tried to tug them away, to no avail. Vivienne was deaf to his advice and worse, her magic was rising to the surface.

Vivienne, no! Alistair tried again, but she ignored him.

Energy permeated the air, raising the hackles on his back. It took him a few moments to realize the potency was more intense than it should have been. He searched past Vivienne's aura, not liking the chaos he perceived.

Ignoring his prying, the enchantress clenched her fists, standing with feet width apart and a tight-lipped smile towards the three men. "You have one chance to back off."

They chuckled derisively, but Alistair was through losing control. He rose to his full height, snarling menacingly. Before they could react, he jumped the leader and fell down wrestling with him.

"Alistair!" Vivienne's cry barely reached him. His jaw clamped on the man's shoulder, biting and tearing at the skin. Screams of pain echoed, then Alistair spoke one word in their minds.

Run.

The man stood, holding his bleeding arm—a flesh wound. Without a glance to them, he and his buddies took off. Alistair turned to Vivienne, dark eyes flashing. The other voice was driven out of his mind, perhaps by the anger—he did not care.

He advanced to his mistress, panting heavily. What the hell were you thinking?

Vivienne glanced to where the men were running, then Alistair. Something passed in her glare, too quick for him to get a read. Then she knelt down in front of him, looking contrite. "I panicked. After everything with Carleigh.... I just panicked, I'm sorry. Thank you for stepping in."

He stared at her for a long time, annoyed at being unable to see past his charge's walls. Finally, he said, *Let's go home.*

* * *

Later that evening, Alistair kept his distance, but his eyes never once strayed from the two lovers.

He watched as Vivienne and Sébastien cooked together, laughing and touching at every opportunity. It was a scene that should have warmed his heart, but did the exact opposite.

Something felt off from their return, but it was only hours later he realized what.

His mistress was chuckling, but her eyes were cold. Lost in her ministrations, Sébastien was either blind or chose to believe the best. Yet whenever she glanced his way, Alistair could practically see her aura flare dark.

And with each passing moment, his worry grew. Merlin had warned him long ago of the dangers behind corrupting Vivienne. In his hubris, he had not listened, assuming they would fine. But though he had been right and her love had saved Sébastien, and his had not tainted her… Something was at odds with the Lady of the Lake.

I need to get in her head, there is no other way.

Alistair waited until they were having dinner, and Vivienne had sipped a few glasses of wine. She was leaning close to Sébastien, enraptured in a story he was telling her, when his chance arose.

Determined, the demon dog pushed his psyche in her direction, trying to broach the confines she kept locked up lately. It was not ethical by any means, but he reasoned that since she could become a danger to herself and to others…. *Something has to give.*

He tried to keep his touch light, and breathed in relief when

Vivienne only moved closer to Sébastien, chatting away. In her mind, Alistair could sense the alcohol flow in her blood and her muscles relax. Desire tinged her every thought —for Sébastien, for carnal consumption.

I did not need to know that, Alistair muttered to himself, then delved deeper still.

The fight with the assailants was alive in Vivienne's memories, but hidden underneath worry for her growing emotions, and a deep sense of unease. She felt at odds with her own mind and body, as though a balance she had previously counted on had ruptured.

And then, further still, Alistair found what he had dreaded: a well of darkness that was developing and latching onto her vital force, feeding off it and replacing it with negative waves.

It existed not in her physical body, where it could have been removed, but rather had latched onto her spiritual force. Like a parasite waiting to be fed, the corruption pulsed and lived off

her. Each time Vivienne gave in to violence, the evil expanded, until she would no longer have control and be under its complete subjugation.

Alistair meant to dig further, but was shoved out of her mind with such brutality it caused him to whine. Vivienne glanced up at him then, her aura dark and eyes shooting warning flames.

Leave her alone, his jailer's voice ordered. *Forget what you have seen, mutt.*

He could not warn Sébastien, but it did not stop him from continuing his surveillance of them. One way or another, a solution would arise. And when it did, he planned to pounce on it.

All I have to do is wait.

* * *

By the end of the night, Sébastien had relaxed and learned to breathe again, enjoying a regular evening with Vivienne—as much as they could.

They were on the couch, having sipped wine and now cuddled in front of the fire. As he glanced in the flames, his mind wandered aimlessly.

"I missed this," he whispered against Vivienne's temple, kissing the side of her head. She snuggled into him, having fallen asleep.

Despite the coziness of the scene, Sébastien could not escape the certainty that something was coming with the force of an unbeatable typhoon, and it was aiming straight for them. He tightened his hold on Vivienne, hoping to keep whatever it was at bay.

The last few days, Sébastien felt as though he had a target painted on his back. Despite his premonition, he resolved that whatever it was, they would deal with it together, as a team.

I have not gotten her back only to lose her again.

Alistair had told him what happened with the assailants, and it had eerily reminded him of his own dealings with violence. Sébastien glanced at his knuckles, now free of bruises. But it had not always been so... Not by a long shot. And the road back had not been easy.

Clenching his jaw, he tried to loosen his stiff muscles and rest his eyes. But his gaze was pulled back into the flames, and he spent the rest of the night wide awake. By the time sunrise came, only one thing was clear in his mind.

I will allow nothing to break us.

CHAPTER 5

The sky shone bright red, violet and yellow. Clouds of silver reflected the many shades onto the ground below, casting an unearthly atmosphere.

It was not a sunrise he recalled, but the tinge of memory was unmistakable. As he stood on the balcony, thunder rolled, lighting struck, and darkness descended.

He was dressed in a dark navy toga, help up by a brooch. His hair was longer, almost past his shoulders. It waved smoothly, curling unlike anything he had before. In his right hand was a golden goblet, clenched so tightly his knuckles had turned white.

In it, he saw his reflection. The pale eyes stared unseeing, pained and brimming with tears. He reeled at this weak version of himself, unwilling to believe it.

Noises distracted him, and he peeked over. Below the balcony, a man and woman were whispering secretly and laughing.

He cringed, stepping backwards. It was impossible to escape them, regardless of where he went. They were in love, and her green eyes shone with adoration to another.

"She should have been mine." His statement was lost on the wind.

But he would not ruin her happiness. So he kept to the corners, unwilling to admit the depth of his pain, or do anything to change it. Though he wanted nothing more than to be far removed from their presence, his feet were rooted to the floor.

Moments later, he had still not moved, listening on until the noises turned to murmurs of love, then moans of desire.

Carleigh's eyes snapped open, flashing in the obscurity of the castle.

What the hell was that?

* * *

Vivienne was asleep, peacefully, when it started. For the first time in a long while she dreamt of a body of water, a soft breeze in her hair and Sébastien's hand in hers.

As often happened with her dreams, the romantic setting quickly turned dark. In a whirl of sensations, she was transported into a field of poppies. She became entranced by their blood red petals and the beauty of the place. But it was not long before she shivered with the odd sensation of feeling watched.

Thunder rolled across the ground, and it vibrated under her naked feet. A quick glance down confirmed Vivienne was only wearing a cloak over a dark shift, the kind of clothing she had worn in her part lives.

She jumped, crying in surprise at another roll of thunder–and this time she caught something out of the corner of her eyes.

Warily, Vivienne turned. He stood a mere few feet away. Black hair, a gaze of the coldest ice, and a smile that was more predatory than enticing.

The big bad wolf.

As the words ran across her mind, he grinned–did he hear?

Vivienne could only stare for a few precious seconds. Everything told her this man was dangerous and she should be as far away from him as possible. Yet the darker part of her that had gained ground, the same side she did not want Sébastien to be aware of, pushed her to the contrary.

Before she knew it, she had taken a few steps towards him. He smiled wider at that, extending a hand in open invitation.

Spooked, Vivienne turned to run–but he was right there! She could sense his energy like a breeze of arctic air.

Their eyes met, and she was puzzled by the intensity in his blue gaze and the conflicting emotions swirling within. "Who are you?" she whispered.

"You know who," he spoke softly, but once more she shivered. "I am the only one who can understand you."

His hand lifted to touch her, but Vivienne balked at the intimacy and took off. Her bare feet hit the ground, and she winced as she stepped on pebbles. Her breath hitched, and she glanced over her shoulder. He was chasing her, quick on her heels...

Vivienne wanted to pick up her pace to avoid him, but found instead that she was slowing down. Butterflies built in her stomach, and an overeager thought blocked everything else: *He's going to catch me!*

But rather than be afraid, Vivienne looked forward to it. She sensed him behind her, and yelped when his hand grabbed a handful of her shift, then tackled her to the ground.

They rolled in the poppies until he ended up pinning her with his body. The blue gaze sparkled with delight and victory, and Vivienne was left dazed once more. Hips pressing against hers, he bent his head, lips inching closer and–

"Vivienne!"

She gasped awake, taking in her surroundings. The bed was soft under her form, but she felt cold and forlorn, as though she had been removed from something vital. Sébastien was frowning over her, worried at whatever she had said, but all Vivienne was aware of were the waves of feelings unfurling within her.

Joy at seeing him. Guilt at visions of another man. Annoyance at being woken up.

The latter won, and she yanked herself out from under Sébastien.

"Vivienne, what–"

"Would you just *stop*!" she exploded, getting up from the bed. She could not be around him and his stifling love—not now, not after what she had dreamt.

The knight frowned, spreading his palms wide open as if to pacify her. "Stop what? You were having another nightmare... I thought I was helping by waking you up."

"Well you didn't!" Vivienne retorted, grappling with her robe.

Sébastien approached her when she was not paying attention, grasping her hands in his. "Talk to me," he pleaded.

She stilled, glancing up at him. But instead of his onyx

stare, all she saw was the sky blue of her dream visitor. Eyes brimming with tears, she pulled away from him.

"Leave me be, Sébastien."

She turned towards the bathroom, but he was there once more, holding onto her wrist. "No." The midnight stare shone with determination, his jaw clenched. "You were there for me at a time

when you could have walked away. And no matter what is going on with you, you have to believe me when I say that I am *here*."

Vivienne opened her mouth to retort something, but Sébastien did not give her a chance to. He tugged on her wrist and pulled her into his arms. His lips descended on hers with the force of a tornado, and she responded in kind.

His mouth melded against hers, coaxing and seducing, and within moments she was melting against him. She returned the kiss, giving in to its power, to his strength, to the reassurance that everything would be alright—that *they* would be alright.

Then the kiss changed. The more she pressed closer, intending to escalate it to its natural conclusion, the more Sébastien became tender. It was no longer about dominance and lust, but about love. The way his hand cupped her cheek, the way he angled her head just so and nibbled on her bottom lip... It was in every pore of his body, in every thought in his mind.

And to Vivienne, it was unbearable.

"Stop!" she cried, wrenching herself out of his arms. Without an explanation, she ran into their en suite bathroom and slammed the door.

She shed her clothes and climbed into the shower, letting the water cascade over her tense muscles and erase everything.

With it, she allowed the tears that had been brimming finally loose, and surrendered to the embrace of the element that knew her best.

Half an hour later, she exited the bath and expected Sébastien to be gone, or asleep. Instead, he was sitting on the bed, arms crossed under his head. Her eyes took in his bare chest, the rippling abs she died to run her hands over, and…

Throat dry, Vivienne shed her robe and got under the blankets. Rather than turn to him like she always did, she rolled over to the side, presenting her back to him.

In the darkness, Sébastien's shock was almost palpable, followed by a roll of frustration. Then he left, and she uneasily slid into a fitful rest.

* * *

Sébastien slunk downstairs, feeling like a lion in a cage. A whine by the door had him look up into Alistair's watchful gaze.

What happened?

"The nightmares again. Vivienne was trashing in bed.

When I woke her up, she was annoyed. I…" He glanced up the stairs, then back at the dog and his shoulders slumped in defeat. "I'm losing her and I don't know why."

Alistair hesitated, waiting to see if the presence would show itself. When nothing happened, he tugged on Sébastien's sweatpants.

Take me for a walk. We both need it.

Sébastien nodded grimly, then set the leash up. They exited and Alistair took off on a sprint, forcing him into a jog to keep up.

The frustration over Vivienne, over not knowing what to

say and how to help, ebbed away. Soon, the beat of the pavement lulled his emotions into a semblance of control.

When Alistair came to a stop, Sébastien was almost sane.

Until he realized where they were—the roundabout known as Place-des-Corps-Saints. It was the same location he had reconnected with Vivienne again, and also where they had last contacted a certain wizard.

He glanced down at his companion, eyebrows narrowed. "Merlin?"

Alistair nodded. *There is no choice. I should have done this sooner but... better late than never.*

He checked their surroundings to ensure no one else was around, before stepping to the fountain. His breath blew in a mist and the water rippled as the curtains between worlds parted. The demon dog felt the tell-tale sign of magic mixing with the spell, and finally the liquid settled.

Except, instead of Merlin's face, Alistair saw a woman. She stood alone, dressed in a long robe and a cloak. At first, her image was blurred, but it soon cleared up. Alistair noticed the lengthy black hair, then the fair skin and stormy gray eyes. He was so entranced by her cold beauty that he almost missed the second person in the frame.

When the man turned, it was impossible to avoid him. Alistair reeled back from the fountain, snarling in shock as he recognized Carleigh.

This isn't possible!

His exclamation drew Sébastien, and he joined Alistair. The knight froze at the sight of their enemy colluding with an unknown woman. Their faces leaned towards each other in mutual complicity, and he sensed nothing good could come of it.

A shiver of rage ran through Sébastien, an almost innate reaction to the necromancer. His fists clenched of their own accord, and he wished nothing more than to jump through time and show him justice.

"Carleigh, you son of a *bitch*!"

As though hearing him, the sorcerer switched his gaze and looked right at them, eyes narrowed. Then the woman focused on them, mouth down turned.

Alistair caught up a second too late to the truth. It had not been another person in their room that drew their attention, but rather the realization they were being surveilled.

"You never learn, do you, mutt?" the woman hissed.

That voice! Alistair started, recognizing it as the presence that had plagued him for the last months.

Before he could speak, pain shot through his body, stopping all rational thought. Lightning blazed over his fur, then under the skin, and he dropped to the cobblestone path, writhing in agony.

"Alistair!" Sébastien knelt beside him, cursing his lack of magic.

The dog's howls of anguish echoed across the empty streets. In the fountain, the image blurred and disappeared, as did the satisfied expressions of the sorcerers.

Sébastien glanced over his shoulder, noticing it was gone – but Alistair was still in torment. "Damn it all to hell!" he growled, running his hands over the dog's coat. He had quieted for a moment, but new convulsions ran through him, and his entire being jerked.

Someone help us! Sébastien screamed mentally. In his

panic, he cast his plea as far as he could, begging from help from anywhere.

* * *

In her realm, Catriona felt the stir of change. She had been hunting for food, but dropped her crossbow and jogged over acres of woods until she was on a cliff. From that spot, the Fae had a straight view of the land.

Everything seemed peaceful—oddly so. Yet in the distance, the horizon was tainted with blood and darkness, and lightning rolled across. Catriona frowned, sensing the electricity

cut through.

Something is coming again. The balance her father had spoken of worsened with each passing day, and still she had not been able to contact Atrox.

Fearing this new development had to do with her brother, Catriona closed her eyes and tried to feel him. Though she sensed his pain, he was alive and in Morgana's clutches as she had last seen him.

Someone help us!

The cry startled the Fae out of her thoughts and she glanced around, half-expecting to see an apparition. Instead, there was an odd vibration on the wind, a discoloration of sorts that caught her eye.

When Catriona touched it, her mind was immediately transported to Avignon and Atrox's plight. She noticed the wolf god writhing on the ground in agony, and fury filled her again.

She was about to hit the man bending over him, but even in her wrath she dimly recognized him as Vivienne's guardian.

Sébastien.

The Fae had only meant his name to center herself, but to her utter surprise the knight turned around. His onyx eyes widened, jaw going slack as he noticed her standing there in a short skirt and a brassiere of leaves. With her flaming red hair and sapphire stare, Catriona was a sight—even in her translucent form.

You can see me? Her fine eyebrows drew together, gaze darting between him and the pained canine.

When Sébastien nodded, she bypassed all niceties. *Move aside, knight. I will not harm Atrox, I swear it on my life.*

It was the determination in her expression, more than the promise, which made Sébastien listen. He stepped away from the demon dog, nervously glancing around to make sure no one was witnessing the encounter. Luckily for them, the night was quiet, and they were the only ones present.

The knight focused back on the redhead, noticing how she knelt next to Alistair and gently ran her hands over him. *Two can play the game,* she muttered in a steely tone, and he took another step away.

He could sense the vibrations of indignation rolling off her and had no doubt a touch from her could send him into oblivion. *But who is she to Alistair?*

Mind reeling with questions, he could do nothing but wait.

* * *

In the castle, Morgana was enjoying the dog's mental anguish, when something slammed into her full force–and blasted her into the wall. She hit it with a thud and dropped down with her head ringing.

"Morgana!"

The necromancer was by her side in a moment, running a hand over her to ensure she was not harmed. It was not concern that motivated his action, rather a dislike of surprises.

And what Carleigh smelled on the Halfling was the scent of an old Fae. He helped Morgana back up to her feet, keeping his thoughts to himself.

She met his gaze then, grimacing in pain. "That was unplanned, but not unbeatable. Do not mistake me for a weakling."

"I would never dare," Carleigh retorted sweetly. "Is this your first contact with this new menace?"

Morgana stilled, lips pressing together in a thin line. "I said I can handle it."

"You may think so, but this is an old power you are dealing with. Be careful your hubris does not cost you your life. It would be such a shame, considering everything your son is willing to do to ensure you live forever..."

Carleigh walked away at that, leaving Morgana in the room alone. She inhaled deeply, then let the breath out shakily. *This is not the time to lose it.*

On trembling legs, she dragged herself to the window sill and took a seat, unable to remain standing. Unaccustomed to the weakness, she scowled at the horizon for long moments.

The sorcerer was right in assuming she was battling an unknown foe, one more powerful than her. And all this to control a mutt who was unhelpful, after all.

The dog needs to show his usefulness, otherwise his life shall end.

* * *

In Avignon, Catriona's translucent form grinned, then centered her attention on her ex-lover. Atrox was groaning, head moving back and forth. After another moment, he blinked awake and his midnight gaze fell on her.

You will be alright, Atrox, she whispered encouragingly.

I used to answer to that name, a long, long time ago. But no longer. The dog peered closer, assessing her bright red hair, sharp blue eyes and barely-there outfit. Past that still, he sensed a wealth of energy similar to one other he had met–Merlin. *Am I dreaming?*

Catriona laughed at that, and something in her warmed at the look in his eyes. *No, you are not.*

Alistair snorted then, though not in amusement. I must have done something to be cursed so. Not one, but two wenches in my head, and one of them happens to be Fae.

She sighed in exasperation, not liking to be put in the same basket as Morgana. *You fool! It is me, Catriona.*

When he did not react, she tried again, reaching for him. To her shock, Atrox stumbled to his feet and moved away from her.

Atrox, it is I. Surely you did not forget me? But all she read in his eyes was confusion. On some level, she had expected it. There was no way the wolf god would have stayed quiet for so long, had he not been forced to.

Still, she chose to fight that particular battle another day. With a sad smile, Catriona stood as well and turned to Sébastien. *He will be alright.*

It was then she noticed, in the aura around Atrox, some

kind of connection trying to be made. With a frown, she flicked her fingers and it disappeared—but she had enough contact to catch Morgana's scent once more.

That witch may have hold of him—but not for much longer. I have stood by as Morgana trampled over Merlin's heart, but enough is enough.

Keeping her thoughts to herself, Catriona moved through space and opened her eyes back in her own realm. In reality, she had never left, and no one was meant to see her unless she chose to let them. Whatever Sébastien had done—she could only assume the discoloration she had touched had been his doing—had caused her soul to travel to his time, and become visible.

Interesting powers for someone who is supposedly only mortal, she mused, before turning her thoughts to Morgana. "It's time you pick on someone your own size, Halfling. Let us see who wins."

* * *

At the fountain, Sébastien waited until the woman was gone, then helped Alistair fully to his feet. When he staggered, the knight realized he was unable to move properly. Without a word, he threw him over his shoulders and walked back home.

I am not a sack of potatoes, Alistair muttered at some point, in between curses.

Sébastien smiled at his outraged tone. "I know. But it's easier this way, and we're almost there."

Another twenty minutes of heavy lifting later, and they finally stepped through the door. Sébastien unceremoniously dropped Alistair on the couch, then headed to the kitchen to grab a bowl of water for the dog—and a glass of scotch for himself.

When he returned to the living room, he was glad to see Alistair was still awake, and glancing into the flames. *I know that face, but I cannot place it. And it does not explain what she was doing with Carleigh—or where Merlin is.*

After he drank some water, Sébastien set it down and sighed, sitting on the couch with his drink. "Are we seriously not going to broach the subject of the gorgeous creature who helped you?"

Alistair threw him a dark look, flames dancing within his gaze. *I do not know who she is, either.*

"You're getting old, buddy," Sébastien laughed, then took a swing of whiskey. "She seemed pretty interested in you—and hurt when you didn't remember her."

So you caught all that.

Sébastien nodded, then cleared his throat. "Can I ask you something?"

I really doubt I could stop you at this stage, Alistair muttered.

"How exactly do you forget someone like *that*?"

At Alistair's growl, Sébastien burst out laughing, his entire frame shaking. "You should see your face right now." He shook his head, biting back more chuckles, then took a larger sip. "She called you Atrox."

It is my old deity name.

"Why did you change it? It has a rather nice ring to it... fitting, almost."

Another glare, then Alistair rolled his eyes. *It should. It means 'bloodthirsty' in the language you call Latin.*

Sébastien opened his mouth to say something, then closed it. After a brief awkward silence, he asked, "So what do we do?

Tell Vivienne?"

Alistair glanced at the stairs, recalling the price they had both paid after hiding things from her once. *Not yet. I do not recognize who either of these women are, but I doubt they mean well. The one we saw tonight is Fae, and they are fickle in their own right. Not to mention blessed with untamable magic–or cursed, depending on how you view it. And the one connected with Carleigh, she…*

He stopped, half-expecting his throat to choke again as it always did around the subject. When nothing happened, Alistair tentatively added, *She is also the presence in my mind.*

No punishment followed his revelation, and he was stunned. Ignoring Sébastien's shocked look, he turned his thoughts inwards, analyzing everything. For whatever reason, the sense of being watched was gone and he was alone in his own head. He realized the Fae must have had something to do with it and resolved to thank her next time—*if* he ever saw her again.

Newly re-energized, Alistair met the knight's knowing gaze. *You were right. I have been keeping something from you, but not of my own accord. I was a prisoner in my own mind—and have been, since we defeated Carleigh.*

"What do you mean?"

After Merlin pulled the evil from Vivienne, and you were together, I noticed a flare of dark aura around her. I wanted to mention it to you, and that's when a woman's voice warned me not to. When I tried, I found I was bound to her in some way— through a very powerful spell, I wager.

"And this kept you from seeking our help?"

Yes. Until tonight, I did not know the woman in my head

was the same one we saw next to Carleigh, I swear. If I had, I would have sought to contact Merlin earlier.

"This mystery aside, it means everything is connected. But what did she want with you?"

Information on Vivienne. I never gave her any, but it sufficed that she was linked to me when things happened with Vivienne, so she is aware of darkness' influence. In a way, I think she wants it to worsen.

Sébastien stood from the couch, pacing around the fireplace instead and sipping the rest of the drink. When he turned back to Alistair, his eyes were sad, and he could read the conflict in his aura. "Alistair, if this woman is in your head, you know what this means."

Yes, I am a liability and it is best I stay away from you both. You are not saying anything I have not thought of before, knight, and I hold no resentment for you speaking the truth. Tonight, my mind is clear, almost as if the woman is gone for good.

Sébastien righted himself, his expression hopeful, but Alistair shook his head. Even if this is true, I have to find out who she is and what she wants. I cannot do so while around you both. Vivienne is in a vulnerable place already, and the last thing I want is to draw more negative energy around her. I dread leaving you both without further protection, but there may be a better way.

"I take no pleasure in asking you to keep a distance," Sébastien knelt by his side. "Please believe me. What is this plan?"

Take Vivienne away–somewhere far from here. I need a few days, a week at most to find out more. This Fae we encountered may help in reinforcing my mental defenses... And if not, I will find a way to free myself. Once that is done, I can join you.

Sébastien hesitated to split up, but it was true Vivienne was no longer safe, and Avignon could not provide the spiritual power needed to ground her. If anything, it might be making things worse. His mind filtered through countries he had visited in his less than stellar past, before landing on one in particular. "Ireland."

What?

"I'll bring Vivienne to Ireland. It's surrounded by more water than Avignon, and the land is ancient. If Carleigh tries something, at least she will be near her strongest element." Sébastien got up and pulled Excalibur free of its leather sheath.

"Time to do our duty," he muttered.

And pray tell, how do you plan to bring that with you on a plane?

"I'll figure out a way." Then he scratched behind the dog's ears, heart squeezing painfully at the thought of being separated.

"Be safe, buddy."

Alistair nodded, then watched as Sébastien went up the stairs to sleep. Once he slid into bed, he pulled Vivienne in his arms, half-afraid she would deny him the contact. To his relief, she melted in his embrace.

"I will not lose you," he vowed. "Never again."

In the dark, Vivienne's eyes fluttered open. She heard the promise but remained silent, at war with her own emotions.

Below them, in the living room, Alistair had a hard time falling asleep despite the exhaustion in his body. The Fae's hurt expression kept dancing in his mind, and when he finally dozed off, he dreamt of blue eyes and soft skin, once more...

CHAPTER 6

"You dare walk away from me!?"

Sébastien had the odd sensation of having stepped mid-way into a scene from a movie. In it, he was the lead, alongside none other than Carleigh.

They were in a hallway richly decorated with gold-wrapped columns and floors of the whitest marble. It echoed with Carleigh's words, but his voice was less croaky, deeper somehow—less evil.

As if the lines were pre-planned, Sébastien turned and faced the sorcerer. Only instead of the pale man he was used to, this one was tanned and wearing a purple toga, pinned with a brooch. His dark hair waved, framing his face and eyes the color of the moon.

"I do not have time to listen to your ramblings," Sébastien said.

Carleigh glared at him, pursing his lips together. "You are arrogant in your deceit!"

Sébastien clenched his fists, taking a step closer. "No, brother. It is no use blaming this on me, when you should have spoken of your intentions towards Light earlier."

"How could I, when you never even allowed me to try!" Carleigh screamed. "You knew I planned to ask for a joining, I revealed this to you in confidence!"

Sébastien was now nose to nose with him. "Our parents gave us freedom of choice for a reason. And if Light picked me, that is her prerogative."

"You think you are so much better, Justice!" Carleigh's nostrils flared, and he was breathing hard. "But you are not."

"I am not superior to you, think what you wish. But I am more suited for her than you, Ambition."

Carleigh flushed, his fists clenching, and for a second Sébastien thought it was time for the fight everyone awaited. He crossed his arms over his chest, feet width apart, and waited with an unwavering gaze.

For days now, the lesser deities had known of the disagreement between the two heirs. The reason behind it was simple, though not quite easily resolved. It was a mutual attraction to another goddess that caused their dissent.

Their parents had thought it important to intervene, but Sébastien had assured them he could fix the matter. Now, staring into his brother's darkening gaze, he had doubts. The aura around Carleigh was shady, and there was an uncharacteristic obscurity to it that made him want to put more distance between them, else he become corrupted as well.

Instead, he dug his feet further in the ground, and held still. To his surprise, Carleigh did not react. Instead, he sneered and took off.

* * *

Sébastien woke up, blinking at the unfamiliar ceiling before he realized where he was. The pale blue walls shone softly with candlelight. His body froze for a minute, fearing another of Vivienne's nightmares. But there was no smoke, only a vanilla smell. It was then he recalled the candles he had bought for her, and the dinner they had in their small room at the local bed and breakfast.

The knight glanced towards his beloved, registering with relief her peaceful expression. No bad dreams disturbed her sleep, and he relished the newfound contentment she had found in their forgotten paradise.

Gone were the chaotic nights, replaced instead with normal ones–except, it seemed, for his own wayward thoughts. Gently, Sébastien removed Vivienne's arm wrapped around his waist and slid out of the bed. He donned a pair of sweatpants over his boxers, then moved barefooted to the window.

Though the seasons had changed to fall, and rather a chilly one, a natural fireplace kept the room they had rented warm. His gaze wandered to the flames, before glancing back outside.

The little house they had chosen was on the edge of a beach, right near the Atlantic Ocean. Managed by a couple as old as they were kind, it had been only one of their many resting places lately. The particular room they had picked even offered them a perfect view of the water.

Though in the night all Sébastien could see was a dark mass, with a blinking red light in the middle—the local lighthouse—he knew in the morning Vivienne's eyes would open to the wonder of the ocean, and the scent of its purity.

Since they had arrived in Ireland, he had rented a car and driven them up and down the coast, maintaining touch with the water at all time. Vivienne had quieted almost as soon as they had descended upon Dublin. After a mere few days, it was impossible to ignore the benefit the trip had on her.

On the other hand, heaviness had settled on Sébastien. Try as he might, he could not shake it off. And with the latest in a series of many dreams, all starring himself and Carleigh having some kind of epic fight, his restless soul could not relax.

Something was coming, and he could not explain it. All Sébastien could sense was danger–and dread at losing the happiness they had fought so hard for.

Gaze lost into the nothingness outside, he tried to grasp at straws, to contact Alistair. The effort was to no use, as the dog would not communicate back—whether because he could not, or by design.

Sébastien flexed his right hand, desperately wishing he could grip Excalibur. On nights like these, the sword had calmed him down in the past, its aura emitting some form of relaxant into him. Unfortunately, his plans to take it with him were doomed from the start, and he had to leave Excalibur behind in Avignon.

Unable to find a resolution, the guardian shuffled back to bed, sliding under the covers and gathering Vivienne back in his arms.

She pressed a kiss to his naked chest, nuzzling sleepily into him. "Where did you go, just now?"

"Nowhere," Sébastien answered, his heart squeezing. *Again, that stupid feeling, like our time is counted!*

Sensing his distress, Vivienne lifted her head, green eyes meeting dark. She searched his gaze for a long moment, then stretched alongside him and kissed him softly.

"Vivienne, I–"

"Shh," she whispered against his lips. "Let me. Whatever worries you, allow me take it away."

When she pressed her mouth to his again, Sébastien was lost. He responded to her kiss, one hand drifting low to her hip, the other cupping her cheek. Vivienne shifted, throwing a leg over him and hoisting herself up to straddle him.

In the dim light, the creaminess of her skin shined, as did the dark emerald of desire in her eyes. His body answered to her siren call, tightening in response. Their lips connected again, and he half-rose to meet her impassioned plea.

"Vivienne…" He groaned this time, dropping back on the bed in surrender.

The enchantress made quick work of his sweatpants and boxers, then straddled him again. She dropped her head closer to his, her hair cascading around their faces. Sébastien looked up at her, his heart in his throat.

"Do you know how much I love you?"

She smiled at that, the angel of his heart, and nodded softly. "I do. And I love you, Sébastien."

On his name, she dropped her hips onto his, taking him deep inside her, and arched back up again. Sébastien could not take his eyes off her. Lips parted, cheeks flushed with desire, Vivienne was alive, vibrant in his arms.

His free hand move between them, finding her center of ecstasy and watching as she came apart above him. He rose and met her mouth in a bruising kiss just as she was coming down from the stars.

Then, he flipped them around until he was hovering over her, unable to get enough. "My turn," he grinned, then moved his hips in a circle.

Vivienne moaned under him, head dropped against the bed, mouth open in a soundless scream of pleasure. He brought his lips to her slender throat, leaving little bite marks everywhere until he reached a particularly sensitive spot. There, he bit her— at the same time he drove inside her repeatedly, chasing lightning until it tore him apart in her arms.

Later, much later once he discovered he could breathe again, Sébastien rolled onto his back, tugging Vivienne half over him. She chuckled sleepily, then snuggled deeper into him and dreams claimed her.

Despite the beauty of what they had just shared, Sébastien could not relax, his mind alight with questions. He squeezed Vivienne closer and tried to join her in dreamland. Only, he ended up looking at the ceiling far more than actually resting.

Damn, Alistair, for once I need your advice.

* * *

Alistair stared at the moonless night from Vivienne's backyard, lost in thought. It had been almost a month since his mistress and Sébastien had left. He had received word–a voicemail every week–to inform him they were fine and Vivienne seemed better.

Despite the distance, he was aware the knight had tried to reach him. It bothered him to cut all contact with them, but it was the only way he knew to protect Vivienne, even if from himself.

News of the lovers' well-being eased his mind—but not the leash wound tightly around his neck. After that one night of peace, the woman had returned in his head with a vengeance. Despite many attempts, Alistair remained bound to the nameless witch that was colluding with Carleigh.

As though catching wind of his wrath, her intrusion shattered the silence of the night. *You have to go to them.*

Alistair knew what would follow, but still he pushed with a single growl. *No.*

The response did not take long, and neither did the punishment. *Foolish mutt.*

Electricity shot through him, and Alistair groaned at the pain. Much like the attack at the fountain, his insides felt scorched. Despite the torture, he gritted his massive jaws and dug his paws into the earth, unwilling to break.

She will not have me. My loyalty is to Vivienne, and no one else. He attempted to defend his mind, though that seemed harder and harder these days. *I cannot let her know where they went.*

The lightning became fiercer and he whined, shaking his head. He realized he would not last long without a distraction, so he changed tactics.

Where. Is. Merlin? Alistair tried to ask instead.

More pain followed, then her voice came, tight with annoyance. *How dare you question me!? Did I not make it clear you are to obey my every command?*

With each word, the shocks became unbearable. The dog dropped to his front paws, his head touching the ground to draw some semblance of respite. Nothing worked, and the world turned.

Alistair gritted his teeth, panting heavily—then the pressure abruptly disappeared.

He slumped on the grass out of pure exhaustion rather than surprise. It was not the first time it happened so. The games had grown longer, as the unknown woman seemed to take an almost sadistic joy in bringing him agony.

Despite her semi-success, they were always interrupted before it continued too far and he was ultimately hurt. Alistair's inability to fight back only strengthened his theory that the intruder was some kind of scorned goddess, with power to rival his own siblings.

But who is helping me?

His thoughts returned to the redheaded beauty that had healed him once, and those blue eyes that were so achingly familiar. Her full identity eluded him still, but he could not get her out of his head.

Alistair pushed off the ground with a loud sigh and dragged himself back in the house, dropping in front of the fireplace. While in the weakened state, he refused to be around Vivienne, fearing what his own predilection would to do her fragile happiness.

Exhausted, he curled into himself and fell asleep with a whine. *At least, Vivienne is safe. For her, I will suffer this for the all eternity if I have to.*

* * *

Catriona withdrew from the tree, panting. For close to a month, she had jumped between Morgana and her torture of Atrox. The Halfling could hold her own in a duel, she would give her that.

But you are still not powerful enough, Morgana.

The Fae took a deep breath, wiping sweat from her brow. She had not spoken to Atrox again, to explain what was happening, and it was imperative she do so.

Now was her chance, as Morgana stood by recuperating. *But first...* Catriona latched onto the sorceress' vibration until she could see her. Morgana was pacing in front of a weakened Merlin, fuming and ranting.

"Who helps the mutt?" she demanded, turning her flashing eyes to him.

Merlin half-smirked, despite his pallor and dark circles. "Wouldn't you like to know, *darling?*"

Brother, hold your tongue! Catriona wanted to warn him. Though she admired his newfound will—or perhaps momentary lapse in sanity—she also knew Morgana was in a foul mood, and needed no additional reason to unleash it onto someone.

As if on cue, the sorceress marched up to Merlin and slapped him. The echo of skin on skin vibrated in the room for a moment, while they glared at each other in silent fury.

"Resorting to violence now, my love?" Despite his stinging cheek, Merlin's tone was taunting, his expression hard. "And here I thought we were making progress."

Morgana got up in his face then, and his nostrils flared in response. "Do you have a death wish? Or perhaps you simply miss my touch?"

She ran a finger down his chest, smiling coldly. Something flashed in Merlin's eyes, an innate reaction as old as time. But agony soon replaced it when Morgana's index shot out blue fire, marking his skin.

As Merlin clenched his jaw, unwilling to give her the satisfaction of his screams, Morgana kept drawing circle upon circle on his torso. When she finished, above his heart were two intertwined circles, overlapping. The skin was red underneath the branding, and he hissed out a breath he had been holding.

"A reminder for what could have been." Morgana searched his gaze, hoping to see something–anything– to use, but instead got lost in the depths of his cerulean eyes.

She moved away, turning her back to him in order to mask her own confusion. Her steps took her by the window, and she overlooked the grounds until her own heartbeat calmed down. *What the hell is wrong with me?*

After another beat, Morgana turned and faced Merlin again. "I get it now. It's a lover of yours, doing your bidding. That is who defends the dog, is it not? You must have a type. She is fairly powerful to constantly stand up to me."

Hurt flashed over his face, but Merlin soon hid it. He was silent as he tried to find a way out of it, but his head ended up dropping to the side. "I do not know. But I am glad someone could face off to you in my stead."

Morgana paused in her pacing, chest heaving. She was almost growling, unused to not getting her way. Her long hair was

gathered to the side, and a faint sheen was on her brow.

Good to see she is even more affected by my magic—and whatever the hell is happening there, Catriona observed in quiet satisfaction.

As Morgana stared at Merlin, something shifted in the air. He straightened up, as though aware of it himself. Once more, their gazes were drawn together like magnets. His eyes burned, and almost despite herself Morgana took a step closer.

Catriona watched them, frowning. Rather than ignore it this time, she waved a hand over the image, and could see their auras—and the connection reflected within. Their colors were mirrors of each other, his dark red on the outside and orange on the inside, and hers the opposite.

What truly astounded the Fae was the lack of darkness around Morgana. *Could it be there is still something worth saving in her?*

Before she could further ponder on it, Carleigh strode in with Mordred. The white walls dimmed, obscurity taking away the light, and both Merlin and Morgana snapped out of their trance.

"How did it go with the dog?" the necromancer inquired.

Morgana was back to scowling, turning towards the window once more. "He is tougher than I remember."

Carleigh assessed her with slanted eyes, then smirked. "Or perhaps *you* are not as strong."

Mordred, whose gaze had been fixed on his father, whirled to face the man. One hand rose, index pointed accusingly. "Watch how you speak to my mother!"

Carleigh laughed, then quickly sobered up. "Forget the mutt. There is something else I require, and only Fae magic can achieve it."

Mordred stood side by side with his mother, chin raised defiantly. "What is it?"

"I need a sacrifice to darkness, of pure light."

"Not Vivienne," Merlin pleaded.

With barely an amused glance to his father, Mordred sneered in response. "Do not fret, old man. Your precious is no longer light, I have seen to that."

Something in his tone had Merlin snap to attention. "You stay away from her!"

Mordred chuckled outright at that, taking a few steps closer. "Or what? You cannot do anything, so save your breath. As for Vivienne," he walked back to Carleigh, "I feel her drawing increasingly to the dark."

"Perfect. Then we will use her as a vessel. Light still prefers her as a champion, else we would have sensed something in the balance by now." When Morgana opened her mouth, he shut her with a glare. "Your new little annoyance, whoever she is, is of no importance."

The sorceress scowled, but did not reply. It was Mordred once more who cut in. "You said the sacrifice has to be of light, but Vivienne is no longer that. How will using her as vessel change anything?"

Carleigh grinned with a secret only he knew. A choked sound behind them had Morgana and Mordred turn to notice Merlin's horrified gaze. "No! You uncouth bastard, I should have killed you when I had the choice!" He struggled against his bindings, nearly tearing out his ligaments in the process.

The necromancer only laughed and with a thrust of his hand a volley of new leeches flew at Merlin. They sucked on his skin, and the trashing warlock soon fell to the clutches of oblivion. Morgana averted her eyes until he was still, and only then looked up to Carleigh.

"What is it you wish? Enough with the riddles."

"Vivienne has a spell around her body that prevents her from being pregnant. I need you to remove it."

Morgana shared a look with her son, who nodded ever so

slightly in response. With a shrug, she went to work on the floor. First she called fire, the element of passion, and cast a symbol of fertility unto the soil. Then she knelt down, passing a hand over it and murmuring in the old Fae language Merlin never meant for her to learn.

"Why now?" Mordred asked Carleigh. "And why not do this yourself?"

"With Darkness so linked with me, it would ruin the purpose. Fae magic is never tainted by something as sinister as what I carry within, only by the emotions of its wearer. At its core, it is exactly what it always was: a force of nature."

Mordred glanced back to his mother, frowning. Her gray eyes shone abnormally in the room, as did the symbol she had drawn on the ground. When it dimmed, she stopped speaking and

looked up. "It is done."

Her eyes darted to Merlin's immobile and unconscious form, and her stomach heaved. *I cannot be around him like this.* She tried to move, but the walls spun and she was unable to keep her balance.

Mordred was there to catch her, then brought her to the adjoining room. "You need rest."

Morgana let him carry her to the small bed, and lay down to sleep. As Mordred pulled a blanket over her, she whispered, "Now we only have to wait."

Catriona reeled away from the image, gnawing on her thumb. "This is not good. I have to tell Atrox."

CHAPTER 7

Alistair was sleeping, lost in a semblance of peace—or so he thought. Amid it all, he arrived in a forest with multi-colored skies. He turned his head up, checking for unfamiliar scents, but found his sense of smell had lessened.

He opened his eyes, but rather than find himself near ground level, he seemed taller. When he moved across the grass, its sharp blades stung between his toes.

Toes!

Alistair glanced down, bemused to realize he was no longer a dog. Rather, he was fully human —and naked, to boot.

"Some dream," he muttered, inspecting the surroundings for something to wear.

"I happen to think it's a fantastic dream," someone purred from behind.

Alistair whirled around, hands automatically lowering to cover his exposed parts. His jaw dropped when he found the same vixen from earlier standing mere feet away from him, dressed in much the same outfit as before. Vaguely, he recalled her name was Catriona.

"My, I do believe this is the first time I see you blush." She laughed, and it sounded like tinkling bells.

Alistair scowled, annoyed at her bubbliness in the face of his dilemma. "Do you *mind*?"

Catriona ran her eyes up and down his frame, unabashedly ogling him. Those starling blue orbs shone a little darker as she nibbled on her lips.

Half-wondering if the Fae planned to eat him, Alistair cleared his throat again. She jumped guiltily, then tossed her head back raised her chin, a smile playing at the edge of her mouth.

"Alright, lover boy!" With a snap of her fingers, he was no longer bare, but was instead clothed in something of her choosing.

Which ended up being a skirt-like garment with a tartan pattern that came to his knees. His chest was bare, and he had no weapons. Alistair's scowl deepened, unimpressed. "A kilt, *really*?"

The Fae giggled, stepping closer. "It was either that, or a toga. I thought you would not appreciate the reminder of your old life, Atrox."

Alistair zeroed in on her face, his entire body stilling at the comment. "How do you know that?"

Her cerulean gaze met his, but she only pursed her lips in response. Alistair could not fathom what possessed him to do it. Maybe it was frustration at having been under a witch's influence for the last months. Perhaps it was more the mocking glint in the woman's eyes.

One minute, he was breathing hard by her side. The next, he had Catriona pinned to a tree, his body pressed against hers and hand at her throat. Nostrils flaring, voice taut, he ordered, "Tell me *exactly* how you came to know my deity name."

The Fae gulped then, any trace of amusement evaporating from her features. Alistair tried to ignore the softness of her skin under his touch, and the rise and fall of her breasts at his proximity. It was only her sincere apology that snapped him out of his desire-hazed thoughts.

"I apologize, Atrox. I meant no harm with my games, but you are right. These are dangerous times, and I owe you an explanation." She glanced down at his hand, then back up at his eyes. "My name is Catriona, and I am Fae queen of this realm. My father is Merlyddus, and you once knew my brother…"

Alistair released his hold on her neck as though scorched, and he stumbled backwards. "Merlin," he breathed in shock.

Catriona nodded, her red curls bouncing with the movement. "Yes. He is imprisoned right now by an enemy you helped him fight in the past."

Alistair snapped out of his trance, focusing back on her face. "Carleigh, you mean?"

"No, another. Her name is Morgana, and she is half-Fae, like Merlin. Long ago, they were lovers. As always with my people's romances, theirs turned for the worst."

Alistair frowned, disbelief etched across his features.

Noticing it, Catriona inched closer. "If you do not believe me, let me show you by means you will understand."

"Which are?" He tilted his head, crossing his arms over his chest.

"Come with me," Catriona entreated, stepping further into the forest.

Despite his better judgment, Alistair followed her. They jogged and moved through the woods, his eyes drifting to her curvy shape every few seconds. It was during one such inspection that light filtered through the trees, hitting her back, and he noticed the translucent wings.

"You weren't lying!"

Catriona heard his gasp and threw him a look over her shoulder. Noticing his dazed expression, she fluttered the wings once—for show. Alistair froze at their movement, gaping at the light that glittered off them and bounced into the trees.

A breeze picked up, carrying the Fae's sweet scent to him. He had to clench his fists at the raging hunger it raised in him. Just when he took a step in her direction, Catriona sauntered away.

Alistair was left alone, blinking in surprise and trying to control his impulses. A few deep breaths later, he chased after her. And all the while he tried to forget that he had dreamt of his hands on her naked skin for the last few weeks.

After a run through the forest, they ended up in a secluded area where a waterfall poured into a small pond. Frothy bubbles met the surface of the water, and he glanced around in surprise.

"This place…"

Catriona stepped to him and grabbed his hand in hers. "Swim with me."

Alistair peered down in the lake, then back to the Fae. Her expression was set in something, but he could not fathom to decrypt it within such a limited time. So he did the next best thing and nodded.

With a joyful cry, Catriona jumped in, clothes and all. She swam under the surface a few feet, then poked her head out. As she floated in the middle of the small lake, her eyes seemed to reflect the sky.

I must be crazy, Alistair mused, but he dropped the kilt and dove in nonetheless.

He stroked the water a few times, surprised at its coolness, then plunged deep. When his head broke the surface, Catriona was there, throwing her arms around his neck.

Alistair froze, unsure what to do with the curvy redhead that was plastered to his body—practically naked. As though guessing his thoughts, the Fae laughed, her petite frame shaking with amusement.

"You can breathe, oh mighty god. There is no need for carnal consumption for what I have in mind." An amused glance, a half-smile, and she teased, "Swim with me, Atrox."

"The name is *Alistair* now."

Catriona met his gaze, unimpressed by his growl, laughter still in her voice. "Sure it is. *Swim.*"

Rolling his eyes, Alistair decided to humor her. She stayed glued to him, shifting over to piggyback him. Thus connected, he cut through the water with powerful movements, somehow keeping them both above the surface.

With each stroke, his breathing stabilized, until he had almost forgotten the Fae he carried. In that moment, Catriona draped herself all over his back and whispered in his ear, "Deep inhale, then go under."

This time, he did not question her—just did as she suggested. Further within they both went, and at first nothing changed. When his breathing became short, Alistair tried to return to the surface.

A swift hand on his ankle deterred him, and Catriona held him down. She shook her head once, lifting an index to indicate he should wait. Rather than panic at the missing air, Alistair surrendered–to her touch, to the surrounding fog and whatever lay beyond.

Water seemed to invade his every sense, but it was more than that. He became one with it, floating around, until Catriona's warmth permeated his skin. There was a familiarity to her, to the scene, to the realm he found himself in.

Alistair tried to think back, and like a dam the memories broke through the barrier of his mind. Overwhelmed, he was drowning, airway closing in. Right when his vision blurred, he burst to the surface, taking in huge gulps of fresh air.

"Well?"

He turned to Catriona, now recalling just why he could never forget the scent of her skin, her kisses, nor the sounds she made when he was above her, driving in deep.

Still submerged to her torso, the Fae froze, her eyes assessing his expression. This time, it was Alistair who approached her, wading through with stony features.

When he was merely a few inches away, he took a moment to inhale the scent of her sun-kissed skin, and the flowery fragrance that seemed to follow her wherever she went. Then he extended a hand, wrapping it to the side of her neck.

Catriona could not tell whether he planned to kiss her or kill her. In that moment, she was only aware of the heat from his body, the fire in his eyes, and the rigid muscles. He drew closer, not once looking away from her–then he crushed his lips to hers.

She inhaled him in, spreading her palms over his chest and pressing on his rock-hard shoulders. Her long legs wrapped around his waist, tugging him that much closer to her center—where he desperately wanted to bury himself.

Despite his innermost desire, Alistair paused, pulling back somewhat and panting. "Wait. Wait, Cat. Tell me one thing. How could I forget this?"

As if his words had thrown cold water over her, Catriona detached herself from him, and swam out. Alistair followed and wrapped the kilt around his lower body—for the sake of modesty, if nothing else.

"Cat?" Using the nickname he had once, long ago, was natural and he did not think twice about it.

The Fae faced him, expression inscrutable, and shrugged. "You chose to reincarnate with Vivienne. I am assuming whatever Morgana did, she must have done at that point in time, for it affected you as well. Regardless, you were reborn without these particular memories, as were Vivienne and Sébastien."

"But you knew all along," he pointed out. "Why not seek me out?"

Catriona's eyes flashed. "Is this you blaming me for the state of things?"

"No!" Alistair approached her, both palms held up in a gesture of supplication. "It was I who drove you away with my callousness, I know that. But how could I have forgotten *you*, Catriona? You're…" He shook his head, at a loss for words. "Please help me understand."

Another shrug, then Catriona explained, "Yes, I remembered. As did Merlin. After our last encounter, I was proud and did not wish to pursue you. By the time I decided to, it was your siblings that set me on the path, and I realized they had chosen the canine punishment for you."

Alistair snorted at that, and the Fae smiled. "You *do* make a cute dog."

"Spare me," he pleaded with an exasperated roll of his eyes. "And Morgana?"

"From what I have gathered while observing her torture my brother, she and Mordred lived in limbo until now. Merlin grew foolish with his experiments, trying to understand and undo what Carleigh had undertaken. It was simple for his son to follow his footprints until they captured him."

Alistair snorted, shaking his head. "Your brother is always running into messes."

"Especially where Morgana is concerned," Catriona agreed. "We have to do something, Alistair."

"You know I wish for nothing more, but that witch is in my head! I can't even be around Vivienne, let alone fight Morgana. Not with these useless powers."

He turned away, clenching his fists in anger. Sensing his distress, Catriona came up behind him and touched his naked back. The broad muscles tensed under her fingertips, then relaxed. Her soft sigh, so close by, was his undoing.

Alistair took her in his arms, his mouth dropping to hers once more. Catriona moaned against his lips, pressing closer until they could not determine where one ended and the other began.

Pieces of clothes flew apart, and before long Alistair was burying himself in her, groaning her name and thanking the fates he had found her again.

Catriona bit his shoulder gently, then harder. At his hiss,

she laughed, a giddy sound of female triumph, whilst throwing her head back and offering her own neck in return.

Alistair stopped an inch above the creamy skin, lips hovering on her pulse point. "You have to get it right this time."

Catriona whined at his whispered order, rolling her hips towards him in an invitation to move deeper. He chuckled darkly, then amended his statement. "*Alistair*, darling. That's the *only* name you should know." Then he gave her what she wanted, and the Fae returned it tenfold.

* * *

Vivienne took in a deep breath, savoring the fresh air. Two days ago, they had been near the Atlantic and now they had entered further inland, towards the magical Killarney National Park. It held acres upon thousands of acres of land, spanning forests, hiking trails and best of all—lakes.

She and Sébastien had been walking for the better part of the day through Killarney's moss green woods, off the trailing paths. There was no particular way they headed, only getting lost in the vastness of the enchanting landscape. In the forgotten oasis, everything seemed surreal.

Hand in hand, Sébastien enjoyed her look of pure wonder as she soaked it all in. The trip had been worth it, regardless of his sleepless nights.

"Have you had any more nightmares?" he asked, squeezing her hand in reassurance.

Vivienne shook her head, flashing a smile his way. "None. This place…. Sébastien, I can't figure out how you knew, but it was exactly what I needed. It's pure magic."

The knight wrapped his arm around her shoulders, pulling

Vivienne closer to him and kissing her forehead, then her lips. "I guessed as much," he admitted with a grin.

In companionable silence, they continued the climb and emerged on a beaten pathway. Across from them, framed by two old trees, was a breathtaking view of the lakes and the sunset.

The sun's rays filtered through just enough to light the road. The trees curbed towards each other like long lost friends, their branches almost touching. Through the space between them, the lake caught the last of the sunlight and reflected its orange shades.

Vivienne froze in her tracks, gasping at the sight. Sébastien chuckled at her delight, then gently moved them both closer to the edge. He placed her back to his chest and wrapped his arms around her, resting his chin on the top of her head.

They were hushed for long moments, basking in the serenity. A lonely hiker passed the same way, then retreated further up the trail.

"I was afraid." Vivienne's admission broke the silence, needing to get the words out. "First not having remembered who I was, then feeling like I was losing myself. I… I am sorry, *so* sorry,

for the hurt I've caused you."

"It's ok, love," Sébastien placed a tender kiss to the side of her head, then to her neck. "I'm only glad to have you back."

"For how long?" Vivienne whispered, pain lacing her voice. "We cannot stay here forever."

Sébastien's heart squeezed at the agony he sensed, and he tightened his hold on her. "Why not, if that's what it takes? If being so close to water, to this place, is forcing your darkness at bay... I would happily spend the rest of my life here, with you, if it means you get to stay just as you are." He paused, unsure if he should continue, but the words tumbled out. "Remember, if you let it affect you and give in, the corruption will only develop. Be strong for me, my love. For us."

Vivienne nodded, blinking back tears and relaxing against his strength. *I will. I swear I will.* Yet deep within her, negative emotions unfurled and a voice warned her not to make promises she could not keep. She squashed it away, determined not to listen.

As they enjoyed the sunset, Sébastien tried to resist the sensation of impending doom. *I will do whatever it takes, so long as it means she's safe.*

Later, once the last rays had disappeared into the water, they wandered down to the rental car. Darkness descended on the trees, yet the moon's soft glow offer some illumination. Vivienne kept her hand in Sébastien's, but the sudden obscurity had shivers racing up her back.

Unknown to Sébastien, she had lied about the nightmares disappearing. They had lessened, yes, and she slept much better in Ireland. But they lingered at the edge of her consciousness, and always *his* voice called–the man in her dreams.

Something existed within her, a part of her that had flourished with each passing month since the fight with Carleigh. And at the sight of shadows, it thrived.

Vivienne tightened her hold on Sébastien, feeling as though the woods were pressing in. Her vision narrowed until all she could focus on was her own shallow breathing.

"Love?" Sébastien paused, frowning at her.

She could only shake her head, and her lungs felt blocked.

Try as she might, Vivienne could not pull in a breath. "The trees." Her agonized whisper forced him into action.

Sébastien squinted at their surroundings, not understanding what she meant. Everything was the same—then he saw it. A shadow slithered on the ground towards them.

No… Not them. *Her.* It was aiming straight for Vivienne.

Sébastien's eyes darted around for an escape, even as he urgently demanded, "Fire, love. Bring forth fire."

When she did not answer, the knight chanced a look her way and bit back a curse. Vivienne seemed frozen and almost in a trance. At a loss, Sébastien angled his frame in front of her, pushing her behind. Jaw clenched, he resolved to get between her and the new menace.

Fighting her own internal demons, the enchantress trembled, warring with herself. The serpent—or whatever it was—was getting closer, and she knew without a doubt it would hurt Sébastien if she did nothing. Yet when she tried to reach the magic, Vivienne only found emptiness and a pit of chaos she did not want to touch. And that scared her more than anything.

Sébastien kept backing away, with Vivienne tucked behind him. In that moment, he fervently wished he had Excalibur. As the shape came closer, his chest burned with the wish, and he could almost envision the blade cutting through evil.

The snake jumped in the air, and his hand tingled–then Excalibur was there.

Sébastien did not bother with guessing what had happened. He grasped the sword one-handed and slashed through the serpent, watching it disintegrate into nothingness. He then grabbed Vivienne behind him and pulled her to his chest, trying to quiet his panting breath.

It was only then he glanced at Excalibur, unsure if it had been a hallucination or not. But the weapon was heavy and familiar in his grip, and its realness was incontestable.

Past his initial reaction, Sébastien snapped back to his regular self. He inspected every obscure corner, no longer trusting what had previously been an amicable atmosphere. "We have to go."

Vivienne nodded against him, still trembling with shock. He moved them down the trail, keeping Excalibur handy in case anything else tried to attack them. Only once he had driven them back to the safe confines of the inn, did he release the sword and take his beloved in his embrace with both arms.

The enchantress stopped her shaking at once, instead kissing him with a desperation that could have made him weep. As it was, Sébastien gave Vivienne the comfort she craved, and held her tight as she fell asleep.

* * *

That same night, Merlin fought against the pull of the leeches, desperately struggling to bring his mind into focus. Rather than manage the feat, his eyes rolled in his head, the whites showing, as a vision assailed him.

> *Vivienne was smiling at Sébastien, her face aglow with happiness. Though her traits seemed thinner, there was a healthy bump where her flat stomach had been.*

Sébastien moved his arm and placed it on her stomach. A wondrous expression came over him, then he chuckled.

"What is it?" Vivienne asked.

"I guess we don't really have to wonder about names," he pointed out, amusement dancing in his eyes.

Vivienne laughed, before nodding. "No, you're right." She intertwined her hand with his, murmuring the name aloud for the first time. "Arthur."

When he came to, Merlin noticed Carleigh's intense gaze on his. "He saw something," the necromancer stated to Morgana. "What was it?"

Merlin grinned, truly at peace. "I will *never* tell you."

"We'll see about that."

He nodded to the sorceress, and she thrust her right palm towards Merlin. Serpents of cold fire escaped her and headed for him. As more pain assailed him at Morgana's hands, Merlin gritted his teeth and kept his secret.

Over my dead body.

* * *

Alistair woke up in his dog form, by the fireplace. He blinked groggily at the sun filtering through the window.

What the... Did I dream all that?

Did it really seem like a dream?

With relief, he recognized Catriona's voice. On the heels of her smartass comment came an apology. *Whatever dizziness you feel is all my fault. I kept you too long in my realm, even if it was only across your dreams.*

Alistair was silent again. *Come again?*

I cannot enter Earth, darling. An old rule I absolutely cannot break. So in order to see you, I have to bring you to me. Since I cannot physically because your body is too weak, I wait until your soul is accessible before pulling you here.

The dog stared into space, his only reaction an incoherent grumble. As he stretched, he tried to wrap his mind around what Catriona had explained. *Are you sure this is possible?*

Fae magic, lover boy. Everything is possible. Now, are you ready to fight back?

His growl echoed in the empty house, where he had maintained residence in his mistress' absence. *Yes. That Halfling is done testing me.*

Good. That sounds more like my Atrox.

Catriona's tone was a little too satisfied for his liking, but he did not bother correcting her. Maybe his thirst for vengeance proved her right, and there was more of his old god identity in him than he cared to admit.

There is one more thing, the Fae added.

I don't like the sound of that.

And you will like my answer even less… Vivienne is pregnant.

Alistair's jaw dropped, his entire body going still. *That's impossible.* He winced, recalling the uncomfortable conversation they had months earlier. *She had protection!*

Morgana's magic threw that for a loop.

But why?

Carleigh needs a sacrifice of Light. And seeing as Vivienne is, well, not herself lately, they plan to use her unborn child. I am not sure if they simply plan to corrupt it or if they would stoop so low as to murder a baby, but…

Snarls the like of rabid dogs escaped Alistair's mouth. Unable to sit still, he paced from one end to the other of the living room, knocking everything out of his way.

He did not want to believe it—yet he knew it was true. When Catriona did not immediately speak after he calmed down, he grew suspicious. *Is there more?*

A pause, followed by a halting confession. *Yes… Though Morgana made this happen, it may be to our advantage.*

How so?

She did not foresee that it would be Arthur.

Alistair blinked in surprise, ears flattening on his head. *How did you even find this out?*

You recall Merlin's visions, do you not? I happened to be watching him when he had his latest one, and had front row seats.

If their connection as siblings surprised him, Alistair did not let it show. *You are right, this could work in our favor. But if they succeed in giving Darkness what it wants….*

Catriona's tone was solemn, aware of the stakes as much as he was. *I know. But we will not allow it.*

He drew a deep breath, determined to trust her faith. *We will keep it quiet, in that case. But I cannot keep my distance any longer. There is no telling how the pregnancy could affect Vivienne. Morgana or not in my head, I have to head to Ireland.*

If he had expected Catriona to talk him out of it, he was sorely mistaken. *Good idea. The land is ancient, and will offer protection if my plan fails. Besides, you might find more than you seek there, Atrox.* With a tinkling laugh, she was gone, and he never got a chance to ask about said plan.

CHAPTER 8

It is time.

Alistair glanced once more at Vivienne's house, making sure the spell he had cast held. The place would be secure until their return— he hoped.

He moved away under cover of darkness, not willing to risk an eager human trapping him. The mission loomed ahead like an untouchable lighthouse, and he intended to reach Ireland at the earliest possibility. His road would take him first towards Reims, east of Paris, in an effort to avoid the over-populated city.

Eventually, the path would lead him to Calais, from where he planned to board a ship with destination to Ireland, or at least the United Kingdom.

It would have been simpler to use magic or ask Catriona to send him where he wanted to, but then Morgana would have sensed such a displacement of energy. And the whole purpose of the affair was to keep her unaware of their plan.

Alistair looked up at the full moon, then took off on a run.

Did you find it? Catriona's voice rang in his mind.

He did not stop on his way, instead shaking his head. *No, Excalibur was gone. I only hope Carleigh did not get his hands on it.*

If it helps, I do not see nor sense the sword's energy anywhere around them. She paused, her silence evocative.

What do you see?

More of them trying to torture Merlin for his vision. He is not giving it up.

And it's just as well he isn't! Alistair growled. *Your brother has done enough to harm.*

I know you think him a nuisance, Catriona grumbled, *but he means no harm.*

I'm sure, the dog muttered, before changing topics. *Excalibur aside, you said you had a plan. What, exactly, is it?*

Morgana preys on you for a reason. You are the closest Vivienne has to family, and by commanding you, she is aiming to control your protégée.

The theory had crossed my mind. Alistair ducked behind some abandoned buildings at that point, passing by the edge of the city. He had a long way ahead before getting to Ireland, but if all went well, he could join Vivienne and Sébastien within the week.

Catriona? He pressed, as the Fae had not answered.

Yes, I am here. I would suggest your best bet is to lie low, but I suppose you will not agree to such an idea.

Damn right I won't!

In that case, our second option is to pretend you are still weak, and lead Morgana on. We have confirmed they wish to use Vivienne once more, Carleigh's obsession with her ensures it. Though I have not been privy to all their conversations, I feel he ultimately wants her death, once he is done with whatever else he seeks.

If only that were news...

In her realm, Catriona grimaced at the thought of everything Vivienne had gone through, all because of her half-brother. *I know. With you in Morgana's clutches—as far as she believes—she might slip up and drop a clue. We can assess better at that point what they intend.*

I agree with the part about me continuing to play a role. But what exactly have we learned? It simply doesn't feel right. The more he talked, the more he felt the truth of his words. *Carleigh is going to all this trouble to, what? Hurt Vivienne again? We're missing something. And the fact he made her get pregnant and plans to use the baby abides nothing good.*

His thoughts turned to his mistress, and Sébastien's last message. The knight had sounded stressed and pleaded for Alistair to join them.

If they corrupt Vivienne further, Catriona started, *it will shift the balance to their side, you know that as well as I. There is no telling what this world with suffer if that happens. Perhaps they are also using this pregnancy as a way to influence Vivienne.*

But the baby will be a force of good... Alistair shook his head, frustrated at going in circles. *Where does Mordred come into all this? You said he's been trying to link with Vivienne. It must be he, the man she was dreaming of and unwilling to speak of. But why?*

His fate and Vivienne's were tied from the beginning, you

have seen it too. And with his awareness of that fact, it became an obsession. It is not love, but it is just as addictive. Mordred desperately wants her by his side.

Alistair snarled at that, thinking of Sébastien. *It will not happen on my watch.*

No. But in the meantime, you have to pretend, lover. See what Morgana asks you to do, as it may give us more information. Whatever they plan, you and Sébastien stand in their way–for now. If they were to make headway, something has to give. On my end, I will continue surveilling them. I sense you are right, and we are missing something valid regarding Carleigh's ambitions. And I expect it has to do with those at the center of this story: Vivienne, Sébastien and Carleigh.

When Alistair did not respond, the Fae sighed. *I can only get through intermittently now, but I will let you know if I pick up anything interesting.*

Carleigh must have sensed your watchful gaze, Alistair pointed out, amused. *That necromancer was never able to handle a little competition.*

Perhaps... Catriona trailed off, recalling what she had seen between Merlin and Morgana. *I do have one last question, and it has to do with my brother and his lady love.*

Alistair's groan echoed through the link. *They are doomed. Were from the start, a fact I warned him against and he did not listen.*

Catriona rolled her eyes at that, realizing full well the wolf god could not see her. *Yes, it is a story I have heard many times before. But do you think there is anything left saving in Morgana?*

The demon dog was startled enough by the question that he stopped running, tilting his head to the side instead. *Why do you ask?*

The other night, Morgana was interrogating Merlin, trying to figure out who was helping you. She lost her temper in jealousy, but there was a moment when they... connected.

Alistair scoffed, biting back a laugh. Undeterred, he picked up his pace once more. *It is but lust, nothing more. They have always been so, drawn to one another. Despite it, mutual destruction happens whenever they do get together.*

Catriona was silent, wondering at his assessment. Atrox had known Merlin longer, but the way them two were gazing at each other gave room for pause.

You are a romantic, darling, Alistair chuckled. *I am sorry to ruin your hopes. But the reality is, there are no happy endings when it comes to beings like us.*

She reeled back at that, the words stinging more than they should. She had picked up her affair with Atrox as easily as it had started the first time, not once making promises nor asking for any in return.

Yet now, her father's cautioning echoed in her head, and she regretted not having listened.

Catriona? I did not mean to offend.

Alistair's contrite tone got a smile out of her, and she eased his worries. *You did not, lover. But I do have to go. Our last encounter has me rather sore, and I am in dire need of some rest.* A pause, then, *And, Atrox? Once you get to Ireland, if you are in the mood for a power surge, let me know.*

He laughed at that, and she left him to his voyage across the countryside.

In her own realm, Catriona leaned against the willow tree, whose branches dropped down to hug her. She allowed its embrace, blinking back tears.

*   *   *

In her dreams, Morgana was still at her father's castle. She was aimlessly wandering the empty corridors until she ended up in the garden where she had met Merlin. This time, the mage was not there, but she moved to the tree, regardless.

Its beauty, its strength called out to her as surely as breathing was important. She placed her palms on it, closing her eyes and inhaling its wooden scent.

The babbling of a child stirred her from the trance, and Morgana blinked. It had not been a hallucination after all. The noises grow louder, and she turned expecting to see a servant with an infant.

Instead, she stared in shock at her innermost desire—and darkest secret.

Merlin entered the courtyard, wearing a pair of loose pants and a tunic opened at the chest. His dark hair was tousled as if having just woke up, his blue eyes shining brilliantly. And in his arms was a baby girl dressed in a beautiful burgundy dress.

The mage walked towards Morgana, cooing softly to the child. When they were in front of her, she fought to keep the tears from spilling. Merlin looked at her, his entire expression softening as he bent and kissed her.

She allowed him, leaning into his body, her own craving his touch. She tilted her head back, deepening the kiss as her nails dug into his chest. Merlin growled in the kiss, then eased it and pulled back. There was a glitter of promise in his darkened gaze, and she shivered all over.

Morgana's attention was turned to the toddler. She touched

her soft black hair, inhaling the vanilla scent that seemed to drift from her skin. The young girl raised her gaze to Morgana's, and she was met by the most astonishing gray eyes she had ever seen, with flecks of gold and silver in them.

The sorceress inhaled shakily, her hand trembling as she kept caressing the child. "Might I hold her?"

Merlin chuckled softly, then carefully passed her the toddler. She glanced up at her mother, eyes rounded and full of trust. Morgana was unable to avoid the tears, and she buried her face in Merlin's chest.

His arms wrapped around her, holding both of them safe even as rivers upon rivers of diamonds cascaded down her cheeks. "Why do you cry, beloved?"

Morgana could only shake her head, unwilling to look at them. When she opened her eyes again, she was in the castle room where she had fallen asleep. And near the foot of the bed was Carleigh, his face a mask of anger.

"Did you not think I would guess your deep, dark secret?"

It took a moment to realize what he meant. But when it sank in that the entire dream had been fabricated by his twisted mind, Morgana turned the sorrow in her heart to blinding rage.

She shot up from the bed as swiftly as a cat, hissing. "You dare try to manipulate me?"

Carleigh snickered at that. "Your desire for what you cannot have—for what you lost—is so obvious it makes me sick. Whoever you think you are, Morgana, you are neither strong nor

ruthless. And I do *not* need a weakling by my side."

Morgana's eyes glowed, and before she could control it her Fae magic acted and slammed Carleigh against the brick wall with enough force to make the ground shake. Another attack followed with air pinning him there until he could not move.

"Release me, now!"

"Not until we get one thing clear." Morgana spoke in a sweet voice, moving closer until she was within an inch of his face. "It was I and Mordred who released you. Without us, you would still be in Merlin's clutches."

Carleigh's eyes burned with hatred and malice, but he kept his mouth shut. "You do not order me around, are we understood?"

It took a moment, but the man nodded. Morgana lifted her hand, showing him the fiery orb that pulsed at her fingertips. "You are wrong in your assumptions, necromancer. Be careful who you push, otherwise you could find yourself... scorched."

She walked away, allowing air to release Carleigh only once she had passed the threshold of the door. The sorcerer dropped to the ground, pounding it with his fist in anger.

* * *

Alistair watched Sébastien tuck Vivienne in bed, then motioned to join him in the adjacent room.

How bad?

It had taken Alistair longer to reach Ireland than intended. He had lost two weeks in the crossing, having to take multiple detours to avoid extra militia set up on the roads. It seemed the humans had yet another war to deal with.

By the time he had reached them at the new cottage they had rented by the water, it was only to notice Vivienne's withdrawal. Whatever peace the enchantress had found was now long gone.

Barely holding on, Vivienne was pale, had lost weight and appeared torn between reality and nightmares. The dark circles were ever-present around her eyes, and Sébastien was looking worse for wear.

The knight followed Alistair into the other room, his steps heavy. He ruffled his hair, then dropped into the couch heavily. His face was tight with worry, shoulders drooping inwards.

"I'm not sure how bad her condition is now," he admitted.

"But it's been going on for the last three weeks, give or take. At first, Vivienne was fine. Ireland really helped, Alistair, she was back to her regular self."

The proximity to water must have benefited her.

"That, but also the land. Everywhere we walked, we can both sense the power in the earth, and I believe it contributed further. But now… Even her element only helps enough to keep Vivienne grounded."

Alistair shook his head, moving closer to him. *What happened? Did it come out of nowhere?*

"No, I… It started when I took her to Killarney National Park. The area is gorgeous, loads of forest and opportunity for nature gazing. It's also close to these lakes in the region, so I brought Vivienne there. As predicted, the trip fuelled her energy, and she was feeling great. Then… At night, we were returning down from a hiking trail and the shadows, they…"

Sébastien stopped, pinching the bridge of his nose, his tone turning anguished. "They came for her. Serpents of evil like the ones around Carleigh, they moved and aimed straight for Vivienne. After I got her back safe, the nightmares returned. I…. *Nothing* I do helps."

Alistair took in all he was saying, mind whirring a mile a

minute. Why would Darkness be so adamant about Vivienne, especially without Carleigh to provoke it? Unless... *Unless it's not only Vivienne it seeks.*

The demon dog focused on Sébastien, assessing his aura. A glint of silver caught his attention and he noticed Excalibur nearby. *Wait, you have the sword? How did this happen? When did this happen? I thought you couldn't figure out a way to bring it with you.*

Sébastien looked at it, his eyes glittering with unspoken emotion. "You will not believe this."

Try me.

Sighing, Sébastien told him the rest of the story. How Excalibur had appeared out of nowhere, and he had used it to slash through the darkness. When he explained what had happened, Alistair headed over to the blade.

He sniffed, but Excalibur only carried Sébastien's aura. He was about to turn away, when he caught a different scent next to the hilt, where Sébastien had recently cut himself. *No, not*

different. More potent. Oddly, it smelled of—

Alistair paused in his thoughts, looking at him in a different light. *Have you had any dreams as well?*

Sébastien seemed surprised at the question, but nodded. "Yes. Of me and Carleigh, battling...as gods."

Shit.

Alistair recalled what Catriona had said, about everything being tied in to Vivienne, Sébastien and Carleigh. Mind reeling at the implications, the pieces finally fell into a more complete picture.

"What is it?"

This has been going on longer than either of us thought. But before we get into it, you have bigger problems. It had only taken one deeper glance at Vivienne to confirm his suspicions. *Brace yourself, knight, for there is no easy way to say this. It is news my mistress should tell you, but I fear she may not. Vivienne is pregnant.*

Sébastien stared in shock, not reacting. His wide gaze darted between the dog and the door to the room, then he bowed his head and focused on his hands. After moments of silence, Alistair prodded him with his muzzle.

Oy, knight! This is not the time to have a crisis of conscience.

"Pregnant?" Sébastien repeated, not looking up.

Yes.

Before Sébastien could add anything, or even digest the news, a crash nearby jerked them to their feet. He jumped to his feet, rushing to Vivienne, but the door would not open.

"Vivienne, open up!"

When no sounds answered from inside, he turned to Alistair, nearly growling with desperation. "Will you? I'll break it otherwise."

Alistair stepped closer and blew into the keyhole. A soft click echoed, and they tumbled in, but Vivienne had disappeared.

"Shit!"

Alistair was tempted to agree.

* * *

Vivienne felt the grass under her bare feet, and could smell the mist from the night. A fog surrounded her, keeping her presence hidden and her mind adrift.

No coherent thought formed, only a deep desire to be by the lake. There was something she had to do, someone she had to see, and nothing else seemed to matter.

Only one thing drew her focus—or rather, a voice.

A little further, the handsome devil of her dreams whispered at the edge of her consciousness, and Vivienne listened.

*   *   *

Sébastien had checked the house, to no avail—and each second brought him closer to panic. *I should have never left her alone!*

Vivienne had not been the same since that night in the forest, but despite her withdrawal she seemed grounded around him. Which was why he had avoided leaving her side until the talk with Alistair.

Sébastien was ready to call the police and report her missing when Alistair ran towards him.

I found her. Hurry! And bring Excalibur.

Without hesitation, Sébastien picked up his sword and took the stairs two at a time. He burst on the ground wearing only sweatpants and the chill of the night hit him full-front, but he did not care.

Excalibur tightly held in his hand, he glanced around. "Where?"

By the lake. Mordred needs her help to open a portal.

"Who?"

Never mind! I'll explain later, just stop her!

Sébastien quickened his pace, heading for the fog that was gathering not far off. It was only after a few moments he realized that Alistair had continued on a different route.

"Where are you going?" he shouted over his shoulder.

Though the dog was a decent distance away, his voice was clear mentally. *To get help.*

* * *

Alistair felt a little guilty, but it was not really a lie. Catriona had been right. If this was to be a fair fight, he needed to stop hiding from who he was. He could sense the ancient land vibrating under his paws, almost in tune with his desires.

The thought had entered his mind once he had clued in to Sébastien's lineage. Whereas before he believed it impossible, now he realized it was quite feasible. Especially with a Fae as his backup.

Catriona?

Yes, lover?

I need you to run interference on Morgana for me. Can you?

Her reply was almost eager. *It would be my pleasure. But why?*

You were right all along. Ireland has something else I require, and I intend to get it.

Now that he was unburdened by Morgana's mental claim—thanks to Catriona's help—was the best time. He tried to center his thoughts on the Fae queen to make one last request. *Of course, a quicker transport would be appreciated, darling. I have absolutely no idea where I'm headed, only following auras and scents. And the clock is ticking.*

As his paws pounded the ground, a circle of light to the side drew his attention. *Hop in,* Catriona chuckled.

The demon dog jumped within, heedless of any consequences. After a few seconds of transition through what felt like a waterfall, he exited into a forest. The hum of power was enough to make him pause, uncertain.

Where am I?

Look around.

Alistair did as Catriona suggested, sniffing the air. A faint scent of metal and electricity permeated the atmosphere, yet he sensed the same vibration under his paws. *Obviously I'm still in Ireland.*

His gaze was pulled to a circle of rocks. Rather than the humongous stones at Stonehenge, these were barely a few inches off the ground. Half-covered in moss, they could be easily dismissed—unless a demon dog with sharpened senses was looking for them.

Alistair noticed the moon at its apex, almost mocking him.

So we have a full moon, a place of power, and...a willing sacrifice? He glanced around uneasily, then shook his head in derision. *Ah, hells be damned. I have nothing to lose.*

After a last deep breath, he stepped inside the circle, by passing the first boulders. For a moment, the rumbling of the ground stopped, then it picked up. The noise of drums filled his ears, but he was alone. Under the beat he could hear a woman singing, her soft voice raising the hairs at the back of his neck.

What is this?

Before he could change his mind, the stones rumbled and shot out golden rays. A band of light tied them together, forming a perfect link between them. Alistair tried to back away, for the first time fearing what he had agreed to, but the ray hit him full chest.

As it vibrated through him, Alistair's form shimmered. The

human shell he once had worn overcame the canine one, flickering in the night.

Alistair howled, screamed and panted, throwing his head back. When he thought he could not take any more, the light evaporated. Shoulders hunched, he was left panting, his fur sticking out at odd ends. He looked down, only to find his still furry paws.

Disappointment filled him, with a large topping of despair. For the first time in eons, he had allowed himself to hope that things could be different, and to no avail. *I will be forever doomed in this form.*

His voice was a little sharper than intended when he addressed Catriona. *It didn't work.*

I beg to differ. The Fae sounded amused. *It's a good thing that what you lack in faith, you make up for in passion, darling.*

What are you getting at?

Picture your human shell, Atrox.

Alistair rolled his eyes at the name he no longer answered to. He hesitated, but eventually did as she asked. His entire body vibrated, and he felt light as a feather, almost lulled to sleep by something much beyond his understanding.

When he next glanced down, it was to see *human* toes. Alistair looked at his hands, then touched his head full of hair. His bemused expression was replaced by a smug one.

"Finally," he spoke aloud, then threw his head back and howled at the moon.

CHAPTER 9

Alistair stared in shock—and some measure of pride—at his reflection. He had found a waterhole filled with rain in the forest and had not moved since, deep in perusal.

The aristocratic features were still the same, all sharp and rugged edges. He had on a day's growth of beard, somehow giving his face a primal look. The dark onyx eyes echoed the moon—and the flames of vengeance within.

When he stood, his muscles stretched sinuously, like a cat's. His nudity did not bother him, but it felt odd to be standing on two feet once more.

Done admiring yourself?

He smirked, and his reflection looked all the more charming for it. *Perhaps, my sweet.* His tone grew serious. *Thank you, Catriona. What you have achieved... I am in your debt forever. You need only say the word.*

You are most welcome.

Sensing she was unused to the gravity of their conversation, he added wryly, *That being said, I will enjoy rewarding you in my arms.*

Her tinkling laugh resounded in his mind. Alistair waited until she paused before asking what weighed on him. *How was this possible? Could I have done it a while ago?*

Not quite, no. As you well know, Fae magic can match a god's curse. What I gifted you only reinforced some of what you had lost.

Same like Merlin did. A recollection nagged at him, of when the mage had found him in a feral state, and had given him back his power of rational thought.

Catriona's smile was clear in her voice when she responded. *Yes, exactly.*

And what did it cost you?

Nothing. Her answer was too quick and he growled in dissent until she relented. *Maybe a bit of trouble with your siblings once they realize it.*

Catriona... No words were strong enough to explain what he felt. His hands clenched in fists, itching to be around her and show her the tenderness she deserved, since his eloquence failed him. *From the bottom of my heart, I thank you. Again.*

I know. Now that you have this ability back, you can morph into a human whenever you wish. Once you do, Morgana cannot reach you.

Why?

Simple, lover. When you transform, you are essentially slipping into the skin of a god. You may not keep it daily, but for the time you do pull it on, the power of your past self protects you.

Alistair shook his head, at a loss for words. *I will believe you on your word, beloved. This puts us one step ahead of Morgana and her pack.*

Yes.

Finally. His thoughts reverted to Vivienne, and what he had been about to reveal to Sébastien before she had left. *Catriona, remember what you mentioned, about the three of them?*

I vaguely recall something, she teased.

Sébastien had dreams of being a god, alongside Carleigh and Vivienne. I expect you may be correct, and this all ties to them.

Twice in one day? The Fae laughed, but sobered soon enough. *I had guessed as much.*

Alistair shook his head at her admission. He had a hard time wrapping his mind around all he had missed, yet Catriona had no problem figuring out. What made you clue in?

The strength of their soul mate bond, for one. Vivienne and Sébastien, for being simple mortals, have an unusual amount of baggage with them. Yet their love transcended time and space, always reuniting them through the ages. There was also the matter of the celestial footprint, deep in their auras.

And Carleigh? How do you explain his... He trailed off, unsure how to describe the necromancer.

Ties with Darkness? Gods are not immune to temptation, you know this as well as anyone.

But I never gave in, and I was living in the blasted underworld!

True.... But then again, you are special, my darling.

Alistair rolled his eyes at her sarcasm, but pressed further. *Tell me. Please.*

I suppose the light inside each god initially protects them against Darkness. When they forego that defense of their own accord, the contract is null and void.

He thought back to their theories regarding Carleigh's true purpose. *Could this be why he is so adamant about Vivienne? He wants to use the baby and drag her into hell alongside him, all as payback for some wrongdoing in their past?*

Catriona was not quick with her response this time, rather mulling it over for a few moments. In the end, her sigh was reflective of her confusion. *I could not say, and we may never know for sure.*

There has to be a way to find out. Does this never affect your kind?

We are much too impulsive for that, lover. There are instances of Faes' negative emotions affecting their magic. Morgana is proof of such things, as her hatred tainted her aura. But gods seem to be easier targets. Another pause, then she reluctantly admitted, *Besides, if I was to guess, whatever happened in Carleigh's past as a deity exacerbated his desire for power, and he surrendered to temptation.*

The proverbial serpent of Eden.

I was not aware you prescribe to mortal religious beliefs, Catriona teased.

Darling, there are many things you don't know about me, Alistair murmured. *But I promise to show you.*

I look forward to it. Her voice deepened when she answered this time. *Have I answered all your questions?*

Yes, Alistair admitted reluctantly, not yet ready for her to go.

Good, because this Fae needs her beauty sleep. Watch

yourself, lover. With the cryptic warning, the contact ended.

Alistair only then realized he had forgotten to inquire about changing back, let alone how to return to Vivienne and Sébastien. He looked down at one of his hands, frowning.

I wonder…

Hesitantly, he waved his palm around clockwise, once, twice. When it felt like he was actually touching air, his eyes widened slightly, but he kept going. Faster and faster he moved until the circle escaped him and dropped parallel to the ground.

Alistair glanced at it, then his naked self. With a shrug he stepped inside and thought of Vivienne. Within moments, he had returned where he had last seen Sébastien.

A quick scan of the area ensured he had remained unseen. Satisfied only acres of land surrounded him–and no nosy humans–he morphed back to his canine form, then headed towards his mistress' scent.

*   *   *

Sébastien reached the lake in time—or so he hoped. Dressed in only a nightgown, Vivienne had one bare foot in the water and the other still on the grass.

"Vivienne!" he screamed, and she jumped, startled.

But when she turned to look at him, her eyes were glazed and unfocused. The knight knew without being told that she was not really seeing him.

Damn!

He advanced towards her, gripping Excalibur tighter, but shadows in the water froze him in his tracks. In front of his astonished gaze, the image of a man formed out of the fog.

He was translucent, almost ghostly, but with blue eyes that

burned colder than sapphires and a mop of dark hair. His face was young, but his body built. Something tugged at the edge of Sébastien's consciousness: images of swords clashing, and another brown-haired opponent fighting him.

Before he could make sense of them, the vision headed toward Vivienne, and she faced it as if drawn to it.

"Vivienne, *no*!" Sébastien ran towards her, already fearing he was too late.

The enchantress stepped with both feet in and raised her hand as though to touch the ghost's cheek. The man turned to Sébastien and grinned smugly.

With a roar that would have made a lion proud, the knight thrust through the specter with Excalibur. The man's furious shout echoed his own, right before he vanished.

The moment he was gone, Vivienne dropped to her knees

in the water, whimpering. With feverish movements, she tried to pull the element out, muttering under her breath.

Sébastien picked her up one-handed by the waist and pulled her out, returning them both to the shore—on solid ground and away from any influences.

He positioned himself to view the lake at all times, unwilling to take any chances. Satisfied by a quick perusal, he dropped Excalibur and gripped Vivienne's shoulders, shaking her gently.

"Vivienne, snap out of it!"

She studied the water, not looking at him until he forced her chin up. Her green eyes were wide and filled with emotions he could not even begin to understand. "What were you doing here, beloved?"

Instead of answering him, she wrenched herself out of his

arms and ran up the hill towards the house. Sébastien turned his gaze back to the lake, rubbing the back of his neck in agitation. Shaking his head, he fought the despair that threatened to overwhelm. Instead, he picked up his sword and followed her inside.

Moments later, when he walked in, Vivienne was sitting by the fireplace, arms wrapped around her knees. Sébastien placed Excalibur on the coffee table and joined her.

He had expected her silence, but received a rather different welcoming when she turned to him. There was something unreadable in her eyes, and it was not a sentiment he liked seeing.

Whatever scenario Sébastien conjured in his mind did not live up to his imagination. There was no fit of crying, no shouting. Instead, Vivienne crawled to him and perched in his lap, wrapping her arms around his neck.

To his utter astonishment, she bent her head to his and kissed him. Rather than give in as he normally did, Sébastien gripped her and pushed her off him. "We are not doing this," he stated firmly, "until you talk to me."

Vivienne glared at him for a beat, then the same eyes shone. "You want to know what's going on with me? Why I'm emotional and barely eating, barely sleeping?"

Though astonished at her scathing tone, so at odds with her expression, Sébastien nodded. "Yes, I do. I think you owe me that much."

"I'm pregnant!" Vivienne shouted, then promptly burst into tears.

* * *

The tree was beaten up, almost ripped apart from the inside out by the time Mordred was through with it. The forest cried at the disrespect, but the Halfling was clueless, lost only in his anger at the knight.

I had her! he cursed inwardly. *I was so bloody close to getting through and I could have had her!*

Another punch to the trunk did not satisfy him, so he tried to call forth fire instead. Rather than the full flames his mother could control, he could only summon the smallest flicker. Still, he threw it at the tree and watched as it blazed, burning until it was a bonfire.

"Having fun?"

Mordred turned to see Morgana, her cape pulled low over her face. Only her mouth was visible, and the tangled black hair that escaped it.

The young man shrugged, presenting his back to her. "As a matter of fact, I was."

He thought his tone would be enough to push her away. Instead, Morgana drew closer and touched his shoulder, hesitantly at first, then firmly.

Her voice was hoarse when she spoke, as though she had been crying. "You should not meddle with things you do not understand."

Mordred faced her, frowning. "What are you going on about?"

Her only response was to push past him to the tree. With one sweep of her hand, water fell upon it and extinguished the fire. While only ashes remained, the sorceress knelt down and grabbed a fistful.

"Rest, now, for you have done your part," she whispered,

and a gentle breeze picked up the dust until it were all gone. Only then did she stand, not meeting Mordred's gaze.

"What happened with Vivienne?"

Mordred's face darkened at the memory. "What do you think? Her knight saved her."

"Carleigh will not be pleased," Morgana murmured, glancing up towards the castle's tower, where the necromancer lay

in wait. The thought of losing her son at his hands squeezed her chest painfully. *He will also not forgive.*

Mordred's next words snapped her out of her ruminations. "I cannot reach Vivienne as I wish with *his* constant interference."

Morgana focused on him, her lips pursed. "Why do you say that?"

"Mother, Sébastien is her soul mate. If anyone can keep me at bay, it's him."

His scowl turned into a surprised look at Morgana's next words. "I will take care of it."

Instead of explaining what she had in mind, Morgana headed to the castle. Astonished at her odd behavior, Mordred ran up to her and tried to fall in step. "What will you do?"

"You say her knight is a problem. I plan to ensure he is no longer one."

* * *

Despite having heard it from Alistair, Sébastien could not speak at first. He opened his mouth to shout his joy at the news, but Vivienne's heart-wrenching sobs quickly dispelled that idea.

Instead, he pulled her into his arms and sat with her on the couch, rubbing her back in a comforting pattern. The crying lasted for long moments after, and with each one Sébastien's chest squeezed.

He caressed Vivienne's hair, pulling her in the cocoon. "Why the tears, love? I, for one, am happy at the news."

Vivienne raised a tear-stained face to his. "We didn't plan this! And I made sure it wasn't possible, I—"

New sobs racked through her frame, and Sébastien realized with dismay she had lost weight. She felt fragile in his arms and infinitely more precious.

"There is no reason to cry," he murmured. "We are more than set financially, we'll care for this baby together."

Despite his reassurance, Vivienne could not settle down, and she dozed off while still upset. Alistair chose that moment to walk in the room, long after her heartbeat settled.

"Where the hell did you go?" Sébastien snapped. "I could have used you out there! I was fighting some pre-pubescent boy playing magic tricks."

Unimpressed, Alistair plopped down on the ground and yawned. *You had it handled, I never had a doubt.*

"Glad to hear it," Sébastien shot sarcastically. "You're making an awful habit of disappearing when I need you most, buddy. Anything you'd like to share?"

Alistair threw him a dark look, but instead his gaze landed on Vivienne. *No, but it seems like you might. What did I miss? I can smell Vivienne's tears.*

Sébastien ran a hand through his hair, expelling a breath. "It appears you were right. I'm going to be a father."

Ah.

At the tone, Sébastien tensed. "What is it?"

I doubt you want me to ruin this moment with the news I have.

"Try me," Sébastien returned his earlier words, not nearly as amicably.

Very well. In truth, I had meant to tell you earlier, but we were disrupted. This development is not an accident, nor is it remotely innocent.

With the free hand that was not holding Vivienne, Sébastien pinched his nose. "Spare me the riddles, Alistair. At least tonight."

Alistair met his gaze and revealed, *This is all Morgana's fault.*

"Who?"

Alistair sighed, then explained to Sébastien everything he could not yet recall. When he had finished, the knight's brow was furrowed in confusion.

"Why can't I remember any of this?"

I couldn't either. Morgana must have erased our memories. Catriona, the Fae you saw the other time, helped me get mine back. That's why I've been secretive.

After another brief silence, Sébastien added, "What about Merlin? You mentioned their powers were a match. Do you think all along...?"

Probably. Merlin knew, but I believe not even he predicted the danger. He would have slipped up otherwise.

Sébastien tightened his grip on Vivienne. "She needs to know this."

Alistair glanced at his mistress, then at the knight. *Come with me. I have to tell you something else.*

Sébastien slid out of Vivienne's embrace and settled her

comfortably on the couch with a pillow and blanket. Only once he was reassured that she was asleep did he follow Alistair in the backyard.

He closed the door to the patio behind them, sighing as though he had the weight of the world on his shoulders. Rolling his muscles to decontract, he turned to Alistair to demand an explanation for his odd behavior.

Instead of finding a massive Caucasian Shepherd, he faced a man not much older than himself—naked.

"What the *hell*!?" Sébastien staggered backwards, eyes widened. "Alistair?"

"It is still me," the dark-haired god confirmed. "*This* is where I disappeared earlier. Catriona helped me regain my ability to morph forms, and this is my godly shell from back in the day."

With a careless hand movement, he was no longer naked but dressed in jeans and a shirt. "Better?"

"Much," Sébastien scowled. "Now we really have to tell Vivienne."

Alistair shook his head, his expression determined. "Not yet. There is more to this pregnancy that we do not understand. Morgana canceled Vivienne's contraceptive spell at the behest of Carleigh. He is after something, and purposefully wanted her pregnant."

"So how do we find out what he wants?"

"Morgana will reveal it–all in due time. She is unaware of what I have gained and still thinks she has control of me. As soon as I learn anything, we can devise a plan and act on it."

Sébastien clenched his jaw, looking away. "I dislike hiding things from Vivienne, especially now."

"I understand," Alistair said, "but to be perfectly honest, I am worried what will happen if we tell her everything while she is in this volatile state."

"What do you mean?" Sébastien frowned.

"The dark side of Vivienne, the part that has grown unstable in the last months—and which you had calmed down while here—has been released again. It is untamed because of the pregnancy, and I fear it may seek to get rid of the child."

"Vivienne would never!"

"You are correct, my mistress would not, *if* she was in her right mind. But she is not while evil can manipulate her. And the

stakes would be high…especially if she found out she was carrying Arthur."

Sébastien took a step back, palming the wall of the house for support as he gaped. *"What* did you just say?"

"Come now," Alistair scoffed. "We all knew Arthur would reincarnate. It is not much surprise fate acted on Morgana's Fae magic and implanted the mortal champion of Light using Vivienne as the vessel."

The knight could barely follow half of what the former dog had said, but one part stuck.

"Mortal? You're talking about Arthur, but what of Vivienne?"

Alistair arched an eyebrow smugly. "She is *im*mortal. Have you not wondered why you two keep being reborn? Over and over? You forever fight darkness, never allowed a single moment of respite."

Sébastien found it hard to remain standing and slouched against the wall, massing his temple. "I don't follow."

"Your love is eternal and your souls joined–beyond everything. That much I realized back when I and Merlin helped you regain your memories. But I missed the other part of the coin in the past: the light illuminating you both."

"Alistair, what… What are you on about?"

The wolf god stepped closer, his gaze intense. "You are deities, both of you. That is why you can now do things you couldn't before –such as materialize a sword out of thin air in a moment of need."

"You...that's not possible."

Unfazed by the knight's glare, Alistair inched nearer still and gripped the man's shoulder. "Sébastien, there is a reason Darkness has tried to latch onto you both. And it's not just because of Carleigh's curses. You are both prime targets, always have been."

Sébastien could only stare in shock as the ground under his feet swayed. A flash of annoyance crossed Alistair's expression.

"You evidently need a little nudge, and we are running out of time."

Not bothering with further explaining, Alistair shoved his palm to Sébastien's forehead. The knight stilled like ice at the contact, then hit the grass with a thud.

CHAPTER 10

Though her dreams were usually turbulent, Vivienne had come to almost expect them. When a particular one changed from swimming into a lake to being dragged under the surface, it did not faze her at first.

Once the murky waters closed in on her and air was missing, she panicked. But through the water, a shape headed towards her. His strong arm wrapped around her waist and he hauled her to the shore, coughing and spluttering.

Vivienne took in a few deep breaths, filling her lungs until she was back to normal. Once she was calmer, she squinted into the face of her savior.

Of course it's him.

The dark hair was plastered to his scalp, the blue eyes intense on her, but that sardonic mouth lifted in a smug grin. "Caught you at a bad time?"

She shook her head, brow furrowed in confusion. "What

are you doing here?"

"And where *is* here, pray tell? Because I thought I was dreaming. And…" His eyes roamed over her skin, where the gown clung to her form, then returned to her face. "Well, in dreams, anything is possible."

Vivienne scowled, but did not walk away. Something about him intrigued her, an inexplicable sense of familiarity. It did not escape her notice that she had had much the same reaction to Sébastien, and found out he was her soul mate shortly after. The recollection made her shift uncomfortably.

"I meant, what do you keep doing in my dreams? And who *are* you?"

The stranger did not respond at first, distracted by his scrutiny. When Vivienne cleared her throat impatiently, amusement danced in his expression. "They call me Mordred. As to my presence here, perhaps your mind keeps conjuring me?"

Vivienne had been about to comment on his name, feeling like they might have met before. But at his teasing implication, she looked away. "I wouldn't… But then again, I have been doing a lot of things I wouldn't normally do."

He knelt in front of her, tilting his head to the side. "Such as?"

Whether because it was a dream, or no consequences to expect, Vivienne poured her heart out to Mordred. "A few months ago, there was an incident and I… I've been dealing with this darkness inside me since. My boyfriend and guardian think there's something wrong with me, and surely there is. I just…"

Her hesitation did not seem to bother him. Instead, he

simply pursed his lips, pondering his words. When he spoke, the simplicity of his reasoning astounded her. "And what if there *is* something wrong with you? Would that be so bad?"

Vivienne met his gaze, surprised. "Well… I suppose no, not really."

"There you have it then," he grinned. "It is all a part of you, like everything else. Life changes us as we go through it; it's only to be expected. For your inner circle to expect that you will always be the same is insane. Not to mention, stifling."

Vivienne could not hold his burning stare any longer. In an effort to escape it, she turned to the water. Instead of the calming effect it normally had on her, all she could recall was the asphyxiation.

"I suppose it is." Words tumbled out of her unbidden, and she did not really pay attention to what she was saying. "I shouldn't feel this torn over something that is out of my control."

When she looked up again, Mordred had disappeared.

* * *

One minute, Sébastien was standing on his two legs, talking with Alistair. The next, a type of vortex sucked him in. Images assailed him, scenes from his previous lives and from Camelot.

The spell dove deeper, further in time – his death in a garden, Vivienne crying over him. A battle in what looked like Ancient Greece and returning home to find his beloved murdered.

On and on it continued, taking him all the way to the beginning, where it had all started.

Sébastien was lying in a bed made of furs and feathers, with

Vivienne resting her head on his chest. His hand drew circles over her naked back, and she nuzzled closer.

"Why do you suppose I'm called Light?" she whispered.

"Because you shine wherever you go, my beloved."

Sensing she was warring with something, he shifted to meet her gaze. "What is bothering you?"

"Ambition is distant these days."

Sébastien shrugged, unwilling to comment.

"I believe he is upset about me...being with you," Vivienne added.

"So let him." When she raised a scandalized expression to him, he softened his response. "Beloved, Ambition will do as he sees fit. We should not allow his issues affect us. If he has a problem, he can come out and announce it or shut up for eternity."

Vivienne nibbled on her bottom lip, not convinced. Sébastien noticed the determination in her gaze and sighed. "I shall speak to him, but not now."

He pushed her on her back, hovering above her with a wicked grin. "I have better things to do."

* * *

Sébastien was searching for Vivienne when he heard shouts in a distant hallway. He turned the corner to see Carleigh pinning her to the wall, one hand roaming over her body. She was trying to push him away, but his face was dark with fury and intent.

Sébastien saw red. Roaring his rage, he marched over and grabbed him by his neck, throwing him as far as he could. "How dare you touch her against her will!?" he snarled.

He briefly turned to Vivienne, to make sure she was

unharmed. At the unspoken question in his eyes, she nodded. "I am fine. Please." Her hand was on his arm, trying to restrain him. "He is your blood."

"Not anymore," Sébastien growled, then faced his brother–his rival. "We will end this, here and now."

In his right hand, a sword of fire materialized. Carleigh sneered, and conjured a double-edged blade, with an aura flaring

dark. Sébastien frowned at the weapon, before tearing his gaze from it to scrutinize his sibling.

For the first time, he noticed the pale skin, the bloodshot eyes, and the edge of evil that surrounded him. "What have you done, fool? Colluded with Darkness?"

Carleigh laughed, but it was a chilling sound. "What do you care? All your attention has been on Light now for a while, despite my feelings about it."

"Leave her out of this. This fight is between you and me, brother."

"As you wish," Carleigh retorted, then launched himself at Sébastien.

Their weapons collided, sparks flying everywhere. Vivienne moved out of the way, her hand on her mouth in horror. She looked at the man she loved, and the one she had unknowingly hurt with her choice.

When Carleigh pulled back to strike Sébastien, she hurled herself in the path of the blade. It pierced her, and she fell in her lover's arms.

"No!" Sébastien cried, crumbling on the floor with Vivienne.

He noted the blood that was pooling into the marble tiles

and looked up at Carleigh. *"What is this madness? What did you do with that sword?"*

Carleigh's stunned gaze met his. *"I turned it into a weapon to kill a god. I... You cannot reverse this."*

Sébastien held Vivienne closer, crying into her neck. *"Do not leave me, beloved!"* His anguished cries echoed in the hallway, where more and more deities gathered. Her blood now stained his hands, his clothes and the floor surrounding them.

No amount of trying to work his healing on her made a difference. Despite his better efforts, Vivienne opened her eyes one last time, smiling at him. Then the angel of his heart exhaled her last breath and stilled forever.

Sébastien tightened his hold on her, refusing to let go as he rocked them back and forth. He tried to inhale the citrus fragrance of her skin, to commit it to memory, but found it was ebbing away already. Fresh tears burned his eyes, and nothing could get through his sorrow.

Until he spoke, haltingly at first, then firmer. *"Brother, I am sorry. I did not mean—"*

Sébastien's head jerked from Vivienne and he glared at his brother. Stumbling backwards, the other god dropped the sword and it clattered on the marble with a resounding pang.

"I... I loved her too, you know that!"

All Sébastien could focus on was the inert blade. It had been the cause of Vivienne's death, wielded by his selfish hand. His gaze rose again and he curled his lip, spitting in his sibling's direction. *"You will pay for this, you piece of—"*

"Enough!"

Before he could get up, two gods passed through the hall— their parents. The blonde-haired woman who was their mother *stared at Vivienne lying dead in his arms.*

Tears streaming down her cheeks, she turned to her eldest son. "How could you, Ambition?"

His eyes shot daggers, but already she dismissed him, walking over to Sébastien and Vivienne. She knelt by their side, running a glowing palm over the young goddess' cold body.

"I am sorry for you loss, my darling. But this does not have to be the end, not for you. The stars aligned long ago, blessing your union. If you decide to give up your life here, I will ensure your reincarnation. You can still be together, my son, as you were meant to be. But you have to choose, now."

Sébastien glanced down at his beloved, then back at his mother. "There is no question about it. I want to be with her, forever."

"Then be it so."

She touched both their foreheads, and their bodies disappeared. Only two glowing orbs remained. She gathered them in her arms and walked to her husband. "I will bring them to the Pool of Reincarnation."

Her mate nodded, then spun on his heels to dispense justice to Carleigh. Only, the god was nowhere to be seen.

"We cannot allow this to happen again. Enough gods have quarreled. It is time to instill a cardinal rule."

Sébastien woke up from the memory, his head fuzzy. He remained seated, meeting Alistair's knowing gaze.

"I... You were right. We are children of the original deities, the ones even before you existed. Carleigh and I were brothers, and Vivienne chose me."

Silence stretched between them for long moments, until Alistair nodded. "As I thought. Now go inside, my mistress needs you. I will try to figure out a solution to this mess, with this new information."

* * *

Alistair watched Sébastien head to the house, waiting until he sensed him next to Vivienne. Once they were asleep, he headed farther to seek whom he needed. Under the stars, he lay down and let his gaze wander, eventually dozing off.

"Atrox."

Catriona stood before him dressed in a silver wrap dress, her wings folded delicately against her back, then disappearing within.

She grinned, taking in his appearance with sparkling eyes. "You look well."

The cocky reply died on his lips. Instead, in two strides he had her in his arms, one hand cupping her cheek.

"I owe you," he breathed against her mouth. "I would never have remembered otherwise. *Thank you*, Catriona."

She shivered at his tone, surprised at the awe she caught between the lines. His dark eyes glittered with something, and it took all her willpower to speak. "There is no need to thank me. I only did—"

Alistair's fierce kiss cut off her air supply, then they forgot themselves and disposed of their clothes.

Later, much later, the wolf god was caressing her naked skin. "Will this ever be fully real?"

Catriona hesitated for a beat, then sighed. "It is as real as it can be. My father's word is law, and I can never enter Earth without his express permission."

"Yet you are able to follow what happens everywhere." At

her nod, he asked, "Have you seen anything else on Morgana's side?"

"Nothing these last few days. But I witnessed what happened to Sébastien."

Alistair pursed his lips thoughtfully. "Yes, his revelations were not surprising considering what we had already theorized. But it bothers me that Carleigh had that much power. No wonder his goals keep escalating. He wants to return to the pantheon of gods."

"But the question remains, does he wish what he once had because he was cast out? Or rather due to paying for his mistakes? If we understood the reason, it could help us form a battle plan more suited to his twisted mind."

Her comment caught Alistair's attention, enough to stop his light touches. "How do you mean?"

"If Carleigh was banished as you were, demoted to being a mortal, he could try to get it back by attaining a god's favor— or a Fae's, such as in your case. If, however, he cast himself out in an effort to chase after Vivienne and Sébastien and ensure they could not be together, then he *chose* the full path of corruption. And the only way to rise higher…"

"… is with Darkness' help," Alistair finished. "Damn."

He stood up from the ground, raising a knee and leaning his forearm against it. "And we are blind to the truth unless one of them makes a mistake and reveals it."

Catriona was silent, so he turned to her for confirmation. "Right?"

She did not meet his gaze, only nodding. He could sense she was lying, but let it drop. Instead, another idea hit him. "You said where Morgana exists now, with Merlin, is in a time dimension of his own making, correct?"

"Yes, what of it?"

"Well, you cannot enter Earth," Atrox thought aloud, brow furrowed as the plan formed. "But the other dimensions..."

"I could, yes." Her eyes sparkled as she caught on to his meaning.

"Even Merlin's?"

"*Especially* his," she smirked.

Atrox returned her grin. "In that case, I need your help. Let us retaliate—properly."

Catriona's trailed an index down his chest, biting her bottom lip. "I am all ears, lover. What did you have in mind?"

* * *

Catriona dug her hands in the tree, using its raw energy as conduit to cast a spell over the castle in Merlin's dimension. Through it, she watched as the time barrier vibrated. Wherever they were, Morgana and her two acolytes would be immobilized.

A flick of her index created a portal and she stepped through, only to emerge in the narrow staircase of the tower moments later. She made her way up to the top, where they had imprisoned Merlin.

When Catriona strode through the door, he did not stir. Still captive by the crystal from hip to toes, he had leeches on his skin that sucked at his power and spirit enough to keep him on the edge. The Fae fought back tears, unable to reconcile the strong mage she had watched from afar with this shadow version.

"Merlin..."

He roused, moving his head from side to side, but did not seem conscious.

Catriona wiped her cheeks, recalling what she had come for. After a deep breath, she stepped closer. "Merlin, wake up! I have little time."

When he still did not blink, she used air to unhook the leeches from his body, tossing them to the ground where they lay inert. His chest blistered and bled from their hooks, but at least his breathing had evened out.

When she called his name next, his eyelids fluttered open, though his blue eyes remained hazy. After a moment, they landed on her face and he frowned.

"Who… are….you…?" he croaked.

Catriona smiled, pushing back a lock of his hair carefully. "Your sister."

"My…"

"Shh!" She placed an index to his lips, nervously glancing over her shoulder. Ignoring his dilated pupils, Catriona insisted, "We really cannot do this right now."

Merlin's gaze flashed at her whispered statement. "Then *make* time. I want to know whom I am speaking with."

Recognizing the stubborn streak in him, Catriona blew an exasperated breath. "Very well." In a few minutes, she summarized everything about Merlyddus, her realm, and her inability to enter Earth—but not other dimensions. He listened carefully, his eyes clearing with each passing second.

"So you know Alistair?" he concluded.

Catriona smirked at that. "I know *Atrox*, yes."

Merlin's brow creased at the correction. "He no longer goes by that name."

"So he keeps saying," the Fae retorted, rolling her eyes. "While I would love to explain to you why your only friend is still

very much the god he once was, we have bigger issues." She gestured to the barrier. "And this will not hold forever. I need answers."

Merlin assessed her for a long moment, searching her gaze, then the walls of suspicion fell away. "What is it you wish to know?"

"Vivienne is pregnant because of what Morgana did." It was not a question, but he inclined his head in agreement nonetheless. "And the heir is Arthur."

"Yes," Merlin confirmed, a faint glimmer of hope shining in his eyes. "I had a vision, a while back. They..." He licked his dry lips, gaze darting to the open door. "They tried to find out, but I would not tell them, even though I saw as much."

"I know," Catriona admitted, shifting on her feet. "There is nothing I wish more than to help you escape, but—"

"Do not worry about me. Morgana and I..." He sighed, stopping himself. "We have unfinished business."

Catriona chose not to speak of what she had already witnessed between them, and instead returned to the topic at hand. "Vivienne is fighting the evil in her. What you could not take out has been eating her up."

She omitted the part about her being the child of the old gods, guessing that Merlin would want all the details and she lacked the time.

As though sensing she was withholding something, Merlin interrupted. "This makes no sense, the way Darkness keeps baiting Vivienne. What I did should have been enough to give her peace."

Catriona crossed her arms, unable to keep the annoyance out of her voice. "It does add up, if you consider their lineage." She followed the comment by disclosing the whole sordid tale, while Merlin listened with wide eyes.

"And I caught none of this?" he said at the end.

"Neither did Atrox, nor I. Nor Morgana. So cut yourself some slack. But the past is gone, brother, and nothing we do will change that. With everything I told you, can you think of anything you overheard that could benefit us? What does Carleigh want?" She uncrossed her arms, inching closer still. "*Why* does want it? Darkness shrouds their plans from us a bit too effectively."

Instead of an answer, Merlin's head abruptly jerked back, hitting the wall. Afraid he was having a fit, Catriona tried to right him, but had to step back in shock.

Only the whites of his orbs showed as he muttered incomprehensible things. Her surprise was not because of his appearance, but rather due to the energy she sensed was animating the vision.

In her childhood, Catriona had witnessed many such scenes when Merlyddus had predictions. It had been something to behold then, and it remained so now.

Overcoming the emotion choking her, the Fae neared her brother once more. His murmurs were louder, enough so that she pressed her ear to his mouth. Her eyes widened at his words and she pulled back, but Merlin had passed out.

"Brother!" she whispered furiously. She wanted to take him with her, unwilling to let him suffer in vain. And if Morgana came after her… *After all, why not?*

"Brother, you say?"

She spun around in shock, meeting Mordred's observing stare. "So that would make you my aunt, I suppose?"

Catriona scowled, not answering. She angled her body in front of Merlin, ready and willing to protect him with her magic if the need arose.

Unfazed, Mordred leaned against the opened door and looked her up and down. "Pleasure to meet you."

The Fae frowned, finally realizing what was bothering her. "How can you move in this spell?"

"The way I always do," he shrugged, glancing between her and Merlin a few times. In the end, he peered over his shoulder and stated, "My mother will have probably freed herself, as well. You had best go before she shows up."

Catriona gaped at him, unable to believe her ears. "Why are you helping me?"

Mordred smirked at that, his gaze twinkling with a secret only he understood. "I'm not."

The Fae spun to Merlin, stretching a hand to help him. In an instant, Mordred was by her side, gripping her wrist and yanking her away.

Instead of the ocean calm, his glare was shooting lightning, reflecting his intention. "*He* stays."

Catriona backed off, already heading towards the vortex that had appeared in a corner. *I will return for you, Merlin,* she promised, before hopping back into her own realm.

* * *

Catriona paced from one end of the forest to the other, wringing her hands and biting her lips until Atrox fell asleep. As soon as she sensed his subconscious. she threw herself in his dream.

"Carleigh *does* plan to sacrifice Vivienne at the stones," she revealed the moment she set eyes on him.

Alistair was headed for her–presumably to embrace her–but he froze at her words. "Merlin confirmed, then?"

"Yes. There's more, Atrox. Carleigh wants to become a god, like us. And he is willing to do anything, including sacrifice Vivienne's baby."

A snarl ripped from his throat and he jerked away, stomping the ground in agitation. Catriona's hand flew to her mouth, holding back her own revulsion at the necromancer's black heart.

She had seen things, yes, in her eons of existence. A selfish man willing to take an innocent life should not have surprised her. But what Carleigh planned to do...

"Merlin heard him mumble about, when Morgana and her son are not around." She paused, hesitant to continue when it seemed Alistair only got more agitated. He was clenching and unclenching his fists, and she had no trouble guessing what he was imagining.

His midnight eyes settled on her, mouth set in a grim line. "Tell me everything, and leave nothing out."

"He intends to tie Vivienne up and bled her dry, offering her essence to Darkness. While she is in its clutches–whether still aligned with Light or not–he will cut her baby out of her and burn him as offer to his master."

Alistair staggered on his way to a tree, then placed a palm against it, taking deep breaths. "Do you know why?"

"Merlin was not coherent enough to tell me, towards the

end, when this all came out." Catriona stepped closer to him, biting her lip. "But you do, am I right?"

"Yes," Alistair sighed, then shuddered in revulsion. "My time in the underworld was very educational on the topic of the occult, unfortunately. By the time human babies are born, their entrance into the world already marks them with good or bad energies. While they are in their mothers' womb, they are protected and at their purest. Except, of course, if the mother is already evil."

"But Vivienne—"

"She is tainted. While the fetus is under three months old, it is protected by a certain, shall we say, psychic barrier. Nothing she feels will get to it. My understanding is, with this being Arthur, once he passes the three month margin he will cleanse Vivienne as well and maintain his Light, no matter what happens to her."

Catriona frowned as a realization struck her. "If it had been any other baby, past that mark he would have been corrupted as well. But then… It would make more sense to wait until she actually gives birth, no?"

"Yes, it would. Of course, Morgana and her lot are unaware that Vivienne is carrying Arthur. They believe in order to get the purest baby they can, they have to cut him out of her womb before the three month period."

"Which explains their rush…" Catriona shook her head, fighting back tears at their atrocious souls. "Those *animals*!"

Alistair pushed away from the tree, muttering under his breath. "You are being too kind with such words, darling. They are depraved, and it will be my pleasure to ensure justice befalls them all."

It took a long time, but Alistair managed to calm down, at least enough to return to the conversation. Nostrils still flaring, fists clenched, he faced Catriona. "Was Merlin able to tell you how Carleigh was banished?" When she shook her head in denial, Atrox frowned darkly. "I suppose that part, if nothing else, makes sense."

"How so?"

"Everything Carleigh is willing to do confirms what we had theorized: he yearns for his original state, and will do anything for it. We *can* stop him, but only if we figure out what really happened."

Catriona folded her arms across her chest, leaning against a tree. "And how do you propose we do that? I cannot go back there. Mordred could somehow move through my spell before the

others. I was lucky he let me leave."

Alistair grew alarmed at that, inching closer to her. "That boy is no saint. Why would he allow it?"

When the Fae only shrugged, Alistair growled in frustration. "Damn the man! We've ended up with more questions than we have answers. I shall speak with Sébastien, perhaps he remembers more. But what about Vivienne? Could Merlin shed light on how to save her from the darkness?"

"Yes," Catriona nibbled on her lip at her brother's last words. "You were almost right, earlier, when you mentioned Arthur. He said that when she gives birth, the act itself will expel the corruption from within. She will be alright—*if* she survives the process."

CHAPTER 11

Sébastien woke up groggy, yet unsure why. Then he realized his arms were empty, and he sat up abruptly. A quick scan of the room confirmed Vivienne's absence, and he panicked.

He rushed downstairs, noticing Alistair passed out in a corner, and continued towards the backyard. Vivienne was sitting on one of the patio chairs, swirling a cube of ice in a glass of water. She was staring at the horizon, her expression inscrutable.

At his bursting in, she glanced up. Rather than the sweet smile he usually saw on her face, Vivienne greeted him with a frown. Sébastien attempted to calm his fast-beating heart, even as he sat at the table next to her.

"You weren't in bed when I woke up."

His words, though spoken softly, only hardened her features. "I didn't realize I was a prisoner there."

Sébastien pulled back his hand, which had been stretching

to touch hers. "What has gotten into you?"

Vivienne snorted, taking a sip of the water. "You should know. I'm pregnant with *your* baby, remember?"

He did not like the way the discussion was headed, but it was too late to steer it otherwise. Any comment from him added to her incensed mood.

"We didn't have time to talk about it. I know you were upset the other night–"

Vivienne knocked the glass off the table, and it smashed to the ground. "Upset?" She stood, nostrils flaring. "*Upset*? I did not expect this, and I *do not* want this baby."

Sébastien paled at the implication, and he slowly got to his feet. "Vivienne, let's talk about this. I will support you in whatever decision you make, you know that."

When she did not react—but neither did she hurl more accusations—he took a chance and lifted his palm to her cheek, caressing it softly.

"I love you, and regardless of what happens, will continue to do so. But please, talk to me. Don't shut me out because of this darkness inside you."

Vivienne jerked away from his touch at that. "Just let me be for now, Sébastien."

Before he could say anything else, she stormed out onto the grounds, her dark hair blowing in the wind.

* * *

After the Fae disappeared, Mordred stared for a few moments. He could not pinpoint what, exactly, had made him let her go. At the very least, her escape with whatever Merlin had told her would ensure a complicated fight.

And after the way Carleigh keeps jabbing at my mother, he deserves complications.

The young sorcerer turned his gaze to his father's unconscious form. He picked up the leeches off the ground and replaced them on his skin. At his hiss of pain, Mordred grinned.

He left Merlin and returned outside, having done his part. In a corner of the castle, he leaned on ramparts and let his mind wander, closing his eyes. It was not long before he dropped into another dream with Vivienne.

The enchantress' aura was scattered all over the place. He could read fear at losing control, doubt over what was happening, and uncertainty about her future... But it was the last emotion that really made him grin: anger at Sébastien.

"Bad day?"

Vivienne turned to him, no longer surprised. "You could say that."

"There is much angst in you..." He tilted his head to the side, hiding a smile. "And fury for being put in a situation you never asked for."

Vivienne frowned at his words. "How would you know all this?"

"I recognize it all because you and I are the same, sweeting. And I understand you better than anyone."

Though she wanted to contest him, deep down the enchantress felt he was not lying.

"I can help you..." Mordred latched onto her dread. "You are right to be afraid. Please, allow me to provide guidance."

"How?"

"You do not know how to handle the corruption inside, but *I* do. I have dealt with enough of it on my own, and survived. It is not a matter to handle alone." He paused, placing a hand on her shoulder. "Let me come to you."

She glanced at him, biting her lip. "Who helped you?"

Mordred's brow creased, then smoothed as he caught her meaning. "You should know him…. He spoke very highly of you. Long white beard, blue eyes, carries a staff?"

Vivienne's mouth opened in surprise. "Merlin!?"

"Yes. I did not know if you would believe me when these dreams started, and he is too busy attempting to undo a certain necromancer's immortality. But he asked me to keep an eye on you." His grip tightened on her, then released. "He would want me to help, considering he is unable to."

The enchantress moved away from him, shaking her head softly. "I doubt there is anything you can do. Whatever it is, it's already inside me. I…" Tears streamed down her cheeks, silent and unwelcome. Never had she felt so alone, so at a loss on what to do.

"I can assist you, if you'll let me," Mordred insisted. "But you have to let me join you on Earth."

Vivienne whirled around, her eyes narrowed in confusion. "Where, exactly, are you?"

"I am in a different dimension, much like Merlin. When he helped me defeat my demons, he also found me a safe place to live in. He promised to come get me, but then…with everything that happened with you…" He ended on a shrug, keeping his face impassive.

Vivienne hesitated for a moment, her gaze searching his. Everything swirled inside her in a mass of confusion, but one thing was clear. This man, whoever he was, did not judge her. On the contrary, he wanted to help her.

Before she could change her mind, she nodded. "What do you need me to do?"

* * *

Alistair looked at the knight, uncomprehending. *What do you mean she is not here?*

Sébastien tried to fight down his own hopelessness at the reminder of Vivienne's hurtful words. "She said she doesn't want to have a baby, and that she needs time."

Time? Alistair growled. *We don't have any!*

In the midst of their argument, Vivienne walked in. She moved about as a ghost would, disregarding them and heading straight to the backyard. Sébastien could only gaze after her, desperately wishing he could do something.

Alistair glanced between them, barely holding down a rumble of irritation. *We need a plan.*

* * *

Vivienne woke up gasping, unable to shake off the feeling of dread. She turned to Sébastien's arms, but after hours of trying to fall asleep, gave up.

She slid out of bed, moving instead towards the window. The moon was high in the sky and the night vibrated, as if expecting some big event.

What is it, highness?

She turned to Alistair, who was watching her warily. These days, her companion kept to himself, and though she did not want to be overprotective, something felt off. "A bad dream, is all. What about you?"

Pardon?

"You feel odd lately…preoccupied. Is everything ok?"

Alistair did his doggy grin and woofed happily. *Of course, majesty. But you should return to bed, you need as much rest as possible.*

Once Vivienne was back under the sheets, the demon dog curled up onto himself, whining.

Good job. Morgana's voice was eager in his mind. *Now remove the knight out of the equation.*

I will not hurt Vivienne!

But you are not hurting her, mutt. You are helping her.

It took his every willpower not to budge from the floor. *This is really pushing it!*

There was silence and for a moment, Alistair almost hoped he had peace. Then her voice returned, taut with disapproval. *Do you wish me to release Carleigh and start this all over again for Vivienne? Or do you want to help her, and in exchange return to your deity self? I offer you a chance, but the ultimate choice is yours.*

Alistair growled, biding his time. What is your command?

Kill Sébastien.

On some level, he had expected such an order, yet it still came as a surprise. After a convincing display of shock, anger and surrender, he pretended to agree to Morgana's latest request.

Once her presence disappeared, he raised his head. Blocking his thoughts, he walked to the knight and shook him awake.

"What is it?" Sébastien whispered, rubbing the sleep out of his eyes.

Morgana wants you out.

"Not surprising, she needs Vivienne alone and weakened." The guardian glanced to his beloved, secure in his arms. "What should we do?"

This is the opportunity we have been waiting for. We have to give in, but I shall pretend to kill you and instead throw you into a coma.

"I don't like this…"

Listen to me, knight. The ruse will fool Morgana and buy us time. All you need to do is dig into your memories and figure out what happened with Carleigh back when you two were gods.

"Why?" Sébastien asked. "What does the past have to do with the present?"

Everything. Carleigh was cast out or left of his own accord. You have to find out which it is. Once you do, I can bring you back with Catriona's help.

"But how can this benefit, other than give us leverage on Carleigh?"

By providing information on what he intends at the stones— their next movement. They plan to tear through time and space to get here and sacrifice Vivienne. The more we know, the better armed we can be for the final battle. We are dealing with seasoned sorcerers here.

Sébastien glanced back to Vivienne and his heart squeezed painfully. "And who will protect her?"

Me. And you. At his confused look, Alistair explained, *I have thought this over, and I am fairly certain that I can bring forth your former self from the past. I will spare you the details, but suffice to say what they plan to do, breaking Carleigh out of his prison, will affect time itself.*

"And that serves our purposes, how?"

You live in one dimension now, but Camelot is not in the past, rather a revolving parallel world. It is only one of the many consequences of Merlin's magic. When Morgana and Mordred break through the portal here, I know I can get you through, as well. Then, once you return from your quest, I will send your past self back.

Sébastien looked away, mulling his words over. His gaze fell on Vivienne and he tugged her closer, caressing her cheek, her hair, lightly enough so she would not wake up. He breathed her scent deeply, then sighed. "Alright. I will do anything for her, you know that. And I trust the me from the past to do an even better job at protecting Vivienne."

Alistair gazed at him steadily, hiding his own discomfort. The magic they would play with was potent, and there was a risk of it going awry. Still, it was the best chance they had.

Good, it is settled. Now get some sleep.

* * *

"Do not do this."

Catriona turned from the tree, to her father's hologram. "Do what?"

"Help the wolf god. What you are plotting will cost everyone."

She hesitated, having sensed changes on the wind herself. Yet it had not been enough to alter her decision. "And what other choice is there?"

He looked at her with pity in his eyes. "Leave it be. All of it. Stay out of it rather than complicate things."

Catriona turned away, hiding her tears. "If there is a small chance I can set this right, I have to take it."

"Even if you are putting yourself in the path of danger by so doing?"

The answer was straight. "Yes."

Only a blast of wind from behind her indicated Merlyddus' departure, and Catriona turned back to the tree.

Your father is correct, child. You do not know what you play with.

"I will accept my chances," she muttered, then dug deeper. "Now, I need you to help me so that I do not screw this up. Sébastien's life depends on it."

When she had caught the line of energy, holding it tightly in her grasp, Catriona intoned, "Let the knight be safe no matter what. His love protected, and his enemy's plans thwarted."

Magic escaped her in a rush of multi-colored streams, and Catriona watched in a pool as they found Sébastien, wrapping him in his sleep. She gasped, bending over in pain at the sudden cramps that seized her. Frowning, she peered at the knight, but he seemed unharmed. He stirred when the wisps disappeared within his skin, but otherwise was not bothered.

For better or worse, it is done.

* * *

When Alistair finally fell asleep and joined Catriona in his dream, he found her lying down. He rushed to her, heart racing at the thought she was injured. "What happened?"

"The spell," she admitted, barely lifting a hand in greeting. "It is not magic easily wielded, lover."

Alistair ran his hands up and down her body, trying to see if there was anything he could do to fix her weakness. Catriona only smiled, "There is nothing you can do, except stay here. You must forgive my inability to provide other entertainment."

His eyes narrowed in confusion, searching her features for the meaning of her words. Her sapphire gaze shone with tears and vulnerability, and the truth dawned on him. With his free hand, he tucked a curl behind her ear. "I am perfectly happy to hold you, darling."

Catriona's only reaction was to bury her face in his arms, blinking back tears.

* * *

Are you ready?

Yes.

Good. Now be a good boy and do my bidding.

Alistair woke up and stepped outside where Sébastien and Vivienne were lying down on the grass. To pacify his beloved, the knight had set up a picnic area. After a fruitful lunch, they had both laid back to relax.

Sébastien was the first who noticed his approach and pointed it out to Vivienne. "Look who stopped being a loner."

She turned to Alistair, opening her arms wide. "Come play, Al."

His heart squeezed at the easygoing smile on her face, the trust in her eyes. *We should have made sure Vivienne does not witness this.*

Sébastien met his gaze upfront and gave a small shrug. *It's too late for that, isn't it?*

Alistair cursed Morgana to all hells and beyond, then focused on Vivienne. *Highness, would you mind getting Excalibur for us? There is something we have to do with it.*

Oblivious to the tension between them, Vivienne stood. Before she could move away, Sébastien grasped her wrist, tugging on it gently to get her attention. Once she humored him, he pulled her fully in his lap.

Vivienne squeaked, then threw her head back and laughed in delight. But Sébastien was a man with a mission. He ran a hand down her throat, then to the back of her neck, forcing her head up so he could stare into those unfathomable emerald eyes one more time.

At first shining with happiness, their gleam dimmed in confusion at his intense expression. "What's wrong?"

He shook his head, unable to be as good an actor as Alistair. Instead, he gently rose until his mouth met hers in a tender kiss. Fighting back panic, trying to quiet his fast-beating heart, Sébastien savored her lips, her touch.

When he let her go, long moments later, Vivienne seemed slightly dazed, but she was smiling. It was the last he saw of her before she got up on shaky feet and headed back into the house.

Alistair bid his time, waiting until Vivienne entered the house, then faced Sébastien. *Are you ready for this?*

The knight tore his gaze from the door his beloved had last vanished through. *Hit me.*

* * *

Vivienne found Excalibur on the living room coffee table and grasped it in her hand. She turned to head back outside, but froze in her tracks.

Alistair was atop Sébastien, his jaws open wide and the two of them were wrestling on the grass. Her lover seemed to have the upper hand, but the dog overpowered him in weight alone.

Vivienne could have believed they were play-fighting. For a moment, she desperately wanted to. But there was no amusement in Sébastien's expression, only tense muscles, and

Alistair's growls resounded inside the house.

Finally snapping out of it, she rushed outside with Excalibur still in her hand.

"Stop! *Stop it*, both of you!"

Alistair glanced up briefly, his midnight eyes glowing red. He noticed the sword in her hand, but dismissed it easily and lunged again for Sébastien's throat. Unwilling to hurt him, but incapable to stand by and watch him maul her lover to death, Vivienne thrust her palm and hit her guardian with air.

The element slammed the demon dog backwards, and he rolled on the grass a few feet away. He still for a beat, shaking his head in confusion, then got up again. Vivienne could not recognize her gentle protector in this monster with foaming jaws and flaming eyes.

"Stop it!"

I cannot, highness. You are best off without him.

Before she could do anything, Alistair opened his jaws wide and fired an orb of magic towards Sébastien. The knight flew off his feet, landing onto his back a good distance away. Vivienne rushed to him, kneeling by him and running glowing palms over his body.

She could sense his pain through their bond, and felt his heaving breaths under her hands. "Sébastien, stay with me!" she pleaded, blinking back tears.

He remained unresponsive, body angled weirdly at the joints, blood seeping from his mouth. Panic flared inside her and her lungs constricted as though air was missing. When she tried to push her magic to mend, a flare of darkness emerged from his chest and wrapped his entire body.

Vivienne fell back in shock, gaping at the cocoon that now held her lover's dying form prisoner. She looked around for help, only to notice Alistair still watching them, a few feet away.

"Why? You were my guardian! *Why* would you do this?"

The red eyes glimmered as he started to back away, snarling. You would not understand. Then he took off, disappearing in the distance.

Vivienne dropped to the ground, unable to keep standing. Through blurry sight she saw Sébastien's body glow, right before it vanished.

"No!" she screamed, but it was to no avail. He was gone—and so was the last remnant of her sanity.

CHAPTER 12

On the edge of the city, Alistair slunk behind an abandoned building and finally settled down. After the so-called victory over Sébastien, he had taken off, unable to bear his mistress' face. Exhausted after hours of trying to shut up his thoughts, he was ready to sleep.

How are you feeling? Catriona's sweet voice breached through. He was grateful to her for having given him the space to get back on track.

As you would expect, he retorted. *Vivienne thinks I betrayed her, and I am fighting the impulse to confess everything to her right now.*

Lover... I feel your pain, but you cannot.

Alistair did not respond. What was there to say?

Vivienne is unstable, we have no idea what she would do if she found out. Perhaps she would want to kill Carleigh once and for all, which would definitely achieve what Darkness desires.

And what do you think not having Sébastien will do to her?
Alistair had not meant his tone to be sharp, but the burden of
the last few hours weighed heavily on his consciousness. He
recalled Vivienne's stricken expression and tried to block his
mind against it. *I am having doubts about this.*

The spell has to work, Catriona stated. *While Sébastien hunts
for the truth, you and I will bring his soul from the past to protect
the Lady of the Lake. Once all is revealed, you can speak to
Vivienne and tell her the full story. Then, at least, you can offer
her a solution to match the problem.*

Alistair sighed and set his massive head on his paws,
closing his eyes. *I shall hope for the best.* He paused, hesitating
to ask what was on his mind. *How is he?*

*Sébastien's body is currently floating above my lake. He is
safe and healthy as far as I can tell. I promise to keep him so.*
There was a slight hesitation, then she said, *Rest. You need it.*

*Wait. You mentioned earlier if Vivienne finds out, she
might give in to a killer instinct. Considering what we have
learned... She really would be able to, despite Carleigh's
darkness-induced immortality now?*

Catriona was silent as she considered it. *I believe so. The
game has changed as have the players. If Vivienne learns to tap
into the reservoir of power she had as a goddess, disposing of
Carleigh would be easy.*

And the opposite is true as well.

*Yes... This makes it easier for him to hurt her, and
Sébastien. I know you will not see it this way, but for better or
worse, Sébastien being in a coma actually ensures he is away
from harm, at least for the time being.*

A wave of warmth passed through his body from the Fae, and he basked in it even as the connection ended. No sooner was Catriona gone that Morgana's voice rang in his head.

Well?

He bit back the retort he wanted to lash out with, and instead kept it simple. *It is done. Sébastien is no longer.*

She was silent, and he could almost imagine her bewildered face. *You didn't think I'd actually do it?*

I had my doubts.

To calm her suspicions—and distract her–he added, *I was a god once, Morgana. I would surrender anything to get that back.*

There was a stunned pause, then her amused voice came. *Since when have you known my true identity?*

From the beginning, he lied. *That is why I know you can give me what I want.*

You truly are a cunning one, mutt. She laughed, but it sounded fake to his own ears. *I might hold my end of the bargain if I cross into your dimension.*

And what makes you think my powers can manage that? He lifted his head, something in him warning he would not like the answer.

Oh, I am aware you are powerless, mutt. Now that you eliminated Sébastien, my son will finish working on Vivienne. She is so close to tipping over that a single push would bring her straight into our hands. Another laugh, this time more genuine as she caught his shock. *You missed that, did you?*

Alistair stumbled to his paws, rooted to the ground, unable to respond. In their haste to find out about Carleigh, and Vivienne's mood swings, never had he considered that someone was working on her subconsciously.

Stupid mistake! he admonished himself.

I would stay and chat further, but I have news to share with my companions. Consider yourself unbound...for now, demon dog. Until next time.

Alistair sensed a ripple across his skin, raising his hair. Then Morgana's presence disappeared from his mind, and he jumped up.

Catriona! What would cut through a portal and destroy it?

The Fae did not respond right away, but finally said, *A sword of justice and light. Something like Excalibur. Why?*

They played us! This entire time we focused on Vivienne's mood swings, and on Carleigh, not once realizing Mordred has been contacting her for the last weeks. I forgot about her nightmares amid all this.

Unable to stand still, he got back on the road—towards his mistress' house.

What does this have to do with what is happening now?

We thought we had time for Sébastien to find out the truth. Alistair pushed his tired muscles, determination sharpening in his mind. *But we don't! They plan to cross over, using Vivienne. And I have no one to wield Excalibur!*

Catriona was struck mute for a moment, but quickly jumped into action. *Are you going by her place?*

Yes, on my way there. Would I be able to use their portal to do what I told Sébastien? Bring his previous self forward?

Maybe, but let me see what else I can find out about their plans first.

Hurry, Alistair pleaded, and redoubled his efforts to get to Vivienne.

* * *

Morgana almost danced in the room they had imprisoned Merlin in. Her ex-lover raised a tired gaze to her, which soon became wary when he noticed her excellent mood.

Carleigh turned to her frowning, but Mordred was already echoing her smile. "Good news, mother?"

"Amazing, as a matter of fact! The demon dog has gotten rid of Sébastien for us." She looked at Merlin, whose gaze was filled with shock and despair. "The knight is gone, and the path is clear."

"He couldn't have!" Merlin croaked. "Alistair would *never* betray Vivienne like that."

Morgana smirked, enjoying his stricken expression a little too much. "But he did. All it took was an enticement—I promised to give him back his deity status."

Merlin's eyes widened as he started between her and the other two. "But you can't possibly!"

Carleigh laughed at that. "Of course not. *I* probably could, but there is no way I am wasting my magic on that mutt." To Morgana, he added, "Good job, my dear. Now it's up to your son."

Mordred grinned at that. "Vivienne is close to tipping. One more dream, and she will be crashing straight into my comforting arms."

Growls from Merlin had them turn to him. "I cannot allow this!" He struggled against his restraints, uncaring of the joints he was hurting. Rage filled him to the point the leeches fell off him, and his entire body glowed from within. "I will *not* permit you to touch Vivienne."

"You don't have a choice, wizard." Carleigh turned to Morgana, jerking his head towards Merlin. "Time to say your goodbyes, my dear, while I make the final preparations."

He whirled around, his cloak billowing in the wind and darkness followed him. Mordred arched an eyebrow towards the mage, waving cheerily. "Until we meet again, father!"

Without so much as a second glance, he vanished. Morgana, however, lingered behind. The smile had slipped from her face, now an inscrutable mask. Her gray shone with the unnatural gleam of her magic.

As they stared at each other, Merlin's gaze lighted in response. "Please, Morgana."

"I do like hearing you beg," she snickered. "Please what, exactly? You want me to free you?"

"No. I care not what you do to me. But do not let Carleigh hurt Vivienne and her unborn child."

His voice was hoarse, heavy with emotion, and something in Morgana stirred. *Foolish thoughts,* she chastised, narrowing her gaze at the mage.

"I will consider keeping an eye on her well-being... *If* you reveal what your last vision was all about."

Merlin tried to think of a way to avoid it, then his shoulders drooped in defeat. There was no escape option he could see, and he absolutely had to take whatever was available to him. *Anything to protect Vivienne and her baby. But Sébastien...* He could not believe that after everything, the knight was dead.

And so the circle starts anew. A muscle ticked in his jaw, then he exhaled. "I will tell you. But give me your vital promise that you shall keep your word. Can you do that?"

"Very well. What was the vision?"

Oh no you don't. "Your oath first, Morgana."

Morgana's eyes narrowed further, but she was eager enough for the information. With a curt nod, she drew up her hand and placed it on his heart, near the carved circle. The glow of her palm ebbed into his skin, and a halo surrounded them both.

"I vow, on my life's essence and my powers as a Fae, that I shall do what I can for Vivienne. And if worse comes to worst, I will ensure her child...survives."

The light vibrated for a second around their bodies, then disappeared. Merlin was smiling smugly when he next met her gaze, and Morgana grew wary. "Why the grin?"

"Because, my darling, the vision I had was of Vivienne's unborn baby. He will be a prodigy, a leader in this new world. And *you* have agreed to protect him."

Morgana's heart stopped, then stuttered to a fast-beating pace. "Who is it?"

Merlin laughed, shaking his head. "Arthur."

The sorceress' expression grew pale, then red with fury. Her eyes blazed, and in an impulsive motion, she slapped him. "How *dare* you!?"

Merlin gritted his teeth, then met her gaze, just as incensed. "I dared because I can. And someone has to keep you sane. I don't know what you did to Alistair to make him kill Sébastien, but I doubt he did so of his own accord. It's my turn now, Morgana."

They were staring daggers at each other when Carleigh stepped back into the room. "Mordred is by the lake, ready for the spell. Are you quite done?"

Morgana scowled his way, before facing Merlin again,

pointing an index his way. "This is not over. When Vivienne is dealt with, and I have regained my immortality, I *will* return for you."

"I shall look forward to it," Merlin promised through clenched teeth.

She stomped out, her own cloak billowing behind. Carleigh stared after her, then his suspicious gaze fell on Merlin. "What did you say to her?"

If he had been able to shrug, he would have. As it was, the wizard simply glared back, lips pursed together and no sound escaping him.

"Mm. Dramatic to the end, I see." Carleigh rolled his eyes, then shuffled about the room. "No matter. Despite what Morgana said, I have a little parting gift for you."

He joined his palms as though in prayer and drew them apart. Between them, an orb formed. It shone black, with a tiny red dot in the middle. Once it was fully developed—about the size of a watermelon—Carleigh set it into the corner of the room.

Merlin glared at the ball of energy, a bad feeling in the pit of his stomach.

"This," Carleigh pointed to it, "is a little conception of mine. A spell designed to detonate at the next full moon. It will be the night when I take your precious Vivienne's life for good. And though you cannot attend, it will ensure you join her shortly after."

"You..." Merlin licked his dry lips, his throat clenching. "You plan to leave this with me?"

"Yes, I do," Carleigh snickered. "Have fun counting down to your doom, Merlin." With a mocking salute, he walked away.

He was almost out the door when he added, "Oh, and the bigger that red dot gets, the more impending your epic end is."

With those parting words, the necromancer stepped out, leaving Merlin to stare at the orb.

* * *

Vivienne had been wallowing in misery, crying all the tears of her body through the night. By the time the sun rose, she was still awake and staring at the ceiling. The fog in her mind drew more present until she eventually passed out from exhaustion.

In her dreams, Mordred appeared once more. "Why so forlorn, darling?"

Without thinking twice about it, she ran into his arms and the sobs came again. "I was betrayed," she choked through tears. "I've lost everything, truly. And this corruption inside me…"

Mordred rubbed her back soothingly. "You still have me. As for the darkness… I think now is as good a time as any to come see you."

Vivienne stared into those blue eyes, so compassionate, so familiar, and surrendered. "How do I help?"

Mordred tried to hide his jubilation, keeping an impassive face. "Go to the lake near your cottage and open a portal. I shall be on the other side, waiting. Then I can show you how to master it, and you will be free."

She sighed, kissing his cheek. "I look forward to seeing you in real life."

The dream dissipated around her, and she was awake once more in the empty household. Alone with her thoughts, the enchantress did not feel a single doubt about letting Mordred pass. He had scared her, at first, but now she realized he was a friend, an ally.

And when he said Merlin sent him, it had calmed any anxiety. She wished she could contact her old mentor, perhaps to see if he had any insight on why Alistair had done what he did. But deep down, Vivienne knew Merlin would be just as flabbergasted as she was.

I trusted him with my life… And he destroyed me.

The darkness in her swirled, and she had a hard time keeping it at bay. She closed her eyes, trying to ground herself in the water that was nearby. But there was no calming hand on her back, no voice whispering in French, no one to love her…

Sébastien is gone, her mind tried to tell her, but her heart could not accept it. Instead, she got up and dressed, heading to the lake, her thoughts a foggy mess. The element answered her urging easily—too much so. She remembered Sébastien's pale face and touched her womb.

Our baby.

The connection to Mordred tugged—he was waiting. She raised her palms parallel to the ground, inhaling deeply.

"I call upon my element to bridge a way," she intoned, and the lake swirled. "Create a conduit my friend can use, and bring him to me."

Much like in previous times, a vortex formed. The waters swirled, picking up speed with each moment. Vivienne sensed the link with Mordred strain, then he stepped through. When he was almost out, she caught another strain, then another… Then it no longer felt like she was controlling the vortex, but rather the opposite.

Her breath was shaky, hands trembling as Mordred

approached her. She only got a chance to meet his gentle blue gaze, before passing out from the power she was using.

The young man was there in a last stride, catching Vivienne before she hit the ground. He picked her up in his arms, then turned to the lake and the other two shapes that emerged.

Morgana was out first, then Carleigh. The portal continued to swirl behind them, as if having a mind of its own. Nothing moved around them, world itself holding its breath.

They joined Mordred, both glancing down at Vivienne. But it was Morgana alone who noticed the enchantress' pallor and thinness. Her cold heart, having hated her for so long, seemed less angry, almost pitying her instead.

Before she could ponder on the surprising thoughts, Mordred threw a warning look to Carleigh. "You said we have a week."

"Yes. Darkness whispers that the sacrifice has to happen on the next full moon, before the baby is fully formed."

Vivienne stirred in his arms, moaning as if in pain. Mordred peered down at her, something softening in his expression. When he spoke again, he was still staring at her. "Stay out of sight until then, she cannot know you are here. She is mine until the sacrifice."

Carleigh nodded, but the evil glint in his eyes when he looked at Vivienne spoke volumes.

* * *

Alistair stepped back from the scene, watching helplessly as Mordred carried Vivienne to the cottage, and Morgana and Carleigh headed in the opposite direction.

He waited until they were out of sight, then rushed to the

closing portal. *Catriona, now!* He thrust his energy into the vortex, but it returned to him tenfold and blew him away, hitting the ground.

By the time he got up, the water was limpid once more and the vortex had disappeared. Alistair found the quickest hidden spot he could, then allowed Catriona to pull him into a dream.

"Anything?" he pressed, the minute he was in her clearing. He scanned their surroundings, noticing Sébastien's floating form nearby.

"Nothing. I tried to connect to his mind, but only reached a blank wall. I cannot tell if he has found out what we need about Carleigh or not."

Alistair paced around Sébastien's body, pinching the bridge of his nose in frustration. "We are already on the clock." Catriona stilled at his revelation, and their worried gazes met. "Vivienne broke the portal to bring Mordred in. Because Morgana and Carleigh tagged along, the entire spell exhausted her and she passed out."

"They are all here, then." Catriona glanced at her blood-red sky. "I sensed the change, but.... What happened to bringing Sébastien in?"

"It didn't work. The path was consumed with Carleigh's darkness and collapsed shortly after."

Alistair stared at the knight, stomach churning. "I had hoped..." He frowned, then moved closer to him and attempted to reach his soul. His mind probed, trying to bypass the walls of his subconscious, to send a message.

"There's nothing there!" He reeled back in shock.

"What?" Catriona rushed by his side, passing her hands over Sébastien. Rather than feel him, like she had previously, all she sensed was a blank wall. "*No!*"

Their shocked gazes met, and she staggered away. "I did everything right, he… He was fine just moments ago."

"Damn all the *hells*!" Alistair turned to the closest tree and unleashed punch after punch until his knuckles bled. Despair threatened at bay for all he had set in motion, and how it had gone wrong. Breathing hard, he leaned his forearm against the trunk, dropping his forehead on it. "This was all useless."

Catriona's hand on his shoulder had him look up in faint hope. But she only shook her head, tears escaping her. "I cannot bring him back. If anyone can, it is only Vivienne through the strength of their bond."

"She thinks he's gone!" Alistair moved away, pacing from side to side, running his hands through his hair. "*Shite*! Damn Fae magic, I should have known better!"

He turned to Catriona, noticing her stricken expression at his words. "It is not what I meant, beloved. This is not your fault."

"Are you sure about that? It was *my* spell," she said bitterly.

"Yes, I'm positive," Atrox stated, moving closer, but she stepped back. "It was my idea. If anyone is to blame, it is me."

He ran a hand through his hair, resisting the urge to tug on it in frustration. "I don't know why, after cleaning Merlin's messes, I thought I could do better. I cannot, and Vivienne is suffering. Worse, she no longer trusts me."

Catriona looked at him in pity, then stepped into his embrace. Atrox tightened his hold on her, inhaling her scent deeply. The squeeze in his heart released, and he sighed. "I have to fix this."

CHAPTER 13

Sébastien stirred awake, and the first thing that hit him was the smell. A mix of vanilla and citrus, not unlike Vivienne's own scent.

The thought of his beloved was enough to wake him up completely. A quick glance around did not clue him in to where he was—at least not at first sight.

Yet once he passed through the clearing and ended up on the edge of a lake, he stopped dead in his tracks. In the middle of it was a familiar castle—after all, he had been there when Vivienne built it from scratch following her father's death and losing her kingdom.

"What the…." He trailed off, unsure what he had stumbled upon.

Step by slow step, he threaded through the grass until he was on its edge. The lake's reflection surprised him with an image of him wearing a toga, much like in the dreams where he was opposing Carleigh.

"Alistair, what the hell did I stumble onto?" Sébastien paced, running a hand through his hair.

"So it *is* my brother that threw you in this mess. I should have known."

He spun, eyes widening when they fell on a beautiful woman with bi-colored eyes. "Brother?"

"Yes. No matter what I do, I seem to keep running into his circle, you included." Her tone was slightly bitter, yet amusement danced in her gaze. "But I forget my manners. I am the goddess Ardea, one of the Three."

Unsure what else to do, Sébastien bowed his head, bending at the waist. "The pleasure is mine. But what brings you

where? And what exactly is this mess you speak of?"

Ardea laughed and stepped closer to Sébastien, linking her arm through his. "Walk with me, and I shall explain everything."

Sébastien glanced back at the castle, then the deity by his side. There was no choice other than obey, it seemed. He tucked her arm closer to his breastbone, and they stepped away side by side like old friends.

* * *

The first thing Vivienne recognized were the signs of an impending migraine. She had the uncanny sensation her head was splitting open, bad enough it caused nausea. The second factor, closely following, was the loud grumbling of her stomach.

She blinked awake, but rather than find herself in some strange land, she was in her own bed at the cottage. She turned to her side, groaning—only to get a full sniff of Sébastien's cologne on the pillow.

Tears streamed silently down her cheeks and before long, she was sobbing into her pillow, grasping Sébastien's close to her chest.

A knock on the door jerked her upright in bed. Absorbed by her own grief, she had forgotten the events she had set in motion. Though she did not regret it, as Mordred would help her deal with the corruption within, wariness crept regardless.

"Come in," she croaked, pulling the blankets up to her chin.

The door opened and in walked the young man. His hair was a familiar jet-black, though much messier than in her dreams. Somehow seeing him there, in the suite she had shared with Sébastien, seemed wrong.

"Stop," she said, then cleared her throat when he paused halfway in. "Sorry, but would you mind waiting for me downstairs instead? I'll only be a minute."

Something flashed in Mordred's eyes, but he nodded and left. Once he had locked up behind him, Vivienne got out of bed and went to shower. The entire affair plus dressing took less than ten minutes, and finally she was ready to head downstairs.

It was only once she was halfway out the door that she realized she had worn a pair of Sébastien's sweatpants, and his t-shirt. She froze in the hallway, fingering the material and pulling the collar up to her nose, inhaling his scent. Her willpower was close to crumbling, but still she gulped past the lump in her throat. With a forced smile, she walked in the living room.

"Welcome, Mordred," she hugged him. "Like any gracious host, I would ask what brings you here, but I think it's clear enough."

He cracked a half-smile, but it dropped when he recognized what she was wearing. His mood shift only lasted for a minute, then he was grinning again. "True enough. How are you feeling these days?"

Vivienne shrugged, dropping onto the couch. "As you would expect, I imagine. That darkness I mentioned, it's...it feels like it's so close to surfacing." Unable to bear his knowing gaze, she turned away.

Mordred was first to move, grabbing her chin and forcing her to look back at him. "I told you I can help. But first, let's see exactly what we're dealing with."

He held his palm up, and Vivienne placed hers atop it. A shock of electricity shot from him to her, and she almost withdrew away—except he tightened his grip and would not let go.

Next thing she knew, everything went dark.

* * *

Mordred laid her down gently on the sofa, then ran his hand on her stomach. With his Halfling senses, he caught the new life growing in there. An insane urge to take it away from her, to remove the baby hit him, and his nails dug into the t-shirt fabric.

"Mordred!"

He snapped to, gaze rising to Morgana's incensed face. "What do you think you're doing?" Her eyes darted around to ensure Carleigh had seen nothing.

The necromancer had arrived in time with her to the house—the minute Mordred put Vivienne to sleep.

"Nothing." Mordred closed off his expression and

wandered away from Vivienne's side.

"*Nothing?*" Morgana followed him, not dropping the matter. "That girl is important! We cannot afford to mess with Carleigh's plans."

"Speak of the devil," Mordred muttered.

The sorceress glanced over her shoulder when Carleigh entered. The room seemed to darken—no, it literally dimmed the moment he stepped in. Only the area around Vivienne remained

light, despite his proximity to her.

"Guess she has more light in her than we give her credit for." Mordred's comment was low, only for his mother's ears.

Morgana did not answer, frowning instead. When Carleigh's gaze fell on Vivienne, for a moment only, she had noticed something flare in his aura. Something akin to empathy.

I must be losing my mind. She joined the necromancer before he tried to do anything else.

"We got you here, as agreed. When do we get what you promised?"

Carleigh's eyes flashed darkness, and the tendrils at his feet hissed. Without him even asking, they moved towards Morgana—but never reached her, blasted by a ray from Mordred.

"Watch it, sorcerer." His glare settled on Carleigh, jaw clenched. "You owe us."

"Very well," Carleigh agreed. "We have a few days yet until the full moon. Once I am released and back to a god, then and only then will you get what I promised. Clear?"

A muscle ticked in Mordred's jaw at the patronizing tone, but Morgana did not even bat an eyelash. Her thoughts were on the vow she had given Merlin—and how he had tricked her. Almost despite herself, her gaze shifted to Vivienne and her pale form. Noticing it, Mordred returned to her side.

"I was about to unleash more darkness in her," he revealed. "All the better to pull her to our side."

"I have seen her face when she gives in to it." Carleigh sneered, his muscle language a little too tense. "It is not pretty."

Ignoring them both, Morgana kneeled by Vivienne's still unconscious body. "I will do it. Go with Carleigh instead and secure this place, so no one can breach the walls we set."

"Are you still thinking about that mutt?" Carleigh snickered.

"No. Rather, the unknown but powerful Fae that has eluded us all for this long." Morgana's contradicting tone was sharp.

Carleigh pursed his lips, then left in a hurry. With one last look to his mother, Mordred followed.

Now alone with Vivienne, Morgana took her hand in hers, and connected much like Mordred had. She sensed the well of corruption inside the enchantress, but also the purity. Its potency

caught her by surprise, and again she recalled what she had witnessed earlier.

A mystery for another day.

Once she had identified where the darkness lay, Morgana sank the power of her psyche in it. Only, instead of bringing it to the surface like Mordred had planned, she absorbed some within her—and the rest she tried to stifle.

When the entire operation concluded, she was panting and wiping away sweat.

For now, at least, you will resist it.

* * *

They had been walking for long enough that Sébastien knew something was up. Though he tried to bide his time, he had no patience for games. After a few more moments, he came to an abrupt stop.

"You said you would explain, yet here we are, and still no word."

Ardea glanced up at him, a half-smile tugging at the corner of her lips. "Very well. Let us start with your presence here. I take it Atrox had some kind of magical idea?"

Sébastien's brow furrowed. "He gave up that life, and no longer goes by that name."

"Funny. Yet he agreed to a deal Morgana offered him to kill you, in exchange for returning to his full capabilities."

He tilted his head to the side, analyzing the goddess' comments. A slow smile spread on his face, then he could no longer contain it and burst out laughing.

"And what, pray tell, is so amusing?" Ardea pursed her lips, removing her arm from his.

The knight sobered up and folded both arms across his chest. "No, you are done asking questions. My turn—or I will figure this out myself."

Ardea scowled, but inclined her head in agreement.

"How did you know about Morgana's deal?"

A long look steadied on him. "Did you really believe we would not keep watch on our brother? Canine or human, he is still blood of my blood—family."

"Right..." Sébastien dragged the word out, getting more suspicious by the second. "So your attention to his every movement had nothing to do with fearing he would rebel and wreak havoc on you again?"

Her eyes darkened, and she pursed her lips. "Watch it, knight. Tread carefully unless you wish to upset the gods."

"Alistair took no deal," Sébastien revealed, watching closely for a reaction.

"That's impossible. We saw him–heard him."

"You only witnessed what we wanted you to see, as did the Halflings and Carleigh."

"And why would he do that?"

"Because it was the only way I could find out what happened eons ago, when I and Carleigh were brothers—and gods."

Ardea did not blink, confirming his suspicion she knew the story.

"So what useful information can you give me, goddess?"

She crinkled her nose, then faced the castle in the lake, pointing to it. "If you swim there and arrive unharmed, there will be a portal. It will take you to the memories you have forgotten, and much more."

Sébastien peered at the area she had outlined for him, squinting against the glare of the sun. "And why do I sense it's not so simple?"

When no answer came, he turned back to Ardea—but she had disappeared.

* * *

Alistair kept watch on Vivienne's house—and it was so he found out they were blocking the area and using spells. *Catriona cannot feel anything now. She will be blind to their plans.*

He cloaked his presence and slunk further into the shadows, choosing for the occasion his demon dog body with dark fur. Night settled on the town, and still he remained there, unmoving.

Eventually, sleep overcame him.

"Took you long enough."

Alistair whirled around, gaping when he noticed Merlin standing there. The wizard was imprisoned—in fact, they were in the room of the castle where he had been all along.

"Took *me* long enough?" Alistair growled, then glanced down when he realized he was in human form.

Merlin's face contorted in pain, and a groan escaped him.

"I have little time—or strength."

"Carleigh really did a number on you, didn't he?" For the first time, Alistair pitied the mage, despite all the havoc he had caused.

Rather than answer, Merlin leveled a narrowed gaze on him. "Alistair, what happened? Why did you betray Vivienne?"

"Rest easy, old man. It was a ruse, one meant to send Sébastien deep into his subconscious and get Morgana off my back."

"Something tells me it did not work quite as you wished."

Alistair looked away, clenching his jaw. "I made the mistake of using Fae magic. But we are trying to fix it."

"Fae magic? *We*?" Merlin's glazed eyes sharpened on Alistair's face, and his obvious discomfort. "You bloody *bastard*! Are you sleeping with my sister?"

Alistair cringed, but tried to recover. "Half-sister, technically."

"That's still too good for you!"

"Oy!" The wolf god took a deep breath, then tried again. "Glad to see color back in those pale cheeks of yours, at least."

They stared at each other for a few tense moments, then a coughing fit shook Merlin. Alistair moved closer, trying to ease his pain but found the mage was still only a ghost in his dreams.

"There is nothing I can do," he whispered. "I'm sorry."

The coughing fit reappeared, lasting longer this time, then Merlin asked another question. "Do you love her, at least?"

"I…" The words stuck in his throat, and Alistair swallowed hard to push them back down. "I will not hurt her, I swear to you."

Merlin met his gaze then and nodded. "I hope Catriona knows what she is doing. Now, as for Sébastien. Tell me what went wrong."

Once Alistair brought him up to speed, including about Mordred's presence in Vivienne's house, Merlin's demeanor darkened considerably. Still, there was some measure of hope he could catch from the wizard—and could not understand.

When he asked him about it, Merlin grinned. "I took a page out of Morgana's book and bound her to me. She cannot let Vivienne or her baby get hurt, on pain of death. And since she is no longer immortal…"

"Still the same cunning old wizard," Alistair laughed and clapped him on the shoulder.

His smile slipped when he noticed the orb in a corner, its center halfway filled with red embers. "What is that?"

Merlin glanced down and sighed. "I had hoped you would not notice, especially now you told me about Catriona. That is Carleigh's parting gift—a magical bomb set to detonate on the full moon when he plans to sacrifice Vivienne."

Alistair stumbled back, eyes wide on the wizard. "He plans to destroy you?"

"Come now, my friend, surely it is not such a shock as that."

Alistair shook his head. "So regardless of whether we save Vivienne, this will still go off?"

"Yes." Merlin's tone was calm, almost resigned. "And you have to promise me you will not let Catriona be around for it. My sister has done enough—more than enough—to help us out. I will not put her more in peril than she already is."

"I will protect her," Alistair said.

"Perhaps. But right now the only thing that keeps her safe is that Carleigh is unaware of her identity. Let us keep it that way, my friend."

Alistair was not on board with the decision, but until he could find a different solution, he might as well agree to it, if only to give Merlin peace of mind.

"I promise," he said, placing a closed fist over his heart. "You have my word I will not endanger Catriona by revealing what is going on."

Merlin's eyes narrowed, trying to find a loophole in the vow, but there was none. Satisfied, he blurred out of the dream.

"Wait!" Alistair took a step closer, arm extended as though to hold him back. "What of Sébastien?"

His face was already fading, but his voice was still strong. "I had a vision that sparked this encounter. Sébastien is alive, and your sister paid him a visit. He has a journey to complete—one can hope he will achieve it before time runs out."

Alistair spoke to what was now an empty landscape, unsure if they would ever meet again. "Thank you. For this, and for your friendship over the centuries, my friend. May fate shine upon you and keep you safe."

From the edge of his subconscious, a single phrase floated back. *And on you.*

CHAPTER 14

It was a dream like any other—or so Vivienne thought. It had not been easy, but Mordred had put her to sleep. There was something at the edge of her consciousness, but the enchantress could not pin it.

After their little experiment, Mordred had declared she was not beyond saving, but that it would take time. He had to remain around her at all times, and she would have to dig deeper than she felt comfortable in the well of darkness in order to both expunge some and also learn to control it.

Though in theory his advice helped ease her worries, Vivienne still struggled. Dark thoughts seemed to follow her around, and at times when they used magic she had the uncanny sensation hers was polluted.

Perhaps to those thoughts, as well as her pregnancy, her sleep had not improved. That same evening, she was tossing and turning, until finally she had slipped into a fitful rest–and the dream that ensued.

The overall environment had everything to do with her past, and nothing with her current reality. By the time the familiarity of the forest sank in, it was too late. Vivienne stepped through in a daze until she was by a lake—and the castle in its midst.

Thoughts of all she had lost, most recently Sébastien, assailed her with an intensity that was crippling. She had to lean against the tree, unable to step further without falling apart.

Vivienne had tried her hardest to hold it together, if only for her baby. It was the reason behind her fighting the darkness– the *only* reason. Nothing else mattered except the little bundle of life growing within her, as it was the last link she had with

Sébastien. Losing him so brutally had cast her into an abyss of loneliness and pain, and she feared she would never be able to escape from it.

The particularly bright moon drew her gaze, though it was only a crescent. "What did I do to deserve all this pain? I have nothing left. *Nothing*!"

A shadow moved, and she jumped away from her hiding place as if scorched. There would be no Sébastien this time around to save her. Her steps brought her by the pool of water and as if her thoughts had conjured him, she heard his voice.

"Vivienne!"

She whirled around, thinking she was going crazy. But there stood Sébastien, dressed in a beige toga, as handsome as when she had last seen him. Her body went utterly still, her legs barely able to keep her upright.

"This is unreal," she breathed, unable to believe what she was seeing.

Sébastien's eyes widened with shock, but he moved closer to her. The corner of his mouth lifted in a half-grin. "Fancy meeting you here, my love."

Still stunned, Vivienne stood unmoving until he was mere inches from her. Tears cascaded down her cheeks, and she took shaky, broken breaths as if to fill her lungs with air she had been missing.

Sébastien's gaze roamed over her, taking her in with just as much intensity, whispering low. "You should not be here."

He caught her frown then, and something flickered in his gaze—almost like a curtain drawing over, masking his thoughts.

"I've missed you." Vivienne's admission tore from her throat, a near-anguished whimper.

Sébastien shifted at that, pulling her into his arms and holding her tightly. He breathed in her citrus fragrance, wishing nothing more than to be with her for real. His mouth moved to the side of her forehead, kissing her. Vivienne's own lips sought his, brushing against him with desperate yearning.

"And I missed you, beloved."

By the time he pulled back from the kiss, Vivienne was crying again. Sébastien wiped them away with careful touches.

"Please don't," he pleaded.

Vivienne shook her head, unable to stop her cascading waterfalls. She clenched his garment in her fists. "You're gone, and Alistair is to blame!"

At his silence, she looked up. "What is it?" Sébastien had the most conflicted look on his face, but all he did was shake his head.

"Nothing." Much as he wished otherwise, they had come

this far without telling her anything. It was imperative she remained in the dark—for the time being at least.

His gaze lowered to her stomach, and he touched her cheek, a swift caress. "Take care of yourself, and our baby."

Vivienne frowned, uncomprehending. Then she scanned their surroundings, finally registering where they were. "Why are we at Aisling Caisleán?"

Another thought followed right on the heels of that one, and Vivienne narrowed her gaze. "This...it doesn't feel like a dream. What's going on? I saw Alistair maul you to death."

He cringed, guilty for the image they had left in her mind and the hurt they caused. *How could we think this was for the better, hiding it all from her? And still he was nowhere closer to learning the truth about Carleigh's choices.*

"Love, I–" He tried to touch her, but Vivienne retreated in anger.

"You swore honesty, no matter what."

Sébastien looked away, running a hand through his hair. "Vivienne, it isn't that simple."

"What isn't?" she shouted. "Are you, or aren't you *dead*?"

He opened his mouth to respond, but the sky darkened and distracted him. He glanced back at Vivienne, and the lightning flashing in her eyes. "Are you doing this?"

The enchantress only stared at him, then looked behind as well. "No, I am not."

As though hearing her confession, the clouds whirled into the tube of a tornado. Before either of them could react, the force of nature headed towards them. Sébastien pulled Vivienne into his arms, holding onto her tightly despite the high-strung wind.

"Sébastien, it's coming for me!"

Vivienne's panicked scream echoed above the deafening noise. She struggled against the pull, trying to return to the safety of his embrace. "I love you, please know that, no matter what. I don't care about the lies, about anything. Just please come back to

me, if you can…" Her vision blurred, and she tried to hold on tighter. "Sébastien, I cannot live without you."

She rose on her tiptoes then and crushed her mouth to his. He answered in kind, deepening the kiss until neither knew where the other began. But still the tornado drew closer, and he felt it yanking Vivienne from him.

"No!" he growled, gripping her hard enough to bruise, but to no avail.

The wind dragged her away, and in a last moment their eyes connected. Sébastien said the one thing he wanted her to remember, above all. "I love you."

Then Vivienne vanished. Only instead of the tornado disappearing with her, it taunted him, circling him until he lost his temper. "What is it you wish!?"

"Vivienne," the wind whispered in a voice he recognized only too well as Mordred's. "And I will have her."

The knight's roar was lost amidst the noise.

* * *

Sébastien could practically hear the clock ticking—it was time. Vivienne was in trouble and would continue to be unless he returned. The thought of Mordred anywhere near her was enough to put him in a blind rage.

Despite this, the knight tried to quiet his fast-beating heart.

He missed her like he missed air, but the entire journey could be in jeopardy if his head was not in the game. What that meant was that he had to forget about anything else except his real purpose.

If it was true, if he was a god—or had been at some long forgotten time in the past—then he had to know. *If there's even a slim chance for me to access those powers like Alistair can...* The opportunities were endless.

Sébastien set his gaze on the castle in the distance and the limpid water. "You better be right about this, Alistair," he complained under his breath. Then he pulled the toga off and waded into the lake, naked.

At first, the cool liquid seemed to embrace him, enough so that he dunked under, then broke through to the surface for air. But as he swam, each stroke became harder, and he had to dispense more energy.

When he opened his eyes to see what the issue was, Sébastien realized the water had become a viscous mass, thicker than pudding. *No wonder I can barely move!* He glanced behind, but the shore had disappeared in a mist.

He kept pushing forward, inhaling and exhaling heavily, his grunts echoing across. Despite his best efforts, his old home remained distant, and the lake seemed to stiffen.

Sébastien caught another breath but immediately sensed the water close in, almost crushing his body. He shifted again, and the mass moved with him. *So either I keep going and fight against the tide, or I stop and get squashed.*

Gritting his teeth against the impossibility of the task, he pushed his sore muscles onwards. *I've come too far to give up now.*

As though the thought alone had started it, his entire body glowed. The brightness that emanated spread across the water, and he had the sensation he was advancing. *Progress!* His jubilation dimmed when right as he got closer to the castle, something dragged him underwater.

To his surprise, what he found in its depths was not some monster, but rather a reflection of himself. The replica was also naked, but cuts, bruises and wounds covered him. His eyes shone cold, mouth pulled into a sneer.

Sébastien understood this was the worst version of himself. *But what the heck am I supposed to do?* At a loss and hoping he was not misinterpreting the vision, he extended a hand in help, trying to communicate his intention. His reflection glanced down at the gesture, then grasped his forearm.

Instead of shaking it in agreement, the twin yanked Sébastien closer and grabbed his throat with his free hand. Caught by surprise, the knight expelled the last bit of air from his lungs. Before he could defend himself, he was pulled deeper and water invaded his nostrils.

A coughing fit gripped him and his entire body twisted to escape the vice-grip hold, in vain. The reflection had grabbed him and did not plan to let him go, it was apparent in the distant gaze.

Sébastien's vision blurred, everything around him disappearing as he narrowed onto his attacker. *If help isn't the answer, what is?* By the time his brain caught up, he was already half unconscious. Still, one word rang loud and clear in his mind.

Fight.

Sébastien lifted a hand, feeling like it weighed a thousand

pounds, and set it to the wrist of his attacker. As he gripped weakly, the same glow from before lighted his body, and permeated the replica.

His eyes widened, mouth open in a scream of horror. He released Sébastien, who floated straight to the surface with the last of his energy. When he finally breached through, he turned to his back, floating as he inhaled large gulps of air.

"Damn!" His sputtered curses echoed above the now tranquil lake. "Who the hell came up with *that* test of endurance?"

Once he had his fill oxygen, Sébastien flipped over and sloppily waded through the remaining distance. He was unsurprised to notice the castle was now closer than before.

After a few more breast strokes, he caught sand under his feet and stepped out of the water. The minute he was clear of the lake, he was once more clothed with the toga from before. No longer fazed by anything that was happening, Sébastien headed towards the entrance.

Oddly, the place was the same as he remembered. Same white walls, same impression of purity and peace. Vivienne had created the sanctuary at a time when her despair had no limits, yet it had become her most precious achievement.

Sébastien sighed, trying to put away thoughts of his beloved from his mind. What had the trail proven? That he had magic? He did not feel changed, only frustrated.

Aimless wandering around the main entrance soon proved him wrong. He noticed a faint light by the sun room. His feet started towards it before he could even decide whether or not he still wanted to learn the truth. Once he passed the corner and entered, he faced what Ardea had described: a portal.

About the size of a regular door, it was brilliant enough to blind anyone. *What is this thing made of, crystal and rainbows?*

Toning down his inner monologue, Sébastien stepped closer, covering his face with one arm. Unseeing, he stumbled straight into the vortex, which then swallowed him whole.

* * *

"He's alive, then?"

Catriona could not hide her relief once Alistair related his encounter with Merlin. He had, of course, left out the part about the wizard's imminent death—though how it escaped her notice, he could only guess.

"Yes," he mumbled distractedly, still pacing and unwilling to rest.

"I thought you would be happier," Catriona pointed out. "What's the problem?"

Alistair sighed at that. *I have to give her something, else it will be my arse on the line. Damn you, Merlin.* He kept his ruminations to himself. "If Sébastien is well, I cannot understand why we are unable to sense it. You, at the very least."

Catriona frowned at that, then glanced at the floating knight. It had been easy enough to get his body into her realm, but perhaps something had gone wrong. When she voiced her worry out loud, Alistair shook his head.

"No, I doubt that is the cause. I've moved plenty between dimensions and never had an issue. Sébastien is a god underneath the mortal façade, the same restrictions should apply."

He joined her, staring at the knight's unconscious form as

they both tried to understand what had happened.

"Perhaps you should look to your own kind, wolf god."

Alistair whirled around at the voice, but found no one. It was Catriona who tugged on his hand, pulling him to the side and pointing to the trunk of a tree. "Over there."

The bark had changed to form the face of a man. Though Alistair did not know him personally, he recognized the familiar jaw and nose. "Merlyddus."

The elder Fae scowled, turning to his daughter. "I warned you to be careful, and still you did not listen."

"You would have let me sit on the sidelines and do nothing," she retorted, tossing her hair back and lifting her chin defiantly. "I could not."

There had been many occasions when Alistair was proud of her, but none quite as in that moment. He squeezed her hand and turned his midnight gaze to Merlyddus.

"With all due respect, majesty, your daughter saved more than just one life."

"I know," Merlyddus admitted. "But she paid a heavy price for it."

Alistair frowned at that, and her father read the expression well. His jaw clenched, voice tight with anger. "Catriona, the least you could have done is told him."

"Tell me what?"

She sighed, looking away as all fight dropped out of her. "I lost a fair amount of vital energy while doing the spell for Sébastien and you."

Alistair tapped his foot, knowing there was more. When she remained silent, he grasped her hand. "What else?"

"I've become linked to the knight."

"Meaning what, exactly?" His tone came out harsher than intended, but he could not stop himself.

Catriona pursed her lips, refusing to answer even when at a disadvantage. It was her father who delivered the missing piece, his voice regretful and jarring. "She can be hurt through him. Which means it is in your best intentions to keep that knight safe, and aware of his own powers."

The revelation struck Alistair quiet, but he kept his cool. His gaze met Catriona's, promising to finish the chat later, then he faced Merlyddus once more.

"I will ensure it," he promised. "But I need to speak with you—in private."

Catriona scowled, but when the elder Fae nodded, she left their sight. Alistair was not convinced she was truly gone, so he morphed into his animal shape and redoubled the efforts to safeguard his mind from intrusion.

Why the dramatic approach, wolf? Merlyddus asked.

Your daughter cannot know of this, Merlin made me swear. He waited a beat for some measure of reaction, but when none came, he continued. *Do I have your word?*

I was not aware the promise of a Fae means so much to you, considering your history.

Alistair growled at that. *Do I or not? Merlin's fate depends on it.*

It was enough to quiet Merlyddus. *I vow not to speak of it to my daughter.*

Very well. You must know what has happened with Morgana and your grandson, I presume?

The man inclined his head, but made no comment once more, leaving Alistair free leave to proceed. *Then you are aware they left Merlin behind. It so happens Carleigh also dropped a magical gadget there. It is set to explode around the same time Vivienne will be sacrificed, killing Merlin as well.*

For a long moment, Merlyddus said nothing. When he spoke again, the hard tone was not what Alistair had expected.

Keep your nose out of this, wolf god. I can protect my son, but I warn you for the last time to stay the hell away from them going forward. Are we understood?

Taken aback, Alistair could only stare. It was in that moment Catriona sprinted around the corner, her pretty face drawn into another scowl. "Are you two quite done?"

Alistair switched back to his human form then and turned to her. In response to her question, he searched her gaze for a brief moment—there was no sign she had heard anything. So he did the only thing he could in the circumstances, and kissed her deeply. When he next glanced at the tree, Merlyddus had vanished.

Unsettled at the pang in his heart, he met Catriona's gaze. "Care to explain why you wouldn't tell me your little issue?"

She sighed, then moved closer and melted her body against his. "I did not wish to worry you. And, I knew you would keep Sébastien safe."

"You put a lot of faith in me, darling," Alistair smirked. "But it is well placed."

He crushed his mouth to hers once more and they dropped to the ground, tangled in a mass of limbs.

* * *

Morgana stirred awake with a start, an unease building in the pit of her stomach. She had left Mordred with Vivienne once more, and she and Carleigh had occupied a spot in the woods nearby, camping under the stars.

She scrutinized their surroundings, looking for the necromancer, and found him a few feet away. In his sleep, he was muttering—it was that which had woken her up.

Intrigued, Morgana threw off the blanket she had on and tiptoed near him. Between incoherent mumbles, she leaned closer and caught a single threat. "She was meant to be *mine*."

The sorceress moved her hand to Carleigh's shoulder, intending to shake him awake. Yet the instant her fingers touched him, a barrier struck her with enough force to fly into the nearest tree. While her body slumped down, her soul joined the sorcerer and one other in the netherworld, in a quest neither was prepared for.

CHAPTER 15

"Are you sure about this?" Alistair turned from the lake to face Catriona, eyes narrowed in thought. "Your father will have my hide if this leads Morgana and her horde straight to you."

The redheaded Fae was facing a large willow tree amid her forest, palms already stretched on its bark, gripping it until her knuckles whitened.

"Yes," she threw over her shoulder. "If Sébastien is safe as you say, one of us needs to tell Vivienne. She is giving in too much to Mordred, and this might buy us some time."

"So let me."

"Lover, you know if you appear out of the blue she will not listen. But I am a stranger, thus more likely to get through."

Alistair continued pacing, not convinced. Noticing his distress, Catriona released the tree and walked over him. She rose on her tiptoes and kissed his cheek. "No harm will come to me, I promise."

In an unusual show of emotion, he grabbed her by the waist and pulled her close, burying his head in her neck. "You had best be," he muttered against her skin.

Then she left his embrace and he allowed the space. His midnight eyes were unreadable, but Catriona could tell by the clenched jaw that he was on edge. She turned back to the willow tree, attempting to clear her mind.

Though she found the wolf god's worry endearing, she could not help but wonder if that was all he felt for her. Months had passed since they had rekindled, and their connection was strong—too much so.

Realizing she was drifting off again, Catriona closed herself to all else except the magic surrounding her. She dug her palms into the trunk to ground herself, then reached out with her psyche across dimensions. It was not long before she encountered Vivienne's subconscious—the enchantress was asleep.

Due to Alistair's worry, Catriona threaded carefully. *It would not do to get caught so close to the end game.* Though she guarded her thoughts, Morgana and Carleigh would be keeping an eye out for any intrusions—hence why the wolf god was concerned.

Not sensing anything odd, the Fae dug deeper into Vivienne's psyche. She felt her pain, her despair over losing her love, and tears streamed down her cheeks in response. Caught as she was at the moment, she did not notice it as first.

Then the darkness was there, and Catriona had nowhere to go. It was closing in, attempting to entrap Vivienne's mind and corrupt it. In so doing, it was reaching out to the Fae as well. She pulled back, recoiling, but a light soon stopped it in its tracks.

Catriona took advantage of the respite to connect with Vivienne. Pressed for time, she had to keep the message short. *Sébastien is alive, Vivienne. Do not despair and do not give in. You will be together again, soon.*

The Fae was about to retreat, hoping it had done the trick. But the magic keeping the darkness at bay intrigued her, and she stopped for a closer look. Once she touched it, Catriona was struck into her own dimension, blasted away from Vivienne's psyche and forcefully returned to her own.

Alistair noticed her rigidity and joined her in two long strides. "What happened?"

Her blue eyes were dark with confusion when she faced him. "I delivered the message, but... Darkness was within her, trying to change her mind. Something stopped it."

Alistair frowned, but the look on her face told him there was more. "Some*thing* or some*one*?"

Catriona shook her head as though not believing it. "It was Morgana."

When Alistair did not react, she became suspicious. "You knew about this?"

"No, darling. I was only aware that Merlin tricked her, and she swore a magical oath. She has to protect Vivienne and, if all else fails, her son."

Catriona gaped in shock, but soon recovered. "My, my.

And you said they were only good for destruction together."

Alistair rolled his eyes, unwilling to admit she had been right. "It is the truth. Did you notice anything else in Vivienne?"

"She is in pain... A lot of it."

A glance to Sébastien, followed by a muttered curse. "Then we should do our best to jerk the knight back to reality, no?"

Catriona tracked his gaze, then nodded. "How?"

"If he is in a deep sleep, only a rather momentous occasion would wake him up." His eyes moved upwards to the sky. "Lightning."

The Fae bit her lip, wondering at the safety. When she voiced her concerns, Alistair stubbornly refused to listen. "If he does not wake up, Vivienne will not recover. And we have less than three days before all hell breaks loose."

Catriona sighed and pointed her to the knight. His floating form moved until he was above the water. Alistair waded deep into it and held out his hand.

"What are you doing?" she asked.

"I need a connection to him. If this does not wake him up, at the very least it might send me wherever he is." His dark gaze fell on Sébastien. "Then I can do the rest."

Though she did not agree, Catriona knew it was a waste to argue. So she raised her other palm and pointed it to the sky, calling lightning to her. Her eyes met Alistair's, and she mouthed, *Be safe.* Then she dropped her hand.

Atmospheric electricity struck them both, illuminating their shapes. By the time she could look again, Alistair had vanished, and Sébastien was still unconscious.

* * *

Carleigh and Sébastien were at a standoff, Vivienne lying dead on the ground. As their parents focused on the couple, the necromancer—then god—slipped away.

Through portals he hopped until he returned to his own

domain. Flames shot out of his hands, destroying everything in his path. Creatures scurried about, unwilling to take the heat from their master.

When he finished—and it took a long time—Carleigh turned to a mirror that occupied the darkest corner of the room.

"You promised me power! Light should not have died in this fight, Justice was meant to!"

The glass shimmered until two red eyes poked out of a fog of darkness. "If she passed on, it was fate's wish."

Carleigh approached threateningly with clenched fists. "I was supposed to control fate!"

Laughter echoed in the room, and he stepped away in fear.

"The only one who controls death is I," the entity whispered. "Now pay me what you promised."

"No!" Carleigh said. "This was not our understanding."

One moment the god was standing, facing off with the entity. The next, he had flown halfway across with an intensity that left him panting on the ground.

Fog then dripped out of the mirror onto the pristine floors and inched towards him, taking its time. And still the voice spoke, unrelenting.

"You can either give me willingly, or I will take it forcefully/"

Carleigh whimpered, then extended one arm. In the other, he materialized a knife and cut across the vein. Blood pooled everywhere, but he did not stop it nor try to heal it. Darkness climbed on him, covering his wrist and sucking away.

"The son of the originals, ripe for the taking," Darkness whispered. "What a prize this is."

Only the sounds of dripping blood resonated for a few

moments, and Carleigh sensed his vision blurring.

"You are mine now, Ambition. Always and forever."

"Light..."

The entity sneered, then said, "If you so wish her, I can send you to where they went."

Carleigh opened drowsy eyes and struggled to focus. "Where..."

"Your precious Light and her lover reincarnated. They chose mortal lives that will allow them to live together, forever, over and over again. You can choose to join them, as the shadow designed to break them apart. But be warned: by becoming my champion, you surrender these memories and godly powers, and will sustain yourself with what I give you." A pause, then, "Do you accept?"

"I do."

The fog fully wrapped him then, and Carleigh dozed off.

"Sleep, little god. For when you wake up, the process will be complete."

* * *

Morgana woke up from the vision with a start. She slowly stood, her gaze never once leaving Carleigh. What she had seen...

As though sensing her discomfort, the necromancer jumped up as well. His eyes could not focus, haunted by the memories he had recovered. Still, he caught Morgana's gaze on him and faced her.

"What is it?" His voice was cold, and she would have thought he was unaffected. But underneath the tone she could detect a faint shaking, and it was enough confirmation of the truth.

"Anything you would like to share?" Morgana threw.

Carleigh's brow furrowed in confusion, then he scowled. "What has gotten into you, woman?"

Morgana stepped closer, glaring and clenching her fists. "How about the fact you forgot to mention your lineage—specifically, that you used to be a god?"

Carleigh paled at the accusation. "How would you know that?"

"Fair is only fair, necromancer. You entered my dreams, I had the right to invade yours."

If he had been shocked before, Carleigh turned incensed. His eyes shot daggers at her, hands clenching as though he wished to wrap them around her neck. "How *dare* you!?"

Morgana raised her chin defiantly, refusing to answer.

Through much willpower, Carleigh controlled his impulse of throttling her. "So what if I am? What business is it of yours? This changes nothing."

"It changes *everything*," Morgana retorted. "Perhaps you didn't know of the Cardinal Rule of gods, put into effect after Vivienne's untimely death back then."

His blank gaze was confirmation, but also further enraged Morgana. *To think we trusted our lives to him!* "You cannot kill Vivienne, Carleigh. And to attempt it would mean cursing everyone involved."

"So?"

His indifferent tone did not fool her. "I will not let my son become a pawn in the game of gods, nor yours. You can do as you wish going forward, but we are done."

She turned to leave, but his laugh stopped her. "And you

think it's that easy, to break contact with me? Where will you go, sorceress? To your precious Merlin? To be one big happy family?"

Something about his snicker had Morgana whirl around to face him. Noticing the real amusement in his gaze, shivers ran up her spine. "What did you do?"

"I made sure Merlin never leaves that prison alive." As he spoke, Carleigh waved his hand in a counter clock circle and a shifting in the air showed Morgana her ex-lover—and the magical device in a corner.

Her gray eyes turned to lightning when she faced the necromancer fully. "You bastard!" she yelled. "Merlin was meant to be mine, you swore!"

"Deals are meant to be broken," Carleigh snickered. "This is our new one: stay with me, and see this to the end, and I will ensure you and your son live. Oppose me, and you will both die atrocious deaths as sacrifices to Darkness."

"You forget who you speak to, necromancer," Morgana retorted and pointed an index his way. "I am the daughter of a king, and he raised me to never bow my head."

To punctuate her statement, she shot two blasts of fire towards him. Caught unawares, Carleigh's cape burned, and he had to throw it off.

He was no longer amused when he squared off with her, now only in a tunic and pants. "Be it so."

He then gathered magic in his joined palms and aimed it at the sorceress. When his attack met with hers, it exploded into filigrees of diamonds—and the surrounding forest shook.

* * *

Vivienne stood overlooking the lake, wringing her hands and biting her lip. Words from a stranger echoed in her head, stuck in a loop.

Sébastien is alive, Vivienne. Do not despair and do not give in. You will be together again, soon.

The possibility of it was enough to give her hope, but she dreaded if it became untrue. *How can I survive losing him again?*

"What is on your mind?"

She turned at Mordred's voice and gratefully took the cup of tea he offered her. As she was about to sip, the tell-tale scent of

alcohol wafted up to her nose.

The enchantress glanced at him, amused. "Trying to get me tipsy?"

He had the good grace to look bashful. "I thought some scotch might help soothe your nerves."

Vivienne shook her head, chuckling. "If only I could. Unfortunately, one downside of pregnancy is I cannot consume alcohol."

"Ah.... Yes, I had forgotten." His gaze dropped to her stomach, then he shrugged. He removed the cup from her hand, downing it in a single gulp. "Why so pensive?"

"I... Sébastien may be alive."

Mordred froze, and it was abrupt enough the surrounding energy shifted. Vivienne glanced at him, surprised. "Are you alright?"

His gaze had darkened, but still he answered, "Fine." After a beat where he inhaled and exhaled slowly, he asked, "What makes you think so?"

"A voice in my head," Vivienne whispered, avoiding his look. She was aware how crazy it sounded, but the tone had been truthful and the message urgent. That, coupled with the dream where she had seen him, had been enough to convince her.

Mordred's laughter snapped her out of her thoughts. She turned to him then, pursing her lips. "How is my plight funny to you?"

"Shouldn't you have stopped hoping, by now?"

Vivienne's eyes widened at his words—and even more so at the tone. "What's wrong?"

Mordred stared back at her for a beat, his gaze heated. She could almost swear he was about to say something when his stare rose a fraction to somewhere over her shoulder. Surprise crossed his face before he could mask it.

Intrigued, Vivienne was about to turn around but Mordred grasped her hand and stopped her. "I do not wish you to hurt again," he answered, though the words sounded forced. "I have been here these last few days, seen your pain at losing Sébastien. Whatever you feel… I would not trust it."

Vivienne nibbled on her bottom lip, trying to gauge the seriousness of his statement. "But what if he is?"

Mordred tore his gaze from what distracted him. "If he was, do you not think he would be by your side, since you are carrying his child?"

She had to admit the reasoning made sense. It was much more plausible that her desperate mind had conjured reasons to convince herself Sébastien was alive when in fact it was a poor attempt at holding onto something that was already lost.

"I don't know what to think anymore," she whispered. The

tea lay forgotten on the table now, and she sensed tears gathering once more.

Mordred was silent again, staring at something in the distance. "What is it that has your attention?" she wondered, turning her face away.

He gripped her chin instead, forcing her gaze on him. That heated gaze was back in his glare and before she could figure out what he was doing, he crushed his lips to hers.

Vivienne recoiled immediately, slamming her palms against his chest and shoving him off her. In her anger, a bit of magic shot out with the movement and Mordred ended up blasted into the bookshelf. As he fell to the ground, groaning, the enchantress turned.

At first, she noticed nothing. Then she realized there was lightning in the forest—no, not lightning. Various colors were shooting back and forth, and her senses picked up a disturbance.

Rather than wait, she stepped out the door and headed towards it. Mordred's muttered curses resonated behind, but she could not care less, instead picking up the pace.

Soon, she was on the edge of the forest and heard shouts.

"You witless sorcerer, how do you think it looks that all this time you've been after her not because you detest her very existence, but because you *love* her?"

"I do not!"

The woman's voice was unfamiliar, but the man...

This is impossible. Still, she stepped through some trees until she ended up in a clearing. And there, in its midst, was Carleigh battling a woman with long black hair.

"You!" Vivienne shouted, unable to believe her eyes.

Carleigh spun to her, jaw slightly agape. The sorceress did, too, her face a mask of surprise and wariness.

"Where is Mordred?"

As if her words had conjured him, the man himself showed up by Vivienne's side, panting.

"I tried to stop her, mother."

"*Mother?*" Vivienne took the scene in, her eyes darting between the three. Things that made little sense previously now mixed about in her head, and the emerging picture was not reassuring in the least. "What is going on?"

"Come back to the house," Mordred entreated, a hand held up in invitation. "I will explain everything."

"No." Vivienne was adamant, her palms already heating in warning. "Tell me *now*. What is Carleigh doing here? Do you know him?"

If Mordred had been about to lie, the necromancer beat him to it. "Of course he knows me! It was him and Morgana that helped me escape, foolish one!"

Vivienne stared, then the implication of his words hit her. *If they supported Carleigh's flight, and it was thanks to me Mordred came through then...* She staggered at the realization, holding onto a trunk for support. "You... I...."

He played me. I was alone, vulnerable, and like an idiot I listened to everything he said.

"Ah, you have caught on," the sorcerer grinned. "How about you be a good girl and forget everything?"

His hand moved up as though to strike her, but Vivienne's eyes flashed and a shield rose to protect her. "I think you're done playing games with me." Her gaze slid over Morgana, then to Mordred. "*All* of you."

Mordred opened his mouth to say something, but Morgana

intervened. "We did not intend to. Carleigh—"

"Shut *up!*" the necromancer yelled, and the attack aimed for Vivienne struck Morgana instead. "I warned you. Stay with me, or oppose me and die."

The sorceress got back to her feet with Mordred's help. She coughed, but seemed otherwise unharmed. When Carleigh was about to shoot again, he found he could not move his arm. Incensed, he glared at Mordred, but the young man was staring elsewhere.

Carleigh followed his gaze to Vivienne, whose outstretched hand was pointed right at him—and restraining him. "You don't want to do this."

"I think I'm done taking advice from all of you," Vivienne retorted darkly. With a flick of her wrist, Carleigh flew into a tree.

The enchantress then stepped closer to Morgana and Mordred, her expression pained. "I trusted you," she told Mordred. "I listened to you, and you tricked me, all to bring this man back."

"It was just business, love," he mocked to hide his own annoyance at having been found out. "I needed something from him, and he agreed in exchange for his freedom."

Somehow, his dismissal hurt more than the actual betrayal. She searched the blue gaze she had thought caring, now recognizing only a cold calculation in its depths.

"And did you get what he promised you?"

Mordred's scowl and shifting gaze were enough answer. Vivienne had to appreciate his acting skill, shaking her head at her own naïveté.

"Too bad. We could have been friends." She ignored his

stricken expression, magic already at work. Her body warmed up and became aglow, then she vanished.

Vivienne reappeared near another lake, by Ross Castle in the same region as the Killarney Park she had visited with Sébastien. She scoured the surroundings to make sure no tourists were there, then found a dark corner inside the walls and curled up. The sobs that wrecked her vibrated through the stone, but only wind and air were witness to it.

CHAPTER 16

Once the enchantress had disappeared, Morgana turned to Mordred. "What scared her off?"

He shrugged, unwilling to admit his weakness. "She has been hard to turn. Do you think we have lost our chance?"

Morgana frowned at the ground, lost in ruminations. "Perhaps."

"Then you had best find a solution," Carleigh threatened as he emerged from the bushes. "Otherwise, mark my words, you will both pay for this."

Mordred scowled at the necromancer, already well past his patience limits. "You forget who freed you, sorcerer."

Morgana's hand on his shoulder had him glance down. Her brow creased infinitesimally, then she addressed Carleigh. "You will have what you want. Come, Mordred."

With one last dark look to Carleigh, he followed his mother until they were well away from him. "What was that about?"

"While you were busy, I found out something interesting about our companion."

Morgana then summarized her findings, eyes unwavering from Mordred's expression. The young man seemed as stunned as she had been at the revelation, though he recovered quickly.

"So what does this change?"

"As far as Carleigh is concerned, nothing. But between you and me, as of today, we no longer support him."

"Why?"

Morgana sighed, knowing it was well past time to reveal the other side of the coin. "Long ago, gods could do whatever it pleased them. When Vivienne died, they came up with a set of

rules. The first one, the Cardinal Rule, was that no god could kill another. The price to pay if infringed was a life for a life."

She paused, trying to gather her thoughts. "Carleigh cannot complete that ritual without our help, which means we would be accomplices in killing Vivienne. But in using Fae magic, we risk it going awry—and then the consequence could fall on any of us: you, me or Carleigh. While I do not mind if he dies because of his hubris, I wish no harm to come to you."

Mordred recalled what she had already paid to revive him, and sighed. "I see your point. What of Vivienne, then?"

"For the moment, we pretend to stay by Carleigh but facilitate nothing for him. When the time of the sacrifice comes in a few days, we will pull away for good."

"And go where?" he pressed.

"To your father," Morgana revealed. "We will force him to help us. With his magic alongside yours and mine, we can open a portal and head somewhere safe."

Mordred wanted to argue, but knew it was useless. So he kept his thoughts to himself—and the intention not to leave Vivienne behind. Instead, he nodded like a dutiful son and left it at that.

* * *

"Atrox, you need to see this."

Catriona's urgent tone had him blink, rubbing at his eyes. He was spread over a large boulder, still naked from their amorous romps. He lifted his head slightly, admiring the Fae's backside as she peered into the lake.

"How about you come back here for another round?" His voice was full of innuendo, even as his body warmed up at the prospect of lovemaking.

Catriona threw him a look over her shoulder, blue eyes dancing with amusement. "Much as that is tempting, this is important. It concerns Vivienne."

Alistair snapped to at that and was by her side in a few lengthy strides. His gaze lowered to where Catriona pointed: an image of Vivienne.

His mistress was pacing on the rampart of a castle, near water from what he could tell. There was no sign of Morgana or her cohorts. "She's alone?"

"It appears so."

"Where is she? My physical body can get to her now."

Catriona could not take her eyes off the image. "What if it's a trap?"

"A risk I have to take," Alistair shrugged.

"Atrox—"

He shut her up with a kiss that went on much longer than intended. "*Not* my name, darling. Where is she?"

Catriona ran her palm over the water once, and the image sharpened. "Seems to be near a large forest."

"I'll find it then. She must have gone to a place Sébastien took her, or close by."

"I can distract Morgana and the rest," Catriona offered, but he was already shaking his head.

"No, I refuse to put you in their path again."

"This protective streak of yours is getting tedious," the Fae mumbled.

"And you still like it, otherwise you would not stand for it," he retorted and stole one more kiss. "Stay out of it, darling, I will handle this."

A few moments later, he woke up in his canine body.

* * *

Alistair moved as a shadow would through the forest. Nature and magic both hid his massive form—as did a sprinkle of Fae dust. His powerful muscles constricted and relaxed as he covered the last bit of distance. The earth shook under his paws, and the breeze hit him full force due to his speed.

It felt good to taste the power humming under the surface again—too good.

Be careful, Catriona warned in his mind. *Morgana and her cohorts may not be around, but perhaps not for long.*

I only need a minute.

For a moment, he pondered over what they had shared, and his own developing feelings for her. Never would he have believed that Catriona could become so entrenched in his life, yet there he was, pining for a Fae.

Alistair shook his head, clearing it of all thoughts. *Now is not the time.*

As the castle came into view, a low growl started down his throat. It was an instant reaction to what lay beyond and the potential to get his mistress back once and for all.

A small bridge stretched over a river that dumped into the lake. Further inland was a hill and atop it stood a gray tower, proud against the darkening sky. Stairs were to the side, and he paused to sniff.

Not catching anything, he ran to the courtyard inside. Though he glanced everywhere, he could not pick up Vivienne's scent—until it was too late.

"What the hell are *you* doing here?"

Alistair spun, ears flattening on his head. She wore a dark green gown that billowed around her body, though her stomach showed a faint bump. Her eyes were dull, features drawn tightly in anger.

Vivienne…

Before he could continue, she lifted a palm and air slammed into him. He ended up smacking the brick wall with a loud thump.

Alistair lay down, stunned for a brief second. Though he had not assumed a warm welcome, he had also not expected a full-on fight. He got back up, groaning. *Highness…*

"No!" Vivienne marching closer to him, eyes blazing and face flushed. "You don't get to use endearments as if I trust you, as if you did not betray me!"

I didn't! All his denial accomplished was to enrage her.

Another waft of air struck him, and Alistair flew further

into the courtyard this time. His head hit the wall, and he blacked out for a second. When he came to, Catriona's urgent voice was ringing in his ear.

Atrox, answer me, you damn fool!

He moved his tongue around, warily glancing at the enchantress that stood only a few feet away. *I am alright,* he addressed the Fae.

You are not! Vivienne is out of control.

Stay out of this, Catriona. Recognizing the harshness of his tone, he amended, *Please.*

No response came, and he sighed. *One more thing to deal with upon my return.* Movement out of the corner of his eye focused his attention on the matter at hand.

Vivienne, I did not betray you.

"And why should I believe that?" There was no softness in her voice, and her palm was already glowing with fire.

Alistair glanced at it uneasily, wondering how close she was to throwing it in his face. Luckily for him, those few moments of scrutiny saved his life. When he noticed her move, he jumped out of the way.

The fire ball aimed at his head shattered on the wall of the castle, leaving a black smudge on it. Cursing in frustration, Vivienne tried to follow him—and directed a few more attacks on his heels.

Alistair dodged them all, but with each one he sensed her uncontrollable anger. Despite being close to water, she was not taking the time to cool off.

The demon dog did the only thing he could think of: turned into his human form. He hoped the surprise would be big enough to give him a breather to speak.

Vivienne blinked in shock at the man now standing in front of her. Her hand lowered of its own accord, and she stood gaping. He was vaguely familiar, with dark hair, an olive complexion and–fully naked.

She averted her eyes until a moment later he had a toga over his well-built body. When she looked back at him, something tugged at her, nagging.

"Who *are* you?"

"You know me, Vivienne. You've seen me in this shape before…"

His rough voice raked her mind, and the memory hit her then.

"It has been a long time, princess." Vivienne turned around, eyes widening as they fell upon a dark haired man. He was clothed in only a toga and smiled paternally at her.

"Who are you?" she questioned in the same breath.

When he grinned, followed by a booming laugh, Vivienne gasped in recognition.

"Alistair!"

Before the full memory took over, Vivienne snapped back to. "You're him." Her tone was neutral, but Alistair noticed her hand was rising again.

He held up both palms in a gesture of peace and forced himself to speak softly. "I am not an enemy, highness."

"How can you say that," Vivienne cried, "when you killed Sébastien?"

With each spoken word, he inched closer. Her eyes now brimmed with tears, but he tried not to let her pain get to him.

"I did not. I would never betray you such."

When she shook her head in denial, he did not hesitate.

There had been another reason for morphing to human. In two quick strides, Alistair slammed against Vivienne—and they disappeared through the portal he had opened at her back.

They materialized by the end of the Killarney lakes, the purity of the water filling the air. Alistair's momentum had thrown them onto the grass, but he had been careful to take the brunt of the fall and play cushion to the enchantress.

Despite this, Vivienne struggled out of his arms. She looked around, eyes narrowed in suspicion. "Where are we?"

"Killarney Lakes, highness. You've been here before, remember? With Sébastien." Alistair waited until the darkness faded and only her regular green gaze remained.

She swayed a little, blinking back tears. "What's the point of all this, of denying your betrayal? You forget I witnessed what you did."

The wolf god moved into a kneeling position and grasped her hand in his. "I swear it was a fabrication, highness. See for yourself."

Same as Sébastien had done long ago, he opened his mind, letting the memories of the past few weeks flow to the surface. He let her discover his predicament, the voice in his head, Catriona, and finally, the plan devised with the knight.

Her eyes glazed over as she witnessed everything, with only the occasional start and whimper of distress. When she came back to, Vivienne frowned. "So it was all planned?"

Relief spread on Alistair's features at the acknowledgement. "Yes. But it failed." His voice lowered at the thought. "We played with Fae magic, and it backfired."

"But Sébastien... He's still here. Unharmed." Vivienne searched his gaze, and his heart squeezed at the anguish etched on her features.

"Indeed, highness. And I believe you can bring him back."

Vivienne gestured for him to stand. "I don't understand. We've been through so much together, you and me. Why not be honest with me from the beginning?"

Once more, he reached for her hand and squeezed it in his.

"You have been grappling with the corruption within you since the battle with Carleigh. Part of my silence was due to an unwillingness to worry you. The rest was because I feared what this revelation would do to you... In your current state."

Vivienne glanced down to her stomach, wrapping her free hand around it protectively. "My baby."

"Yes. The pregnancy has had both good and bad influences on you. When you give birth, you will expel the remnants of the darkness from you, and you will be a Lady of Light once more."

She tilted her head in response, catching the meaning between the lines. "But there is potential for worse?"

Alistair paused for a moment, but eventually nodded. "Yes. You could lose yourself before the it comes to completion."

The silence that followed had him tense, mainly in expectation of her reaction. But rather than a blowout, all Vivienne had were more questions. "Tell me more. Who is Morgana?"

Instead of jumping on the chance to explain, Alistair hesitated. "There is much more than that to find out. And all the memories are in you."

"Why wouldn't they have come to the surface when I remembered everything else?"

Alistair shrugged, unsure of the answer himself. "If I had to guess, I would say it is because of Morgana's spell. Fae magic takes actual concentration to break... Especially when dispensed in the amount she did."

"So how do I get to the truth?"

The wolf god jerked his chin towards the water. Vivienne followed his gaze, then glanced back at him, eyes full of questions.

"Lose yourself within these waters. They are the most similar to your lake from the past. The ancient powers underneath should be enough to help you break the cycle."

With an encouraging nod, Alistair put some distance between them, enough to avoid the lake's influence. Vivienne, meanwhile, inhaled a big gulp of air and stepped in the icy water, uncaring of her gown getting wet.

When she was hip-deep, Vivienne threw her head back and raised her palms to the sky. "What was forgotten..." She struggled for a moment, unsure how to voice what she needed.

Water sloshed around her, reassuring, calming and patient. Vivienne took her strength from it, then tried again. "Long ago, memories were stolen from me. Let what was taken be returned, given free and willing." In a whisper, she finished, "Release the walls in my mind, *please*."

Alistair watched, awed anew at how easily the elements responded to Vivienne. The sky darkened as lightning struck the lake. He stepped forward, but was blasted into a tree by the force conjured.

By the time he got up and looked at Vivienne, she was aglow with illumination. Everything seemed suspended as she slowly turned to him, and Alistair was speechless at the infinity in her gaze. The green eyes shone with unspoken emotion, yet their depths hid secrets from the beginning of...everything.

This is not Vivienne.

When the enchantress met his stare fully, he dropped to his knees. A sense of awareness ran through him, sharper than ever before. Whether due to his own lineage, or some genetic code engrained in him, he had no issue recognizing the goddess that now inhabited Vivienne.

"Gaia?"

Vivienne tilted her head to the side, smiling warmly. "I was called that, once. And many other names since, wolf god."

She stepped towards him fluidly, never quite leaving the water. A slim hand rose to his forehead, running a gentle touch through the soft dark hair, like a mother petting a child.

"You were greedy, eons ago." Her voice had changed too, holding within it the wisdom of all ages.

Alistair recalled the goddess had been the initial Mother, the original Light that had coursed through the universe. She had created gods and goddesses in her image, and his family branch stemmed from them.

Whatever her connection to Vivienne, he now understood the inexplicable urge he had had from the beginning, to protect his mistress. Even at four years old when they had first met she had radiated light.

It all makes sense.

"You do not speak, Atrox?"

"I..." Alistair glanced up fearfully at the goddess, but she smiled encouragingly. "I no longer go by that name, Gaia, having given it up."

Her head tilted to the side, a gleam of amusement in her gaze. "Why?"

"Because I shamed it and used my powers for the wrong side. I had to commit an unspeakable act to fix my mistakes."

The green eyes stared into his for so long he felt lost. Eventually, Gaia spoke again.

"You have done well by my daughter."

"*Daughter?*"

Gaia laughed at his surprised tone, and it sounded like stars. "All my children are me, and I them. Vivienne, as you call her now, was born to shine. She was my favorite, of all my daughters."

Alistair swallowed hard, wanting to ask a burning question. "What of Sébastien, her knight?"

"He is her half. The only piece in this entire universe that matches her."

"And Carleigh?"

The smile disappeared, replaced by sadness. "A product of another. As I was Light, influencing them all for good, he was Dark, adding negativity to every somber corner of their hearts."

Alistair could not recall a deity that rivaled Gaia. As though reading his mind, she nodded thoughtfully. "You would not. But Vulper would."

Gaia chuckled at his gaping jaw. "Rest easy, wolf god. Your secret is safe with me. For all that you have done and everything you have tried to prevent, you earn my gratitude."

"I am... overwhelmed, Gaia," he choked past the lump in his throat.

The goddess smiled, then her hand on top of his head warmed. "As a token of my faith in you, I allow you to reprise your full identity. All your powers, all your capabilities, they shall be returned if you so wish." A half-smile played on her lips. "Needless to say, this offer comes with no fears of reprisal for your past actions."

"A pardon, then?"

"Yes."

There was no contest to the answer, but Alistair paused long enough to make sure it was what he wanted. Then, voice rough with emotion, he spoke. "I would very much like that, goddess."

The heat above his head spread to his entire body. Similar to what happened at the stones, it was mixed with both pain and pleasure, and left him panting when all was said and done. But amidst the effort to draw in breaths, he now sensed the power deep in his belly.

Yet the change was more than energy coursing through, electrocuting his joints and snapping him to attention. It was in his mind, his demeanor. There was no hesitation in him, no more second guessing, the path crystal clear to the end. His thoughts turned to Catriona in that moment, and he knew exactly what he wanted to do when he was next by her side.

The goddess' last words rang in his ears, bringing him back to the present. "Take good care of my daughter, Atrox."

By the time Vivienne blinked, she was back to herself, and it was regular voice that echoed around them, thick with emotion. "I remember everything, to the dawn of the ages. I... Carleigh. Morgana was right, he was never after me because he hated me, but because he once loved me and I did not return it."

Atrox inclined his head, silently agreeing. "As you saw in my memories, Sébastien sacrificed himself in order to find out how, exactly, the god became Darkness' puppet–whether by his own choice, or forced."

"But what does Carleigh want with me now, Alistair?"

A faint smile tugged on his lips at the name, but he focused on Vivienne's question, trying to rein in the hum of his energy. "I hate to be blunt, majesty, but he wants your death–as usual. He intends to sacrifice you and your baby to Darkness in a few days."

Though her gaze saddened, her determination to understand did not waver. "What of Morgana?"

Atrox hesitated, unsure how to summarize the Halfling in a few words. "She is rather more complicated, but it is not you she has something against. Merlin is the focus of her rage, because of their past and respective betrayals."

"Yet she is colluding with Carleigh against *me*."

A breath of exasperation escaped him, and Atrox knew it was time he revealed everything. "That's because they already captured Merlin, highness. It was how they were able to rescue Carleigh... Your magic was not solely responsible for his return to this world."

His words offered a measure of comfort, but still Vivienne felt restless, trying to grasp at straws and understand all she had missed. The loss of Sébastien, the pregnancy, along with the corruption within, had blinded her to many things.

"And Mordred?" It was in a whisper the last question escaped her, mainly because she was afraid of the answer.

"His role was to facilitate your transition to their side..." Atrox paused, and despite his ruthlessness being returned to him alongside the rest of his identity, he chose not to burden Vivienne with all he knew about the chaotic sorcerer. *Especially the fact he nearly caused a miscarriage.* Instead, he chose a noncommittal answer. "The further you were from Light, the easier it would have been to kill you."

The enchantress shook her head, one hand closing in a fist. Mordred's betrayal stung most, as did the realization she had been only a pawn in a game to him, nothing else. She had believed him, trusted him as she would a brother…

A breeze lifted her hair, and clouds gathered above, the elements sensing her agitation. Dimly, she was aware her magic was causing the changes and willed it to stop. Within moments, she blinked and everything was back to normal. Or, almost.

Vivienne focused her gaze on her guardian, finally registering he had been kneeling during their entire conversation. "Why are you…?" Her second shock came when she looked deeper into the midnight stare and felt its burning intensity. "You… Alistair?"

Atrox laughed at that, rising to his feet and shaking his head. "Much as I have enjoyed the name, highness, I have been freed. My identity of old has been returned to me, with all its perks."

Vivienne's eyes widened. "You have your god-like strength back?" When he grinned, she matched it. "Then put it to good use. Bring me to Sébastien before it is too late."

"It would be my pleasure." He bowed, offering his hand. When she took it, he drew a portal with his index. The atmosphere shimmered, and they stepped through.

CHAPTER 17

From the portal, Atrox and Vivienne emerged into the other side of the Park, by the trailing paths. He had brought them away from the final destination on purpose, in case the sorcerers planned to follow them.

A quick glance around ensured they were alone, and he shifted into his large wolf form. Plastering himself to the ground, he allowed his mistress to mount him.

Vivienne gripped onto his fur and held on as he cut across the distance with utmost speed. *Where exactly are you taking me?*

Somewhere you have been before, and which has water nearby. I do not know what is needed to break the spell on Sébastien, but I am sure it will come to you.

She nodded, knowing he could not see her but could sense her intent. Her thoughts turned inward, reflecting on what she had seen.

Vivienne had thought it a shock finding out that in this new life Carleigh was her half-brother. But it was nothing compared to discovering the true reason behind his hate—his unrequited love for her.

Atrox...She hesitated, waiting until he turned his muzzle sideways to continue. *This thing with Carleigh, did Merlin know?*

I do not believe so, highness. Not even I was aware—and I used to be a god. Am one again, now... He shook his head, hardly believing it. *I am fairly certain had Merlin realized the truth, he never would have intervened as he did with Carleigh's life.*

I suppose so, Vivienne agreed. *So where is Sébastien? With a trusted friend.*

Atrox blocked his mind from Vivienne then contacted Catriona directly. *Darling... I have Vivienne and am heading to the waterfall. Can you get Sébastien here if I help you?*

Yes.

He wanted to enquire about her curt response, but bit back his questions for another time. *Thank you.*

My pleasure, lover.

Once Atrox cut through the last of the trees, they emerged on a semi-paved road, marking the trail of the park. In the dark of the night, no tourists were around—and he was thankful for the privacy.

He ran them under a small bridge and exited the tunnel onto yet another path, though this one curved upwards and disappeared into mossy green trees.

"I've been here before," Vivienne whispered above him, but he heard her loud and clear.

I am aware, highness. It was the best place to bring Sébastien back.

He pushed on, panting as the path grew steeper. Noticing it, Vivienne smiled. "I can walk, you know."

Do you really think I would let you exert yourself in your condition?

She rolled her eyes and tightened her grip on his fur. The last time she had been in the area, shadows had attacked her and sparked a new form of despair.

Nothing will happen, Atrox reassured her, having sensed her wariness.

Vivienne did not reply, but kept a close eye on obscure corners. When they neared the waterfall, its calm flow pulled her attention away. Without quite realizing it, she dismounted Atrox and inched closer to the ledge.

Watch your step.

The warning fell on deaf ears as she felt a pull unlike before. "What is this?"

Atrox moved by her side, gently prodding her until she stepped backwards a few steps to avoid the slippery edge. *Nothing you have to worry yourself over.*

Then the wolf god turned his full attention to the waterfall. His eyes glowed red for a moment as he reached to help Catriona with the spell. The water shimmered, then the cascade parted and through it floated Sébastien.

Vivienne took another step forward, but it was not to the upper ledge that Alistair brought him. Instead, he set the knight on the lower part of it, where a different pathway led straight to under the waterfall.

I will keep watch up here, Atrox advised, then retreated until he was out of sight.

By the time Sébastien was fully lying down, Vivienne was

already rushing to him. She knelt down and pulled his head in her lap, smoothing down his mess of wet hair.

Her eyes searched his features, the curve of his lips, remembering their touch on hers. Tears burned her eyes at the memories of their fondest moments, and the recollections of all he had given up for her– all he had *done* for her.

How did I ever hurt this man? A wave of guilt hit her for everything she had put Sébastien and their relationship through.

Atrox was in her mind, sending calming waves of energy. You will have all the time in the world to set it right–after you bring him back.

Vivienne fought back tears, then bent over and kissed his cold lips. "Love, wake up." Her plea was a whisper against his mouth, but it remained unanswered.

When he did not stir, she grasped his hand in hers, pulling it to her belly. "Please. For both of us."

Despair threatened at bay when Sébastien still remained immobile. "Atrox, he's not waking up!"

The wolf god poked his head over the ledge, peering down at them. His gaze was pensive, if panicked. *Catriona, any advice?*

The Fae's answer was halting. *Vivienne's entire aura is full of dark matter. If this is ever to work, she needs to pull onto light as her strength, not darkness.*

Thanking her, he then relayed the information to his mistress. Vivienne raised a tear-stained face to his. "I cannot control my feelings!"

You had best figure out a way, highness, if you want Sébastien back. Stick to light—only light.

Vivienne curled up over Sébastien, unable to hold back her

sobs. Thoughts of what their future could be, with their baby, ran through her mind. An almost too vivid vision of them having a regular picnic by a beach choked her with emotion.

As she cried on him, a river of tears became silvery wisps and fell on him. Shining, the rivulets ran down his chin, his throat,

and under his shirt, covering his chest. Sébastien's entire body responded with a glow and he gasped, coming awake with a start. His glazed eyes peered around, then focused on Vivienne. The first words out of his lips were not what she had expected.

"They're here."

At the warning, Atrox looked to the other side–too late.

Mordred emerged from the forest across the ledge where Vivienne and Sébastien were, followed by Morgana and Carleigh.

"Well if it isn't the love birds reunited." Mordred cackled, an evil glint in his eyes. "Tired of me so soon, my sweet?"

Sébastien growled low, standing up and putting himself between Mordred and Vivienne. He wobbled on his feet, but an arm draped casually over the enchantress' shoulders covered it.

Atrox jumped off the top ledge and dropped by his other side. His massive form leaned against the knight's left thigh, lending him support.

Sébastien gripped his fur with his free hand, tugging on it. *Thank you.*

Atrox said nothing, but he could sense a weakness in him. Sébastien needed rest—*real* rest. The wolf god glanced at Vivienne, trying to communicate the sentiment. She nodded her understanding and leaned her weight into her lover, supporting his other side.

Mordred zeroed in on the touch, scowling like a child who had lost his favorite toy. "Much changed while you were away, knight."

Sébastien clenched his jaw so tightly Vivienne could have sworn she heard his teeth grind together. "Not that much," he retorted, tightening his hold.

They stared at each other for a beat, the tension thick in the air. Vivienne placed a restraining hand on Sébastien's chest, fearing they would come to blows. Sensing someone was watching her, she turned to the trio and met Morgana's unreal silvery gaze, steady on hers.

It was the first time they met in person while aware of each other's identities. Now that she knew Morgana had imprisoned Merlin, she should have automatically hated the woman. Yet an odd sense of pity overcame her, her magic capturing the sorceress' distress and regrets.

Carleigh was the one to break the standoff, not easily distracted. "I beg to differ. Your precious has something I need."

"I guess you'll just have to do without," Sébastien threatened.

The necromancer only smirked. "It's too late. The child was promised to Darkness. He *will* be mine."

"Over my dead body." Sébastien's growl rumbled in his chest, shocking Vivienne. Over her shoulder, she sensed his fist clenching in aggravation.

Carleigh's eyes darted to the tell-tale sign of impending violence and he grinned. "That can be arranged."

Atrox kept his silence, only watching the men's aura while

they verbally sparred. He could sense the strength in each male, though Darkness masked the sorcerer's.

Watch out!

His warning came just as an orb rose from Carleigh's palm, and he threw it towards Sébastien. The wolf dog jerked as if to take the hit himself, but he need not have worried. The knight moved so quick they were all taken aback.

One minute he was by Vivienne's side, weak and unarmed. The next he was across the shore, in Carleigh's face. A hand grasped his neck in an iron grip. In his other was Excalibur, its deadly blade pointed at the necromancer's neck.

"You sure you can finish what you start?" Sébastien's glare was fixated only on Carleigh, dismissing the other two, despite their proximity.

Mordred closed his gaping mouth, then clapped humorously. "Impressive. Where did you hide that little trick?"

Sébastien threw him a look that shut him up, his dark gaze intense and commanding. What had once seemed like a regular man now presented power only an ancient one would have. Mordred recalled his mother's words, and stepped back.

Morgana, silent until then, chose that moment to speak up. "Best be careful with your threats, knight. Especially when you cannot carry them to fruition."

Carleigh's eyes sparkled in understanding, but Sébastien did not move. "And what makes you think I will not?"

Though she kept a soft, firm tone, Morgana made no effort to step closer. "Your lineage. The Cardinal Rule prohibits killing another god, under pain of paying the price with your own life."

"And?" Sébastien countered, not the least fazed.

Careful, knight.

I know what I'm doing.

Morgana stared at Sébastien for a beat, trying to read past his expression to see if he was bluffing or not. Nothing changed in his demeanor, and the blade inched closer to Carleigh.

She stepped around them, making sure to keep her distance from Excalibur, and touched the necromancer's shoulder. "Time to recognize a lost battle, sorcerer." Though she spoke matter-of-factly, her gaze never wavered from Sébastien. "The war will still be ours. Come."

And like a mother calling her cubs home, she turned and left. Mordred followed first, walking backwards, but Carleigh was glaring at Sébastien.

When the knight pushed the blade's tip closer to his throat, Carleigh lifted both palms up and stepped away. Sébastien let him go, shoving him away in the same movement.

"We will finish this another time."

"I won't hold my breath." Sébastien ignored the man's sneer and hopped over the water, landing by Vivienne's side once more.

His gaze raked over her body, taking in the thin features and the slight bump. He glanced behind to make sure Carleigh had vanished, then grabbed her hand in his and started up the path that led them to the forest. Atrox followed in their wake, casting his senses about to ensure no else was around.

Not catching anything, he focused his attention on Sébastien and noticed the anger had still not left him.

What is it?

Rather than answer, Sébastien halted. He headed to the right where the trees were denser, and shadows cast everything in darkness. When Vivienne tried to stop him, he threw over a shoulder, "You'll be safe with me."

Though his presence reassured her, Vivienne bit her lip at his tone. Within moments, they reached an area that was to Sébastien's liking. He let go of his beloved and paced away, then back, repeating the movement a few times like a caged panther.

When he next faced Vivienne, his eyes flashed. Without looking at Atrox, he ordered, "Leave us."

After a quick glance to his mistress, the wolf god obeyed and left them alone. *Don't do anything stupid,* he advised the knight in parting. *She did not betray you.*

Though his words were meant to be reassuring, they did nothing to calm the turmoil inside Sébastien. Months' worth of frustration, hopelessness and wariness built to the surface and he could not push them back down.

He inhaled deeply, then moved closer to Vivienne, taking measured steps as if holding himself in check. His entire body was rigid, looming in the darkness, yet not threatening.

Vivienne could only stand and watch, conflicting emotions warring within her. She was perplexed as to the reason for his behavior, but mesmerized by the attraction pulling them together.

When she met his gaze, it was darker than ever—and not in desire.

"Are you... mad... at me?" Vivienne finally asked.

Another flash of lightning passed in his eyes, and Sébastien's jaw clenched harder. "Mad is an understatement."

"But... *why*?"

"You really could not guess?" She cringed at his flat voice, unused to being berated by him.

"I know I was difficult these last months, Sébastien," she tried to step closer, to touch him, but he shook his head in warning.

"I would not trust myself right now," he warned. "*Difficult*, you say? Do you have any idea what it did to me when you pushed me away? Refused to let me help you. You preferred to delve deeper and deeper down a hole I could not follow, rather than talk it out!"

"Sébastien, I—"

"No!" he cut angrily. "I am not chasing after an apology. No words can erase the fact you told me you did not want our baby—and needed space."

Tears filled her eyes at the memory, but Vivienne tried to hold them back. "I know you don't want an apology, but I owe you a rather large one."

Sébastien stared at her for a beat, and something in him softened at her obvious distress. But then he recalled Mordred's smug expression, and found he had more to stay.

"You put your life in danger, love. Pushed *me* away." He ran a hand through his hair, messing it up in agitation. "You nearly tore us apart—for *him*?"

Vivienne's gaze widened at the implication. "You must be joking! Sébastien, nothing ever happened with Mordred!"

"You dreamt of him!" Sébastien accused. "And whatever he told you was enough to turn your head around. You put him above what we had, gave in to his lies."

Vivienne opened her mouth to speak, but any statement she planned was stuck in her throat.

"Tell me the truth."

Vivienne glanced towards the woods where Mordred had disappeared. They were alone, she knew that. But how could she explain to Sébastien what her connection to the other man was?

She met her lover's darkening stare and took a step closer. "Mordred is…" She paused, trying to find the words. Her dry lips bothered her, and she licked them.

Sébastien's gaze latched on to the movement, then his mouth descended on hers with a fierce rush that left her gasping—and practically hanging on to him for dear life.

"Want to try that again?" Sébastien rumbled against her lips.

"Nothing," Vivienne finished on a breathless whisper, desperately searching his gaze. "Mordred is *nothing* to me. The darkness in me feels his chaos, that is all. We are nemesis, our fates tied. But he is nothing. I am yours, Sébastien."

He observed her every movement, a muscle ticking in his jaw. Yet his hold on her was gentle, if firm.

"Only yours."

Her pleading whisper seemed to be his undoing, as Sébastien groaned and bent his forehead to hers. "Great answer, beloved." Then his mouth dropped to hers once more, pulling her closer.

CHAPTER 18

Ross Castle was welcoming after the chill of the forest. Vivienne and Atrox—in human form—helped Sébastien past the threshold, then settled him in a corner. Already on the verge of passing out, the knight gave in and let sleep claim him.

Not looking forward to spending another night on the bare floor, Vivienne conjured up a bed for their comfort. Atrox declined something for him, instead helping her move Sébastien on the soft mattress.

"It is you two who need the most rest." His gaze fell to her bump, and he smiled. "Especially you, highness."

Too tired to argue, Vivienne settled down and laid her head on Sébastien's chest, cuddling closer and pulling a blanket over them. Though he was dead asleep, his arm tightened around her instinctively.

Vivienne breathed his woodsy scent in, snuggling deeper. Something in her had been set right, now that they were together again. It was like every part of her aligned with every part of him, to form a larger picture.

It is not just Sébastien that has returned, Atrox pointed out wryly, now in his dog form.

Vivienne met his eyes, unflinching and unashamed. "Yes, you are correct. It was a long road."

He tilted his head to the side, his tone speculative when he next spoke. *And?*

"And I do not intend to give in to it ever again."

I am glad to hear it. But, be that as it may, highness, Mordred believes otherwise.

Vivienne nibbled on her bottom lip, knowing full well the main reason was because of her own interaction with him. "So if

I'm the champion of Light, what is he? Why is our connection so strong?"

Atrox was not ready to answer that particular question, but he knew it was best to, anyway. *You know how the soul mate bond works to you find each other even across different lifetimes. Well, for every contender of good, there is one for evil.*

"Which was Carleigh for me… no?"

Yes. But as you have much good in you, someone was born to counteract you, to balance the scales. And that was Mordred.

Vivienne took in the information, pondering how her life had changed. Her hand drifted lower to her tummy, cradling her womb. "I need to keep this baby safe."

You have no idea, highness. At her intrigued look, he only added, *Ask Sébastien when he wakes. This is his news to share, not mine.*

She sighed, then curled further into Sébastien and closed

her eyes. Sleep evaded her at first, but soon she fell in a peaceful slumber while Atrox kept watch.

* * *

Carleigh emerged out of the portal back at Vivienne's house, Morgana and Mordred close behind. Though he tried to control his rage, by the time they were all together the tendrils of darkness at his feet were hissing.

Morgana glanced at them, then met his unwavering stare full on. "What seems to be the problem?"

"You are," Carleigh snarled, stepping closer. Mordred moved between him and his mother, extending a hand to keep him at bay.

"Watch yourself, sorcerer," he growled, his palm heating in response to the tension.

Carleigh glared at him, then directed his gaze to Morgana. "Why did you intervene?"

"Are you daft?" she sneered. "Sébastien would have killed you."

"He wouldn't have."

"Are you so lost in your hubris to believe your own lies?" Mordred intervened. "I saw the knight, sensed his anger and power. It would have taken but a movement to end you."

"Fools!" Carleigh lashed out, but moved away rather than towards them. After pacing for a few moments, he faced them once more. "You seem to know so much about my lineage, yet you tell me you are unaware he cannot kill me because his sword is not fit for it?"

Mordred glanced to his mother, frowning at the retort, but Morgana did not appear fazed by the sorcerer's reasoning. "You would think so. But Excalibur is a weapon of Light. You are a being of Darkness. If a god wields it, imbued with power, it *would* end you."

Her eyes glittered menacingly, then she added, "Of course, there is also the small matter of the flower that can kill gods. Should you have forgotten, long ago I poisoned Vivienne. The powder I had gathered in the realm of the Faes was from that same plant."

"Meaning?"

"The poison coursed through Vivienne's veins, but it was also absorbed by what was in the immediate area. And considering Mordred was battling Arthur, who was wielding Excalibur…"

Carleigh paled at the implication, but it was Mordred who finished the thought. "The blade consumed the nectar, thus now contains it. Talk about a double-edged sword, mother."

Morgana shrugged in response, but her glare never left Carleigh. "Are you catching on, sorcerer? I *was* saving your life."

His eyes turned to slits as he assessed her, trying to gauge her honesty. As his powers stretched to see beyond, he caught sight of something else—an eavesdropper. A sneer on his lips, he said to Morgana, "You can lie to yourself as much as you want, Halfling. But I know your heart is not in it."

Then he strode out on the grounds, his cape billowing behind. Mordred crossed his arms over his chest, facing his mother. "What does he mean?"

"Nothing, my son." She gazed out the window, pensive. "Nothing at all."

* * *

Catriona pulled back from watching the sorcerers, wondering at the sudden block. She had kept an eye on them despite Atrox's warnings, intrigued at what Morgana was doing.

Though the Halfling pretended—and very well, at that—to be on Carleigh's side, all she had done recently was diffuse situations between the two camps.

Could it be Atrox was wrong, and there really is something worth saving in her? Or is she only doing this because of what Merlin demanded?

Lost in thoughts, the Fae shed her clothing and jumped in the lake, letting the water wash off her doubts. Once she felt cleansed, she exited and conjured another outfit. It was when she stepped out of the lake that Catriona noticed it.

The skies had darkened considerably, the shadows in her forest growing longer. The air, which had been warm, now chilled her skin. Even the reflection of the pool had dulled, almost gray rather than the sparkling blue it normally was.

The Fae frowned and headed to the willow tree, thrusting her palms into its trunk. "What is it?" she whispered. "What is happening to my realm?"

Its response, when it came, was faint. *You were warned, child. But you chose not to listen.*

"Warned about what?"

The balance… the sorcerer…

"I do not understand!" Catriona cried.

It is too late… Pay heed.

When the connection stopped, the Fae stepped back in shock. Her eyes darted around the forest, taken aback at the darkness she felt.

Movement out of the corner of her eye caused Catriona to spin—only to face Carleigh.

"So you are the pain in my neck lately," he stated, eyeing her up and down.

Catriona refused to show fear, going on the offensive. "How did you get here? You have no right to enter my realm!"

The necromancer scanned the surroundings, laughing. "It was much too easy to follow your trail. Then again, that happens when you eavesdrop on conversations you have no part of."

Catriona did not reply, instead let the elements respond to her call. "You have no business here, your very presence makes me sick. I would suggest you leave."

Carleigh only narrowed his eyes towards her flaming palms. "Ah, yes. I sense an ancient power within you, Fae. But I cannot understand why you would meddle in these affairs, especially at your own detriment."

The redhead laughed at the implication in his words. "If you expect me to entertain your delusions and answer your

questions, you are sorely mistaken, sorcerer. Your kind is not welcome here."

To illustrate her point, Catriona let loose the fireballs. Having not expected the attack so soon, Carleigh had to step out of the way and block them. With each movement he backed away, the Fae countered by pushing forward.

"I see you will not stand for civilized conversation," he muttered.

"Civilized? *You?* After what you did to Merlin?"

The hate in her voice gave her away, and it was enough of

a clue for the sorcerer to pounce on. "So your issue with me is because of the wizard... Interesting."

Another set of fireballs flew at him, and this time he narrowed his eyes and clenched his fists. "I am trying to show you respect, Fae, but you render my task rather hard."

"Bite me," she scowled. "I said leave my realm, you do not belong here!"

When she raised her hand to attack him again, he jumped on the opportunity and struck back. The ball of darkness hit Catriona full-force, and she flew into the willow tree.

"I tried to be reasonable," he continued as he stepped forward, "but you are very stubborn. Why is Merlin so important to you?"

Her blue eyes glared daggers at him, mouth pursed in defiance. She refused to speak, and it enraged him further. "Is he an old lover? A friend?"

Carleigh took in her red hair, then the set of her lips, the sapphires glowing of an unnatural light—

"No, not a lover," he corrected himself. "Brother. Or, half-brother, judging by your physical differences and amplified powers. *That* is why you have been meddling in things that did not concern you."

Catriona straightened her back and clapped. "Congratulations, you connected the dots. Now what?"

"Well," Carleigh pretended to think, but tendrils gathered for a strike at his feet. "I suppose I cannot let you live. You will only continue to get in my–"

Before he could finish, the Fae had already sent a fireball slam into him with enough force to push him in the lake. Once tangled in its depths, he was hers. She allowed water to curl around his neck, pulling tighter as he lost all air.

His face became blue, and she relished the power—the kill. But before she could end the matter, the sorcerer disappeared.

Catriona stepped closer, scanning the water with her senses, but could not catch sight of him. "Where the bloody hell did he go?"

"Somewhere you cannot follow."

She whirled around at her father's voice. Only this time, instead of the hologram made of leaves, it was the real man who stood in her forest. Dressed in a long monk-like cape the color of ivory, he leaned on a staff of white oak. Its tip spiraled into an intricate Fae design that symbolized elderly wisdom and immortality.

"Father," she breathed, unsure of how to react.

Merlyddus scanned the surrounding area, and his glare fell on the darkened forest and silent willow tree. "The sorcerer did a number on your sanctuary."

"It is nothing I cannot fix."

The elder Fae met her eyes then, his own sparkling. "I know, child. But perhaps it is time to go elsewhere."

"What do you mean? I need to help Merlin, and Atrox!"

"You have done enough as it is. Now to put yourself in the path of that necromancer…" A glance to the lake, as icy as its reflection. "He will not bother you further, but I would still prefer you leave."

Catriona glanced between him and the spot Carleigh had disappeared in. "You did this? You kicked him out?"

"I was not about to stand by and let my daughter commit murder," Merlyddus retorted. "Now come, it is time you join me."

Catriona reeled back at the authority in his voice. "No. Father, please. I... I have a life here. I care for Atrox."

Merlyddus said nothing for a moment, only watched her steadily. When he spoke, each word was a dagger to her heart. "Would you still love him if you knew he hid your brother's discomfort from you? Merlin is dying. Carleigh ensured he would the minute Vivienne is sacrificed. Yet your precious wolf god did not see fit to tell you."

"You..." Catriona tried to speak past the lump in her throat, but had to swallow first. "That is a lie."

"He needed you willing to perform for him, and you have done so selflessly, my dear. But I cannot sit by while my offspring suffers. You are coming with me."

"No! Even if Atrox did not tell me everything, I refuse to let them face Morgana without my help."

Merlyddus clenched his jaw, pinching the bridge of his nose with one wrinkled hand. "I thought I could reasonably convince you, but I see that is not the case. Very well, my beautiful yet stubborn daughter. You wish to help your wolf? I will tell you how to go about killing the necromancer."

"How to..." Catriona's brow furrowed and she stepped closer, almost despite herself. "What are you talking about? What about the immortality spell?"

"The one named Carleigh was already immortal. Darkness only transferred what was in his soul –eternal life– into his physical body. The only reason this was possible was due to his godly lineage. As for the knight, he went about his quest and learned what you needed about his past. But you know this will never end until Carleigh is dead. Of course, there is the small matter of the Cardinal Rule. If any of them kill your villain, they will also pay with their lives."

Shivers ran up her back at the realization her father was correct. *How did we miss this? We were so focused on the larger picture, we never bothered to think about what would need to happen in the end.*

"Then…how will they be able to win this battle?"

Merlyddus shuffled closer, leaning on his cane more than was actually necessary. Whether he did it to plead for her sympathy or due to real necessity, Catriona could not figure out. Nonetheless, the moment came when he faced her, only inches away.

He lifted a hand and stroked her cheek, smiling. "You are so very beautiful, like your mother before you. And so proud, my dear." His gentle tone hardened, and his hand fell down to his side. "But this is where you submit. Vow to me that you will return to my realm, and forget all this foolishness behind you. Then, I will tell you what you need to know in order to win."

Catriona gaped at her father, unable to believe her ears. Here stood her one parent, blood of her blood, and he was blackmailing her. Before her magic got out of control, she pushed it back and took a deep breath. "I swear, father."

Merlyddus searched her gaze, narrowing his eyes. She could feel his psyche trying to breach hers in an attempt to confirm her commitment. The Fae straightened her back and took it, allowing him to see she was being truthful.

Satisfied, Merlyddus nodded. "For your wolf and his friends to survive, a Fae should be the one to kill Carleigh, and no one else."

Catriona understood then why he wanted her out of the picture. *No matter the outcome, I would have been in danger.*

"Thank you, father. I agree to your terms, but you have to know… I will never forgive you for forcing my hand." Catriona blinked back her tears, maintaining as much dignity as she could. "Allow me one last contact, then I shall join you."

Merlyddus watched her closely, then nodded. "Very well." He pointed to a nearby tree, turning it into a portal with a single snap of his fingers. "When you are ready, step through and it will lead you to me."

"And Merlin?"

"He is only half-Fae, thus I cannot bring him forth. However, I can ensure he survives his plight."

The redhead inclined her head and waited until he disappeared. Then she crumbled to the ground, sobs wrecking her slim body.

* * *

Sébastien was the first to wake up, glancing around at the unfamiliar surroundings. He noticed Atrox in a corner, passed out, and Vivienne at the bottom of the bed, smiling faintly at him.

"How are you feeling?"

"Good enough," he replied, sitting up.

Vivienne inched closer, rearranging the pillow at his back. Her eyes filled with tears, lips trembling with emotion. "I am *so* sorry. This is all my fault, I brought them here and–"

Sébastien pulled her in his arms, cutting her off. "They would have come regardless. Whatever part you played, I believe it only amplified things that had already been set in motion."

Vivienne nuzzled his neck, burrowing deeper in the embrace. They were both quiet, enjoying the simplicity of being together. After a while, Sébastien spoke.

"With all the craziness, we never talked about the baby."

She glanced up at him, surprised. Then she recalled what Atrox had said and mentioned it to her lover. Sébastien got the most peculiar look on his face, half-way between panic and amusement.

"It's not a good idea to keep secrets from a pregnant woman," Vivienne pointed out.

Sébastien chuckled at that, then kissed the top of her head. "Right. Well, the fact of the matter is somewhere in between conceiving this baby, we got lucky. Because it's not just a regular newborn, but rather a king of the past... One Merlin was waiting for to reincarnate."

Vivienne's eyes widened in shock, her mouth gaping slightly as the pieces clicked into place. "Arthur?"

Sébastien nodded, watching her face carefully for any sign of distress. Instead, Vivienne moved the blanket off her stomach and rubbed it in soft circles with an awed smile. "I'm carrying the heir to Camelot?"

"More like the new leader of this world," the knight retorted with a grin. "You're ok with this, then?"

"Of course! Why wouldn't I be?"

Sébastien opened his mouth, about to tell her everything he had been warned against. But the joy in her, the beauty of the moment, was too pure to shatter. He only kissed Vivienne instead, making it last until they had to pull away for air.

Foreheads touching, he moved his arm and placed it on her slight bump. A wondrous expression came over him, then he chuckled.

"What is it?" Vivienne asked.

"I guess we don't really have to wonder about names," he pointed out, amusement dancing in his eye

Vivienne laughed, before nodding. "No, you're right." She intertwined her hand with his, murmuring the name aloud. "Arthur."

The enchantress then glanced at the sleeping Atrox, and whispered, "Since we're sharing, you should probably know Alistair is no longer Alistair. He regained his deity form– Atrox."

Sébastien stared in the corner, his mouth rising in a half-smile. "Did Catriona have anything to do with it?"

"The redheaded Fae from his memories?" At his nod, she shrugged. "Maybe. I'm not too sure, to be honest. He brought me

to Killarney to unlock the memories of Morgana, and then when I came out of a trance he was... him."

"It was about time," Sébastien held her tighter. "It is no fun being only half of what you could be."

He fell silent, the words triggering his own memories. Being without Vivienne for two lifetimes, then again while he was in a coma, had nearly torn him apart. He ran his hands through her hair, enjoying the softness of it over his skin. *I never want to be without her again.*

After a faint silence, Sébastien shrugged out of her embrace and Vivienne frowned. "Where are you going?"

"I'll only be a minute," he whispered. Though the room spun, he was able to stand and inch closer to the corner Atrox was in.

Next to the demon dog, leaning against the wall, was Excalibur. He knelt by the sword, focused on the jewels encrusted in its hilt. Sapphires and rubies swirled around the hilt, strategically placed to enhance the dragon figurine.

Sébastien thought of his deity powers and envisioned what he wanted, eyes shut tight. When he opened them, nothing had happened.

Damn.

What is it you are trying to do?

Sébastien glanced towards the dog, who still looked asleep, then to the sword.

He imagined the object he needed created, and Alistair let out a small, *Ah.* After a beat, he added, *Allow me to help, while you recover your faculties.*

No.... I appreciate it, but tell me how. I want to do this for Vivienne.

On the fifth try, Sébastien finally had in his hand the product of his hard work. He closed his fist over it, then walked back to the bed. Vivienne had fallen asleep, her mouth parted slightly, hair spread over his pillow.

He knelt by the side of the bed, gently tucking a tendril behind her ear. The movement stirred Vivienne awake and she blinked at him, smiling happily. "What were you doing?"

Sébastien felt his heartbeat increasing as he arranged himself so he was kneeling on one knee, Excalibur held between them with its tip pointed to the floor. Vivienne's eyes widened,

darting between the blade and him repeatedly.

A fist closed over his heart, the knight took her left hand in his. "I never got a chance in our past, as we were too busy surviving. But I have utmost faith we will live to see a bright future in this life, together. With that in mind, my beautiful enchantress, will you allow me to spend the rest of my days as your partner, protector and soul mate?"

Vivienne's eyes shone when he presented the ring. A perfect fit for her finger, it had a solitaire in the shape of a heart, made of both sapphire and ruby. In the fireplace light, the stones caught the flames and reflected them, adding further depths to the gift.

Sébastien fit the ring over her ring finger, and Vivienne laughed shakily through her tears, unable to look away. When she finally met his gaze, reading all the love, she threw her arms around him. "Yes."

The single word was enough to make Sébastien's soul sing, and Atrox barked happily behind them.

CHAPTER 19

Merlin stared into nothingness, his legs and hands still encased in the crystal. Occasionally, his gaze shifted to the orb in the corner—and its growing red center. It now almost dominated the entire device, to his ascending despair.

To think I will end thus... Unable to even help Vivienne. Where did I go so wrong?

The answer to the question was evident, if not entirely appreciated. He had been warned against taking up with Morgana—and against what followed. But despite his better judgment, he had not only fallen for her, but he had trained her and harmed her.

At the thought of what had broken them apart, Merlin felt a different wave of despair hit him. It was not the first instance he had reflected on the past, nor would it be the last. It was simply one more sleepless night he spent wishing he could have done things differently.

Lost in ruminations, he did not notice the light atop the stairs. No bigger than a regular palm, it floated closer and grew. By the time Merlin's suspicious gaze set on it, the brilliance had grown to the size of a watermelon.

"What the...?"

As though his words had sparked it into action, rays of pure brightness streaked out of the orb and hit the crystal encasing him. The entire tower burst white, so much so that Merlin had to shut his eyes or risk going blind.

With the new illumination, the leeches on his skin fell apart. And with each passing minute, he could sense some of his own strength returning.

"Who goes there?" he questioned, determined to know the identity of his savior.

"No one of importance."

Despite the shortness of the answer, Merlin froze at the tone, so like his own. He forced himself to look straight at the light. And sure enough, within its depths he could make out the blurred contour of an elderly man. His long, black hair fell to his waist, blue eyes sparkling almost white.

"Father?" Merlin choked out, unable to believe what he was seeing.

Merlyddus sighed, and a breeze blew out in that same moment. Merlin could taste the sweetness of a peach, feel the sun's rays, smell the flowers... He blinked, noticing the man was not truly there, but rather in ghostly form.

"Why have you come?"

"Someone needs to save you from yourself," he chastised.

Merlyddus then pointed his staff at the orb. A shot of light, and the makeshift explosive shattered. He faced his son, arching an eyebrow. "I trust you could do the rest yourself. There is only so much I can use my magic without it getting ideas of its own... Especially where it concerns you."

The nerve of him to act like a parent when he's been missing my whole life! Merlin flushed, but refused to retort in anger. Instead, he inclined his head gratefully. "Thank you, father. I will handle it from here."

The elder Fae stood staring at him for a moment until something akin to respect passed through his irises. Then, he clapped his hands and vanished.

Merlin glanced down at the crystal, brow furrowed in concentration. He called forth all magic he possessed, though most of it lay dormant thanks to the leeches. Still, enough answered that he heard a crack in his bindings.

A small smile formed on his lips, despite his sweaty forehead. *Baby steps...*

* * *

Atrox knew the moment he entered the dream—and Catriona's realm—that something was wrong. One shrewd glance around registered the darkened atmosphere, the dying trees and their mistress, alone in the middle of all the chaos.

His other senses picked up Carleigh's scent—and that of his ever-master, Darkness itself. "What happened here?"

Catriona had on a black sheath, in mourning for her lost realm. The sorrow in her eyes turned them almost gray and reminded him of another queen who had suffered so at the hands of the same man.

He ran to her and dragged her into his arms, grateful she was unharmed. "Talk to me." His whispered plea fell against her hair, even as he tightened his hold.

Catriona remained frozen in the embrace, not quite crying but trembling. Her words, when they came, hit him with the force of a tsunami. "Like you talked to me, about Merlin?"

Atrox pulled back enough to examine her expression. Though her features were taut, there was no anger in those eyes—only regret. And that hurt more than anything else.

"I meant to, I promise I did." When she looked away, he grabbed her chin between his thumb and index, forcing her to meet his gaze. "I *swear*."

"And why didn't you?" she countered.

"Because Merlin made me promise. He did not want you risking yourself, or for Carleigh to follow you here." He glanced around, taking in the destruction. "Evidently, we both had good intentions—and we both failed."

The tears came then, streaking down her cheeks until the trembling became violent and sobs escaped. Hearing her choke them down, Atrox wished nothing more than to put his fist through Carleigh's nose.

Instead, he pulled Catriona closer, letting her bury her face in the crook of his neck and cry it all out. It was long moments until she could speak again, and even then emotion roughened her voice.

"Was it about Merlin, that you spoke to my father?"

Atrox nodded, recalling the time he had asked her to leave them alone. "Yes."

"And what did he say? You were quiet after."

He hesitated to answer her, not wanting to cause a rift with Merlyddus. But when she turned her tear-streaked face to him, Atrox lost all will to keep silent. "He told me to stay away, and out of his business. That you were best off without me."

Catriona stared at him for a beat, and he felt suspended. Then, almost in slow motion, she raised herself up on her tiptoes and kissed him. What started out soft and tender soon morphed into something a lot more primal.

His free hand moved down to her throat, then to the back of her head to grab onto her hair. He angled her mouth, all to better plunder it at his leisure.

And he did. Atrox took his time, enjoying her moans, breathing in her scent, getting high off the way her body melted against his.

Underneath it, he was aware of a change—of something coming. She felt fragile and strong all at once, real and ethereal. And still he sensed she was slipping through his fingers, soon to be gone from his life.

Desperation took over and Atrox pulled the redhead closer to him, his hands on her hips, moving under her butt, hoisting her until she came full center with the proof of his arousal. He groaned, she moaned in delight.

He moved them until she was leaning against the willow tree, and he was holding her up. One hand drifted between her legs, finding her moist and willing. He locked gazes with her then, frowning at the emotions he could not read.

Catriona did not let him think. She grasped his hips and pulled him closer, hissing when he slid home in a single thrust. Then she held on to him, hiding her tears as she enjoyed his touch for last time.

Fevered by each other's caresses, on edge from being apart, it did not take them long to climax together. Atrox dropped his head to her shoulder, panting and trying to quiet his breath.

Catriona ran her hand through his hair, keeping all proof of her sadness at bay.

When he moved off her, she had control over her emotions. So it was with a straight face she righted her clothing, then looked at him and announced, "I am glad you could come tonight. Because it will be the last we see of each other... I am leaving."

Still recovering from the fog of sex, Atrox could only stare in disbelief. "What do you mean you're leaving?"

"Look around, Atrox. There is nothing left for me here."

"I can help you rebuild!"

"Carleigh would find me anytime," she countered.

"I will murder him before he comes near you again," Atrox vowed, his midnight stare intent with purpose.

Still, Catriona shook her head. "You cannot change my mind, Atrox. This relationship is long past its expiration date, and it is time for it to end."

He gritted his jaw at that, trying to fight the panic rising within. Catriona would not meet his eyes, and even the flush in her cheeks from their lovemaking was fading.

"You cannot walk away," he whispered, grasping her hand and holding tightly. "This makes no sense, Catriona! At least give me a plausible enough reason!"

She met his glare then, her own blazing—but not from anger. "I have said what I wished. Why can't you accept it and let me go?"

He moved closer to her, his entire body pinning her again to the tree. Catriona's gaze darkened at the memory of what they had just shared, and Atrox smiled. "Because I know you want me, Fae. And I want *you*. We are good together. Why do you wish to break this?"

Catriona glanced away then and wrestled out of his grip. She put a distance between them, but he was there in a heartbeat, grasping her wrist and pulling her close.

"You are *not* leaving me," he growled. In some dim part of his brain, Atrox knew he was not going about it rationally. But there was nothing he could to stifle the panic inside him.

I cannot lose her.

Catriona met his gaze then, noticing the confusion flaring underneath the anger. "I am sorry," she apologized, "you have no idea how much."

She kissed him then, her lips lingering, and Atrox sensed all the pent-up frustration and love.

Love!

His eyes flew open, but already she was moving away. "Catriona, wait!" he shouted, no longer caring of the desperation that tinged his voice.

"Please, I–" He stopped, the words locked in his throat.

Catriona turned around, a faint glimmer of hope in her expression. They stared at each other for a breath, Atrox panting heavily, his outstretched hand clenching in a fist.

"Before I leave, you have to know something for the final battle. For you all to survive, only a Fae should kill Carleigh. Please…be safe, Atrox."

Shocked beyond speaking, the wolf god could only stare as Catriona smiled sadly and blew him a kiss. She disappeared before he could react, and he only had himself to blame. Growling in rage, he willed himself awake.

* * *

Wake up, knight.

Sébastien blinked awake, his mind still in the fog of a dream. He met Atrox's midnight eyes, close by the bedside. "What is it?" he whispered, not wanting to disturb Vivienne, who was still sleeping.

Have you secured the castle?

The knight struggled to understand the question. He glanced outside, noticing it was pitch black. "Can this wait until morning?"

No. Answer me, and I will take care of it.

Sébastien sighed at that and moved Vivienne off him gently. Once he had her tucked in bed, he grabbed Excalibur and walked down the stairs with the wolf god.

"No, I did not," he admitted. "What's the rush?"

I sense Carleigh is on the move. We had best be prepared.

He glanced up towards where they had left Vivienne. *Are you confident we can leave her alone?*

"Yes," Sébastien frowned. "It'll only take a minute." He peered down at Atrox, then asked what was on his mind. "What's going on with you?"

Nothing, Atrox growled.

"You sure? My instinct tells me it has to do with a woman."

Atrox's silence was more than confirmation, but Sébastien knew to leave it be. Once they were outside the castle, they each headed to opposite ends of the embankment while the god shot off a single instruction. *Copy me.*

Sébastien saw him place his paws on the wall, then sensed his magic rise to the surface. He mimicked his movements, surprised when a well of energy answered from within him.

Now demand that it protects Vivienne.

The knight closed his eyes, touching the energy and feeling it within his chest. When the command came, it was friendly, not at all like ordering someone but more similar to working alongside one another.

*　*　*

By the time Vivienne woke up, she was already on the edge of the lake, feet dipped in the water. She sensed the darkness before she saw him.

Across the distance, Mordred's form stood unmoving, just like in her memories. Only, she knew he was there and what he wanted.

"You belong with us." The wind carried his voice carried for her ears alone.

"I do not," Vivienne retorted firmly. "Only in your delusional mind."

"Tell yourself what you wish, enchantress, but your rage betrays you."

Vivienne glanced down, noticing her palms had already lighted. Her magic wanted to protect her, and the baby in her womb. She stared to where he awaited, gritting her teeth.

"Your lies no longer bother me."

She was about to leave, determined to forget him to his own delusions. But his shout came from across the distance, vibrating the earth under her feet.

"You belong with *me*!"

Vivienne turned in time to see a wave lifting. The waters which had once been peaceful were now turbulent, angry at his presence. Yet his Fae abilities broke the balance once more, forcing water to respond.

The enchantress refused to back down, set in her determination to show he would not intimidate her—not any longer.

Amongst the unruly waves, one rose, coming to her with menacing intent. Vivienne lifted a palm, and her element responded eagerly. The wave diffused, returning tranquil once more.

No sooner had the lake calmed that a ball of fire followed. With each inch it neared, it increased in size. By the time it was halfway to her, it had doubled.

Vivienne sent a breeze to catch it before it got any closer, and snuff it out. Though it resisted—presumably from Mordred's influence—the fireball was soon diffused.

Air was next—and with it, a rather fierce tornado. It hit Vivienne from behind this time, aiming to push her further in the

lake. The surprise element was enough to destabilize her. Her feet sank in the sand underneath the body of water, feeling like they were caught in moving sand and unable escape. Vivienne gasped, realizing she was close to being outwitted.

Not just yet.

Instead, she stuck her hand in the water, drawing strength from her element. She focused on her baby, on their safety, on returning to Sébastien's arms.

Rather than respond, all the elements moved her closer to Mordred until she was hip-deep, and drawing further from shore.

Damn!

* * *

Sébastien and Atrox were deep in the spell when they heard Mordred's voice.

"You belong with me!" the sorcerer shouted.

He was about to drop the magic, but it was Atrox who stopped him. *No! Finish this first, it may be a distraction. We are close, knight. Focus!*

Sébastien did as instructed though his entire being screamed Vivienne was in danger once more. Still, he concentrated until the last of it was complete, and Atrox came to nudge him.

Let's go.

They followed the wall of the castle until it gave onto a picnic area which faced the lake. There, in turbulent waters, they saw Vivienne fighting against the elements. Slowly but surely, she moved further in and closer to the other side.

Sébastien moved before he had made the conscious decision to do so. Grasping Excalibur with both hands, he ran in after her. His sword struck the water once, twice, then a blinding light escaped.

When he blinked against it, Vivienne had stilled. He knew her body enough to recognize she was angry, and sure enough both water and air responded in kin. They expelled him out of the lake, then the elements circled around and targeted Mordred.

A wave of rage unlike any other unfurled over the enchantress, and Vivienne's eyes shone like glittering emeralds.

Her hands moved over each other, forming an orb of flames that she hurled towards the sorcerer without a second thought. She willed it to find its target, to harm him in the same

way he had tried to hurt her.

She envisioned it strong, pushing through any barrier, aided by water and air. Next thing she heard was Mordred's scream of pain, then the sound of a body hitting something hard.

Vivienne was panting, trying to calm down her own nerves–scared at what she could do.

"Did I kill him?" she whispered, unable to bear the thought.

As though hearing her, Mordred's laugh echoed across the distance–an unwelcome reminder he had been right, and she could not control herself.

Before she could give in to the despair, Atrox was in the water, pushing her backwards into Sébastien's arms. The knight turned her around and crashed his lips against hers, putting an immediate stop to the chaos of her thoughts.

Vivienne snuggled closer, burying herself in Sébastien's embrace. Before Alistair could intervene, he pushed her gently away and grasped her chin in his hand. "Love, hear me out. I know you're confused and afraid, but darkness cannot control you. You are light, you are a guardian of peace. No matter what Mordred says, remember that. You. Are. *Good.*"

The enchantress slumped in his grip, unable to stand on her shaking legs. Relief passed her gaze—right before she passed out in his arms.

CHAPTER 20

Atrox was staring out the window, his senses attuned to every movement out in the darkness. Another day had passed and yet another night ended without seeing Catriona. He had woken from a dream crying for her, disgusted at his own weakness but unable to let go of the pain.

"What troubles you, old pal?"

The wolf god turned his massive head towards Sébastien, ears flattening against it as a whine escaped him. *Nothing.*

The knight hoisted himself up on a shoulder, even as Vivienne curled up deeper in his back, seeking his heat. He hissed as her cold skin touched his, then relaxed and dozed off.

They had tried to get as much rest as possible, knowing their time was limited, and he felt awake. At least enough to take a long, hard look around and notice his friend's distress.

"You may lie to yourself," Sébastien whispered, "but something is bothering you. Is it Morgana again?"

Atrox shook his head in denial, then leaned it against the window and stared, forlorn, at the grounds beneath. *It has nothing to do with her.*

"Then what is it?" He tried to think back to the last few days and what might have put him in such a mood. It had not been until the previous evening that Atrox had become restless.

Night... A thought nagged at him, and then he knew. "Is it Catriona?"

Atrox stood frozen for a moment, then his head dropped in confirmation. Sébastien read the pain in his stance, the buried emotions.

"What happened?"

She had to leave.

Sébastien frowned, unsure he had heard correctly. "Leave? As in for a short time or...?" Atrox's silence provided the answer once more, and he knew no words of consolation would help.

After a beat, it was the wolf god who spoke. *I had a choice to keep her, to admit my feelings. Perhaps it would have changed things, perhaps not. But I did not take it, and instead I let her walk away.*

"Why?"

Carleigh followed her in her realm, and they fought until she chased him out. When I last saw it, her entire kingdom had been destroyed.

"Like Vivienne's," Sébastien murmured, grasping his lover's hand in his tightly, an instinct for shelter and contact taking over.

Yes, Atrox nodded. *I could tell you the reason I let her leave is for her own good...* His gaze drifted far away. *But I would be lying. I was only thinking of protecting myself, and my heart.*

Sébastien slid out of bed at that and knelt next to the demon dog, placing a hand on his fur. "If you made a mistake, you can fix it. Find her and tell her how you feel."

The midnight eyes shone with tears when they met his. *She has gone where I cannot follow: her father's realm.*

"Why would you be unable to go there? You're Atrox, one of three rulers of a pantheon. Whatever would stop you from getting to your lady love?"

A bark of laughter escaped Atrox. *You give me too much credit, knight. I can do many things as a god, but impeding upon a Fae king's domain without his approval... Is not one of them.*

"So *get* his approval."

His snort was loud in the small encampment, but Atrox nudged Sébastien's hand. *Maybe after a few centuries—* He halted, his fur rising as his gaze fixated on the forest.

They are here. Wake Vivienne and meet me downstairs.

Sébastien nodded, all business now. He pulled on a t-shirt and grabbed Excalibur, then stepped to the bed and kissed Vivienne awake.

"Time to get ready, love. Morgana and her lot are here."

A determined glint replaced the haze of desire in her eyes. "About time." She moved off and with a hand movement dressed in a silver gown, a cape thrown over her shoulders.

Sébastien smiled at the attire, knowing she had chosen it for comfort as much as nostalgia. "Ready?"

"Yes." She walked to him, resting her palm on his chest for a brief contact. "Be careful out there."

His gaze fell to her stomach, and he rubbed his palm over the slight bump. "And you—*both* of you."

Hand in hand, they stepped out of the castle's protection, determined to meet Carleigh on empty land.

* * *

Atrox kept his glare on Carleigh, Morgana and Mordred as they inched closer. When they were only a few meters away, he turned his head to the side. *Now.*

Vivienne focused her attention on the lake, inhaling its strength as much as possible, knowing she would soon be without its power. She then directed a jet of water and made it circle the trio of sorcerers that faced them. They all watched, unperturbed, as the transparent liquid surrounded them all by a thin string-like arc.

"I thought we were done playing tricks, sister," Carleigh greeted Vivienne. Morgana and Mordred remained quiet, eyes fixated on their opponents.

The enchantress only smirked in return. She flicked her finger and the band circling them pulled taut, then vibrated. Unseen, unfelt, Atrox added his own mix to the spell. A cocoon of light encompassed them all, then they disappeared.

When they reappeared, it was in an opposite landscape. As far as the eye could tell it was only rock and earth, large boulders and little. Mountains were all around, but no soul was in sight, not even a road.

"Where the hell are we?"

The angry question came from Mordred, who was looking around rather agitated. Sébastien was the one to answer, his voice the opposite in its calmness. "They call it the Burren, but it's in fact a historical site. It was the farthest we could find to get you all away from anyone you could use as collateral damage."

As Mordred was busy glaring, Carleigh sneered. "And you think this will help? Tourists fill these places."

"Perhaps," Vivienne mused, "but none wander this far out where no trails exist. It's just you and me, Carleigh."

The necromancer snickered, his eyes raking over Vivienne, Sébastien and Atrox's unmoving forms. "Aren't you a

person short?"

Atrox had not planned to reveal himself so soon, but between his emotions over Catriona leaving and facing the sorcerer, anger took over. His body shook, snarls escaping his wide jaws as light covered his fur.

A low growl and a shake of his head later, he was standing as a human—naked—and enjoying their stunned looks. With a simple hand movement, he donned his darkest toga, the wolf brooch glinting in the moonlight.

As he surveyed their faces, they each stood frozen in stupefaction—and fear. Even Morgana took a step back when the wave of his power hit her, full front and unabashed.

Atrox grinned coldly. "You asked. Here I am."

"Who the *hell* are you?" Carleigh snarled, not liking surprises. He shot a dark look to Morgana by his side, silently accusing her of having hidden this from him.

"Do not berate the Halfling, sorcerer," Atrox intervened in his rough voice. "She could not have sensed my power if she tried."

"She was linked to you!" Carleigh countered with another hateful glare. Still, Morgana remained silent, eyes wide and unmoving from the wolf god.

"And I am one of a trinity, too powerful for your senses to

detect." Atrox's tone left no room for argument.

Despite this, Carleigh made a move towards Morgana. Only Mordred's tight grip on his arm and shuttered expression stood in his way. "Leave my mother alone."

"We will finish this—after," Carleigh threatened, then turned his attention to Vivienne. "I will look forward to this."

The battle started in an almost synchronized dance. Of unspoken agreement, Sébastien moved towards Mordred, the lines of his body taut. "It's about time someone teaches you a lesson, boy."

"I hope you don't mean you," Mordred laughed and unsheathed a sword off his hip.

Vivienne stepped to Carleigh, her hand lighted pre-emptively, a focused expression on her face. The necromancer stepped back, pulling her away from the others—intending to get what he had come for all along.

Atrox glanced towards Vivienne, planning to keep an eye on her. He then turned his cold gaze on Morgana, noticing the flicker of unease in those gray orbs.

"Looks like it's you and me, sorceress."

* * *

Before he was even close enough to Mordred, Sébastien lifted Excalibur to block off an attack. The Halfling made up what he lacked in training with pure aggression, forcing the knight to stay on his toes.

They broke off and danced around each other, trying to find weaknesses to exploit. Sébastien's gaze drifted over Mordred's shoulder, where he could see Vivienne engaged in a fight with Carleigh.

A sword in his field of vision brought his attention back to his own battle, and Excalibur hissed when its blade connected with Mordred's.

"Focus on me, knight," the sorcerer ordered.

As he evaded another attack and parried with a counter one, Sébastien smirked. "It's called multi-tasking, *boy*. You should try it."

He ducked Mordred's enraged hit and elbowed him in the stomach instead. "Plus, you really should learn to defend all areas."

Mordred's eyes flashed at the advice, and it was all the warning Sébastien had before a gust of wind struck him full force and he went flying.

Sébastien had a déjà vu to his first fight with Carleigh, and their swords clashing. The necromancer had used magic, trying to cheat, until Alistair—*Atrox*, he corrected mentally—had stopped him.

Now, there were no limits.

He will not play fair, knight. Watch your back. Atrox's voice disappeared as swiftly as it came, and Sébastien risked a glance at him.

He was circling—no, *assessing*—Morgana, taking his time. *In the way a cat plays with its food,* he thought in amusement. Then his gaze focused on Mordred, standing over him smugly.

Sébastien stood, curling his palm around his sword's hilt. "I hadn't realized you wanted to play with magic. You should have just said so."

Gripping Excalibur, Sébastien imbued the blade with force. When it connected with Mordred, the backlash from both blades threw the young man backwards.

When he next got to his feet, he was no longer amused. Face darkened with rage, he lashed at Sébastien with all he had.

Mordred moved furiously, chaotically with his sword. A swordsman he was not, but his recklessness grew with each failed attempt. In contrast, Excalibur was an extension of Sébastien. The weapon parried and thrust with barely any effort on his part.

When neither magic nor fight were enough to shake him off, Mordred delved into the personal. "Did Vivienne ever tell you what happened while you were not around?"

Sébastien's clenched jaw was the only sign his comment had gotten through. That, and a particularly nasty kick Mordred received to the stomach. Though it left him coughing, Mordred was not one to back down.

"She was so vulnerable," he taunted, "so sweet and…. needy."

Sébastien was aware he was only trying to get a rise out of him, but the male inside him, the one who had staked his claim over Vivienne, did not intend to listen further.

He tore off from their interlaced swords and threw a punch instead, catching Mordred under the chin. When the young sorcerer flew backwards from the force of the blow, Sébastien followed. "You think your words get to me?"

"It's pretty obvious they do." Mordred spit out blood, then grinned. "Why else would you be losing your cool?"

Sébastien picked him off one-handed, fisting his shirt. Excalibur's tip pointed towards the ground, but his grip on it was tightening.

"Her lips were sweet, like berries," Mordred laughed.

Before he had rationally intended to, Excalibur was at the

sorcerer's throat, and Sébastien was panting. Through narrowed eyes, he saw the possibilities pass in front of his face like a movie in a fog.

Kill Mordred, and Morgana would go insane. She would try to slay Vivienne, pursuing them both with a passion akin to insanity. And she would not cease until they were both dead.

Let him live, be the better man, and Mordred would disappear. Fate was letting him choose, and his choice would affect more than one outcome.

"Do you want me to tell you how she kissed me back?"

The fog broke, and Sébastien tilted his head. "What kind of fool do you take me for?" he snarled, then released him abruptly. "I trust my fiancée's loyalty more than your poisoned words. Pick up your sword, boy. Let us finish this."

Mordred's eyes flashed in annoyance. *I almost had him!*

"She could have been mine," he tried again during a close call when they ended face to face.

Sébastien shoved him off. "Not likely. We were soul mates before you were born."

* * *

Vivienne glanced over her shoulder, distracted for a moment by the flare of darkness she sensed in Sébastien. He had Mordred up by his throat, Excalibur pointed at him with murdering intent.

Right as she was about to contact him, to calm him down from whatever frenzy had possessed him, Sébastien's aura went back to its regular color and he dropped the young man to the ground.

Her attention returned to Carleigh, who had also been

watching the exchange. "Looks like your knight learned to control the corruption within. What a pity."

Vivienne narrowed her eyes at his smug tone. Rather than give in to him, she brought up something she knew would destabilize the necromancer.

"I would have thought learning the truth, all the memories from the past, would have convinced you not to hurt me. After all, you pleaded your love for me far and wide, did you not?"

If possible, Carleigh became even paler at her question than his regular pasty skin tone. "How dare you bring this up?"

"Because as sick as it makes me to think you might have had a thing for me, it's even worse to realize how depraved you've become," Vivienne retorted.

Carleigh's strike came as no surprise, neither did the one he sent on the heels of the first. Angry beyond words, face deformed by the rage, he shot attack after attack at Vivienne.

With her shield, she deflected every single hit and waited for when she could counter him. In between strikes, he stopped to take a breath, and that was when the enchantress let loose both fire

and air, hitting him straight in the chest.

Carleigh flew backwards, landing hard on boulders a few feet away. When he got up, groaning, his eyes had gone full black. "You want to talk about love? You chose *him* over me! Not only content with discarding me, you had to parade him around the entire pantheon. The precious daughter of Light, happy at last."

"You should have been thrilled for your brother, if not for me."

Carleigh glared daggers at Sébastien's back, before turning

the hateful look onto her. "It was your choice that pushed me down this path!"

"Spare me," Vivienne said scathingly. "I did not force you to surrender to Darkness. It courted each of us, me included. Yet we never gave in to it! You were weak-willed from the start, nothing more."

"Never gave in to it?" Carleigh laughed. "And what do you say now, oh queen? Darkness in your belly, in your precious knight. Are you still pure?"

Vivienne's eyes glittered menacingly, her voice as even as she could keep it. "We may not be the perfect beings of light we were once. But we fight evil at every turn, and support each other through it. That is why Sébastien was my choice, and not you. Because you would have dragged me down in your filthy misery."

A semblance of emotion flickered over his face—Fury? Regret? Shame?

Whatever it was, it disappeared too quickly for Vivienne to read it. Instead, Carleigh gathered another orb of magic and thrust it towards her. This time, she caught it in her hand.

Carleigh gaped, unable to believe his sight—when the last time she had done so was after giving in to temptation during their last battle. Yet her gaze was clear, her face soft and as far from marble as possible.

Noticing his surprise, Vivienne smiled, twirling the orb between her fingers. "You do not scare me, now that I understand you. And I do not fear the dark, because I know I can fight it." *If nothing else, Mordred's tricks have taught me that—whether he willingly meant them to, or not.*

Carleigh narrowed his eyes, unsure where Vivienne's

strength came from. He had thought to squash his half-sister, get her unborn child and become a god again. Instead, he was stuck in

a duel with no way to escape it.

"Sad now that things aren't going according to your plan?" Vivienne taunted.

He gritted his teeth, clenching one hand against his power.

* * *

Atrox deflected Morgana's superficial attempt to fight once more, his expression amused. "If I didn't know better, I would say you are biding your time."

Gray eyes flared in anger, and she threw another orb of fire towards him. With a flick of his wrist, the wolf god diverted it and the sorceress had to jump out of the way.

Only rather than land on ground, she landed in his arms—he had moved at the last minute. He used the moment to grab Morgana closer, twisting until her back was to his chest.

"Look!" he rasped, pointing her in Vivienne's direction. "Do you not see the precious life she carries within? Will you really be an accessory to taking that away—when you suffered so yourself?"

Morgana stilled her struggling in his arms, and he sensed her attention on the enchantress. His tone hardened, recalling everything Catriona had divulged. "Do you really believe it is right to not only kill her, but tear the not-yet-developed unborn from her womb and burn him as sacrifice? Answer me!"

When he let her go, Morgana dropped to the ground as if stunned.

CHAPTER 21

Atrox watched Morgana for a moment, recalling what Catriona had tried to tell him. He had doubted the sorceress could ever change, considering the number of times she had fooled Merlin.

Yet now, looking at her crumpled form on the ground, he could sense no malicious intent. Gaze still wary, he ran a hand over their heads and a circle of light protected them—and hid them.

He then circled Morgana, casting his senses to feel her emotions. "Tell me truly, as we are alone. No one can hear us. Why are you doing this, helping Carleigh?"

"Merlin has to pay," she whispered. It was a phrase he had heard many times before, but none as unconvincingly as in that moment.

Aware of what he was risking, he knelt in front of her and met her darkened gaze. "I know he made you promise." When she was silent, he pressed, "Merlin. He tricked you, like you did in the past."

Morgana looked away, but still did not stand. "Then what is it you wish from me?"

"I want the truth. Why help Carleigh? Does it not disgust you, as a creature of nature, how he uses you? Does being around his darkness not bother you?"

There was a glint of life in her expression when she glared at him. "Of course it does! It sickens me that I have helped him, but he knows of my lost immortality. There is nothing I can do if he kills me—or Mordred."

Her gaze shifted over his shoulder to where her son and Sébastien were in a frenzied fight. "I will not watch him die again."

"No, instead you prefer to cause the world to suffer, all for one life? Is his the most important existence on this realm?"

"Yes," Morgana whispered, tears gathering in her eyes. "He is all I have left."

And for the first time in eons, Atrox watched as she crumbled in front of him, sobbing into her palms, her entire body trembling with contained emotion.

Morgana had known what Carleigh planned—or at least, she had guessed parts of it. But when Atrox had so cruelly outlined the facts, revulsion had filled her, for everything she had done and all she had *almost* done.

The wolf god observed her, then shamelessly used the moment to probe into her emotions, to sense that which the Halfling would have hid from his eyes. But there was nothing left in Morgana other than the deep sorrow she showed, and a pile of regrets.

Catriona was right. There really is something salvageable in her.

He glanced over his shoulder, pensively looking over Mordred and Carleigh. *If I could turn Morgana to our side...*

"I will help you keep Mordred safe—as long as he stays away from Vivienne. And I can give you back your immortality, Halfling."

Morgana stopped sobbing, raising her tear-streaked face to him. "Why would you do that, demon dog? You owe me nothing."

"Perhaps not, and perhaps I do it to make up for what happened in the past. I could not steer Merlin from the path that ruined you both, but I will not stand by and watch Vivienne harmed." He flexed his palm, a glow already within it. "Especially not now."

The sorceress dropped her gaze to the light, longing on her features. He could tell she wanted to take him up on his offer, but something held her back.

"What do you need from me in exchange?"

"Your loyalty," Atrox replied honestly.

"Nothing more, nothing less?" Morgana pressed, glancing towards her son once more.

"Exactly."

I hope Mordred can forgive me, because I only do this for his own good. She was silent for the span of a few breaths, then nodded. "What do you wish me to do?"

"For starters, we return your immortality." At her stunned gaze, he thought he had offended her. "What is it?"

"You intend to give me that which I wish most, without a single shred of proof that I will hold my word?"

Atrox leaned in to her until his stare caught hers, his hand on her shoulder. At first gentle, his touch firmed until it made her flinch. "Make no mistake, sorceress. I show my good faith thus, but if you cross me, you *will* pay. As will your son."

Morgana clenched her jaw, then nodded once more and shrugged him off. "Very well."

Atrox stared at her for a beat. *I hope to all hells I'm not making yet another error in judgment.* Then he lifted his palm and placed it upon her head.

"Stay very still."

* * *

Mordred deflected a hit from the knight, and out of pure habit turned to check on his mother. Instead of finding her, there was only nothingness.

"Where the hell did they go?"

Sébastien stopped midway another strike, checking the surroundings as well. Atrox had, for all intents and purposes, vanished.

Playing hide and seek?

It took a moment, but the wolf god answered. *Just taking care of something. Keep an eye on Vivienne.*

Sébastien was a second too late in focusing on Mordred, whose gust of air hit him full blast and sent him flying on the ground. His head smacked the pavement with a resounding crack, and he groaned.

Everything went blurry, but he could still see Mordred heading towards Carleigh and Vivienne.

"Hell no!" Sébastien breathed, his hand seeking Excalibur and closing around it in relief. He got back to his feet, gritting his teeth. Though the world spun, he caught sight of the sorcerers and headed their way.

* * *

Vivienne ducked another of Carleigh's curses, her eyes scanned the surrounding area. Moments ago, she had sensed a burst of energy, and could have sworn she had heard a woman cry. Thinking it had been Morgana, she had sought the sorceress— but both she and Atrox had vanished.

Distracted in her perusal, she took the next hit straight in the chest and barely remained standing. Her hand went to her womb and her unborn baby.

Keep my baby safe! Her magic rose at the command, and an invisible spell surrounded her with a barrier.

"Afraid you might lose your precious child?" Carleigh sneered. "Good. It is him I need for my sacrifice, with or without you."

Vivienne gritted her teeth and allowed the energy loose, a lioness defending her own. "You will not have my baby!"

By the time she noticed movement out of the corner of her eye, it was too late. Her hand was grasped into an iron grip, and she turned to meet Mordred's cold blue gaze.

"Let me go!" She tried to yank out of his grasp, but her shouts had no effect. Mordred's grip only tightened, mouth curling into a smirk.

"Not quite yet, love. You and I have things to finish."

Carleigh grinned at the turn of events. "Well played, Mordred. Take her and we can get out of here before that blasted wolf god returns."

"What about my mother?"

"She will join us—later."

Mordred's narrowed gaze fell on the necromancer, his entire body frozen with anger. When he spoke, his voice was low. "I do not think so. Find her. Otherwise, we stay here until she shows up."

Carleigh scowled, his expression on the verge of a blowout. "We had a deal."

"And nowhere did it say I am to abandon my mother at the hands of a god," Mordred retorted icily. He yanked Vivienne into his body, wrapping his free hand around her waist for good measure. "*Find her.*"

Muttering under his breath about insolent young men, Carleigh curled his fist and called darkness forth. It crawled on the ground in search of her and stopped at the same spot as before, to no avail.

"There is nothing there!" Mordred screamed. "Do better!"

"No," Carleigh denied. "I have had quite enough of you and your mother."

"Watch yourself, necromancer." Mordred recognized the glint of madness in Carleigh's eyes and was not about to lose his precious prize to a madman. Gaze glued to him, he pushed Vivienne backwards, getting her out of harm's way but still within his reach.

Carleigh smirked as though he knew something he did not—then darkness crawled up his leg. Mordred jumped backwards, but it followed him, climbing further up. Distracted by his own plight, he did not see Sébastien come up behind the necromancer.

And neither did Carleigh.

When Excalibur slashed across his back, his mouth opened in horror. *Not the poisoned sword!* He spun with wide eyes, unable to believe what he was seeing. "You…"

"Time to say goodbye, brother. You have poisoned this world enough."

He went to drop Excalibur on his head, but it flew out of his hands. He whirled, stunned—as did Mordred and Vivienne. Everything seemed to stop while they registered what happened.

Morgana had appeared out of thin air, dressed no longer in her dark robes, but rather in an emerald green gown with a cape of the same color. Her expression, previously gaunt and drawn, was now almost rosy. Her eyes sparkled with power, hair wavy and shiny.

"She's stunning!" Vivienne breathed behind Mordred, faced with the Halfling's true face.

Mordred himself was speechless, able only to watch—but not intervene. The darkness on his leg had crawled away, returning to its master whose back it tried to heal.

"I knew I could count on you," Carleigh cackled.

Sébastien glanced from Morgana to Atrox, who was standing nearby. The wolf god made the smallest head gesture—and the knight remained silent.

As Carleigh tried to rise, curbed in two because of his wound, Morgana kept inching closer.

Step away, Atrox warned Sébastien, who was the closest in the vicinity.

He did as instructed, now reading the intention in Morgana's eyes. Carleigh did not.

When she was only a few inches away, Morgana gripped Carleigh's chin. The necromancer froze, searching her gaze.

With a smile as cold as ice itself, she brought her free hand up—and blew powder in his face. Carleigh stood frozen for a moment, then fell to the ground, contorting in pain.

In front of their bewildered stares, he became nothing—returned to whence he had been born.

Out of them all, it was the youngest that recovered first.

"How could you!?" Mordred shouted at Morgana. He glanced again at Carleigh's dead body, even now turning to dust. His jaw was tight, fists clenched and expression darkening in fury at the betrayal.

"He was an aberration from birth," Morgana stated. "And we are not."

Mordred looked at the wolf god, reappeared as magically as his mother. "No. You're lying," he accused. "You've turned against me!"

Morgana's expression fell. "I did not!"

"You did!"

He evaded her touch when she tried to hug him, shaking his head and marching backwards. Mordred diverted his wrath to Vivienne and in a surge of unprecedented display of violence, launched himself at her.

Focused on protecting her baby, Vivienne wrapped her arms around her mid-section, calling another spell for defense. But it was her throat Mordred aimed for.

His hand wrapped her neck in a vice grip, and he lifted her off the ground. Sébastien moved to attack him, but Atrox was there to hold him back.

"You will injure Vivienne," he warned. "Stay within his sight. He hates you and will wish to hurt you as much as possible."

Sébastien clenched his jaw hard enough to chip a few teeth,

ready to launch. Atrox's hand tightened on his forearm until he met the god's firm gaze. "Hear me, Sébastien. Work with me like you have in the past, and I swear we will save Vivienne."

The knight nodded tightly, and Atrox released him. They turned their gazes to where Mordred still held Vivienne. With his mother nearing them, the sorcerer had shifted stances and placed the enchantress before him, her back to his chest, and was now

holding her by the waist.

By the time he looked to Sébastien with hateful eyes, Atrox had already sunk into the shadows available, morphing to his wolf form.

The knight met Mordred's gaze full on. "Let her go."

"No." The sorcerer grinned. "In fact, I think I'll have some fun."

His palm slid to Vivienne's stomach, settling right over the bump. She struggled against him, but his free hand moved to her neck and squeezed until she was immobile once more.

"Do not move," he ordered in her ear. Then the touch over her stomach lighted, even as he smirked, his gaze still on Sébastien. "I think it's time I taught you who is in charge here."

"Mordred!" Morgana screamed, snapped out of her stupor when faced with the result of her own thirst for vengeance. She would not have believed he was capable of harming an innocent, a baby, but there was no denying the evidence.

Her eyes brimming with tears, she looked upon the son she would have given all to—the one she should have raised better. Her thoughts turned to Merlin, probably dead by now because of Carleigh's contraption.

I cannot lose him again.

"Please, son," she murmured, inching closer to him. "Let Vivienne go."

"No!" he snarled, face twisted in rage. Vivienne whimpered in his arms, gasping for air.

"You're suffocating her!" Sébastien yelled, taking a step closer.

Mordred backed away, tightening his grip further on the enchantress. Vivienne's panicked eyes met Sébastien's, and he read the pain in there.

"Mordred, what is it you wish?" He pleaded, trying to keep his voice firm. It shook with rage at seeing Vivienne's skin marred with bruises, her existence at his mercy.

"I want you to beg," the sorcerer smirked. "Beseech me for her life."

Sébastien did not hesitate. With Vivienne turning blue in the face, he dropped to his knees, his gaze never once leaving her. "I beg you. Please let her breathe. Please!"

Mordred pretended to think, and he wanted nothing more

than to use Excalibur to cut off his head. But at the last moment, while Vivienne's eyes rolled in her head, he loosened his grip.

She bent over in two—still in his arms—and Mordred watched her, grinning, as she tried to gulp as much air in her lungs as possible.

"You *bastard*!" Sébastien shouted, standing.

"No! *Stay*, knight—god of whatever—until I tell you otherwise." He then shifted his sparkling eyes to his mother. "See this, mum? I have a deity on his knees." He laughed wildly. "Who would have thought it?"

He focused his attention to Vivienne then, whispering in

her ear. It was all Sébastien could do to remain immobile. *Atrox!*
Almost there.

The wolf moved in the shadows, even as Sébastien trembled with rage.

"This is all your fault," Mordred hissed in Vivienne's ear. "If only you had listened and come with me, it would not have ended thus."

The enchantress tried to stay calm, when all she wanted was to scream. "Please don't do this, Mordred. It's not necessary...."

"Oh, but it is."

Vivienne's eyes widened when she sensed the power building behind them. She was dimly aware of him opening a portal. The same realization dawned on Morgana's features.

"You're coming with me," Mordred confirmed.

Her panicked gaze flew to Sébastien. He was a second too late realizing what was happening, only catching sight of the exit with his senses.

"Say bye to your lover, darling, because it's the last time you'll see him. No one can follow us where we are going."

Before Vivienne could open her mouth to speak, Mordred grabbed her and used air to propel them towards the vortex. They were a few feet from their standing spot when shouts echoed from below.

"Vivienne!"

"No!"

Sébastien let loose the rage within and thrust his palms at the sorcerer. Light escaped him and headed straight for the man's chest. It was not alone, as a set of fiery magic joined it.

The knight glanced to his right, to where Morgana had also

shot a ray towards her son. Her gaze flickered to him, and they both dropped their hands in unison.

Mordred stayed suspended in air for a moment—and Vivienne with him—then sank like a boulder. He let go of the enchantress and their bodies drifted apart.

As she fell, Atrox jumped from the forest as a massive dog and picked Vivienne up on his back, returning her to Sébastien's arms. The knight grasped her tightly, murmuring in her hair while she held onto his neck and trembled.

"You're safe now," he kept repeating. "You're protected. He's gone."

Atrox was the first to turn away from them, allowing them their privacy. He stepped a few feet to where Morgana stood in a trance staring where the vortex still swirled—and where Mordred had disappeared.

The wolf god read the sorrow in her eyes and touched her shoulder lightly. Morgana lifted a teary gaze to him. "You don't have to." His words were low, reading her intent. "You're free now. Mordred got what he deserved."

"But I do," Morgana smiled. "I have to see this through. He is my son, *my* mistake."

Atrox said nothing, aware more than most of what the weight of regret could do.

"Thank you."

Morgana glanced up at the couple's heartfelt gratitude. Vivienne had joined them, resting heavily on Sébastien. His arm was wrapped around her middle, their auras aligned in perfect synchrony.

"I don't know what, exactly, happened between you and my mentor, Merlin." Vivienne took a step forward, at first hesitantly, then more sure. She and Morgana were of the same height, so she had no trouble looking her in the eyes. "But whatever it was, it brought you on my path, and I would not be here without your help. So again, *thank you*, from the bottom of my heart."

Morgana blinked back the tears threatening at bay. "You have nothing to thank me for, Lady of the Lake. It is I who need to thank *you* for giving me the chance to set things right. I hope one day, you can accept my apology for all that nearly happened."

"I do," Vivienne smiled, then hugged her. When she pulled back and returned to Sébastien's embrace, the Halfling's radiant grin reflected hers.

Her gaze lowered to the enchantress' stomach. "Take care of my little brother, will you?"

"I promise."

Sébastien chose that moment to act, touching Morgana's shoulder much like Atrox had done. His voice was thick with emotion at what she had done. "Thank you, *enchantress*."

Morgana inclined her head graciously, and stepped towards the lake. Sensing eyes on her, she glanced behind one more time and shared a look with Atrox. The wolf god's knowing gaze was unwavering, even as she dove into the vortex headfirst.

Wish him a good life from me, Morgana, his voice echoed in her mind.

She closed her eyes, blocking all else except the feel of the waves, the swirling of the water. Deep in her heart, she begged her Fae powers to take her to her utmost hidden desire, to where she had to be...

CHAPTER 22

Vivienne!

The enchantress jumped, turning away guiltily from the mirror. *I'm coming!*

Hurry, would you? Your knight is about to have a heart attack.

She chuckled and glanced once more at her reflection, then walked down the stairs. It had been Sébastien's idea to have the ceremony held at Ross castle. Somehow it seemed fitting, considering it had been where he had proposed.

She stepped on the last stair and stopped for a minute, enough to catch her breath. Though only two weeks had passed from when they had their final battle, the pregnancy was advancing—and Vivienne sensed it would be anything but normal.

As if conjured by thin magic, Atrox showed up—in human form, and dressed to boot. His dark eyes glittered as they fell on her.

"You are a vision, highness."

She chuckled weakly, grasping his elbow when he offered it. "You do realize you outrank me now, right?"

He smiled mysteriously. "If only you knew."

Ignoring her curious gaze, he kissed her cheek and almost pulled her down another set of stairs, only slowing his pace when they reached the corner of the castle.

"Why stop now?" Vivienne teased. "You practically hauled me here."

His expression was full of something when he faced her. His voice had roughened, as it only got when he was emotional. "I need you to know how much I love you, like a sister. You have been... a treasure to see grow, and I am the luckiest guardian to have had such a mistress."

Tears gathered in her eyes, some escaping despite her efforts. "Why speak as if you are leaving me?"

Atrox opened his mouth to reply, but the words would not come. Instead, he kissed her forehead and wiped her cheeks, then smiled. "Never, highness. I will always be by your side."

Once Vivienne pulled in a few more breaths, he stepped around the corner and had the pleasure of witnessing Sébastien's expression a split second before Vivienne.

The knight had been restless all day, but even more so as the night approached and the apex of the full moon. It had taken all of Atrox's coaxing to dress him in black slacks and a chemise fit for a god, with threads of silver.

With his black hair and rugged features, Sébastien was the picture of a dark angel—one who would spend the rest of his life looking after Vivienne and loving her as she deserved.

I wish you were here to witness this, old friend, Atrox thought of Merlin.

Sébastien now stood rigid, his expression frozen in stupor as he looked at the vision walking towards him, eyes downcast. Her long dark hair framed her face freely, falling in cascading waves. A crown of flowers rested atop her head, the only ornament she had allowed.

As she moved, the white dress flowed with her body, both embracing her femininity and hinting at her beauty. Her cheeks were flushed from the exertion, but when she looked up at Sébastien, her entire being lighted.

Atrox saw their auras, and at once felt the loneliness that had plagued him the last few weeks. Determined not to let it affect this moment, he shook it off and stopped in his tracks.

"I believe she is yours now, knight," he grinned, then handed Vivienne's right hand to Sébastien.

As they both stood holding hands, Atrox moved between them and the lake. He raised a palm to the moon, open and outstretched. "On this holy night, I am here to serve as witness to the union of two who were meant to be long before this world ever evolved."

In his hand appeared a silver band which he purified with water, before getting back up and facing the couple. Vivienne and Sébastien were too engrossed in each other and he had to clear his throat.

"Are you with me, lovebirds?" He laughed as Vivienne blushed, and shared a wink with Sébastien, then he gestured between them. "Please join your right hands."

They did as they were told, sharing a secret look like they so often did—one of both love and the promise of what was to come. Atrox then bound the silver cord around their wrists until it had been set in a solid figure eight—the symbol of infinity.

The two soul mates had grown silent, awed by the beauty of the moment. Atrox placed his hands on their wrist, his palms already imbuing their bindings with a soft glow. "Your lives have always been linked, but never such as in this moment. On this day, you have both chosen to stand before me, before the world as you know it, and to choose each other—for life."

Vivienne smiled, her body leaning towards Sébastien's. The knight's aura warmed in response, and Atrox smiled.

"Until this moment, fate separated you. Obstacles streamed your paths. But you rose above them because you were together—united. You may have been separate in thought and action, but your intentions always aligned. As your hands are bound by this cord, so too, shall your lives be bound as one."

He looked from one to the other, his voice hoarse with emotion. "May you be forever happy, sharing in all things, in love and loyalty for all time to come." *May you always be safe, protected from all harms, by my guidance I beseech it.* Aloud, he continued, "Blessed be, my friends. Sébastien, you may kiss your bride."

The knight did not wait to be told twice. He wrapped an arm around Vivienne's waist and pulled her closer, mouth dropping to hers in a kiss of promises.

When they drew apart, Vivienne was laughing and crying all at once. "Damn these hormones!" she cursed, then hugged Atrox tightly.

"You're the best," she whispered in his ear.

* * *

Three weeks later...

Vivienne and Sébastien had honeymooned at a few castle resorts in Ireland and finally ended up renting a cottage by the water. They had been there for a week when Atrox joined them.

He kept his dog shape, accustomed to it now. It helped keep his thoughts more focused on needs rather than wants and idiotic dreams. Still, his restlessness became clear enough to bother his mistress.

"What is it, Atrox?" Vivienne asked him one morning.

Nothing, highness, he denied as he usually did. *The weather makes me moody, is all.* It had rained for the last two days in a row, and it seemed like a plausible excuse.

Vivienne, senses sharpened by her pregnancy, did not fall for it. "I doubt that's the truth. Please, talk to me." She settled down on the rug next to him, petting his fur with a soft touch. *"Please."*

He looked up into her pleading green eyes and was at a loss. *I...* Atrox trailed off, unsure of how to voice what was in his mind.

"He needs to leave, love," Sébastien rescued him.

The enchantress gaped at her husband, who now leaned against the wall, watching Atrox with an expression that dared him to contradict. "I think it's high time you go find your Fae, wolf god. After everything you did for us, I need to know you can be happy too."

Vivienne glanced to him for confirmation, and Atrox nodded, sighing. Her eyes filled with tears, and no amount of nuzzling her was enough to ease the pain. Like the rock he was, Sébastien moved closer and threw his arm around her shoulders.

I will take care of her, I swear.

I know.

"Will I ever see you again?" Vivienne choked.

Atrox turned human. "Of course, highness. I'll always return to you. Just, maybe, not alone."

His smirk was all male, and Vivienne laughed between her tears. Sébastien only gave him a knowing grin, a silent acknowledgement in his stance.

"Promise you'll bring her to visit," Vivienne pleaded, and he nodded.

"Good. How can we help?" Sébastien intervened.

"I need passage to a particular Fae realm."

Vivienne frowned at Sébastien. "Didn't you tell me she was with her father?"

The knight shrugged, then met Atrox's gaze. "You try keeping anything from Catriona once you get her back... *then* give me that look." When the wolf god only shook his head in amusement, Sébastien continued, "Aye, I did. And for Atrox to sneak in there, it'll take all of us."

"Very well," Vivienne agreed. "Then what are we waiting for?"

Together, they headed to the lake, ducking under the rain. Vivienne and Sébastien joined hands first, acting as a conduit. Atrox stepped in the water, then turned and placed both his palms on theirs.

The rain poured harder, its repetitive drip-drip mixing with the sound of the wind. Vivienne shared a look with her old guardian, then smiled and let go. Their magic mixed, strong enough to cause a few trees to fall over.

When all was said and done, a passage opened in the lake.

Knowing he had limited time, Atrox broke contact and pulled Vivienne in a bear hug. He swallowed past the lump in his throat, then released her back in Sébastien's arms, his eyes darting between them. "Be happy."

Vivienne's cheeks were wet, both with rain and tears. But the gleam in her eyes was understanding, and her smile encouraging. "Safe travels, Atrox."

Their eyes met and held for a long moment, centuries of friendship passing between them. It was not a goodbye —only a temporary departure. At least, that was what Atrox tried to tell himself when he turned his back on the couple and dove into the water headfirst.

He emerged a few feet farther, almost near the vortex, and glanced back. *Until we meet again.*

Then he allowed the current to drag him further in, and closed his eyes to think of Catriona.

* * *

Back on the shore, Vivienne leaned against Sébastien. She would miss her friend, her companion, and no words could explain how much. But they had another life to care for, and she hoped Arthur, at least, would fill the void Atrox's departure left.

She ran her hands down her stomach, holding onto her ever-growing bump. "How will we ever explain all this to Arthur?"

Sébastien chuckled in her ear. "Oh love, we'll find a way. Or at least we can try."

His mouth descended on hers and he took his time savoring the taste of her lips, in a promise of tomorrow. Hand in hand, they returned to the cottage—and their new life.

EPILOGUE

Morgana stepped out of the vortex, wary at what she would find. She had known it would bring her to her heart's desire, but did not feel ready to face what she was bound to discover there.

She tiptoed inside, headed to where he had last been. Rather than locate remnants of broken stone and shattered glass, she found the room the same way it had been. Only, the restraints were empty, and Merlin nowhere to be seen.

"What the hell are *you* doing here?"

She whirled, noticing him in a corner, pale and trying to regain his strength. The fire in his eyes died as he noticed her burning hands.

"Come to see me dead, have you?"

When she did not answer, he sneered. "Well, have at it. I have nothing to give you except my life."

Morgana stared back at him, panting. "I will take it."

Her palms stood towards him, extended and trembling. The

light was ready to part, almost burning to be loose and end him as she had wished countless times before. Yet Morgana stood immobile, breathing hard, her grey eyes latched onto his.

Merlin's gaze went from incensed, to confused in the span of a few heartbeats. Then he dropped his eyes to her lips, and Morgana's mouth parted in response to his intensity.

In front of his bewildered gaze, she lowered her hand. "Atrox said to wish you a good life."

The End

A small spinoff ☺

Liked *The Avalon Chronicles*, but missing Alistair/Atrox already? His story is nowhere close to finished. In fact, it's only beginning!

> *Atrox barely stepped out of the vortex when he knew he was in trouble. Rather than a clearing similar to the one he was used to in Catriona's realm, he found himself surrounded by Faes – males. In armor. With spears.*
>
> *"Shite!" he cursed under his breath.*
>
> *"I thought I was clear when we last saw each other, mutt."*
>
> *Atrox whirled around, his midnight gaze falling on Merlyddus, sitting on his throne. "You were warned to stay out of my business."*
>
> *Rather than cower, the wolf god rose to his full stature, eyes flashing red. "I heard you loud and clear, Fae king. But I did not come here for you. I've come to take home what is mine."*
>
> *The king's eyes glittered menacingly, but still he asked. "And what would that be?"*
>
> *"Catriona."*

Don't miss out on the novella wrapping up his
story, coming 2019!

If you liked _The Avalon Chronicles,_ try one of my other series!

For a sneak peek at my urban fantasy (young adult) series, check out **The Sage's Legacy**!

If you're in the mood for a different type of paranormal romance, the _Moonlight Rogues_ are waiting for you ☺

Or there's always my standalone novels!

Preview of First to Fall
(Moonlight Rogues, Book 1)

∞ 1 – Începuturi ∞
"The beginning is the most important part of the work."
-Plato-

L u c r e z i a

My feet crunch in the snow, and for the tenth time this morning I thank my lucky stars I invested in my fuzzy warm boots. It may have been money I didn't have, but with the way the winter is acting up, it will only get worse.

Rockland Creek, Wyoming, is renowned for its harsh winters—not that it's the real reason I ended up here. It was the most remote place near the border with Canada and having that quick escape possible eases the tightness in my back somewhat.

Memories of a much darker time linger at the edge of my consciousness, but I shake them off. Distance and months of breathing freely have made it easier to compartmentalize, and I'm determined to get in to work chipper despite the chilly Monday morning.

An icy gust of wind sweeps up, and I huddle in my coat, wishing I had grabbed an extra sweater underneath it.

Almost there. As if to spite me, Mother Nature throws in some nice flurries—and more wind. Gritting my teeth against it, I quicken my step towards Claws Auto Shop, which I see in the distance. I'm one of those lucky few who can walk to work rather than have to drive or bus, which keeps me in an overall nice shape and clears my mind most mornings.

Most times, it only takes me about half an hour to

get there. It's a breeze in summer, but not so much in winter. I vaguely consider asking one of my colleagues

for a lift for the rest of the season and then dismiss the idea. The last thing I want them to feel is obligated to protect the only girl in their pack.

By the time I finally reach the side door of Claws Auto Shop, where I work as receptionist, my cheeks are frozen and my fingers refuse to cooperate. I fumble with the key, dropping it three times in the snow, before I get the blasted thing open.

After taking off my coat and switching into some comfortable sneakers, I sit down at my small desk and get started on my day. Within the next hour, as I answer calls and confirm appointments, the guys pile in one by one.

Guys, no. These are *men* and so damn gorgeous my heart hurts every time I notice them. Unfortunately, other body parts I've neglected for a while also poke their head out. Normally, I have a tight control on my hormones. These last few weeks, however…

I tear my eyes away from them and focus on my paperwork, going through the previous week's sales and amounts for collection. Having studied accounting and business while in university, numbers always fascinated me. They make sense, more so than people ever do—to me, at least. But this time around, not even the dry accounts payable booklet is enough to keep me focused. With every ring of the bell announcing someone's presence, I glance up.

First Finn McConnell shows up, his mischievous green eyes twinkling already. With his mop of unruly dark hair and the lithe body of an athlete, he could easily be an actor or model. The lilt in his voice hints at his Irish background, and yeah it's sexy as hell. You would never peg him for a lawyer, but he once dabbled in the trade before leaving Ireland for the States—a long, long time ago like he says.

Next comes Tristan Cayne, brooding about another sleepless night, if the circles under his eyes are any indication. He's a war vet, honorably discharged from the Marines with PTSD—post-traumatic stress disorder. He lost his entire unit in an ambush in the desert and still has the nightmares about it. His skin is tanned even in winter, due to his Brazilian blood, but the man knows how to pull off jeans and a simple shirt like no other. With his shaved head, gentle hazel gaze and square jaw, he's the most aloof of the four.

Third in is Dominic Kosta, with blue eyes that capture me every time and the sinful body of Apollo. Dark blonde hair, clean-cut jaw and muscular build, he's the gentlest of the bunch. At first he told me he was born and bred here, but after many late evening conversations, he revealed he was adopted from a Romanian orphanage by an American couple who couldn't have children of their own.

The story answered a lot of questions about him, and it gave me more insight into this gentle giant who I've seen break more than one heart with all his womanizing. Despite it, there's a quiet confidence in him I respond to, and he puts me at ease in a way no other man has. I've been working here for the last year, but it's Dominic I connected with more than all the others.

His grin lights his face when he sees me, and he moves in

for a hug. I squeal out of his grip, shivering at the wind drafting in with him. "Get away, you're ice cold!"

Dom picks me up snorting and twirls me around, before putting me back down. I'm still recovering from the closeness, when the last of them walks in.

"Already wasting time, I see?" Lucas Bianchi's remark would have stung, had it not been delivered with his side-smirk and glittering onyx eyes. The man is Italian to the bone, and his commanding presence tends to leave me shaking at the knees.

Lately, it's morphed into more than that. Whenever he's around, I lose my words—and I haven't crushed on anyone since high school.

"Morning, Lucrezia," he murmurs in his gravelly voice, and I smile feebly in return. To this day, Lucas is the only one who calls me by my full name, all the others having picked up on the nickname Dom gave me: Luz, for light.

As can be guessed, the mixed nationalities have definitely increased my vocab, at least where swearing is concerned. Both Tristan and Lucas lose it in their respective native tongues, and it's almost fun watching them when it happens.

With a nod to Dominic, Lucas heads to the back, already barking orders to Finn and Tristan. Two other guys help around the store in summer, but they're only teenagers from high school, learning the trade. Mostly, it's just us five: me on the paperwork and phones, and the guys tinkering and fixing the cars of Rockland Creek—and of the people passing through.

And I was the lucky one who got to work with them every week, day in and day out.

"Why the long sigh?"

Oops. I'm uncannily aware of Dom's steady gaze on me—

and his keen sense of observation.

"Bah, it's Monday," I try to joke, but even I don't fall for it. I peek towards Lucas, who's now opening the doors of the garage—a tell-tale sign announcing they're ready for work.

The inside of their working environment has heat blasting so even with the cool air wafting in, they're comfortable. Not that it seems to matter to these four—

they're so hot-blooded a hug from them will have you sweating in no time!

Thankfully for me, a transparent window and well-insulated door separates me from the garage area, and I get to stay indoors and enjoy the warmth.

My gaze is drawn to the two cars already driving in, one of which is a sporty red Mustang convertible. The other is a pickup truck that has seen better days. It's no surprise when Lucas walks over to the Mustang, with Tristan heading to the other car to greet the clients.

"Who the hell drives a car like that in winter?" My eyes narrow in annoyance.

The answer soon makes itself known. A leggy brunette steps out of the car, dressed in dark leggings, thigh-high boots with six-inch stilettos and a white fur coat. Even from afar, I notice her makeup is done to perfection.

Though I'm confident in my flaming locks and exotic features, I don't tend to flaunt my looks. Working with the guys gives me the perfect excuse for casual dress and flying under the radar in jeans and t-shirts.

It's better this way, the reasonable voice in my mind warns. *Remember what happened last time?*

A snort from Dom has me focus back on him, in time to

see his grimace.

"What?"

"The girl," he rolls his eyes. "She'll be a handful. I better go, Lucas might need help."

I watch him go, trying to stifle an exasperated sigh—and failing. "You sure it's not *her* you want to get a closer look at?"

Dom turns around at that, a flash of surprise crossing his features. It's gone so quick I might have imagined it. He grins instead and winks. "Not with you around, Luz."

He's gone before I can figure out what he means, and I turn my attention to my regular tasks. At least until

the brunette comes for payment. "I was told to come here to pay for the services," she says huskily, and I wonder for a second if she fakes that voice.

I force a polite smile, realizing how mean my thoughts are turning. "Of course. May I see their quote?" She hands me the paper—perfectly manicured nails, I notice—and I plug it into the computer and issue her a formal invoice.

Once she pays I staple a receipt to the invoice and hand it back to her. Eliza Porting is her name, and if it didn't fit her so classically I would laugh about it. She sounds so posh, dresses to a T, yet here she is in the middle of nowhere with a car that broke down.

You once ended up here in a similar way... I try to ignore the reasonable voice nagging me. A lecture would be bad right about now.

Oddly put off, I hand Eliza back the card and return to my computer. I figure this will be it and she'll go wait in the seating area, but she sees fit to hang around.

"How do you work with all that man candy around?" An

annoying giggle follows her whispered words.

I track her gaze to the guys, for a moment detracted when Lucas bends down to check under the car, giving us both a perfect view of his, err, assets. Eliza's practically panting in delight, eyes glued to him solely now.

Mine, I want to growl, and hold back. This possessive nature is new for me, as is the jealousy. I have no right, but Lucas is that kind of man. The type you want to lock up and have your way with, day and night... *especially* night.

"Not sure what you mean," I mutter, focusing on papers that need no more organizing.

She turns to peer at me then—really looks at me, assessing me from head to toe—and smirks knowingly. "Oh, I get it. It's ok; I have nothing against people who play for the other team."

The diva goes back to ogling the guys lasciviously, dismissing me in the process. "More for me."

My palm itches, consumed by an almost insane urge to slap her. Just because I dress a certain way, she needs to label me already? *Bitch.*

I'm about to comment, when her next words hit me hard. "So, seen Tommy lately?" Her lips turn upwards into a sneer at my shocked expression, but those eyes are emotionless.

Shit. I thought I escaped this.

D o m i n i c

I stare at Luz for who knows how long this particular time. At first, I tried to keep my distance. She was new, different, and mortal. But something in her calls to me as sure as the full moon, and the more I've known her these last months, the more

I want her.

Unfortunately, she only has eyes for Lucas. She doesn't understand the reason for her attraction is linked to his status as chieftain of our pack. Nor that he officially took the lead as alpha in the summer, causing a hell of a lot of hormonal changes in his scent over the last weeks that affect even the most hardened females.

Then again, Luz also has no idea she's living and working in the midst of a town ruled by werewolves.

Some secret, huh?

We've kept it on the down low from the uninitiated—basically, people like Luz who think the world is normal. Her working for us was a complication at first. We were so used to joking around and acting like mutts in heat that needing to censor ourselves seemed like chaining.

It would have built resentment, were it not for Luz's open perspective on life. She quickly—and bossily—got us all in check, ordering us to treat her like one of the guys. It established a certain professional relationship.

Which is why I'm loath to break it. That, and there was something wounded about her when she first appeared in town. I still remember the day she got off the bus with nothing but a backpack, looking lost and so damn vulnerable it tore at my heart. I was in wolf form, and her scent acted like an aphrodisiac I had a hard time letting go of.

Not many humans are supposed to affect us this way. Not many *do*.

Except Luz.

Back then, despite morphing into my human form, I'd still struggled to quiet my wolf down. I can recall, even to this day, the anxiety in her expression when I first asked if she was new to town. After a few moments of awkward talk, I offered to show her around.

It might have been the loneliness or her quick assessment of me, but Luz agreed. Within the day, we ended up at a diner. No matter how much I tried to probe back then—and since then—the only information I got was that she recently moved to Rockland Creek and was searching for a job.

Before I thought things through, I was already telling her our mechanic's shop direly needed a receptionist. Lucas had been none too happy when I showed up with her in tow, but after some discussion, he relented. Luz was hired the next day, and Lucas has admitted on more than one occasion since that it was the best decision he ever made.

My thoughts of Luz must have intruded on my senses because my wolf is growling. *Danger.*

And no, I don't make a habit of hearing voices, at least not in the losing-my-mind way. But I do have a second facet to my personality, and that's my wolf.

He lives within me, like a subconscious part of me, not an alter ego but more... a voice of reasoning. On a regular basis, he pokes his head out only when strong emotions control me, luring me away from my more human side.

But this time...

I listen to the warning and look towards the reception desk where Luz's anger reverberates across the distance. The high-maintenance gal who's with her irks me, and she annoys my wolf.

"Don't," Finn mutters next to me.

I glance at my buddy, surprised he read me so easily. Then

again, with Finn, you're an open book more often than not. That's the thing when you're around werewolves with special *gifts*, like I call them.

"You know she has feelings for Lucas." His eyes narrow in disapproval, darting from Luz back to me.

"And you know *why* she has them," I retort, going back to what I'm supposed to be doing— hammering back into shape a beat-up bumper.

Finn follows me to the long table meant for the task, not dropping the conversation. "You're assuming," he accuses, and I hammer the metal a little too hard.

My back muscles tense, and my wolf jumps to defense when I turn to him. "Back off, Finn."

He notices my glare, because after a few tense moments of staring at each other he steps away, hands held up in the air. "I'm only saying, mate. Keep in mind, Luz may have real feelings and more than a crush on our boss."

I don't believe that. *Won't* believe it, is more like it.

And as I sense Luz's annoyance go up a notch, my wolf whines. *We can't sit by and do nothing.*

"Need a coffee." My mutter is barely audible, but I don't wait for an answer, instead storming toward the doors. I step through, and the gal from the city moves towards me like a cat pouncing on her favorite toy. Her overwhelming perfume makes me cough and I take a step sideways.

"Aw, poor baby's got a cold?"

I don't know what my face conveys at her idiotic question, but she backs away so fast she almost trips over her heels. "No, just allergic to perfumes, *miss*." I stress the term for professionalism's sake, before dismissing her and turning to

Luz.

Luz's eyes flash towards the client and the scent of anger hits me again, something I seldom see in her. It makes the gold stand out against the green of her eyes, and the image of a cat superimposes itself for a moment in my imagination.

Cats and dogs don't mix, my wolf points out. I stifle a smile at that, and Luz stops glaring at the fake Barbie long enough to spare me a concerned look. "You ok, Dom?"

I fake cough this time and force a sheepish grin. "On second thought, I may be coming down with something. Want to make me one of your special teas?"

Whenever any of us is sick, we go to Luz. She has an insane knowledge of herbal teas and their best properties, which comes in handy. My eyes roam over her as she moves from behind the desk, noticing the jeans and long-sleeved purple top she's wearing. She's shorter than me by a head at least, but damn those curves have my mind wandering in a not-so-innocent way, one too many times a day.

Then Luz grins at my words, and it's quick and bright like the sun appearing after a morning of clouds. I swallow past everything else I want to add—this is not the time. Instead, I pout in supplication, hoping the ruse will work.

Luz glances over at the client, undecided and unwilling to slack on the job. "I'll watch her." My promise comes in a mutter, as I'm none too pleased about spending alone time with the snotty client.

After a moment, Luz bites her lip, but relents and moves to the back. "Her name's Eliza."

I'm staring in confusion after her. Why would she give me the useless piece of information? It's not like I'm planning to ask this girl out. Still, once Luz disappears around the corner, I turn to Eliza. "I'm not sure where you think you've landed, miss, but I would loathe rejecting your business because you're upsetting our staff."

She gapes, evidently used to getting her way. *Spoiled*, my wolf snorts, and I can't help but agree when she yells, "Upset your staff? How dare you!?"

The urge to roll my eyes is strong, but I hold back—barely. "In case you haven't noticed, we're a quiet town here. Tight-knit group of people. We notice when someone upsets one of us."

Eliza continues to scowl, but now there's a stubborn lift to her chin as if she's thinking of disputing my words. "Not my fault your girl can't take a joke."

A growl slips past my clenched teeth then, and she widens her eyes.

"Leave. Now."

"You can't do that, I already paid!"

"There is such a thing as a refund," I drawl, crossing my arms over my chest.

"I didn't even *do* anything!" She stomps her foot at that—I wish I was joking, trust me.

"Either you keep your mouth shut around Luz, or I kick you out." When I move towards her, she gives up and sits on the far couch. "Thank you. Now stay there until your car is ready."

I turn away, ignoring her glare, and follow Luz to the kitchen, determined to make sure she's ok.

L u c r e z i a

Dom's a sweetheart, and his actions warm my heart. Even if he offered to stick around so he could chat up little Miss Princess.

I'm aggravated with myself for caring, and even more so for not being able to let it go. Dom fools around, I know this. He's not a player per se, but he dates enough. In a small town like ours, he's known as a catch—in bed. But never for good.

Enough.

I go about making the honey and cinnamon mixture in the small kitchenette, adding some of the ginger root I keep in the fridge here. Once it steeps enough, I pour it all in a cup and am about to return to the reception area.

I almost smack into Dom, who apparently snuck up behind me and was watching me work.

"Easy," he cups my hands, grabbing the mug from them before it spills and burns me everywhere.

After placing it on the side cabinet, he turns his attention back to me. "You ok?"

I want to answer him, really I do. But I'm struck dumb by his proximity, now in my internal bubble, as I call it. Have I never been this close to him? Or have I only been blind to his charm until today? And why in the hell does it feel like I'm left staring at a real-life Apollo, instead of my best friend?

The broadness of his back seems to dwarf me, and every nerve in my body is aware of our secluded presence. *He could do anything...* My brain tries to backtrack, memories pushing forth, and I half-expect a panic attack.

Yet nothing happens, and that scares me more than the opposite. Either I've lost my mind, or there is something about Dom that makes me feel safe. *Maybe it's because I've known him for so long.*

If I was to reach out, I could touch the muscles of his chest. Even from where I am, heat radiates off him, and something in my stomach unfurls in response.

My breath turns shaky, and this time I can't tell if it's a panic attack, or emotions…or something else.

"Luz, you ok?"

I glance up at his worried tone and manage a nod that's too stiff. "Yeah, fine. Just…out of breath. Sorry."

He frowns then, those beautiful blue eyes warm and scanning me up and down. My skin tingles, and I take a minute to realize he's holding my elbow, as though afraid I'll topple over.

"You sure?"

"Mhm," is my only intelligent answer. Then, like a coward, I side-step him. "Your tea is getting cold," I mutter over my shoulder, and take off the minute he releases his grip.

D o m i n i c

After the morning incident, the day goes by fairly smooth. Eliza leaves with her damn Mustang, and we get no more high class maintenance clients, only our regular clientele. Finn keeps his mouth shut, and I stay busy with as many things as I can take.

Despite my best efforts, I can't stop watching Luz. I see her blush when Lucas asks her out to lunch to go over the sales reports—which they end up doing on the couch in the reception area. I can smell the waves of arousal off her and want to rip his throat out.

Finn steps in at that point, not fooled in the least by my resenting silence. "He's our alpha, Dom."

I ignore how in my face he is, trying to keep my tone curt

as I continue to fiddle with the timing belt. "I'm well aware."

"We promised him loyalty."

I throw the piece on the table, ignoring the clank of metal on metal that echoes. I face Finn, failing to appear calm. "He's still new as alpha. And if I recall correctly, I promised him my obedience as his beta, but not my allegiance—and not forever."

Finn glances towards Luz and Lucas, then back at me. "Pack law is clear, mate."

"He hasn't made a claim." The words are more than a growl, but enough to quiet even my wolf.

Then Lucas gets up to go in his office, and Luz watches him with longing. A thought strikes me and before I have time to reason it through, I'm already moving.

This is a terrible idea.

Or so I keep telling myself, even as my feet inch towards Luz. Before I know it, my mouth is running off again—without me. "I can help."

Luz turns those otherworldly eyes to me, the gold more clear up close, and I gulp. I've never had an issue with women, but hell, this one will be the death of me.

"Dom?"

I snap back to with a very unintelligent, "Huh?"

Luz laughs, and I rub the back of my neck.

"Help me with what?" Again, her eyes slide to where Lucas disappeared to.

"With him."

She turns so fast I'm afraid she got whiplash.

"What are you talking about?"

"I can help you with Lucas." I drop on the couch, ignoring her stunned expression and those lips I want to kiss so bad my mouth tingles. "You like him, right?"

Her face falls as she whispers, "Am I that obvious?"

"Only to me," I answer truthfully. "But you *do* like him?"

She nods, her eyes big pools of uncertainty.

"Let me help. I know Lucas, we've been buds forever. If he has feelings for you, he may let rules get in the way. Guy always had a thing for not breaking them."

"What rules?"

I want to smack myself—the reference to our werewolf life slipped too quickly. "Dating work colleagues." I save face and change the subject before she inquires further. "Either way, nothing like dating someone to get him to make a move if he's interested."

"I'm not good at dating," she whispers, looking away.

My wolf points its head, sniffing her scent, which changed in a few seconds. *Fear.* I sense it, too. But of what? *Surely it can't be me.* Either way, this is a chance to find out more.

"It won't really be dating. We'll fake it for his benefit. If it makes you more comfortable, we can even put a time limit on it. A week, two weeks, whatever you want."

She glances back again towards Lucas as he steps out of his office and back into the garage. The longing in her expression crushes my heart, but I promise myself to rein it in.

"And what's in it for you?" Her gaze is wary when it meets mine.

I shrug. "A chance to annoy him." *And make you happy. And show you he's not the one for you.* That last part, I don't say out loud.

Luz is silent for so long, I'm sure she'll end up saying no.

Besides, what am I thinking? Nothing except selfish thoughts. I want her first kiss, and I want her to at least have the memory of my lips imprinted in her mind before she ends up with Lucas. I want to stake my claim even if it won't be permanent.

"Ok," she surprises me by saying. "How will this work?"

I'm too stunned for a moment to react, but already my wolf is roaring in victory and a grin spreads on my face. "Leave it to me. Meet me tonight for drinks at The Cave, eight o'clock sharp."

When she nods, I lean forward and kiss her cheek, not even surprised when she jumps at the contact. "It'll be fun, you'll see."

And no kidding, I walk away whistling. Yup, like a poor sap who won the girl—not the one who promised to help her get the man of her dreams.

Bite me.

Continue reading!
Visit www.alexawhitewolf.com/books for more

ABOUT THE AUTHOR

Alexa Whitewolf was born in Romania a little after the fall of Communism, 1992 to be exact. Growing up in the Transylvania region surrounded by epic mountains and a never ending stream of legends and stories was bound to create an overactive imagination. From a young age, she started rescuing pets–abandoned dogs in warehouses, kittens about to be drowned–and spent her childhood talking to animals. This devotion to the furry creatures shows up in her writing, as most of her series will have one–or more–pets involved (think Alistair if you read **The Avalon Chronicles**, Tyr in **The Sage's Legacy**).

The move to Canada in her teens was a sometimes rough adjustment, and Alexa overcame it by burying herself in books–both reading and writing. She started her young adult series at that time, and continued with the fantasy of Avalon in university. Nowadays? She's working on a few other upcoming series, among which a werewolf paranormal romance.

Alexa currently lives nearby picturesque Ontario, where Starbucks locations abound. When not at home writing–or awake in the middle of the night trying to put her characters to sleep–Alexa can be found enjoying walks with her husband and two masters of mischief, Zeus and Achilles. Her social media feed is always inundated with animal posts, so if you're looking for some sunshine in your day, you know where to find it: Facebook, Twitter or Goodreads, so don't be shy!

When the mood strikes, Alexa also dabbles in handmade jewelry and stationery for special occasions, as well as the occasional website creation for friends. And if that's not enough to keep this night owl busy, she's still trying to convince her husband to get another puppy–sadly, a work in progress.

You can read more on her books, enter giveaways and follow her blog on travel, dogs and life in general at **alexawhitewolf.com**.

ALSO BY THE AUTHOR

The Avalon Chronicles series
Avalon Dreams
Avalon Wishes
Avalon Nightmares

The Sage's Legacy – YA series
The Dragon Medallion
The Dragon Manuscript
Relics of the Underworld

Moonlight Rogues series
First to Fall
Second to Surrender
Third to Tumble
Last to Love

Standalone novels
Blood Ties, Love Binds
Unconditional Love
Blazing in a Storm of Ashes (Coming Soon)
More novels coming soon!

Sign up for my readers' group **at
www.alexawhitewolf.com/contact** and
receive a copy of *Unconditional Love* for **FREE,**
as well as first dibs on cover reveals,
discounts, giveaways, prizes **and more!**